P9-BYV-023

Daughter of SMOKE & BONE

STEVENS MEMORIAL LIBRARY
20 Memorial Drive
Ashburnham, MA 01430
978-827-4115
Fax 978-827-4116

WITHDRAWN

Daughter of SMOKE & BONE

Laini Taylor

Little, Brown and Company

New York Boston

Copyright © 2011 by Laini Taylor

All rights reserved. Except as permitted under the U.S. Copyright Act of 1976, no part of this publication may be reproduced, distributed, or transmitted in any form or by any means, or stored in a database or retrieval system, without the prior written permission of the publisher.

Little, Brown and Company

Hachette Book Group
237 Park Avenue, New York, NY 10017
Visit our website at www.lb-teens.com

Little, Brown and Company is a division of Hachette Book Group, Inc.
The Little, Brown name and logo are trademarks of Hachette Book Group, Inc.

The publisher is not responsible for websites (or their content) that are not owned by the publisher.

First Edition: September 2011
First International Edition: September 2011

The characters and events portrayed in this book are fictitious. Any similarity to real persons, living or dead, is coincidental and not intended by the author.

Library of Congress Cataloging-in-Publication Data

Taylor, Laini.
Daughter of smoke and bone / by Laini Taylor. — 1st ed.
p. cm.
Summary: Seventeen-year-old Karou, a lovely, enigmatic art student in a Prague boarding school, carries a sketchbook of hideous, frightening monsters—the chimaerae who form the only family she has ever known.
ISBN 978-0-316-13402-6 (hc) / ISBN 978-0-316-19902-5 (int'l)
[1. Supernatural—Fiction. 2. Chimera (Greek mythology)—Fiction. 3. Mythology, Greek—Fiction. 4. Angels—Fiction. 5. Demonology—Fiction. 6. Boarding schools—Fiction. 7. Schools—Fiction. 8. Artists—Fiction. 9. Prague (Czech Republic)—Fiction. 10. Czech Republic—Fiction.] I. Title.
PZ7.T214826Dau 2011
[Fic]—dc22   2010045802

10 9 8 7 6 5 4 3 2 1

RRD-C

Printed in the United States of America

Book design by Alison Impey

38179000565646
B+T
10/11

For Jane,
for a whole new world of possibilities

Once upon a time,
an angel and a devil fell in love.

It did not end well.

1

Impossible to Scare

Walking to school over the snow-muffled cobbles, Karou had no sinister premonitions about the day. It seemed like just another Monday, innocent but for its essential Mondayness, not to mention its Januaryness. It was cold, and it was dark—in the dead of winter the sun didn't rise until eight—but it was also lovely. The falling snow and the early hour conspired to paint Prague ghostly, like a tintype photograph, all silver and haze.

On the riverfront thoroughfare, trams and buses roared past, grounding the day in the twenty-first century, but on the quieter lanes, the wintry peace might have hailed from another time. Snow and stone and ghostlight, Karou's own footsteps and the feather of steam from her coffee mug, and she was alone and adrift in mundane thoughts: school, errands. The occasional cheek-chew of bitterness when a pang of heartache intruded, as pangs of heartache will, but she pushed them aside, resolute, ready to be done with all that.

She held her coffee mug in one hand and clutched her coat closed with the other. An artist's portfolio was slung over her shoulder, and her hair—loose, long, and peacock blue—was gathering a lace of snowflakes.

Just another day.

And then.

A snarl, rushing footfall, and she was seized from behind, pulled hard against a man's broad chest as hands yanked her scarf askew and she felt teeth—*teeth*—against her neck.

Nibbling.

Her attacker was *nibbling* her.

Annoyed, she tried to shake him off without spilling her coffee, but some sloshed out of her cup anyway, into the dirty snow.

"Jesus, Kaz, get off," she snapped, spinning to face her ex-boyfriend. The lamplight was soft on his beautiful face. *Stupid beauty*, she thought, shoving him away. *Stupid face.*

"How did you know it was me?" he asked.

"It's always you. And it never works."

Kazimir made his living jumping out from behind things, and it frustrated him that he could never get even the slightest rise out of Karou. "You're impossible to scare," he complained, giving her the pout he thought was irresistible. Until recently, she wouldn't have resisted it. She would have risen on tiptoe and licked his pout-puckered lower lip, licked it languorously and then taken it between her teeth and teased it before losing herself in a kiss that made her melt against him like sun-warmed honey.

Those days were so over.

"Maybe you're just not scary," she said, and walked on.

Kaz caught up and strolled at her side, hands in pockets. "I *am* scary, though. The snarl? The bite? Anyone normal would have a heart attack. Just not you, ice water for blood."

When she ignored him, he added, "Josef and I are starting a new tour. Old Town *vampire* tour. The tourists will eat it up."

They would, thought Karou. They paid good money for Kaz's "ghost tours," which consisted of being herded through the tangled lanes of Prague in the dark, pausing at sites of supposed murders so "ghosts" could leap out of doorways and make them shriek. She'd played a ghost herself on several occasions, had held aloft a bloody head and moaned while the tourists' screams gave way to laughter. It had been fun.

Kaz had been fun. Not anymore. "Good luck with that," she said, staring ahead, her voice colorless.

"We could use you," Kaz said.

"No."

"You could play a sexy vampire vixen—"

"No."

"Lure in the men—"

"No."

"You could wear your cape...."

Karou stiffened.

Softly, Kaz coaxed, "You still have it, don't you, baby? Most beautiful thing I've ever seen, you with that black silk against your white skin—"

"Shut up," she hissed, coming to a halt in the middle of Maltese Square. *God*, she thought. How stupid had she been to fall for this petty, pretty street actor, dress up for him and give him memories like that? Exquisitely stupid.

3

Lonely stupid.

Kaz lifted his hand to brush a snowflake from her eyelashes. She said, "Touch me and you'll get this coffee in your face."

He lowered his hand. "Roo, Roo, my fierce Karou. When will you stop fighting me? I said I was sorry."

"Be sorry, then. Just be sorry somewhere else." They spoke in Czech, and her acquired accent matched his native one perfectly.

He sighed, irritated that Karou was still resisting his apologies. This wasn't in his script. "Come on," he coaxed. His voice was rough and soft at the same time, like a blues singer's mix of gravel and silk. "We're meant to be together, you and me."

Meant. Karou sincerely hoped that if she were "meant" for anyone, it wasn't Kaz. She looked at him, beautiful Kazimir whose smile used to work on her like a summons, compelling her to his side. And that had seemed a glorious place to be, as if colors were brighter there, sensations more profound. It had also, she'd discovered, been a *popular* place, other girls occupying it when she did not.

"Get Svetla to be your vampire vixen," she said. "She's got the vixen part down."

He looked pained. "I don't want Svetla. I want you."

"Alas. I am not an option."

"Don't say that," he said, reaching for her hand.

She pulled back, a pang of heartache surging in spite of all her efforts at aloofness. *Not worth it*, she told herself. *Not even close.* "This is the definition of stalking, you realize."

"Puh. I'm not stalking you. I happen to be going this way."

"Right," said Karou. They were just a few doors from her

4

school now. The Art Lyceum of Bohemia was a private high school housed in a pink Baroque palace where famously, during the Nazi occupation, two young Czech nationalists had slit the throat of a Gestapo commander and scrawled *liberty* with his blood. A brief, brave rebellion before they were captured and impaled upon the finials of the courtyard gate. Now students were milling around that very gate, smoking, waiting for friends. But Kaz wasn't a student—at twenty, he was several years older than Karou—and she had never known him to be out of bed before noon. "Why are you even awake?"

"I have a new job," he said. "It starts early."

"What, you're doing *morning* vampire tours?"

"Not that. Something else. An…*unveiling* of sorts." He was grinning now. Gloating. He wanted her to ask what his new job was.

She wouldn't ask. With perfect disinterest she said, "Well, have fun with that," and walked away.

Kaz called after her, "Don't you want to know what it is?" The grin was still there. She could hear it in his voice.

"Don't care," she called back, and went through the gate.

* * *

She really should have asked.

2

An Unveiling of Sorts

Monday, Wednesday, and Friday, Karou's first class was life drawing. When she walked into the studio, her friend Zuzana was already there and had staked out easels for them in front of the model's platform. Karou shrugged off her portfolio and coat, unwound her scarf, and announced, "I'm being stalked."

Zuzana arched an eyebrow. She was a master of the eyebrow arch, and Karou envied her for it. Her own eyebrows did not function independently of each other, which handicapped her expressions of suspicion and disdain.

Zuzana could do both perfectly, but this was milder eyebrow action, mere cool curiosity. "Don't tell me Jackass tried to scare you again."

"He's going through a vampire phase. He bit my neck."

"Actors," muttered Zuzana. "I'm telling you, you need to tase the loser. Teach him to go jumping out at people."

"I don't have a Taser." Karou didn't add that she didn't need a Taser; she was more than capable of defending herself without electricity. She'd had an unusual education.

"Well, get one. Seriously. Bad behavior should be punished. Plus, it would be fun. Don't you think? I've always wanted to tase someone. *Zap!*" Zuzana mimicked convulsions.

Karou shook her head. "No, tiny violent one, I don't think it would be fun. You're terrible."

"I am not terrible. Kaz is terrible. Tell me I don't have to remind you." She gave Karou a sharp look. "Tell me you're not even considering forgiving him."

"*No*," declared Karou. "But try getting *him* to believe that." Kaz just couldn't fathom any girl willfully depriving herself of his charms. And what had she done but strengthen his vanity those months they'd been together, gazing at him starry-eyed, giving him…everything? His wooing her now, she thought, was a point of pride, to prove to himself that he could have who he wanted. That it was up to him.

Maybe Zuzana was right. Maybe she *should* tase him.

"Sketchbook," commanded Zuzana, holding out her hand like a surgeon for a scalpel.

Karou's best friend was bossy in obverse proportion to her size. She only passed five feet in her platform boots, whereas Karou was five foot six but seemed taller in the same way that ballerinas do, with their long necks and willowy limbs. She wasn't a ballerina, but she had the look, in figure if not in fashion. Not many ballerinas have bright blue hair or a constellation of tattoos on their limbs, and Karou had both.

The only tattoos visible as she dug out her sketchbook and handed it over were the ones on her wrists like bracelets—a single word on each: *true* and *story*.

As Zuzana took the book, a couple of other students, Pavel and Dina, crowded in to look over her shoulder. Karou's sketchbooks had a cult following around school and were handed around and marveled at on a daily basis. This one—number ninety-two in a lifelong series—was bound with rubber bands, and as soon as Zuzana took them off it burst open, each page so coated in gesso and paint that the binding could scarcely contain them. As it fanned open, Karou's trademark characters wavered on the pages, gorgeously rendered and deeply strange.

There was Issa, serpent from the waist down and woman from the waist up, with the bare, globe breasts of Kama Sutra carvings, the hood and fangs of a cobra, and the face of an angel.

Giraffe-necked Twiga, hunched over with his jeweler's glass stuck in one squinting eye.

Yasri, parrot-beaked and human-eyed, a frill of orange curls escaping her kerchief. She was carrying a platter of fruit and a pitcher of wine.

And Brimstone, of course—he was the star of the sketchbooks. Here he was shown with Kishmish perched on the curl of one of his great ram's horns. In the fantastical stories Karou told in her sketchbooks, Brimstone dealt in wishes. Sometimes she called him the Wishmonger; other times, simply "the grump."

She'd been drawing these creatures since she was a little girl, and her friends tended to talk about them as if they were real. "What was Brimstone up to this weekend?" asked Zuzana.

"The usual," said Karou. "Buying teeth from murderers. He got some Nile crocodile teeth yesterday from this awful Somali poacher, but the idiot tried to steal from him and got half strangled by his snake collar. He's lucky to be alive."

Zuzana found the story illustrated on the book's last drawn pages: the Somali, his eyes rolling back in his head as the whip-thin snake around his neck cinched itself as tight as a garrote. Humans, Karou had explained before, had to submit to wearing one of Issa's serpents around their necks before they could enter Brimstone's shop. That way if they tried anything fishy they were easy to subdue—by strangulation, which wasn't always fatal, or, if necessary, by a bite to the throat, which was.

"How do you make this stuff up, maniac?" Zuzana asked, all jealous wonderment.

"Who says I do? I keep telling you, it's all real."

"Uh-huh. And your hair grows out of your head that color, too."

"What? It totally does," said Karou, passing a long blue strand through her fingers.

"Right."

Karou shrugged and gathered her hair back in a messy coil, stabbing a paintbrush through it to secure it at the nape of her neck. In fact, her hair did grow out of her head that color, pure as ultramarine straight from the paint tube, but that was a truth she told with a certain wry smile, as if she were being absurd. Over the years she'd found that that was all it took, that lazy smile, and she could tell the truth without risk of being believed. It was easier than keeping track of lies, and so it became part of who she was: Karou with her wry smile and crazy imagination.

In fact, it was not her imagination that was crazy. It was her life — blue hair and Brimstone and all.

Zuzana handed the book to Pavel and started flipping pages in her own oversize drawing pad, searching for a fresh page. "I wonder who's posing today."

"Probably Wiktor," said Karou. "We haven't had him in a while."

"I know. I'm hoping he's dead."

"Zuzana!"

"What? He's eight million years old. We might as well draw the anatomical skeleton as that creepy bonesack."

There were some dozen models, male and female, all shapes and ages, who rotated through the class. They ranged from enormous Madame Svobodnik, whose flesh was more landscape than figure, to pixie Eliska with her wasp waist, the favorite of the male students. Ancient Wiktor was Zuzana's least favorite. She claimed to have nightmares whenever she had to draw him.

"He looks like an unwrapped mummy." She shuddered. "I ask you, is staring at a naked old man any way to start the day?"

"Better than getting attacked by a vampire," said Karou.

In fact, she didn't mind drawing Wiktor. For one thing, he was so nearsighted he never made eye contact with the students, which was a bonus. No matter that she had been drawing nudes for years; she still found it unsettling, sketching one of the younger male models, to look up from a study of his penis — a necessary study; you couldn't exactly leave the area blank — and find him staring back at her. Karou had felt her cheeks flame on plenty of occasions and ducked behind her easel.

Those occasions, as it turned out, were about to fade into insignificance next to the mortification of today.

She was sharpening a pencil with a razor blade when Zuzana blurted in a weird, choked voice, "Oh my god, Karou!"

And before she even looked up, she knew.

An *unveiling*, he had said. Oh, how clever. She lifted her gaze from her pencil and took in the sight of Kaz standing beside Profesorka Fiala. He was barefoot and wearing a robe, and his shoulder-length golden hair, which had minutes before been wind-teased and sparkling with snowflakes, was pulled back in a ponytail. His face was a perfect blend of Slavic angles and soft sensuality: cheekbones that might have been turned on a diamond cutter's lathe, lips you wanted to touch with your fingertips to see if they felt like velvet. Which, Karou knew, they did. Stupid lips.

Murmurs went around the room. *A new model, oh my god, gorgeous . . .*

One murmur cut through the others: "Isn't that Karou's boyfriend?"

Ex, she wanted to snap. So very, very *ex*.

"I think it is. *Look* at him. . . ."

Karou *was* looking at him, her face frozen in what she hoped was a mask of impervious calm. *Don't blush*, she commanded herself. *Do not blush.* Kaz looked right back at her, a smile dimpling one cheek, eyes lazy and amused. And when he was sure he held her gaze, he had the nerve to wink.

A flurry of giggles erupted around Karou.

"Oh, the evil bastard . . ." Zuzana breathed.

Kaz stepped up onto the model's platform. He looked straight

11

at Karou as he untied his sash; he looked at her as he shrugged off the robe. And then Karou's ex-boyfriend was standing before her entire class, beautiful as heartbreak, naked as the *David*. And on his chest, right over his heart, was a new tattoo.

It was an elaborate cursive *K*.

More giggles burst forth. Students didn't know who to look at, Karou or Kazimir, and glanced from one to the other, waiting for a drama to unfold. "Quiet!" commanded Profesorka Fiala, appalled, clapping her hands together until the laughter was stifled. Karou's blush came on then. She couldn't stop it. First her chest and neck went hot, then her face. Kaz's eyes were on her the whole time, and his dimple deepened with satisfaction when he saw her flustered.

"One-minute poses, please, Kazimir," said Fiala.

Kaz stepped into his first pose. It was dynamic, as the one-minute poses were meant to be — twisted torso, taut muscles, limbs stretched in simulation of action. These warm-up sketches were all about movement and loose line, and Kaz was taking the opportunity to flaunt himself. Karou thought she didn't hear a lot of pencils scratching. Were the other girls in the class just staring stupidly, as she was?

She dipped her head, took up her sharp pencil — thinking of other uses she would happily put it to — and started to sketch. Quick, fluid lines, and all the sketches on one page; she overlapped them so they looked like an illustration of dance.

Kaz was graceful. He spent enough time looking in the mirror that he knew how to use his body for effect. It was his instrument, he'd have said. Along with the voice, the body was an actor's tool. Well, Kaz was a lousy actor — which was why he got by on ghost tours and the occasional low-budget production of *Faust*—but he made a fine artist's model, as Karou knew, having drawn him many times before.

His body had reminded Karou, from the first time she saw it...unveiled...of a Michelangelo. Unlike some Renaissance artists, who'd favored slim, effete models, Michelangelo had gone for power, drawing broad-shouldered quarry workers and somehow managing to render them both carnal and elegant at the same time. That was Kaz: carnal and elegant.

And deceitful. And narcissistic. And, honestly, kind of dumb.

"Karou!" The British girl Helen was whispering harshly, trying to get her attention. "Is that him?"

Karou didn't acknowledge her. She drew, pretending everything was normal. Just another day in class. And if the model had an insolent dimple and wouldn't take his eyes off her? She ignored it as best she could.

When the timer rang, Kaz calmly gathered up his robe and put it on. Karou hoped it wouldn't occur to him that he was free to walk around the studio. *Stay where you are*, she willed him. But he didn't. He sauntered toward her.

"Hi, Jackass," said Zuzana. "Modest much?"

Ignoring her, he asked Karou, "Like my new tattoo?"

Students were standing up to stretch, but rather than dispersing for smoke or bathroom breaks, they hovered casually within earshot.

"Sure," Karou said, keeping her voice light. "K for *Kazimir*, right?"

"Funny girl. You know what it's for."

"Well," she mused in Thinker pose, "I know there's only one

13

person you really love, and his name does start with a K. But I can think of a better place for it than your heart." She took up her pencil and, on her last drawing of Kaz, inscribed a K right over his classically sculpted buttock.

Zuzana laughed, and Kaz's jaw tightened. Like most vain people, he hated to be mocked. "I'm not the only one with a tattoo, am I, Karou?" he asked. He looked to Zuzana. "Has she shown it to you?"

Zuzana gave Karou the suspicious rendition of the eyebrow arch.

"I don't know which you mean," Karou lied calmly. "I have lots of tattoos." To demonstrate, she didn't flash *true* or *story*, or the serpent coiled around her ankle, or any of her other concealed works of art. Rather, she held up her hands in front of her face, palms out. In the center of each was an eye inked in deepest indigo, in effect turning her hands into hamsas, those ancient symbols of warding against the evil eye. Palm tattoos are notorious for fading, but Karou's never did. She'd had these eyes as long as she could remember; for all she knew of their origin, she could have been born with them.

"Not those," said Kaz. "I mean the one that says *Kazimir*, right over your heart."

"I don't have a tattoo like that." She made herself sound puzzled and unfastened the top few buttons of her sweater. Beneath was a camisole, and she lowered it by a few revealing inches to demonstrate that indeed there was no tattoo above her breast. The skin there was white as milk.

Kaz blinked. "What? How did you—?"

"Come with me." Zuzana grabbed Karou's hand and pulled

her away. As they wove among the easels, all eyes were on Karou, lit with curiosity.

"Karou, did you break up?" Helen whispered in English, but Zuzana put up her hand in an imperious gesture that silenced her, and she dragged Karou out of the studio and into the girls' bathroom. There, eyebrow still arched, she asked, "What the hell was that?"

"What?"

"*What?* You practically flashed the boy."

"Please. I did not flash him."

"Whatever. What's this about a tattoo over your heart?"

"I just showed you. There's nothing there." She saw no reason to add that there *had* been something; she preferred to pretend she had never been so stupid. Plus, explaining how she'd gotten rid of it was not exactly an option.

"Well, good. The last thing you need is that idiot's name on your body. Can you believe him? Does he think if he just dangles his boy bits at you like a cat toy you'll go scampering after him?"

"Of course he thinks that," said Karou. "This is his idea of a romantic gesture."

"All you have to do is tell Fiala he's a stalker, and she'll throw his ass out."

Karou had thought of that, but she shook her head. Surely she could come up with a better way to get Kaz out of her class and out of her life. She had means at her disposal that most people didn't. She'd think of something.

"The boy is not terrible to draw, though." Zuzana went to the mirror and flipped wisps of dark hair across her forehead. "Got to give him that."

15

"Yeah. Too bad he's such a gargantuan asshole."

"A giant, stupid orifice," Zuzana agreed.

"A walking, talking cranny."

"Cranny." Zuzana laughed. "I like."

An idea came to Karou, and a faintly villainous smirk crossed her face.

"What?" asked Zuzana, seeing it.

"Nothing. We'd better get back in there."

"You're sure? You don't have to."

Karou nodded. "Nothing to it."

Kaz had gotten all the satisfaction he was going to get from this cute little ploy of his. It was her turn now. Walking back into the studio, she reached up and touched the necklace she was wearing, a multistrand loop of African trade beads in every color. At least they looked like African trade beads. They were more than that. Not much more, but enough for what Karou had planned.

3

CRANNY

Profesorka Fiala asked Kaz for a reclining pose for the rest of the period, and he draped himself back across the daybed in a way that, if not quite lewd, was certainly suggestive, knees just a bit too skewed, smile bordering on bedroom. There were no titters this time, but Karou imagined a surge of heat in the atmosphere, as if the girls in the class—and at least one of the boys—needed to fan themselves. She herself was not affected. This time when Kaz peered at her from under lazy eyelids, she met his gaze straight on.

She started sketching and did her best, thinking it fitting that, since their relationship had begun with a drawing, it should end with one, too.

He'd been sitting two tables away at Mustache Bar the first time she saw him. He wore a villain's twirled mustache, which seemed like foreshadowing now, but it was Mustache Bar after all. Everyone was wearing mustaches—Karou was sporting a

Fu Manchu she'd gotten from the vending machine. She'd pasted both mustaches into her sketchbook later that night—sketchbook number ninety—and the resulting lump made it easy to locate the exact page where her story with Kaz began.

He'd been drinking beer with friends, and Karou, unable to take her eyes off him, had drawn him. She was always drawing, not just Brimstone and the other creatures from her secret life, but scenes and people from the common world. Falconers and street musicians, Orthodox priests with beards to their bellies, the occasional beautiful boy.

Usually she got away with it, her subjects none the wiser, but this time the beautiful boy caught her looking, and the next thing she knew he was smiling under his fake mustache and coming over. How flattered he'd been by her sketch! He'd shown it to his friends, taken her hand to urge her to join them, and kept hold of it, fingers laced with hers, even after she'd settled at his table. That was the beginning: her worshipping his beauty, him reveling in it. And that was more or less how it had continued.

Of course, he'd told her she was beautiful, too, all the time. If she hadn't been, surely he'd never have come over to talk to her in the first place. Kaz wasn't exactly one to look for *inner* beauty. Karou was, simply, lovely. Creamy and leggy, with long azure hair and the eyes of a silent-movie star, she moved like a poem and smiled like a sphinx. Beyond merely pretty, her face was vibrantly alive, her gaze always sparking and luminous, and she had a birdlike way of cocking her head, her lips pressed together while her dark eyes danced, that hinted at secrets and mysteries.

Karou *was* mysterious. She had no apparent family, she never

talked about herself, and she was expert at evading questions—
for all that her friends knew of her background, she might have
sprung whole from the head of Zeus. And she was endlessly
surprising. Her pockets were always spilling out curious things:
ancient bronze coins, teeth, tiny jade tigers no bigger than her
thumbnail. She might reveal, while haggling for sunglasses
with an African street vendor, that she spoke fluent Yoruba.
Once, Kaz had undressed her to discover a knife hidden in her
boot. There was the matter of her being impossible to scare
and, of course, there were the scars on her abdomen: three shiny
divots that could only have been made by bullets.

"Who *are* you?" Kaz had sometimes asked, enchanted, to
which Karou would wistfully reply, "I really don't know."

Because she really didn't.

She drew quickly now, and didn't shy away from meeting
Kaz's eyes as she glanced up and down between model and
drawing. She wanted to see his face.

She wanted to see the moment his expression changed.

Only when she had captured his pose did she lift her left
hand—continuing to draw with her right—to the beads of
her necklace. She took one between her thumb and forefinger
and held it there.

And then she made a wish.

It was a very small wish. These beads were just scuppies,
after all. Like money, wishes came in denominations, and scuppies were mere pennies. Weaker even than pennies, because
unlike coins, wishes couldn't be compounded. Pennies you could
add up to make dollars, but scuppies were only ever just scuppies, and whole strands of them, like this necklace, would never

add up to a more potent wish, just plenty of very small, nearly useless wishes.

Wishes, for example, for things like *itches*.

Karou wished Kaz an itch, and the bead vanished between her fingers. Spent and gone. She'd never wished an itch before, so, to make sure it would work, she started with a spot he wouldn't be shy to scratch: his elbow. Sure enough, he nudged it casually against a cushion, scarcely shifting his pose. Karou smiled to herself and kept drawing.

A few seconds later, she took another bead between her fingers and wished another itch, this time to Kaz's nose. Another bead disappeared, the necklace shortened imperceptibly, and his face twitched. For a few seconds he resisted moving, but then gave in and rubbed his nose quickly with the back of his hand before resuming his position. His bedroom expression was gone, Karou couldn't help noticing. She had to bite her lip to keep her smile from broadening.

Oh, Kazimir, she thought, *you shouldn't have come here today. You really should have slept in.*

The next itch she wished to the hidden place of her evil plan, and she met Kaz's eyes at the moment it hit. His brow creased with sudden strain. She cocked her head slightly, as if to inquire, *Something wrong, dear?*

Here was an itch that could not be scratched in public. Kaz went pale. His hips shifted; he couldn't quite manage to hold still. Karou gave him a short respite and kept drawing. As soon as he started to relax and...unclench...she struck again and had to stifle a laugh when his face went rigid.

Another bead vanished between her fingers.

Then another.

This, she thought, *isn't just for today. It's for everything.* For the heartache that still felt like a punch in the gut each time it struck, fresh as new, at unpredictable moments; for the smiling lies and the mental images she couldn't shake; for the shame of having been so naive.

For the way loneliness is worse when you return to it after a reprieve—like the soul's version of putting on a wet bathing suit, clammy and miserable.

And this, Karou thought, no longer smiling, *is for the irretrievable.*

For her virginity.

That first time, the black cape and nothing under it, she'd felt so grown up—like the Czech girls Kaz and Josef hung out with, cool Slavic beauties with names like Svetla and Frantiska, who looked like nothing could ever shock them or make them laugh. Had she really wanted to be like them? She'd pretended to be, played the part of a girl—a *woman*—who didn't care. She'd treated her virginity like a trapping of childhood, and then it was gone.

She hadn't expected to be sorry, and at first she wasn't. The act itself was neither disappointing nor magical; it was what it was: a new closeness. A shared secret.

Or so she'd thought.

"You look different, Karou," Kaz's friend Josef had said the next time she saw him. "Are you...*glowing?*"

Kaz had punched him on the shoulder to silence him, looking at once sheepish and smug, and Karou knew he'd told. The girls, even. Their ruby lips had curled knowingly. Svetla—the

21

one she later caught him with—even made a straight-faced comment about capes coming back in fashion, and Kaz had colored slightly and looked away, the only indication that he knew he'd done wrong.

Karou had never even told Zuzana about it, at first because it belonged to her and Kaz alone, and later because she was ashamed. She hadn't told anyone, but Brimstone, in the inscrutable way he had of *knowing things*, had guessed, and had taken the opportunity to give her a rare lecture.

That had been interesting.

The Wishmonger's voice was so deep it seemed almost the shadow of sound: a dark sonance that lurked in the lowest register of hearing. "I don't know many rules to live by," he'd said. "But here's one. It's simple. Don't put anything unnecessary into yourself. No poisons or chemicals, no fumes or smoke or alcohol, no sharp objects, no inessential needles—drug *or* tattoo—and…no inessential penises, either."

"Inessential penises?" Karou had repeated, delighted with the phrase in spite of her grief. "Is there any such thing as an *essential* one?"

"When an essential one comes along, you'll know," he'd replied. "Stop squandering yourself, child. Wait for love."

"Love." Her delight evaporated. She'd thought that *was* love.

"It will come, and you will know it," Brimstone had promised, and she so wanted to believe him. He'd been alive for hundreds of years, hadn't he? Karou had never before thought about Brimstone and love—to look at him, he didn't seem such a candidate for it—but she hoped that in his centuries of life he'd accrued some wisdom, and that he was right about her.

Because, of all things in the world, that was her orphan's craving: *love*. And she certainly hadn't gotten it from Kaz.

Her pencil point snapped, so hard was she bearing down on her drawing, and at the same moment a burst of anger converted itself to a rapid-fire volley of itches that shortened her necklace to a choker and sent Kaz scrambling off the model stand. Karou released her necklace and watched him. He was already to the door, robe in hand, and he opened it and darted out, still naked in his haste to get away and find a place where he could attend to his humiliating misery.

The door swung shut and the class was left blinking at the empty daybed. Profesorka Fiala was peering over the rim of her glasses at the door, and Karou was ashamed of herself.

Maybe that was too much.

"What's with Jackass?" Zuzana asked.

"No idea," said Karou, looking down at her drawing. There on the paper was Kaz in all his carnality and elegance, looking like he was waiting for a lover to come to him. It could have been a good drawing, but she'd ruined it. Her line work had darkened and lost all subtlety, finally ending in a chaotic scribble that blotted out his... *inessential penis*. She wondered what Brimstone would think of her now. He was always reprimanding her for injudicious use of wishes—most recently the one that had made Svetla's eyebrows thicken overnight until they looked like caterpillars and grew right back the moment they were tweezed.

"Women have been burned at the stake for less, Karou," he'd said.

Lucky for me, she thought, *this isn't the Middle Ages.*

23

❧ 4 ❧

POISON KITCHEN

The rest of the school day was uneventful. A double period of chemistry and color lab, followed by master drawing and lunch, after which Zuzana went to puppetry and Karou to painting, both three-hour studio classes that released them into the same full winter dark by which they'd arrived that morning.

"Poison?" inquired Zuzana as they stepped out the door.

"You have to ask?" said Karou. "I'm starved."

They bent their heads against the icy wind and headed toward the river.

The streets of Prague were a fantasia scarcely touched by the twenty-first century—or the twentieth or nineteenth, for that matter. It was a city of alchemists and dreamers, its medieval cobbles once trod by golems, mystics, invading armies. Tall houses glowed goldenrod and carmine and eggshell blue, embellished with Rococo plasterwork and capped in roofs of uniform red. Baroque cupolas were the soft green of antique copper, and Gothic steeples stood ready to impale fallen angels. The wind carried the memory of magic, revolution, violins, and the cobbled lanes meandered like creeks. Thugs wore Mozart wigs and pushed chamber music on street corners, and marionettes hung in windows, making the whole city seem like a theater with unseen puppeteers crouched behind velvet.

Above it all loomed the castle on the hill, its silhouette as sharp as thorns. By night it was floodlit, bathed in eerie light, and this evening the sky hung low, full-bellied with snow, making gauzy halos around the street lamps.

Down by the Devil's Stream, Poison Kitchen was a place rarely stumbled upon by chance; you had to know it was there, and duck under an unmarked stone arch into a walled graveyard, beyond which glowed the lamp-lit windowpanes of the cafe.

Unfortunately, tourists no longer had to rely on chance to discover the place; the latest edition of the Lonely Planet guide had outed it to the world—

The church once attached to this medieval priory burned down some three hundred years ago, but the monks' quarters remain, and have been converted to the strangest cafe you'll find anywhere, crowded with classical statues all sporting the owner's collection of WWI gas masks. Legend has it that back in the Middle Ages, the cook lost his mind and murdered the whole priory with a poisoned vat of goulash, hence the cafe's ghoulish name and signature dish: goulash, of course. Sit on a velvet sofa and prop your feet up on a coffin. The skulls behind the bar may or may not belong to the murdered monks....

—and for the past half year backpackers had been poking their heads through the arch, looking for some morbid Prague to write postcards about.

This evening, though, the girls found it quiet. In the corner a foreign couple was taking pictures of their children wearing gas masks, and a few men hunched at the bar, but most of the tables—coffins, flanked by low velvet settees—were unoccupied. Roman statues were everywhere, life-size gods and nymphs with missing arms and wings, and in the middle of the room stood a copy of the huge equestrian Marcus Aurelius from Capitoline Hill.

"Oh, good, Pestilence is free," said Karou, heading toward the sculpture. Massive emperor and horse both wore gas masks, like every other statue in the place, and it had always put Karou in mind of the first horseman of the Apocalypse, Pestilence, sowing plague with one outstretched arm. The girls' preferred table was in its shadow, having the benefit of both privacy and a view of the bar—through the horse's legs—so they could see if anyone interesting came in.

They dropped their portfolios and hung their coats from Marcus Aurelius's stone fingertips. The one-eyed owner raised his hand from behind the bar, and they waved back.

They'd been coming here for two and a half years, since they were fifteen and in their first year at the Lyceum. Karou had been new to Prague and had known no one. Her Czech was freshly acquired (by *wish*, not study; Karou collected languages, and that's what Brimstone always gave her for her birthday) and it had still tasted strange on her tongue, like a new spice.

She'd been at a boarding school in England before that, and

though she was capable of a flawless British accent, she had stuck with the American one she'd developed as a child, so that was what her classmates had thought she was. In truth, she had claim to no nationality. Her papers were all forgeries, and her accents—all except one, in her first language, which was not of human origin—were all fakes.

Zuzana was Czech, from a long line of marionette artisans in Český Krumlov, the little jewel box of a city in southern Bohemia. Her older brother had shocked the family by going into the army, but Zuzana had puppets in the blood and was carrying on the family tradition. Like Karou, she'd known no one else at school and, as fortune would have it, early in the first term they'd been paired up to paint a mural for a local primary school. That had entailed a week of evenings spent up ladders, and they'd taken to going to Poison Kitchen afterward. This was where their friendship had taken root, and when the mural was finished, the owner had hired them to paint a scene of skeletons on toilets in the cafe's bathroom. He'd paid them a month of suppers for their labor, ensuring they would keep coming back, and a couple of years later, they still were.

They ordered bowls of goulash, which they ate while discussing Kaz's stunt, their chemistry teacher's nose hair—which Zuzana asserted was braidable—and ideas for their semester projects. Soon, talk shifted to the handsome new violinist in the orchestra of the Marionette Theatre of Prague.

"He has a girlfriend," lamented Zuzana.

"What? How do you know?"

"He's always texting on his breaks."

"That's your evidence? Flimsy. Maybe he secretly fights

crime, and he's texting infuriating riddles to his nemesis," suggested Karou.

"Yes, I'm sure that's it. *Thank you.*"

"I'm just saying, there could be other explanations than a girlfriend. Anyway, since when are you shy? Just talk to him already!"

"And say what? *Nice fiddling, handsome man?*"

"Absolutely."

Zuzana snorted. She worked as an assistant to the theater's puppeteers on the weekends and had developed a crush on the violinist some weeks before Christmas. Though not usually bashful, she had yet to even speak to him. "He probably thinks I'm a kid," she said. "You don't know what it's like, being child-size."

"Marionette-size," said Karou, who felt no pity whatsoever. She thought Zuzana's tininess was perfect, like a fairy you found in the woods and wanted to put in your pocket. Though in Zuzana's case the fairy was likely to be rabid, and *bite.*

"Yeah, Zuzana the marvelous human marionette. Watch her dance." Zuzana did a jerky, puppetlike version of ballet arms.

Inspired, Karou said, "Hey! That's what you should do for your project. Make a giant puppeteer, and you be the marionette. You know? You could make it so that when you move, it's like, I don't know, reverse puppetry. Has anyone done that before? You're the puppet, dancing from strings, but really it's your movements that are making the puppeteer's hands move?"

Zuzana had been lifting a piece of bread to her mouth, and she paused. Karou knew by the way her friend's eyes went dreamy that she was envisioning it. She said, "That would be a really big puppet."

"I could do your makeup, like a little marionette ballerina."

"Are you sure you want to give it to me? It's your idea."

"What, like I'm going to make a giant marionette? It's all yours."

"Well, thanks. Do you have any ideas for yours yet?"

Karou didn't. Last semester when she'd taken costuming she had constructed angel wings that she could wear on a harness, rigged to operate by a pulley system so she could lift and lower them. Fully unfolded, they gave her a wingspan of twelve magnificent feet. She'd worn them to show Brimstone, but had never even made it in to see him. Issa had stopped her in the vestibule and—gentle Issa!—had actually *hissed* at her, cobra hood flaring open in a way Karou had seen only a couple of times in her whole life. "An *angel*, of all abominations! Get them off! Oh, sweet girl, I can't stand the sight of you like that." It was all very odd. The wings hung above the bed now in Karou's tiny flat, taking up one entire wall.

This semester she needed to come up with a theme for a series of paintings, but so far nothing had set her mind on fire. As she was pondering ideas, she heard the tinkle of bells on the door. A few men came in, and a darting shadow behind them caught Karou's eye. It was the size and shape of a crow, but it was nothing so mundane.

It was Kishmish.

She straightened up and cast a quick glance at her friend. Zuzana was sketching puppet ideas in her notebook and barely responded when Karou excused herself. She went into the bathroom and the shadow followed, low and unseen.

Brimstone's messenger had the body and beak of a crow but

the membranous wings of a bat, and his tongue, when it flicked out, was forked. He looked like an escapee from a Hieronymus Bosch painting, and he was clutching a note with his feet. When Karou took it, she saw that his little knifelike talons had pierced the paper through.

She unfolded it and read the message, which took all of two seconds, as it said only, *Errand requiring immediate attention. Come.*

"He never says please," she remarked to Kishmish.

The creature cocked his head to one side, crow-style, as if to inquire, *Are you coming?*

"I'm coming, I'm coming," said Karou. "Don't I always?"

To Zuzana, a moment later, she said, "I have to go."

"What?" Zuzana looked up from her sketchbook. "But, dessert." It was there on the coffin: two plates of apple strudel, along with tea.

"Oh, damn," said Karou. "I can't. I have an errand."

"You and your errands. What do you have to do, so all of a sudden?" She glanced at Karou's phone, sitting on the coffin, and knew she had gotten no phone call.

"Just things," said Karou, and Zuzana let it drop, knowing from experience that she'd get no specifics.

Karou had things to do. Sometimes they took a few hours; other times, she was gone for days and returned weary and disheveled, maybe pale, maybe sunburned, or with a limp, or possibly a bite mark, and once with an unshakable fever that had turned out to be malaria.

"Just where did you happen to pick up a tropical disease?" Zuzana had demanded, to which Karou had replied, "Oh, I don't know. On the tram, maybe? This old woman did sneeze right in my face the other day."

"That is *not* how you get malaria."

"I know. It was gross, though. I'm thinking of getting a moped so I don't have to take the tram anymore."

And that was the end of that discussion. Part of being friends with Karou was resignation to never really knowing her. Now Zuzana sighed and said, "Fine. Two strudels for me. Any resulting fat is your fault," and Karou left Poison Kitchen, the shadow of an almost-crow darting out the door before her.

5

ELSEWHERE

Kishmish took to the sky and was gone in a flutter. Karou watched, wishing she could follow. What magnitude of wish, she wondered, would it take to endow her with flight?

One far more powerful than she'd ever have access to.

Brimstone wasn't stingy with scuppies. He let her refresh her necklace as often as she liked from his chipped teacups full of beads, and he paid her in bronze shings for the errands she ran for him. A shing was the next denomination of wish, and it could do more than a scuppy—Svetla's caterpillar eyebrows were a case in point, as were Karou's tattoo removal and her blue hair—but she had never gotten her hands on a wish that could work any real magic. She never would, either, unless she earned it, and she knew too well how humans earned wishes. Chiefly: hunting, graverobbing, and murder.

Oh, and there was one other way: a particular form of self-mutilation involving pliers and a deep commitment.

It wasn't like in the storybooks. No witches lurked at crossroads disguised as crones, waiting to reward travelers who shared their bread. Genies didn't burst from lamps, and talking fish didn't bargain for their lives. In all the world, there was only one place humans could get wishes: Brimstone's shop. And there was only one currency he accepted. It wasn't gold, or riddles, or kindness, or any other fairy-tale nonsense, and no, it wasn't souls, either. It was weirder than any of that.

It was teeth.

Karou crossed the Charles Bridge and took the tram north to the Jewish Quarter, a medieval ghetto that had given way to a dense concentration of Art Nouveau apartment buildings as pretty as cakes. Her destination was the service entrance in the rear of one of them. The plain metal door didn't look like anything special, and in and of itself, it wasn't. If you opened it from without, it revealed only a mildewed laundry room. But Karou didn't open it. She knocked and waited, because when the door was opened from *within*, it had the potential to lead someplace quite different.

It swung open and there was Issa, looking just as she did in Karou's sketchbooks, like a snake goddess in some ancient temple. Her serpent coils were withdrawn into the shadows of a small vestibule. "Blessings, darling."

"Blessings," Karou returned fondly, kissing her cheek. "Did Kishmish make it back?"

"He did," said Issa, "and he felt like an icicle on my shoulder. Come in now. It's freezing in your city." She was guardian of the threshold, and she ushered Karou inside, closing the door behind her so the two of them were alone in a space no bigger than a closet. The outer door of the vestibule had to seal completely before the inner one could be opened, in the manner of safety doors at aviaries that prevent birds from escaping. Only, in this case, it wasn't for birds.

"How was your day, sweet girl?" Issa had some half dozen snakes on her person—wound around her arms, roaming through her hair, and one encircling her slim waist like a belly dancer's chain. Anyone seeking entry would have to submit to wearing one around the neck before the inner door would unseal—anyone but Karou, that is. She was the only human who entered the shop uncollared. She was trusted. After all, she'd grown up in this place.

"It's been a day," Karou sighed. "You won't believe what Kaz did. He showed up to be the model in my drawing class."

Issa had not met Kaz, of course, but she knew him the same way Kaz knew her: from Karou's sketchbooks. The difference was that while Kaz thought Issa and her perfect breasts were an erotic figment of Karou's imagination, Issa knew Kaz was real.

She and Twiga and Yasri were as hooked on Karou's sketchbooks as her human friends were, but for the opposite reason. They liked to see the normal things: tourists huddled under umbrellas, chickens on balconies, children playing in the park. And Issa especially was fascinated by the nudes. To her, the human form—plain as it was, and not spliced together with other species—was a missed opportunity. She was always scrutinizing Karou and making such pronouncements as, "I think antlers would suit you, sweet girl," or "You'd make a lovely serpent," in just the way a human might suggest a new hairstyle or shade of lipstick.

Now, Issa's eyes lit up with ferocity. "You mean he came to your school? The scandalous rodent-loaf! Did you draw him? Show me." Outraged or not, she wouldn't miss an opportunity to see Kaz naked.

Karou pulled out her pad and flipped it open.

"You scribbled out the best part," Issa accused.

"Trust me, it's not that great."

Issa giggled into her hand as the shop door creaked open to admit them, and Karou stepped across the threshold. As always, she felt the slightest wave of nausea at the transition.

She was no longer in Prague.

Even though she had lived in Brimstone's shop, she still didn't understand where it was, only that you could enter through doorways all over the world and end up right here. As a child she used to ask Brimstone where exactly "here" was, only to be told brusquely, *Elsewhere.*

Brimstone was not a fan of questions.

Wherever it was, the shop was a windowless clutter of shelves that looked like some kind of tooth fairy's dumping ground—if, that is, the tooth fairy trafficked in all species. Viper fangs, canines, grooved elephant molars, overgrown orange incisors from exotic jungle rodents—they were all collected in bins and apothecary chests, strung in garlands that draped from hooks, and sealed in hundreds of jars you could shake like maracas.

The ceiling was vaulted like a crypt's, and small things scurried in the shadows, their tiny claws scritch-scritching on stone. Like Kishmish, these were creatures of disparate parts: scorpion-mice, gecko-crabs, beetle-rats. In the damp around the drains were snails with the heads of bullfrogs, and overhead, the ubiquitous moth-winged hummingbirds hurled themselves at lanterns, setting them swaying with the creak of copper chains.

In the corner, Twiga was bent over his work, his ungainly long neck bowed like a horseshoe as he cleaned teeth and banded them with gold to be strung onto catgut. A clatter came from the kitchen nook that was Yasri's domain.

And off to the left, behind a huge oak desk, was Brimstone himself. Kishmish was perched in his usual place on his master's right horn, and spread out on the desk were trays of teeth and small chests of gems. Brimstone was stringing them into a necklace and did not look up. "Karou," he said. "I believe I wrote 'errand requiring *immediate* attention.'"

"Which is exactly why I came immediately."

"It's been"—he consulted his pocket watch—"forty minutes."

"I was across town. If you want me to travel faster, give me wings, and I'll race Kishmish back. Or just give me a gavriel, and I'll wish for flight myself."

A gavriel was the second most powerful wish, certainly sufficient to grant the power of flight. Still bent over his work, Brimstone replied, "I think a flying girl would not go unnoticed in your city."

"Easily solved," said Karou. "Give me *two* gavriels, and I'll wish for invisibility, too."

Brimstone looked up. His eyes were those of a crocodile, luteous gold with vertical slit pupils, and they were not amused. He would not, Karou knew, give her any gavriels. She didn't ask out of hope, but because his complaint was so unfair. Hadn't she come running as soon as he'd called?

"I could trust you with gavriels, could I?" he asked.

"Of course you could. What kind of question is that?"

She felt his appraisal, as if he were mentally reviewing every wish she'd ever made.

Blue hair: frivolous.

Erasing pimples: vain.

Wishing off the light switch so she didn't have to get out of bed: lazy.

He said, "Your necklace is looking quite short. Have you had a busy day?"

Her hand flew to cover it. Too late. "Why do you have to notice everything?" No doubt the old devil somehow knew exactly what she'd used these scuppies for and was adding it to his mental list:

Making ex-boyfriend's cranny itch: vindictive.

"Such pettiness is beneath you, Karou."

"He deserved it," she replied, forgetting her earlier shame. Like Zuzana had said, bad behavior should be punished. She added, "Besides, it's not like you ask your traders what they're going to use their wishes for, and I'm sure they do a hell of a lot worse than make people *itch*."

"I expect you to be better than them," Brimstone said simply.

"Are you suggesting that I'm *not?*"

The tooth-traders who came to the shop were, with few exceptions, about the worst specimens humanity had to offer. Though Brimstone did have a small coterie of longtime associates who did not turn Karou's stomach—such as the retired diamond dealer who had on a number of occasions posed as her grandmother to enroll her in schools—mostly they were

37

a stinking, soul-dead lot with crescents of gore under their fingernails. They killed and maimed. They carried pliers in their pockets for extracting the teeth of the dead—and sometimes the living. Karou loathed them, and she was certainly better than them.

Brimstone said, "Prove that you are, by using wishes for good."

Nettled, she asked, "Who are you to talk about *good*, anyway?" She gestured to the necklace clutched in his huge clawed hands. Crocodile teeth—those would be from the Somali. Also wolf fangs, horse molars, and hematite beads. "I wonder how many animals died in the world today because of you. Not to mention people."

She heard Issa suck in a surprised breath, and she knew she should shut up, but her mouth kept moving. "No, really. You do business with killers, and you don't even have to see the corpses they leave behind. You lurk in here like a troll—"

"Karou," Brimstone said.

"But I've seen them, piles of dead creatures with bloody mouths. Those *girls* with their bloody mouths; I'll never forget as long as I live. What's it all for? What do you do with these teeth? If you would just tell me, maybe I could understand. There must be a *reason*—"

"*Karou*," Brimstone said again. He did not say "shut up." He didn't have to. His voice conveyed it clearly enough, on top of which he rose suddenly from his chair.

Karou shut up.

Sometimes, maybe most of the time, she forgot to *see* Brimstone. He was so familiar that when she looked at him she saw not a beast but the creature who, for reasons unknown, had

38

raised her from a baby, and not without tenderness. But he could still strike her speechless at times, such as when he used that tone of voice. It slithered like a hiss to the core of her consciousness and opened her eyes to the full, fearsome truth of him.

Brimstone was a monster.

If he and Issa, Twiga, and Yasri were to stray from the shop, that's what humans would call them: monsters. Demons, maybe, or devils. They called themselves chimaera.

Brimstone's arms and massive torso were the only human parts of him, though the tough flesh that covered them was more hide than skin. His square pectorals were riven with ancient scar tissue, one nipple entirely obliterated by it, and his shoulders and back were etched in more scars: a network of puckered white cross-hatchings. Below the waist he became *elsething*. His haunches, covered in faded, off-gold fur, rippled with leonine muscle, but instead of the padded paws of a lion, they tapered to wicked, clawed feet that could have been either raptor or lizard—or perhaps, Karou fancied, dragon.

And then there was his head. Roughly that of a ram, it wasn't furred, but fleshed in the same tough brown hide as the rest of him. It gave way to scales around his flat ovine nose and reptilian eyes, and giant, yellowed ram horns spiraled on either side of his face.

He wore a set of jeweler's lenses on a chain, and their dark gold rims were the only ornament on his person, if you didn't count the other thing he wore around his neck, which had no sparkle to catch the eye. It was just an old wishbone, sitting in the hollow of his throat. Karou didn't know why he wore it, only that she was forbidden to touch it, which, of course, had always made her long to do so. When she was a baby and he used to rock her on his knee, she would make little lightning grabs for it, but Brimst... was always faster. Karou had never succeeded in laying so ... as a fingertip to it.

Now that she was gr... she showed more decorum, but she still sometimes found he... itching to reach for the thing. Not now, though. Cowed by ...mstone's abrupt rising, she felt her rebelliousness subside. T... g a step back, she asked in a small voice, "So, um, what ab... his urgent errand? Where do you need me to go?"

He tossed her a case... ed with colorful banknotes that turned out to be euros. A... of euros.

"Paris," said Brimston... ave fun."

6

THE ANGEL OF EXTINCTION

Fun?

"Oh, yes," Karou muttered to herself later that night as she dragged three hundred pounds of illegal elephant ivory down the steps of the Paris Metro. "This is just so much fun."

When she'd left Brimstone's shop, Issa had let her out through the same door by which she'd entered, but when she stepped onto the street she was not back in Prague. She was in Paris, just like that.

No matter how many times she went through the portal, the thrill never wore off. It opened onto dozens of cities, and Karou had been to them all, on errands like this one and sometimes for pleasure. Brimstone let her go out and draw anywhere in the world where there wasn't a war, and when she had a craving for mangoes he opened the door to India, on the condition that she bring some back for him, too. She had even wheedled her way into shopping expeditions to exotic bazaars, and right here, to the Paris flea markets, to furnish her flat.

Wherever she went, when the door closed behind her, its connection to the shop was severed. Whatever magic was at work, it existed in that other place — *Elsewhere*, as she thought of it — and could not be conjured from this side. No one would ever force his way into the shop. One would only succeed in breaking through an earthly door that didn't lead where he hoped to go.

Even Karou was dependent on the whim of Brimstone to admit her. Sometimes he didn't, however much she knocked, though he had never yet stranded her on the far side of an errand, and she hoped he never would.

This errand turned out to be a black-market auction in a warehouse on the outskirts of Paris. Karou had attended several such, and they were always the same. Cash only, of course, and attended by sundry underworld types like exiled dictators and crime lords with pretensions to culture. The auction items were a mixed salad of stolen museum pieces — a Chagall drawing, the dried uvula of some beheaded saint, a matched set of tusks from a mature African bull elephant.

Yes. A matched set of tusks from a mature African bull elephant.

Karou sighed when she saw them. Brimstone hadn't told her what she was after, only that she would know it when she saw it, and she did. Oh, and wouldn't they be a delight to wrangle on public transportation?

Unlike the other bidders, she didn't have a long black car waiting, or a pair of thug bodyguards to do her heavy lifting.

She had only a string of scuppies and her charm, neither of which proved sufficient to persuade a cab driver to hang seven-foot-long elephant tusks out the back of his taxi. So, grumbling, Karou had to drag them six blocks to the nearest Metro station, down the stairs, and through the turnstile. They were wrapped in canvas and duct-taped, and when a street musician lowered his violin to inquire, "Hey lovely, what you got there?" she said, "Musicians who asked questions," and kept on dragging.

It could have been worse, certainly, and often was. Brimstone sent her to some god-awful places in pursuit of teeth. After the incident in St. Petersburg, when she was recovering from being shot, she'd demanded, "Is my life really worth so little to you?"

As soon as the question was out of her mouth, she'd regretted it. If her life *was* worth so little to him, she didn't want him to admit it. Brimstone had his faults, but he was all she had for a family, along with Issa and Twiga and Yasri. If she was just some kind of expendable slave girl, she didn't want to know.

His answer had neither confirmed nor denied her fear. "Your life? You mean, your *body*? Your body is nothing but an envelope, Karou. Your soul is another matter, and is not, as far as I know, in any immediate danger."

"An *envelope*?" She didn't like to think of her body as an envelope—something others might be able to open up and rifle through, remove things from like so many clipped coupons.

"I assumed you felt the same way," he'd said. "The way you scribble on it."

Brimstone didn't approve of her tattoos, which was funny, since he was responsible for her first, the eyes on her palms. At least Karou suspected he was, though she didn't know for sure, since he was incapable of answering even the most basic questions.

"Whatever," she'd said with a pained sigh. Really: *pained*. Getting shot *hurt*, no surprise there. Of course, she couldn't argue that Brimstone shoved her unprepared into danger. He'd seen to it that she was trained from a young age in martial arts. She never mentioned it to her friends — it was not, her sensei had taught her early, a bragging matter — and they would have been surprised to learn that Karou's gliding, straight-spined grace went hand in hand with deadly skill. Deadly or not, she'd had the misfortune to discover that karate went only so far against guns.

She'd healed quickly with the help of a pungent salve and, she suspected, magic, but her youthful fearlessness had been shaken, and she went on errands with more trepidation now.

Her train came, and she wrestled her burden through the doors, trying not to think too much about what was in it, or the magnificent life that had been ended somewhere in Africa, though probably not recently. These tusks were massive, and Karou happened to know that elephant tusks rarely grew so big anymore — poachers had seen to that. By killing all the biggest bulls, they'd altered the elephant gene pool. It was sickening, and here she was, part of that blood trade, hauling endangered species contraband on the freaking Paris Metro.

She shut the thought away in a dark room in her mind and stared out the window as the train sped through its black tunnels. She couldn't let herself think about it. Whenever she did, her life felt gore-streaked and nasty.

Last semester, when she'd made her wings, she'd dubbed herself "the Angel of Extinction," and it was entirely appropriate. The wings were made of real feathers she'd "borrowed" from Brimstone—hundreds of them, brought to him over the years by traders. She used to play with them when she was little, before she understood that birds had been killed for them, whole species driven extinct.

She had been innocent once, a little girl playing with feathers on the floor of a devil's lair. She wasn't innocent now, but she didn't know what to do about it. This was her life: magic and shame and secrets and teeth and a deep, nagging hollow at the center of herself where something was most certainly missing.

Karou was plagued by the notion that she wasn't *whole*. She didn't know what this meant, but it was a lifelong feeling, a sensation akin to having forgotten something. She'd tried describing it to Issa once, when she was a girl. "It's like you're standing in the kitchen, and you know you went in there for a reason, but you can't think of what that reason is, no matter what."

"And that's how you feel?" asked Issa, frowning.

"All the time."

Issa had only drawn her close and stroked her hair—then its natural near-black—and said, unconvincingly, "I'm sure it's nothing, lovely. Try not to worry."

Right.

Well. Getting the tusks *up* the Metro steps at her destination was a lot harder than dragging them down had been, and by the top Karou was exhausted, sweating under her winter coat, and extremely peevish. The portal was a couple more blocks away, linked to the doorway of a synagogue's small storage

45

outbuilding, and when she finally reached it she found two Orthodox rabbis in deep conversation right in front of it.

"Perfect," she muttered. She continued past them and leaned against an iron gate, just out of sight, to wait while they discussed some act of vandalism in mystified tones. At last they left, and Karou wrangled the tusks to the little door and knocked. As she always did while waiting at a portal in some back alley of the world, she imagined being stranded. Sometimes it took long minutes for Issa to open the door, and each and every time, Karou considered the possibility that it might *not* open. There was always a twinge of fear of being locked out, not just for the night, but forever. The scenario made her hyperaware of her powerlessness. If, some day, the door didn't open, she would be alone.

The moment stretched, and Karou, leaning wearily against the doorframe, noticed something. She straightened. On the surface of the door was a large black handprint. That wouldn't have been so very strange, except that it gave every appearance of having been burned into the wood. *Burned*, but in the perfect contours of a hand. This must be what the rabbis were talking about. She traced it with her fingertips, finding that it was actually scored into the wood, so that her own hand fit inside it, though dwarfed by it, and came away dusted with fine ash. She brushed off her fingers, puzzled.

What had made the print? A cleverly shaped brand? It sometimes happened that Brimstone's traders left a mark by which to find portals on their next visit, but that was usually just a smear of paint or a knife-gouged X-marks-the-spot. This was a bit sophisticated for them.

The door creaked open, to Karou's deep relief.

"Did everything go all right?" Issa asked.

Karou heaved the tusks into the vestibule, having to wedge them at an angle to fit them inside. "Sure." She slumped against the wall. "I'd drag tusks across Paris every night if I could, it was such a treat."

7

BLACK HANDPRINTS

Around the world, over a space of days, black handprints appeared on many doors, each scorched deep into wood or metal. Nairobi, Delhi, St. Petersburg, a handful of other cities. It was a phenomenon. In Cairo, the owner of a shisha den painted over the mark on his back door only to find, hours later, that the handprint had smoldered through the paint and showed just as black as when he'd discovered it.

There were some witnesses to the acts of vandalism, but no one believed what they claimed to have seen.

"With his bare hand," a child in New York told his mother, pointing out the window. "He just put his hand there, and it glowed and smoked."

His mother sighed and went back to bed. The boy was an established fibber, worse luck for him, because this time he was not lying. He had seen a tall man lay his hand on the door and scorch the mark into it. "His shadow was wrong," he told his mother's retreating back. "It didn't match."

A drunken tourist in Bangkok witnessed a similar scene, though this time the handprint was made by a woman of such impossible beauty that he followed her, spellbound, only to see her — as he claimed — *fly away.*

"She didn't have wings," he told his friends, "but her shadow did."

"His eyes were like fire," said an old man who caught sight of one of the strangers from his rooftop pigeon coop. "Sparks rained down when he flew away."

So it was in slum alleys and dark courtyards in Kuala Lumpur, Istanbul, San Francisco, Paris. Beautiful men and women with distorted shadows came and scorched their handprints onto doors before vanishing skyward, drafts of heat billowing behind them with the *whumph* of unseen wings. Here and there, feathers fell, and they were like tufts of white fire, disintegrating to ash as soon as they touched the ground. In Delhi, a Sister of Mercy reached out and caught one on her palm like a raindrop, but unlike a raindrop it burned, and left the perfect outline of a feather seared into her flesh.

"Angel," she whispered, relishing the pain.

She was not exactly wrong.

8

GAVRIELS

When Karou stepped back into the shop, she found that Brim-stone was not alone. A trader sat opposite him, a loathsome American hunter whose slab-of-meat face was garnished by the biggest, filthiest beard she had ever seen.

She turned to Issa and grimaced.

"I know," agreed Issa, coming across the threshold in a ripple of serpentine muscle. "I gave him Avigeth. She's about to molt."

Karou laughed.

Avigeth was the coral snake wound around the hunter's thick throat, forming a collar far too beautiful for the likes of him. Her bands of black, yellow, and crimson looked, even in their dulled state, like fine Chinese cloisonné. But for all her beauty, Avigeth was deadly, and never more so than when the itch of impending molt made her peevish. She was wending now in and out of the massive beard, a constant reminder to the trader that he must behave if he hoped to live.

"On behalf of the animals of North America," whispered Karou, "can't you just make her bite him?"

"I could, but Brimstone wouldn't be happy. As well you know, Bain is one of his most valued traders."

Karou sighed. "I know." For longer than she had even been alive, Bain had been supplying Brimstone with bear teeth—grizzly, black, and polar—and lynx, fox, mountain lion, wolf, and sometimes even dog. He specialized in predators, always of premium value down here. They were also, Karou had pointed out to Brimstone on many occasions, of premium value to the world. How many beautiful carcasses did that pile of teeth amount to?

She watched, dismayed, as Brimstone took two large gold medallions out of his strongbox, each the size of a saucer and engraved with his own likeness. Gavriels. Enough to buy her flight and invisibility, and he pushed them across the desk to the hunter. Karou scowled as Bain pocketed them and rose from his chair, moving slowly so as not to irritate Avigeth. Out of the corner of one soulless eye, he cut Karou a look that she could almost swear was a gloat, and then had the gall to wink.

Karou clenched her teeth and said nothing as Issa escorted Bain out. Had it been only that morning that Kaz had winked at her from the model stand? What a day.

The door closed, and Brimstone gestured Karou forward. She heaved the canvas-wrapped tusks toward him and let the bundle collapse on the shop floor.

"Be careful," he barked. "Do you know the value of these?"

"Indeed I do, since I just paid it."

"That's the *human* value. The idiots would carve them to bits to make trinkets and baubles."

"And what will you do with them?" asked Karou. She kept her voice casual, as if Brimstone might forget himself and reveal, at last, the mystery at the core of everything: what in the hell he *did* with all these teeth.

He only gave her a weary look, as if to say, *Nice try.*

"What? You brought it up. And no, I don't know the *inhuman* value of tusks. I have no idea."

"Beyond price." He started sawing at the duct tape with a curved knife.

"It's a good thing I had some scuppies on me, then," said Karou, flopping into the chair Bain had just vacated. "Otherwise you'd have lost your priceless tusks to another bidder."

"What?"

"You didn't give me enough money. This little bastard war criminal kept bidding them up and—well, I'm not *sure* he was a war criminal, but he had this certain indefinable *war-criminaliness* about him—and I could see he was determined to get them, so I...maybe I shouldn't have, though, since you don't approve of my...pettiness, did you call it?" She smiled sweetly and dangled the remaining beads of her necklace. It was more of a bracelet now.

She'd used her new itch trick on the man, wishing a relentless onslaught of cranny itches on him until he fled the room. Surely Brimstone knew; he always knew. It would be nice, she thought, if he would say thank you. Instead, he just slapped a coin onto the table.

A measly shing.

"That's it? I dragged those things across Paris for you for a *shing*, while beardy gets away with double gavriels?"

Brimstone ignored her and extricated the tusks from their shroud. Twiga came to consult with him, and they muttered in undertones in their own language, which Karou had learned from the cradle in the natural way, and not by wish. It was a harsh tongue, growlsome and full of fricatives, with much of it rising from the throat. By comparison, even German or Hebrew seemed melodious.

While they talked about tooth configurations, Karou helped herself to the scuppy teacups and set about replenishing her string of nearly useless wishes, which she decided to keep as a multistrand bracelet for now. Twiga hauled the tusks over to his corner for cleaning, and Karou contemplated going home.

Home. The word always had air quotes around it in her mind. She'd done what she could to make her flat cozy, filling it with art, books, ornate lanterns, and a Persian carpet as soft as lynx fur, and of course there were her angel wings taking up one whole wall. But there was no help for its real emptiness; its close air was stirred by no breath but her own. When she was alone, the empty place within her, the *missingness* as she thought of it, seemed to swell. Even being with Kaz had done something to keep it at bay, though not enough. Never enough.

She thought of the little cot that used to be hers, tucked behind the tall bookcases in the back of the shop, and wished whimsically that she could stay here tonight. She could fall asleep like she used to, to the sound of murmured voices, Issa's soft slither, the scritch of wee elsething beasties scampering in the shadows.

"Sweet girl." Yasri bustled out of the kitchen with a tea tray. Beside the teapot was a plate of the custard-filled pastries in the shape of horns that were her specialty. "You must be hungry," she said in her parrot voice. With a sideward glance at Brimstone, she added, "It's not healthy for a growing girl, always running off hither and thither at not a moment's notice."

"That's me, hither-and-thither girl," said Karou. She grabbed a pastry and slumped in her chair to eat it.

Brimstone spared her a glance, then said to Yasri, "And I suppose it's healthy for a growing girl to live on pastry?"

Yasri tutted. "I'd be happy to fix her a proper meal if you ever gave me warning, you great brute." She turned to Karou. "You're too thin, lovely. It isn't becoming."

"Mmm," agreed Issa, caressing Karou's hair. "She should be leopard, don't you think? Sleek and lazy, fur hot from the sun, and not too lean. A well-fed leopard-girl, lapping from a bowl of cream."

Karou smiled and ate. Yasri poured tea for them all, just how they liked it, which meant four sugars for Brimstone. After all these years, Karou still thought it was funny that the Wishmonger had a sweet tooth. She watched as he bent back to his never-ending work, stringing teeth into necklaces.

"*Oryx leucoryx*," she identified as he selected a tooth from his tray.

He was unimpressed. "Antelopes are child's play."

"Give me a hard one, then."

He handed her a shark's tooth, and Karou was reminded of the hours she'd sat here with him as a child, learning teeth. "Mako," she said.

"Longfin or shortfin?"

"Oh. Uh." She went still, holding the tooth between her

54

thumb and forefinger. Brimstone had trained her in this art since she was small, and she could read the origin and integrity of teeth from their subtle vibrations. She declared, "Short."

He grunted, which was about as close as he came to praise.

"Did you know," Karou asked him, "that mako shark fetuses eat each other in the womb?"

Issa, who was stroking Avigeth, gave a *tch* of disgust.

"It's true. Only cannibal fetuses survive to be born. Can you imagine if people were like that?" She put her feet up on the desk and, two seconds later, at a dark look from Brimstone, took them down again.

The shop's warmth was making her drowsy. The cot in its little nook called to her, as did the quilt Yasri had made her, so soft from years of snuggling. "Brimstone," she said, hesitant. "Do you think—?"

At that moment, a thudding sounded, violent.

"Oh, dear," said Yasri, clicking her beak in agitation as she gathered up the tea things.

It was the shop's other door.

Back behind Twiga's workspace, in the shadowed reaches of the shop where no lantern ever hung, there was a second door. In all Karou's life, it had never been opened in her presence. She had no idea what was behind it.

The thudding came again, so hard it rattled the teeth in their jars. Brimstone rose, and Karou knew what was expected of her—that she rise, too, and leave at once—but she slouched down in her chair. "Let me stay," she said. "I'll be quiet. I'll go back to my cot. I won't look—"

"Karou," said Brimstone. "You know the rules."

"I hate the rules."

He took a step toward her, prepared to help her out of the chair if she didn't obey, and she shot to her feet, hands up in surrender. "Okay, okay." She put on her coat as the banging continued, and grabbed another pastry from Yasri's tray before letting Issa usher her into the vestibule. The door closed behind them, sealing out sound.

She didn't bother asking Issa who was at the other door — Issa never gave away Brimstone's secrets. But she said, a little pitifully, "I was just about to ask Brimstone if I could sleep in my old cot."

Issa leaned forward to kiss her cheek and said, "Oh, sweet girl, wouldn't that be nice? We can wait right here, the way we did when you were small."

Ah, yes. When Karou was too small to shove out into the world's streets on her own, Issa had kept her here. *Hours* they had sometimes crouched in this tiny space, Issa trying to keep her entertained by singing songs or drawing — in fact, it was Issa who had started her drawing — or crowning her with venomous snakes, while inside Brimstone confronted whatever lurked on the other side of that door.

"You can come back in," Issa continued, "after."

"That's okay," Karou said with a sigh. "I'll just go."

Issa squeezed her arm and said, "Sweet dreams, sweet girl," and Karou hunched her shoulders and stepped back out into the cold. As she walked, clock towers across Prague started arguing midnight, and the long, fraught Monday came at last to a close.

9

THE DEVIL'S DOORWAYS

Akiva stood at the edge of a rooftop terrace in Riyadh, peering down at a doorway in the lane below. It was as nondescript as the others, but he knew it for what it was. He could feel its bitter aura of magic as an ache behind his eyes.

It was one of the devil's portals into the human world.

Spreading vast wings that were visible only in his shadow, he glided down to it, landing in a rain of sparks. A street sweeper saw him and dropped to his knees, but Akiva ignored him and faced the door, his hands curling into fists. He wanted nothing so much as to draw his swords and storm inside, end things quick right there in Brimstone's shop, end them bloody, but the magic of the portals was cunning and he knew better than to attempt it, so he did what he had come here to do.

He reached out and laid his hand flat against the door. There was a soft glow and a smell of scorching, and when he took away his hand its print was scored into the wood.

That was all, for now.

He turned and walked away, and folk cringed close to walls to let him pass.

Certainly, they couldn't see him as he truly was. His fiery wings were glamoured invisible, and he should have been able to pass as human, but he wasn't quite pulling it off. What people saw was a tall young man, beautiful — truly, breath-stealingly beautiful, in a way one rarely beholds in real life — who moved among them with predatory grace, seeming no more mindful of them than if they were statuary in a garden of gods. On his back a pair of crossed swords were sheathed, and his sleeves were pushed up over forearms tanned and corded with muscle. His hands were a curiosity, etched both white with scars and black with the ink of tattoos — simple repeating black lines hatched across the tops of his fingers.

His dark hair was cropped close to his skull, with a hairline that dipped into a widow's peak. His golden skin was bronzed darker across the planes of his face — high ridges of cheek-bones, brow, bridge of the nose — as if he lived his life in drenching rich honey light.

Beautiful as he was, he was forbidding. It was difficult to imagine him breaking into a smile — which indeed Akiva hadn't done in many years, and couldn't imagine doing ever again.

But all of this was just fleeting impression. What people fixed on, stopping to watch him pass, were his eyes.

They were amber like a tiger's, and like a tiger's they were rimmed in black — the black both of heavy lashes and of kohl, which focused the gold of his irises like beams of light. They were pure and luminous, mesmerizing and achingly beautiful, but something was wrong, was *missing*. Humanity, perhaps, that quality of benevolence that humans have, without irony, named after themselves. When, coming around a corner, an old woman found herself in his path, the full force of his gaze fell on her and she gasped.

There was live fire in his eyes. She was sure he would set her alight.

She gasped and stumbled, and he reached out a hand to steady her. She felt heat, and when he continued past, his unseen wings brushed against her. Sparks shivered from them and she was left gaping in breathless, paralyzed panic at his receding form. Plainly she saw his shadow wings fan open and then, with a gust of heat that blew her headscarf off, he was gone.

In moments Akiva was up in the ether, scarcely feeling the sting of ice crystals in the thin air. He let his glamour fall away, and his wings were like sheets of fire sweeping the black of the heavens. He moved at speed, onward toward another human city to find another doorway bitter with the devil's magic, and after that another, until all bore the black handprint.

In far reaches of the world, Hazael and Liraz were doing the same. Once all the doors were marked, the end would begin.

And it would begin with fire.

❧ 10 ❧

HITHER-AND-THITHER GIRL

In general, Karou managed to keep her two lives in balance.
On the one hand, she was a seventeen-year-old art student in
Prague; on the other, errand girl to an inhuman creature who
was the closest thing she had to family. For the most part, she'd
found that there was time enough in a week for both lives. If
not every week, at least most.

This did not turn out to be one of those weeks.

Tuesday she was still in class when Kishmish alighted on the
window ledge and rapped at the glass with his beak. His note
was even more succinct than yesterday's and read only *Come*.
Karou did, though if she'd known where Brimstone was sending
her, she might not have.

The animal market in Saigon was one of her least favorite
places in the world. The caged kittens and German shepherds,
the bats and sun bears and langur monkeys, were not sold as
pets, but *food*. An old crone of a butcher's mother saved teeth

in a funerary urn, and it was Karou who had to collect them every few months and seal the deal with a sour swig of rice wine that left her stomach churning.

Wednesday: Northern Canada. Two Athabascan hunters, a sickening haul of wolf teeth.

Thursday: San Francisco, a young blonde herpetologist with a cache of rattlesnake fangs left over from her unfortunate research subjects.

"You know, you could come into the shop yourself," Karou told her, irritated because she had a self-portrait due the next day and could have used the extra hours to perfect it.

There were various reasons why traders might not come into the shop. Some had lost the privilege through misbehavior; others weren't yet vetted; many were simply afraid to submit to the serpent collars, which shouldn't have been a problem in this case, since this particular scientist spent her days with snakes by choice.

The herpetologist shuddered. "I came once. I thought the snake-woman was going to kill me."

Karou smothered a smile. "Ah." She understood. Issa was no friend to reptile killers, and had been known to coax her snakes into semi-strangulation as the mood arose. "Well, okay." She counted out twenties into a decent stack. "But you know, if you do come in, Brimstone will pay you wishes worth much more than this." He did not, to Karou's bitterness, entrust her to dispense wishes on his behalf.

"Maybe next time."

"Your choice." Karou shrugged and left with a little wave, to head back to the portal and through it, taking note as she did that a black handprint was scorched into its surface. She was going to mention it to Brimstone, but he was with a trader and she had homework to get to, so she went on her way.

Up half the night working on her self-portrait, she was groggy on Friday and hopeful that Brimstone wouldn't summon her again. He usually didn't send for her more than twice a week, and it had already been four times. In the morning, while drawing old Wiktor in nothing but a feather boa—a sight Zuzana almost did not survive—she kept an eye on the window. All through afternoon painting studio, she kept fearing that Kishmish would appear, but he didn't, and after school she waited for Zuzana under a ledge out of the drizzle.

"Well," said her friend, "it's a Karou. Get a good look, folks. Sightings of this elusive creature are getting rarer all the time."

Karou noted the coolness in her voice. "Poison?" she suggested hopefully. After the week she'd had, she wanted to go to the cafe and sink into a couch, gossip and laugh and sketch and drink tea and make up for lost normal.

Zuzana gave her the eyebrow. "What, no *errands*?"

"No, thank god. Come on, I'm freezing."

"I don't know, Karou. Maybe *I* have secret errands today."

Karou chewed the inside of her cheek and wondered what to say. She hated the way Brimstone kept secrets from her, and she hated even more having to do the same thing to Zuzana. What kind of friendship was based on evasions and lies? Growing up, she'd found it almost impossible to have friends; the need for lies always got in the way. It had been even worse then because she'd lived in the shop—forget about having a friend over to play! She would exit the portal in Manhattan each morning for school, followed by her lessons in karate and aikido, and go back to it each evening.

It was a boarded-up door of an abandoned building in the East Village, and when Karou was in fifth grade a friend named Belinda had seen her go in and had come to the conclusion that she was homeless. Word got around, parents and teachers got involved, and Karou, unable to produce Esther, her fake grandmother, on short notice, was taken into DHS custody. She was put into a group home, from which she escaped the first night, never to be seen again. After that: a new school in Hong Kong and extra caution that no one saw her using the portal. That meant more lies and secrecy, and no possibility of real friends.

She was old enough now that there was no risk of social services sniffing around, but as for friends, that was still a tight-rope. Zuzana was the best friend she'd ever had, and she didn't want to lose her.

She sighed. "I'm sorry about this week. It's been crazy. It's work—"

"Work? Since when do you *work*?"

"I work. What do you think I live on, rainwater and daydreams?"

She'd hoped to make Zuzana smile, but her friend just squinted at her. "How would I know what you live on, Karou? How long have we been friends, and you've never mentioned a job or a family or anything—"

Ignoring the "family or anything" part, Karou replied, "Well, it's not exactly a *job*. I just run errands for this guy. Make pick-ups, meet with people."

"What, like a drug dealer?"

"Come on, Zuze, really? He's a…collector, I guess."

"Oh? What does he collect?"

"Just stuff. Who cares?"

"I care. I'm interested. It just sounds *weird*, Karou. You're not mixed up in something weird, are you?"

Oh no, thought Karou. *Not at all.* Taking a deep breath, she said, "I really can't talk about it. It's not my business, it's his."

"Fine. Whatever." Zuzana spun on one platform heel and walked out into the rain.

"Wait!" Karou called after her. She *wanted* to talk about it. She wanted to tell Zuzana everything, to complain about her crappy week—the elephant tusks, the nightmarish animal market, how Brimstone only paid her in stupid shings, and the creepy banging on the other door. She could put it in her sketchbook, and that was something, but it wasn't enough. She wanted to *talk*.

It was out of the question, of course. "Can we please go to Poison?" she asked, her voice coming out small and tired. Zuzana looked back and saw the expression that Karou sometimes got when she thought no one was watching. It was sadness, *lostness*, and the worst thing about it was the way it seemed like a default—like it was there all the time, and all her other expressions were just an array of masks she used to cover it up.

Zuzana relented. "Fine. Okay. I'm dying for some goulash. Get it? Dying. Ha ha."

The poisoned goulash; it was an old groaner between them, and Karou knew everything was okay. For now. But what about next time?

They set out, umbrella-less and huddled together, hurrying through the drizzle.

"You should know," Zuzana said, "Jackass has been hanging around Poison. I think he's lying in wait for you."

Karou groaned. "Great." Kaz had been calling and texting, and she had been ignoring him.

"We could go somewhere else—"

"No. I'm not letting that rodent-loaf have Poison. Poison's ours."

"*Rodent-loaf?*" repeated Zuzana.

It was a favorite insult of Issa's, and made sense in the context of the serpent-woman's diet, which consisted mainly of small furry creatures. Karou said, "Yes. Loaf of rodent. Ground mouse-meat with bread crumbs and ketchup—"

"Ugh. Stop."

"Or you could substitute hamsters, I suppose," said Karou. "Or guinea pigs. You know they roast guinea pigs in Peru, skewered on little sticks, like marshmallows?"

"Stop," said Zuzana.

"Mmm, guinea pig s'mores—"

"Stop *now*, before I throw up. *Please*."

And Karou did stop, not because of Zuzana's plea, but because she caught a familiar flutter in the corner of her eye. *No no no*, she said to herself. She didn't—wouldn't—turn her head. *Not Kishmish, not tonight*.

Noting her sudden silence, Zuzana asked, "You okay?"

The flutter again, in a circle of lamplight in Karou's line of sight. Too far off to draw special attention to itself, but unmistakably Kishmish.

Damn.

"I'm fine," Karou said, and she kept on resolutely in the direction of Poison Kitchen. What was she supposed to do, smack her forehead and claim to have remembered an errand, after all that? She wondered what Zuzana would say if she could see Brimstone's little beast messenger, his bat wings so bizarre on his feathered body. Being Zuzana, she'd probably want to make a marionette version of him.

"How's the puppet project coming?" Karou asked, trying to act normal.

Zuzana brightened and started to tell her. Karou half listened, but she was distracted by her jumbled defiance and anxiety. What would Brimstone do if she didn't come? What *could* he do, come out and get her?

She was aware of Kishmish following, and as she ducked under the arch into the courtyard of Poison Kitchen, she gave him a pointed look as if to say, *I see you. And I'm not coming.* He cocked his head at her, perplexed, and she left him there and went inside.

The cafe was crowded, though Kaz, blessedly, was nowhere to be seen. A mix of local laborers, backpackers, expat artist types, and students hung out at the coffins, the fume of their cigarettes so heavy the Roman statues seemed to loom from a fog, ghoulish in their gas masks.

"Damn," said Karou, seeing a trio of scruffy backpackers lounging at their favorite table. "Pestilence is taken."

"Everything is taken," said Zuzana. "Stupid Lonely Planet book. I want to go back in time and mug that damn travel writer at the end of the alley, make sure he never finds this place."

"So violent. You want to mug and tase everybody these days."

"I *do*," Zuzana agreed. "I swear I hate more people every day. *Everyone* annoys me. If I'm like this now, what am I going to be like when I'm old?"

"You'll be the mean old biddy who fires a BB gun at kids from her balcony."

"Nah. BBs just rile 'em up. More like a crossbow. Or a bazooka."

"You're a brute."

Zuzana dropped a curtsy, then took another frustrated look around at the crowded cafe. "Suck. Want to go somewhere else?"

Karou shook her head. Their hair was already soaked; she didn't want to go back out. She just wanted her favorite table in her favorite cafe. In her jacket pocket, her fingers toyed with the store of shings from the week's errands. "I think those guys are about to leave." She nodded to the backpackers at Pestilence.

"I don't think so," said Zuzana. "They have full beers."

"No, I think they are." Between Karou's fingers, one of the shings dematerialized. A second later, the backpackers rose to their feet. "Told you."

In her head, she fancied she heard Brimstone's commentary: *Evicting strangers from cafe tables: selfish.*

"Weird," was Zuzana's response as the girls slipped behind the giant horse statue to claim their table. Looking bewildered, the backpackers left. "They were kind of cute," said Zuzana.

"Oh? You want to call them back?"

"As if." They had a rule against backpacker boys, who blew through with the wind, and started to all look the same after a while, with their stubbly chins and wrinkled shirts. "I was simply making a diagnosis of cuteness. Plus, they looked kind of lost. Like puppies."

Karou felt a pang of guilt. What was she doing, defying Brimstone, spending wishes on mean things like forcing innocent backpackers out into the rain? She flopped onto the couch. Her head ached, her hair was clammy, she was tired, and she couldn't stop worrying about the Wishmonger. What would he say?

The entire time she and Zuzana were eating their goulash, her gaze kept straying to the door.

"Watching for someone?" Zuzana asked.

"Oh. Just . . . just afraid Kaz might turn up."

"Yeah, well, if he does, we can wrestle him into this coffin and nail it shut."

"Sounds good."

They ordered tea, which came in an antique silver service, the sugar and creamer dishes engraved with the words *arsenic* and *strychnine*.

"So," said Karou, "you'll see violin boy tomorrow at the theater. What's your strategy?"

"I have no strategy," said Zuzana. "I just want to skip all this and get to the part where he's my boyfriend. Not to mention, you know, the part where he's aware I exist."

"Come on, you wouldn't really want to skip this part."

"Yes I would."

"Skip *meeting* him? The butterflies, the pounding heart, the blushing? The part where you enter each other's magnetic fields for the first time, and it's like invisible lines of energy are drawing you together—"

"*Invisible lines of energy?*" Zuzana repeated. "Are you turning into one of those New Age weirdos who wear crystals and read people's auras?"

"You know what I mean. First date, holding hands, first kiss, all the smoldering and yearning?"

"Oh, Karou, you poor little romantic."

"Hardly. I was going to say the beginning is the good part, when it's all sparks and sparkles, before they are inevitably unmasked as assholes."

Zuzana grimaced. "They can't all be assholes, can they?"

"I don't know. Maybe not. Maybe just the pretty ones."

"But he *is* pretty. God, I hope he's not an asshole. Do you think there's any chance he's both a non-orifice *and* single? I mean, seriously. What are the chances?"

"Slim."

"I know." Zuzana slumped dramatically back and lay crumpled like a discarded marionette.

"Pavel likes you, you know," said Karou. "He's a certified non-orifice."

"Yes, well, Pavel's sweet, but he does not give of the butterflies."

"The butterflies in the belly." Karou sighed. "I know. You know what I think? I think the butterflies are always there in your belly, in everyone, all the time —"

"Like bacteria?"

"*No*, not like bacteria, like *butterflies*, and some people's butterflies react to other people's, on a chemical level, like pheromones, so that when they're nearby, your butterflies start to dance. They can't help it — it's chemical."

"Chemical. Now *that's* romantic."

"I know, right? Stupid butterflies." Liking the idea, Karou opened her sketchbook and started to draw it: cartoon intestines and a stomach crowded with butterflies. *Papilio stomachus* would be their Latin name.

Zuzana asked, "So, if it's all chemical and you have no say in the matter, does that mean Jackass still makes your butterflies dance?"

Karou looked up. "God no. I think he makes my butterflies *barf*."

Zuzana had just taken a sip of tea and her hand flew to her mouth in an effort to keep it in. She laughed, doubled over, until she managed to swallow. "Oh, gross. Your stomach is full of butterfly barf!"

Karou laughed, too, and kept sketching. "Actually, I think my stomach is full of dead butterflies. Kaz killed them."

She wrote, *Papilio stomachus: fragile creatures, vulnerable to frost and betrayal.*

"So what," said Zuzana. "They had to be pretty stupid butterflies to fall for him anyway. You'll grow new ones with more sense. New *wise* butterflies."

Karou loved Zuzana for her willingness to play out such silliness on a long kite string. "Right." She raised her teacup in a toast. "To a new generation of butterflies, hopefully less stupid than the last." Maybe they were burgeoning even now in fat little cocoons. Or maybe not. It was hard to imagine feeling that magical tingling sensation in the pit of her belly anytime soon. *Best not to worry about it,* she thought. She didn't need it. Well. She didn't *want* to need it. Yearning for love made her feel like a cat that was always twining around ankles, meowing *Pet me, pet me, look at me, love me.*

Better to be the cat gazing coolly down from a high wall, its expression inscrutable. The cat that shunned petting, that needed no one. Why couldn't she be that cat?

Be that cat!!! she wrote, drawing it into the corner of her page, cool and aloof.

Karou wished she could be the kind of girl who was complete unto herself, comfortable in solitude, serene. But she wasn't. She was lonely, and she feared the missingness within her as if it might expand and . . . *cancel* her. She craved a presence beside her, solid. Fingertips light at the nape of her neck and a voice meeting hers in the dark. Someone who would wait with an umbrella to walk her home in the rain, and smile like sunshine when he saw her coming. Who would dance with her on her balcony, keep his promises and know her secrets, and make a tiny world wherever he was, with just her and his arms and his whisper and her trust.

The door opened. She looked in the mirror and suppressed a curse. Slipping in behind some tourists, that winged shadow was back again. Karou rose and made for the bathroom, where she took the note that Kishmish had come to deliver.

Again it bore a single word. But this time the word was *Please.*

11

PLEASE

Please? Brimstone never said please. Hurrying across town, Karou found herself more troubled than if the note had said something menacing, like: *Now, or else.*

Letting her in, Issa was uncharacteristically silent.

"What is it, Issa? Am I in trouble?"

"Hush. Just come in and try not to berate him today."

"Berate *him*?" Karou blinked. She'd have thought if anyone was in danger of being berated, it was herself.

"You're very hard on him sometimes, as if it's not hard enough already."

"As if what's not hard enough?"

"His life. His work. His life *is* work. It's joyless, it's relentless, and sometimes you make it harder than it already is."

"Me?" Karou was stunned. "Did I just come in on the middle of a conversation, Issa? I have no idea what you're talking about—"

"Hush, I said. I'm just asking that you try to be kind, like when you were little. You were such a joy to us all, Karou. I know it's not easy for you, living this life, but try to remember, always try to remember, you're not the only one with troubles."

And with that the inner door unsealed and Karou stepped across the threshold. She was confused, ready to defend herself, but when she saw Brimstone, she forgot all that.

He was leaning heavily on his desk, his great head resting in one hand, while the other cupped the wishbone he wore around his neck. Kishmish hopped in agitation from one of his master's horns to the other, uttering crickety chirrups of concern, and Karou faltered to a halt. "Are . . . are you okay?" It felt odd asking, and she realized that of all the questions she had barraged him with in her life, she had never asked him that. She'd never had reason to—he'd scarcely ever shown a hint of emotion, let alone weakness or weariness.

He raised his head, released the wishbone, and said simply, "You came." He sounded surprised and, Karou thought guiltily, relieved.

Striving for lightness, she said, "Well, please *is* the magic word, you know."

"I thought perhaps we had lost you."

"*Lost* me? You mean you thought I'd *died?*"

"No, Karou. I thought that you had taken your freedom."

"My . . ." She trailed off. *Taken her freedom?* "What does that even mean?"

"I've always imagined that one day the path of your life would unroll at your feet and carry you away from us. As it should, as it must. But I am glad that day is not today."

73

Karou stood staring at him. "Seriously? I blow off one errand and you think that's it, I'm gone forever? Jesus. What do you think of me, that you think I'd just vanish like that?"

"Letting you go, Karou, will be like opening the window for a butterfly. One does not hope for the butterfly's return."

"I'm not a freaking butterfly."

"No. You're human. Your place is in the human world. Your childhood is nearly over—"

"So...what? You don't need me anymore?"

"On the contrary. I need you now more than ever. As I said, I'm glad that today is not the day you leave us."

This was all news to Karou, that there would come a day when she would leave her chimaera family, that she even possessed the freedom to do so if she wished. She didn't wish. Well, maybe she wished not to go on some of the creepier errands, but that didn't mean she was a butterfly fluttering against glass, trying to get out and away. She didn't even know what to say.

Brimstone pushed a wallet across the desk to her.

The errand. She'd almost forgotten why she was here. Angry, she grabbed the wallet and flipped it open. Dirhams. Morocco, then. Her brow furrowed. "Izîl?" she asked, and Brimstone nodded.

"But it's not time." Karou had a standing appointment with a graverobber in Marrakesh the last Sunday of every month, and this was Friday, and a week early.

"It is time," said Brimstone. He gestured to a tall apothecary jar on the shelf behind him. Karou knew it well; usually it was full of human teeth. Now it stood nearly empty.

"Oh." Her gaze roved along the shelf, and she saw, to her

surprise, that many of the jars were likewise dwindling. She couldn't remember a time when the tooth supply had been so low. "Wow. You're really burning through teeth. Something going on?"

It was an inane question. As if she could understand what it meant that he was using *more* teeth, when she didn't know what they were for to begin with.

"See what Izîl has," Brimstone said. "I'd rather not send you anywhere else for human teeth, if it can be helped."

"Yeah, me, too." Karou ran her fingers lightly over the bullet scars on her belly, remembering St. Petersburg, the errand gone horribly wrong. Human teeth, despite being in such abundant supply in the world, could be . . . interesting . . . to procure.

She would never forget the sight of those girls, still alive in the cargo hold, mouths bloody, other fates awaiting them next.

They may have gotten away. When Karou thought of them now, she always added a made-up ending, the way Issa had taught her to do with nightmares so she could fall back to sleep. She could only bear the memory if she believed she'd given those girls time to escape their traffickers, and maybe she even had. She'd tried.

How strange it had been, being shot. How *unalarmed* she'd found herself, how quick to unsheathe her hidden knife and use it.

And use it. And use it.

She had trained in fighting for years, but she had never before had to defend her life. In the flash of a moment, she had discovered that she knew just what to do.

"Try the Jemaa el-Fna," Brimstone said. "Kishmish spotted

75

Izîl there, but that was hours ago, when I first summoned you. If you're lucky, he might still be there." And with that, he bent back over his tray of monkey teeth, and Karou was apparently dismissed. Now there was the old Brimstone, and she was glad. This new creature who said "please" and talked about her like she was a butterfly—he was unsettling.

"I'll find him," Karou said. "And I'll be back soon, with my pockets full of human teeth. Ha. I bet that sentence hasn't been said anywhere else in the world today."

The Wishmonger didn't respond, and Karou hesitated in the vestibule. "Brimstone," she said, looking back, "I want you to know I would never just ... leave you."

When he raised his reptilian eyes, they were bleary with exhaustion. "You can't know what you will do," he said, and his hand went again to his wishbone. "I won't hold you to that."

Issa closed the door, and even after Karou stepped out into Morocco, she couldn't shake the image of him like that, and the uneasy feeling that something was terribly wrong.

🌿 12 🌿

SOMETHING ELSE ENTIRELY

Akiva saw her come out. He was approaching the doorway, was just steps from it when it swung open, letting loose an acrid flood of magic that set his teeth on edge. Through the portal stepped a girl with hair the improbable color of lapis lazuli. She didn't see him, seeming lost in thought as she hurried past.

He said nothing but stood looking after her as she moved away, the curve of the alley soon robbing him of the sight of her and her swaying blue hair. He shook himself, turned back to the portal, and laid his hand on it. The hiss of the scorch, his hand limned in smoke, and it was done: the last of the doorways that were his to mark. In other quarters of the world, Hazael and Liraz would be finishing, too, and winging their way toward Samarkand.

Akiva was poised to spring skyward and begin the last leg of his journey, to meet them there before returning home, but a heartbeat passed, then another, and still he stood with his feet on the earth, looking in the direction the girl had gone.

Without quite deciding to do it, he found himself following her.

How, he wondered, when he caught the lamp-lit shimmer of her hair up ahead, had a girl like that gotten mixed up with the chimaera? From what he'd seen of Brimstone's other traders, they were rank brutes with dead eyes, stinking of the slaughterhouse. But her? She was a shining beauty, lithe and vivid, though surely this wasn't what intrigued him. All of his own kind were beautiful, to such an extent that beauty was next to meaningless among them. What, then, compelled him to follow her, when he should have taken at once to the sky, the mission so near completion? He couldn't have said. It was almost as if a whisper beckoned him onward.

The medina of Marrakesh was labyrinthine, some three thousand blind alleys intertwined like a drawer full of snakes, but the girl seemed to know her route cold. She paused once to run a finger over the weave of a textile, and Akiva slowed his steps, veering off to one side so he could see her better.

There was a look of unguarded wistfulness on her pale, pretty face—a kind of *lostness*—but the moment the vendor spoke to her, it transmuted to a smile like light. She answered easily, making the man laugh, and they bantered back and forth, her Arabic rich and throaty, with an edge like a purr.

Akiva watched her with hawklike fixedness. Until a few days ago, humans had been little more than legend to him, and now here he was in their world. It was like stepping into the pages of a book—a book alive with color and fragrance, filth and chaos—and the blue-haired girl moved through it all like a fairy through a story, the light treating her differently than it did others, the air seeming to gather around her like held breath. As if this whole place were a story about *her*.

Who was she?

He didn't know, but some intuition sang in him that, whoever she was, she was not just another of Brimstone's street-level grim reapers. She was, he was sure, something else entirely.

His gaze unwavering, he prowled after her as she made her way through the medina.

13

THE GRAVEROBBER

Karou walked with her hands in her pockets, trying to shake her uneasiness about Brimstone. That stuff about "taking her freedom"—what was that about? It gave her a creeping sense of impending aloneness, like she was some orphaned animal raised by do-gooders, soon to be released into the wild.

She didn't want to be released into the wild. She wanted to be *held dear*. To belong to a place and a family, irrevocably.

"Magic healings here, Miss Lady, for the melancholy bowels," someone called out to her, and she couldn't help smiling as she shook her head in demurral. *How about melancholy hearts?* she thought. Was there a cure for that? Probably. There was real magic here among the quacks and touts. She knew of a scribe dressed all in white who penned letters to the dead (*and* delivered them), and an old storyteller who sold ideas to writers at the price of a year of their lives. Karou had seen tourists laugh as they signed his contract, not believing it for a second, but she believed it. Hadn't she seen stranger things?

As she made her way, the city began to distract her from her mood. It was hard to be glum in such a place. In some *derbs*, as the wending alleyways were called, the world seemed draped in carpets. In others, freshly dyed silks dripped scarlet and cobalt on the heads of passersby. Languages crowded the air like exotic birds: Arabic, French, the tribal tongues. Women chivvied children home to bed, and old men in tarboosh caps leaned together in doorways, smoking.

A trill of laughter, the scent of cinnamon and donkeys, and color, everywhere color.

Karou made her way toward the Jemaa el-Fna, the square that was the city's nerve center, a mad, teeming carnival of humanity: snake charmers and dancers, dusty barefoot boys, pickpockets, hapless tourists, and food stalls selling everything from orange juice to roasted sheep's heads. On some errands, Karou couldn't get back to the portal fast enough, but in Marrakesh she liked to linger and wander, sip mint tea, sketch, browse through the souks for pointy slippers and silver bracelets.

She would not be lingering tonight, however. Brimstone was clearly anxious to have his teeth. She thought again of the empty jars, and furious curiosity strummed at her mind. What was it all about? *What?* She tried to stop wondering. She was going to find the graverobber, after all, and Izîl was nothing if not a cautionary tale.

"Don't be curious" was one of Brimstone's prime rules, and Izîl had not obeyed it. Karou pitied him, because she understood him. In her, too, curiosity was a perverse fire, stoked by any effort to extinguish it. The more Brimstone ignored her questions, the more she yearned to know. And she had *a lot* of questions.

The teeth, of course: What the hell were they all for?

What of the other door? Where did it lead?

What exactly were the chimaera, and where had they come from? Were there more of them?

And what about her? Who were her parents, and how had she fallen into Brimstone's care? Was she a fairy-tale cliché, like the firstborn child in "Rumpelstiltskin," the settlement of some debt? Or perhaps her mother had been a trader strangled by her serpent collar, leaving a baby squalling on the floor of the shop. Karou had thought of a hundred scenarios, but the truth remained a mystery.

Was there another life she was meant to be living? At times she felt a keen certainty that there was — a phantom life, taunting her from just out of reach. A sense would come over her while she was drawing or walking, and once when she was dancing slow and close with Kaz, that she was supposed to be doing something else with her hands, with her legs, with her body. Something else. Something else. Something *else*.

But what?

She reached the square and wandered through the chaos, her movements synchronizing themselves to the rhythms of mystical Gnawa music as she dodged motorbikes and acrobats. Billows of grilled-meat smoke gusted thick as houses on fire, teenage boys whispered "hashish," and costumed water-sellers clamored "Photo! Photo!" At a distance, she spotted the hunchback shape of Izîl among the henna artists and street dentists.

Seeing him at one-month intervals was like watching a

time-lapse of decline. When Karou was a child, he was a doctor and a scholar—a straight and genteel man with mild brown eyes and a silky mustache he preened like plumage. He had come to the shop himself and done business at Brimstone's desk, and, unlike the other traders, he always made it seem like a social call. He flirted with Issa, brought her little gifts— snakes carved from seedpods, jade-drop earrings, almonds. He brought dolls for Karou, and a tiny silver tea service for them, and he didn't neglect Brimstone, either, casually leaving chocolates or jars of honey on the desk when he left.

But that was before he'd been warped by the weight of a terrible choice he'd made, bent and twisted and driven mad. He wasn't welcome in the shop anymore, so Karou came out to meet him here.

Seeing him now, tender pity overcame her. He was bent nearly double, his gnarled olivewood walking stick all that kept him from collapsing on his face. His eyes were sunk in bruises, and his teeth, which were not his own, were overlarge in his shrunken face. The mustache that had been his pride hung lank and tangled. Any passerby would be taken with pity, but to Karou, who knew how he had looked only a few years earlier, he was a tragedy to behold.

His face lit up when he saw her. "Look who it is! The Wishmonger's beautiful daughter, sweet ambassadress of teeth. Have you come to buy a sad old man a cup of tea?"

"Hello, Izîl. A cup of tea sounds perfect," she said, and led him to the cafe where they usually met.

"My dear, has the month passed me by? I'm afraid I'd quite forgotten our appointment."

"Oh, you haven't. I've come early."

"Ah, well, it's always a pleasure to see you, but I haven't got much for the old devil, I'm afraid."

"But you have some?"

"Some."

Unlike most of the other traders, Izîl neither hunted nor murdered; he didn't kill at all. Before, as a doctor working in conflict zones, he'd had access to war dead whose teeth wouldn't be missed. Now that madness had lost him his livelihood, he had to dig up graves.

Quite abruptly, he snapped, "Hush, thing! Behave, and then we'll see."

Karou knew he was not speaking to her, and politely pretended not to have heard.

They reached the cafe. When Izîl dropped into his chair, it strained and groaned, its legs bowing as if beneath a weight far greater than this one wasted man. "So," he asked, settling in, "how are my old friends? Issa?"

"She's well."

"I do so miss her face. Do you have any new drawings of her?"

Karou did, and she showed them to him.

"Beautiful." He traced Issa's cheek with his fingertip. "So beautiful. The subject *and* the work. You are very talented, my dear." Seeing the episode with the Somali poacher, he snorted, "Fools. What Brimstone has to endure, dealing with humans."

Karou's eyebrows went up. "Come on, their problem isn't that they're human. It's that they're *sub*human."

"True enough. Every race has its bad seeds, one supposes. Isn't that right, beast of mine?" This last bit he said over his

84

shoulder, and this time a soft response seemed to emanate from the air.

Karou couldn't help herself. She glanced at the ground, where Izîl's shadow was cast crisp across the tiles. It seemed impolite to peek, as if Izîl's...*condition*...ought to be ignored, like a lazy eye or birthmark. His shadow revealed what looking at him directly did not.

Shadows told the truth, and Izîl's told that a creature clung to his back, invisible to the eye. It was a hulking, barrel-chested thing, its arms clenched tight around his neck. This was what curiosity had gotten him: The thing was riding him like a mule. Karou didn't understand how it had come about; she only knew that Izîl had made a wish for knowledge, and this had been the form of its fulfillment. Brimstone warned her that powerful wishes could go powerfully awry, and here was the evidence.

She supposed that the invisible thing, who was called Razgut, had held the secrets Izîl had hungered to know. Whatever they were, surely this price was far too high.

Razgut was talking. Karou could make out only the faintest whisper, and a sound like a soft smack of fleshy lips.

"No," Izîl said. "I will *not* ask her that. She'll only say no."

Karou watched, repelled, as Izîl argued with the thing, which she could see only in shadow. Finally the graverobber said, "All right, all right, hush! I'll ask." Then he turned to Karou and said, apologetically, "He just wants a taste. Just a tiny taste."

"A taste?" She blinked. Their tea had not yet arrived. "Of what?"

"Of *you*, wish-daughter. Just a lick. He promises not to bite."

Karou's stomach turned. "Uh, *no*."

"I told you," Izîl muttered. "Now will you be quiet, *please?*"

A low hiss came in response.

A waiter in a white djellaba came and poured mint tea, raising the pot to head height and expertly aiming the long stream of tea into etched glasses. Karou, eyeing the hollows of the graverobber's cheeks, ordered pastries, too, and she let him eat and drink for a while before asking, "So, what have you got?"

He dug into his pockets and produced a fistful of teeth, which he dropped on the table.

* * *

Watching from the shadow of a nearby doorway, Akiva straightened up. All went still and silent around him, and he saw nothing but those teeth, and the girl sorting through them in just the way he knew the old beast sorcerer did.

Teeth. How harmless they looked on that tabletop—just tiny, dirty things, plundered from the dead. And if they stayed in this world where they belonged, that was all they'd ever be. In Brimstone's hands, though, they became so much more than that.

It was Akiva's mission to end this foul trade, and with it, the devil's dark magic.

He watched as the girl inspected the teeth with what was clearly a practiced hand, as if she did this all the time. Mixed with his disgust was something like disappointment. She had seemed too clean for this business, but apparently she was not. He'd been right, though, in his guess that she was no mere trader. She was more than that, sitting there doing Brimstone's work. But what?

* * *

"God, Izîl," said Karou. "These are nasty. Did you bring them straight from the cemetery?"

"Mass grave. It was hidden, but Razgut sniffed it out. He can always find the dead."

"What a talent." Karou got a chill, imagining Razgut leering at her, hoping for a taste. She turned her attention to the teeth. Scraps of dried flesh clung to their roots, along with the dirt they'd been exhumed from. Even through the filth, it was easy to see that they were not of high quality, but were the teeth of a people who had gnawed at tough food, smoked pipes, and been unacquainted with toothpaste.

She scooped them off the table and dropped them into the dregs of her tea, swishing it around before dumping it out in a sodden pile of mint leaves and teeth, now only slightly less filthy. One by one, she picked them up. Incisors, molars, canines, adult and child alike. "Izîl. You know Brimstone doesn't take baby teeth."

"You don't know everything, girl," he snapped.

"Excuse me?"

"Sometimes he does. *Once*. Once he wanted some."

Karou didn't believe him. Brimstone strictly did not buy immature teeth, not animal, not human, but she saw no point in arguing. "Well"—she pushed the tiny teeth aside and tried not to think about small corpses in mass graves—"he didn't ask for any, so I'll have to pass."

She held each of the adult teeth, listening to what their hum told her, and sorted them into two piles.

Izîl watched anxiously, his gaze darting from one pile to the other. "They chewed too much, didn't they? Greedy gypsies! They kept chewing after they were dead. No manners. No table manners at all."

Most of the teeth were worn blunt, riddled with decay, and no good to Brimstone. By the time Karou was through sorting, one pile was larger than the other, but Izîl didn't know which was which. He pointed hopefully to the larger pile.

She shook her head and fished some dirham notes out of the wallet Brimstone had given her. It was an overly generous payment for these sorry few teeth, but it was still not what Izîl was hoping for.

"So much digging," he moaned. "And for what? Paper with pictures of the dead king? Always the dead staring at me." His voice dropped. "I can't keep it up, Karou. I'm broken. I can barely hold a shovel anymore. I scrabble at the hard earth, digging like a dog. I'm through."

Pity hit her hard. "Surely there are other ways to live—"

"No. Only death remains. One should die proudly when it is no longer possible to *live* proudly. Nietzsche said that, you know. Wise man. Large mustache." He tugged at his own bedraggled mustache and attempted a smile.

"Izîl, you can't mean you want to *die*."

"If only there was a way to be free..."

"Isn't there?" she asked earnestly. "There must be *something* you can do."

His fingers twitched, fidgeting with his mustache. "I don't

like to think of it, my dear, but...there *is* a way, if you would help me. You're the only one I know who's brave enough and good enough— Ow!" His hand flew to his ear, and Karou saw blood seep through his fingers. She shrank back. Razgut must have bitten him. "I'll ask her if I want, monster!" cried the graverobber. "Yes, you are a monster! I don't care what you once were. You're a monster now!"

A peculiar tussle ensued; it looked as if the old man were wrestling with himself. The waiter flapped nearby, agitated, and Karou scraped her chair back clear of flailing limbs both visible and invisible.

"Stop it. Stop!" Izîl cried, wild-eyed. He braced himself, raised his walking stick, and brought it back hard against his own shoulder and the thing that perched there. Again and again he struck, seeming to smite himself, and then he let out a shriek and fell to his knees. His walking stick clattered away as both hands flew to his neck. Blood was wicking into the collar of his djellaba—the thing must have bitten him again. The misery on his face was more than Karou could bear and, without stopping to consider, she dropped to his side, taking his elbow to help him up.

A mistake.

At once she felt it on her neck: a slithering touch. Revulsion juddered through her. It was a *tongue*. Razgut had gotten his taste. She heard a loathsome gobbling sound as she lurched away, leaving the graverobber on his knees.

That was enough for her. She gathered up the teeth and her sketchbook.

"Wait, please," Izîl cried. "Karou. Please."

His plea was so desperate that she hesitated. Scrabbling, he dug something from his pocket and held it out. A pair of pliers. They looked rusted, but Karou knew it wasn't rust. These were the tools of his trade, and they were covered in the residue of dead mouths. "Please, my dear," he said. "There isn't anyone else."

She understood at once what he meant and took a step back in shock. "No, Izîl! *God*. The answer is *no*."

"A bruxis would save me! I can't save myself. I've already used mine. It would take another bruxis to undo my fool wish. You could wish him off me. Please. *Please!*"

A bruxis. That was the one wish more powerful than a gavriel, and its trade value was singular: The only way to purchase one was with one's own teeth. All of them, self-extracted.

The thought of pulling her own teeth out one by one made Karou feel woozy. "Don't be ridiculous," she whispered, appalled that he would even ask it. But then, he *was* a madman, and right now he certainly looked it.

She retreated.

"I wouldn't ask, you know I wouldn't, but it's the only way!"

Karou walked rapidly away, head down, and she would have kept walking and not looked back but for a cry that erupted behind her. It burst from the chaos of the Jemaa el-Fna and instantly dwarfed all other noise. It was some mad kind of keening, a high, thin river of sound unlike anything she had ever heard.

It was definitely not Izîl.

Unearthly, the wail rose, wavering and violent, to break like a wave and become language — susurrous, without hard conso-

90

nants. The modulations suggested words, but the language was alien even to Karou, who had more than twenty in her collection. She turned, seeing as she did that the people around her were turning, too, craning their necks, and that their expressions of alarm were turning to horror when they perceived the source of the sound.

Then she saw it, too.

The thing on Izîl's back was invisible no more.

❦ 14 ❦

Deadly Bird of the Soul

If the language was alien to Karou, it was not so to Akiva.

"Seraph, I see you!" rang the voice. "I know you! Brother, brother, I have served my sentence. I will do anything! I have repented, I have been punished enough—"

Akiva stared in blank incomprehension at the thing that materialized on the old man's back.

It was all but naked, a bloated torso with reedy arms wrapped tight around the human's neck. Useless legs dangled behind, and its head was swollen taut and purple, as if it were engorged with blood and ready to pop in a great, wet burst. It was hideous. That it should speak the language of the seraphim was an abomination.

The absolute wrongness of it held Akiva immobile, staring, before the amazement at hearing his own language turned to shock at what was being said in it.

"They tore off my wings, my brother!" The thing was staring

at Akiva. It unwound one arm from the old man's neck and reached toward him, imploring. "Twisted my legs so I would have to crawl, like the insects of the earth! It has been a thousand years since I was cast out, a thousand years of torment, but now you've come, you've come to take me home!"

Home?

No. It was impossible.

People were shrinking away from the sight of the creature. Others had turned, following the direction of its supplication to fix their eyes on Akiva. He became aware of their notice and swept the crowd with his burning gaze. Some fell back, murmuring prayers. And then his eyes came to rest on the blue-haired girl, some twenty yards distant. She was a calm, shining figure in the moiling crowd.

And she was staring back.

* * *

Into kohl-rimmed eyes in a sun-bronzed face. Fire-colored eyes with a charge like sparks that seared a path through the air and kindled it. It gave Karou a jolt—no mere startle but a chain reaction that lashed through her body with a rush of adrenaline. Her limbs came into the lightness and power of sudden awakening, fight or flight, chemical and wild.

Who? she thought, her mind racing to catch up to the fervor in her body.

And: *What?*

Because clearly he was not human, the man standing amid the tumult in absolute stillness. A pulse beat in the palms of her hands and she curled them into fists, feeling a wild hum in her blood.

Enemy. Enemy. Enemy. The knowledge pounded through her on the rhythm of her heartbeat: the fire-eyed stranger was the enemy. His face—oh, beauty, he was perfect, he was *mythic*—was absolutely cold. She was caught between the urge to flee and the fear of turning her back on him.

It was Izîl who decided her.

"*Malak!*" he screamed, pointing at the man. "*Malak!*"

Angel.

Angel?

"I know you, deadly bird of the soul! I know what you are!" Izîl turned to Karou and said urgently, "Karou, wish-daughter, you must get to Brimstone. Tell him the seraphim are here. They've gotten back in. You must warn him! Run, child. Run!"

And run she did.

Across the Jemaa el-Fna, where those attempting to flee were being hampered by those drawn to the commotion. She shouldered her way through them, knocked someone aside, spun off a camel's flank and leapt over a coiled cobra, which struck out at her, defanged and harmless. Hazarding a glance over her shoulder, she could see no sign of pursuit—no sign of *him*—but she felt it.

A thrill along every nerve ending. Her body, alert and alive. She was hunted, she was prey, and she didn't even have her knife tucked into her boot, little thinking she'd need it on a visit to the graverobber.

She ran, leaving the square by one of the many alleys that fed into it like tributaries. The crowds in the souks had thinned and many lights had been snuffed, and she raced in and out of pools of darkness, her stride long and measured and light, her footfall nearly silent. She took turns wide to avoid collisions, glanced behind again and again and saw no one.

Angel. The word kept sounding in her mind.

She was nearing the portal — just one more turn, the length of another blind alley, and she would be there, if she made it that far.

Rushing from above. Heat and the bass *whumph* of wingbeats.

Overhead, darkness massed where a shape blotted out the moon. Something was hurtling down at Karou on huge, impossible wings. Heat and wingbeats and the skirr of air parted by a blade. A blade. She leapt aside, felt steel bite her shoulder as she slammed into a carved door, splintering slats. She seized one, a jagged spear of wood, and spun to face her attacker.

He stood a mere body's length away, the point of his sword resting on the ground.

Oh, thought Karou, staring at him.

Oh.

Angel indeed.

He stood revealed. The blade of his long sword gleamed white from the incandescence of his wings — vast shimmering wings, their reach so great they swept the walls on either side of the alley, each feather like the wind-tugged lick of a candle flame.

Those eyes.

His gaze was like a lit fuse, scorching the air between them. He was the most beautiful thing Karou had ever seen. Her first thought, incongruous but overpowering, was to memorize him so she could draw him later.

Her second thought was that there wasn't going to be a later, because he was going to kill her.

He came at her so fast that his wings painted blurs of light on the air, and even as Karou leapt aside again she was seeing his fiery imprint seared into her vision. His sword bit her again, her arm this time, but she twisted clear of a killing thrust. She was quick. She kept space around her; he tried to close it, and she danced clear, lissome, fluid. Their eyes met again, and Karou saw past his shocking beauty to the inhumanity there, the absolute absence of mercy.

He attacked again. As quick as Karou was, she couldn't get clear of the reach of his sword. A strike aimed at her throat glanced off her scapula instead. There was no pain—that would come later, unless she was *dead*—only spreading heat that she knew was blood. Another strike, and she parried it with her slat of wood, which split like kindling, half of it falling away so she held a mere dagger's length of old wood, a ridiculous excuse for a weapon. Yet when the angel came at her again she dodged in close to him and thrust, felt the wood catch flesh and sink in.

Karou had stabbed men before, and she hated it, the gruesome feeling of penetrating living flesh. She pulled back, leaving her makeshift weapon in his side. His face registered neither pain nor surprise. It was, Karou thought as he closed in, a dead face. Or rather, the living face of a dead soul.

It was utterly terrifying.

He had her cornered now, and they both knew she wouldn't get away. She was vaguely aware of shouts of amazement and fear up the alley and from windows, but all of her focus was on the angel. What did it even mean, *angel*? What had Izîl said? *The seraphim are here.*

She'd heard the word before; seraphim were some high order of angels, at least according to the Christian mythos, for which Brimstone had utter contempt, as he did for all religion. "Humans have gotten glimpses of things over time," he'd said. "Just enough to make the rest up. It's all a quilt of fairy tales with a patch here and there of truth."

"So what's real?" she'd wanted to know.

"If you can kill it, or it can kill you, it's real."

By that definition, this angel was real enough.

He raised his sword, and she just watched him do it, her attention catching for a moment on the bars of black ink tattooed across his fingers—they were fleetingly familiar but then not, the feeling gone as soon as it registered—and she just stared up at her killer and wondered numbly *why*. It seemed impossible that this was the final moment of her life. She cocked her head to the side, desperately searching his features for some hint of...*soul*...and then, she saw it.

He hesitated. Only for a split second did his mask slip, but Karou saw some urgent pathos surface, a wave of feeling that softened his rigid and ridiculously perfect features. His jaw unclenched, his lips parted, his brow furrowed in an instant of confusion.

At the same moment, she became aware of the pulse in her palms that had made her curl her hands into fists at her first sight of him. It thrummed there still, a pent-up energy, and she was jolted by the certainty that it emanated from her tattoos. An impulse overcame her to throw up her hands, and she did, not in cringing surrender, but with palms powerfully outthrust, inked with the eyes she'd worn all her life without ever knowing why.

And something happened.

It was like a detonation—a sharp intake, all air sucked into a tight core and then expelled. It was silent, lightless—to the gape-jawed witnesses it was nothing at all, just a girl throwing up her hands—but Karou felt it, and the angel did, too. His eyes went wide with recognition in the instant before he was flung back with devastating force to hit a wall some twenty feet behind him. He crumpled to the ground, wings askew, sword skittering away. Karou scrambled to her feet.

The angel wasn't moving.

She spun and sprinted away. Whatever had happened, a silence had risen from it, and it followed her. She could hear only her own breathing, weirdly amplified like she was in a tunnel. She rounded the bend in the alley at speed, skidding on her heel to avoid a donkey standing stubborn in the middle of the lane. The portal was in sight, a plain door in a row of plain doors, but something was different about it now. A large black handprint was burned into the wood.

Karou flung herself at it, hammering with her fists in a frenzy such as she had never unleashed on a portal before. "Issa!" she screamed. "Let me in!"

A long, awful moment, Karou looking back over her shoulder, and then the door finally swung open.

She started to dart forward, then let out a choked cry. It was not Issa or the vestibule, but a Moroccan woman with a broom. Oh no. The woman's eyes narrowed and she opened her mouth to scold, but Karou didn't wait. She pushed her back inside and shoved the door closed, staying outside. Frantically she knocked again. "Issa!"

She could hear the woman shouting and feel her trying to push the door open. Karou swore and held it shut. If it was open, the magic of the portal couldn't connect. In Arabic she hollered, "Get away from the door!"

She looked over her shoulder. There was a commotion in the street, arms waving, people shouting. The donkey stood unimpressed. No angel. Had she killed him? No. Whatever had happened, she knew he wasn't dead. He would come.

She pounded on the door again. "Issa, Brimstone, please!"

Nothing but irate Arabic. Karou held the door closed with her foot and kept pounding. "Issa! He's going to kill me! Issa! Let me in!"

What was taking so long? Seconds hung like scuppies on a string, vanishing one after another. The door was jumping against her foot, someone trying to force it open—could it be Issa?—and then she felt a draft of heat at her back. She didn't hesitate this time but turned, jamming her back up against the door to hold it closed, and raised her hands as if to let her tattoos *see*. There was no detonation this time, only a crackling of energy that raised her hair like Medusa's serpents.

The angel was stalking toward her, head lowered so he was looking at her from the tops of his burning eyes. He didn't move with ease, but as if against a wind. Whatever power in Karou's tattoos had hurled him against that wall, it hindered him now but didn't stop him. His hands were fists at his sides, and his face was ferocious, set to endure pain.

He stopped a few paces away and looked at her, really looked at her, his eyes no longer dead but roving over her face and neck, drawn back to her hamsas, and again to her face. Back and forth, as if something didn't add up.

"Who *are* you?" he asked, and she almost didn't recognize the language he spoke as Chimaera, it sounded so soft on his tongue.

Who *was* she? "Don't you usually find that out *before* you try to kill someone?"

At her back, a renewed pressure at the door. If it wasn't Issa, she was finished.

The angel came a step closer, and Karou moved aside so the door burst open.

"Karou!" Issa's voice, sharp.

And she spun and leapt through the portal, pulling it shut behind her.

＊ ＊ ＊

Akiva lunged after her and yanked it back open, only to come face-to-face with a hollering woman who blanched and dropped her broom at his feet.

The girl was already gone.

He stood there a moment, all but unaware of the madness around him. His thoughts were spinning. The girl would warn Brimstone. He should have stopped her, could easily have killed her. Instead he'd struck slowly, giving her time to spin clear, dance free. Why?

It was simple. He'd wanted to look at her.

100

Fool.

And what had he seen, or thought he'd seen? Some glimpse of a past that could never come again—the phantom of the girl who had taught him mercy, long ago, only to have her own fate undo all her gentle teaching? He'd thought every spark of mercy was dead in him now, but he hadn't been able to kill the girl. And then, the unexpected: the hamsas.

A human marked with the devil's eyes! *Why?*

There was only one possible answer, as plain as it was disturbing.

That she was not, in fact, human.

15

THE OTHER DOOR

In the vestibule, Karou fell to her knees. Breathing hard, she leaned into the coil of Issa's serpent body.

"Karou!" Issa gathered her into an embrace that left them both sticky with blood. "What happened? Who did this to you?"

"You didn't see him?" Karou was dazed.

"See who?"

"The angel..."

Issa's reaction was profound. She reared back like a serpent ready to strike and hissed, *"Angel?"* All her snakes—in her hair, around her waist and shoulders—writhed along with her, hissing. Karou cried out, her wounds wrenched by the violent motion.

"Oh, my dear, my sweet girl. Forgive me." Issa softened again, cradling Karou like a child. "What do you mean, *angel?* Surely not—"

Karou blinked up at her. Shadows were closing in. "Why did he want to kill me?"

"Darling, darling," Issa fretted. She pulled away Karou's sword-slashed coat and scarf to see her wounds, but the blood was heavy and still flowing and the light in the vestibule was dim. "So much blood!"

Karou felt as if the walls were swinging in a slow arc around her. She was waiting for the inner door to unseal, but it didn't. "Can't we go in?" Her voice was faint. "I want Brimstone." She remembered how he'd picked her up and held her when she came in bleeding from St. Petersburg. How she'd felt perfect trust and calm, knowing he would fix her. And he had, and would again....

Issa bunched up Karou's blood-soaked scarf and tried to stanch her wounds. "He's not here right now, sweet girl."

"Where is he?"

"He...he can't be disturbed."

Karou whimpered. She wanted Brimstone. Needed him. She said, "Disturb him," and then she was losing herself, drifting.

Falling.

Issa's voice, far away.

And then nothing.

By and by, flickering images like badly spliced film: Issa's eyes and Yasri's, close, anxious. Soft hands, cool water. Dreams: Izîl and the thing on his back, its bloated face the brown-purple of bruised fruit, and the angel staring straight at Karou like he could ignite her with his eyes.

Issa's voice, hushed and secretive. "What can it mean, that they are in the human world?"

Yasri. "They must have found a way back in. It took them long enough, for all their high opinion of themselves."

This was not part of the dream. Karou had come back into consciousness like swimming to a distant shore—effortfully—and she lay silent, listening. She was on her childhood cot in the back of the shop; she knew that without opening her eyes. Her wounds stung, and the smell of healing salve was pungent in the air. The two chimaera stood at the end of the aisle of bookcases, whispering.

"But why attack Karou?" Issa hissed.

Yasri. "You don't think . . . ? They couldn't know about her."

Issa. "Of course not. Don't be ridiculous."

"No, no, of course not." Yasri sighed. "Oh, I wish Brimstone would come back. Do you think we should go and get him?"

"You know he can't be interrupted. But it shouldn't be long now."

"No."

After a fraught pause, Issa ventured, "He'll be very angry."

"Yes," agreed Yasri, a tremor of fear in her voice. "Oh, yes."

Karou felt the two chimaera looking at her and tried her best to appear unconscious. It wasn't hard. She felt sluggish, and pain blossomed across her chest, arm, and collarbone. Slash wounds to keep her bullet scars company. She was thirsty, and knew she had only to let out a murmur for Yasri to scurry toward her with water and a soothing hand, but she kept silent. There was too much to think about.

Yasri had said, "They couldn't know about her."

Know *what*?

It was maddening, this secrecy. She wanted to sit up and scream, "Who am I?" but she didn't. She feigned sleep, because there was something else nudging at her thoughts.

Brimstone wasn't here.

He was *always* here. She had never before been granted admittance to the shop in his absence, and only the extraordinary circumstance of her nearly dying accounted for this breach.

This opportunity.

Karou waited until she heard Yasri and Issa moving away, peering through her lashes to be certain they had gone. She knew that as soon as she shifted her weight to stand the springs of the cot would creak and give her away, so she reached for the strand of scuppies around her wrist.

Yet another use for nearly useless wishes: to silence creaking bedsprings.

She stood and steadied herself, head spinning, wounds burning, without making a sound. Yasri and Issa had taken her boots off, along with her coat and sweater, so she was wearing only bandages and a blood-streaked camisole and jeans. She went barefoot around a pair of cabinets and under hanging strings of camel and giraffe teeth, then paused, listened, and peered out into the shop.

Brimstone's desk was dark, and so was Twiga's, no lanterns lit for the hummingbird-moths to flutter to. Issa and Yasri were in the kitchen, out of sight, and the whole shop was cast in gloom, which made the other door stand out all the more, a crack of light giving away its edge.

For the first time in Karou's life, it was ajar.

Heart pounding, she approached it. She paused for a beat with her hand on the knob, then eased the door open a fraction and peered through it.

🌿 16 🌿

FALLEN

Akiva found Izîl cowering behind a garbage pile in the Jemaa el-Fna, his creature still clinging to his back. A half circle of frightened humans crowded in on them, menacing, but when Akiva dropped from the sky in an explosion of sparks, they fled in all directions, squealing like slapped pigs.

The creature reached out to Akiva. "My brother," it crooned. "I knew you'd come back for me."

Akiva's jaw clenched. He forced himself to look at the thing. Bloated as its face was, its features held an echo of long-ago beauty: almond eyes, a fine, high-bridged nose, and sensuous lips that were perverse on such a wretched face. But the key to its true nature was at its back. From its shoulder blades protruded the splintered remnants of wing joints.

Incredibly, this thing was a seraph. It could only be one of the Fallen.

Akiva knew the story as legend and had never wondered

whether it was true, not until this moment, faced with the proof of it. That there were seraphim, exiled in another age for treason and collaborating with the enemy, cast into the human world forever. Well, here was one of them, and indeed, he had fallen far from what he once had been. Time had curved his spine, and his flesh, pulled taut, seemed to snag on every ridge of vertebrae. His legs dangled uselessly behind him — that was not the work of time, but of violence. They had been pulverized with cruel purpose, that he should never walk again. As if it were not punishment enough that his wings were torn away — not even cut, but *torn* — his legs were destroyed, too, leaving him a crawling thing on the surface of an alien world.

A thousand years he had lived like this, and he was beside himself with joy to see Akiva.

Izîl was not so happy. He cowered against the stinking mound of refuse, more afraid of Akiva than he had been of the mob. While Razgut gibbered, "My brother, my brother," in an ecstatic chant, the old man shook with a palsy and tried to back away, but there was nowhere for him to go.

Akiva loomed over him, the brilliance of his unglamoured wings lighting the scene like daylight.

Razgut reached longingly toward Akiva. "My sentence is up, and you've come to bring me back. That's it, isn't it, my brother? You're going to take me home and make me whole again, so I can walk. So I can *fly* — "

"This has nothing to do with you," said Akiva.

"What . . . what do you want?" Izîl choked out in the language of the seraphim, which he had learned from Razgut.

"The girl," Akiva said. "I want you to tell me about the girl."

🏵 17 🏵

WORLD APART

On the far side of the other door, Karou discovered a passage of dull black stone. Peering out, she could see that the corridor went on for some ten feet before turning out of sight. Just before it did, there was a window—a narrow, barred niche at the wrong angle for her to see through from where she stood. White light washed in, painting rectangles across the floor. *Moonlight*, Karou thought, and she wondered what landscape she would see if she crept over and looked out. Where was this place? Like the shop's front door, did this rear one open onto myriad cities, or was this something else altogether, some depth of Brimstone's Elsewhere that she couldn't begin to fathom? A few steps and she might know that, if nothing else. But did she dare?

She listened hard. There were sounds but they seemed far away, echoing calls in the night. The passage itself was silent.

So she did it. She prowled out. Quick silent steps, high on

the balls of her bare feet, and she was over to the window. Peering through its heavy iron bars. Seeing what was there.

Her facial muscles, tense with anxiety, abruptly slackened with the onset of total awe, and her jaw actually dropped. It was a second before she realized it and snapped it closed, wincing when the sharp report of her teeth broke the silence. She leaned forward, taking in the scene before and below her.

Wherever this was, she was sure of one thing: It was not her world.

In the sky were two moons. That was the first thing. *Two moons*. Neither was full. One was a radiant half disc high overhead, the other a pale crescent just rising to clear a crust of mountain. As for the landscape they illuminated, she saw she was in a vast fortress. Huge, bermed defensive walls met at hexagonal bastions; a generous town was laid out in the center of it all, and crenellated towers—in one of which, Karou gauged by her high vantage point, she must be—reared above it all, with the silhouettes of guards pacing at their peaks. But for the moons, it might have been a fortified town of old Europe.

It was the bars that made it something else.

Extraordinarily, the city was banded over by iron bars. She'd never seen anything like it. They arched over the whole of the place from one expanse of rammed-earth walls to the next, beetle-black and ugly, enclosing even the towers. A quick study gave away no gaps; the bars were spaced so closely that no body could possibly squeeze between them. The streets and plazas of the town were entirely screened from above as if they existed within a cage, and moonlight cast rickrack shadows over everything.

What was it about? Were the bars meant to keep something *in* or *out*?

And then Karou saw a winged figure sweeping down out of the sky and she flinched, thinking she had her answer. An angel, a seraph—that was her first thought, her heart starting to hammer and her wounds to throb. But it wasn't. It passed overhead and out of sight, and she clearly saw that its form was animal—some sort of winged deer. A chimaera? She had always supposed there must be more, though she had only ever seen her four, who would never say if there were others.

It hit her now that this whole city must be inhabited by chimaera, and that beyond its walls lay an entire world, a world with *two moons*, also inhabited by chimaera, and she had to grip the bars to hold herself upright as the universe seemed to tremble and grow larger around her.

There was another world.

Another world.

Of all the theories she'd dreamed up about the other door, she'd never imagined this: a world apart, complete with its own mountains, continents, moons. She was already light-headed with blood loss, and the revelation made her reel so she had to clutch at the window bars.

It was then that she heard voices. Near. And also familiar. She had listened to their murmurs all her life as their incongruous heads bent together in discussions of teeth. It was Brimstone and Twiga, and they were coming around the corner.

"Ondine has brought Thiago," Twiga was saying.

"The fool," Brimstone breathed. "Does he think the armies

can afford the loss of him at a time like this? How many times must I tell him, a general need not fight at the front?"

"It is because of you that he knows no fear," said Twiga, to which Brimstone only snorted, and that snort sounded dangerously close.

Karou almost panicked. Her eyes darted back to the door she had come from. She didn't think she could reach it. Instead, she pressed herself into the window niche and held stone-still.

They passed her, near enough to touch. Karou feared that they would go into the shop and close the door behind them, trapping her in this strange place. She was ready to cry after them to prevent it, but they bypassed the door. Her panic subsided. In its wake, something else flared: anger.

Anger at the years of secrets, as if she weren't worthy of trust or even the barest details of her own existence. Her anger made her bold, and she determined to find out more—as much as she could while she was here. This chance, she suspected, would never come again. So when Brimstone and Twiga turned into a stairwell, she followed.

They were tower stairs, a tight corkscrew down. The spiraling descent made Karou dizzy: down, around, down, around, hypnotic, until it seemed as if she were caught in a purgatory of stairs and would go down like this forever. There were small slot windows for a while, and then they disappeared. The air grew cool and still, and Karou had the impression of being belowground. She heard Brimstone and Twiga in snatches, and could make no sense of their conversation.

"We will need more incense soon." Twiga.

"We will need more of everything. There has not been an onslaught like this in decades." Brimstone.

"Do you think they have their eye on the city?"

"When have they not?"

"How long?" Twiga asked with a quaver. "How long can we hold them off?"

Brimstone. "I don't know."

And just when Karou thought she couldn't bear any more turning, they reached the bottom. It was here that things got interesting.

Really interesting.

The stairs spilled out into a vast, echoing hall. Karou had to hold herself back to make sure Brimstone and Twiga had gone on, but when she heard their voices moving away, rendered small by the immensity of the space that swallowed them, she crept out after them.

It seemed she was in a cathedral—if, that is, the earth itself were to dream a cathedral into being over thousands of years of water weeping through stone. It was a massive natural cavern that soared overhead to a near-perfect Gothic arch. Stalagmites as old as the world were carved into pillars in the shapes of beasts, and candelabras hung so high they were like clusters of stars. A scent was heavy in the air, herbs and sulfur, and smoke wreathed among the pillars, teased into wisps by breezes emanating from unseen openings in the carven walls.

And below it all, where Brimstone and Twiga walked down the cathedral's long nave, there weren't pews for worship, but tables—stone tables huge as menhirs, so huge they must have required elephants to haul them there. Indeed, they were large

112

enough to accommodate an elephant reclining, though only one of them actually *did*.

An elephant, laid out on a table.

Or...no. It was not an elephant. With clawed feet and a head that was some nightmare of a massive, tusked grizzly bear, it was elsething. Chimaera.

And it was dead.

On each of the tables lay a dead chimaera, and there were dozens of them. Dozens. Karou's gaze fluttered, erratic, from table to table. No two of the dead were alike. Most had some human quality to them, head or torso, but not all. There, an ape with the mane of a lion; an iguana-thing so huge it could only be called a dragon; a jaguar's head on the nude body of a woman.

Brimstone and Twiga moved among them, touching them, examining. They paused the longest over a man.

He was naked, too. He was what Karou and Zuzana would have called, with the smug smiles of connoisseurs, a "physical specimen." Heavy shoulders tapering to neat hips, abdomen corrugated, all the muscles Karou could identify from life drawing study ruggedly pronounced. On his powerful chest was a down of pure white hair, and the hair of his head was white, too, long and silken on the stone table.

A fug of incense hung thick around him. It was coming from a kind of ornate silver lantern suspended from a hook above his head, exhaling a steady fume. A *thurible*, Karou thought, like those twirled about in Catholic Mass. Brimstone laid a hand to the dead man's chest, let it linger there a moment in a gesture Karou couldn't decipher. Fondness? Sadness? When he and

113

Twiga moved on and vanished into the rearing wall of shadow at the far end of the nave, she crept out of hiding and went to the table.

Up close, she saw that the man's white hair was an incongruity. He was young, his face unlined. He was very handsome, though blank and waxen in death, and seeming not quite *real*.

He was also not quite human, though nearer to it than most of the chimaera here. The flesh and musculature of his legs transitioned at mid-thigh to become the white-furred haunches of a wolf, with long backward-bending canine feet and black claws. And his hands, she saw, were hybrid: broad and furred across the backs like paws, with human fingers tapering to claws. They were lying palm up, as if they had been arranged that way, and that was how Karou saw what was etched on his skin.

In the center of each palm was a tattooed eye identical to her own.

She took a startled step back.

This was something. Something critical, something *key*, but what did it mean? She turned to the next table, the lion-maned creature. Its hands were simian, the flesh black, but she could still make out the hamsas on them.

She went to the next table, and the next. Even the elephant-creature: The soles of its mammoth forefeet were marked. Each of these dead creatures wore the hamsas, just like she did. Her thoughts hammered in her head the way her heart thumped in her chest. What was going on? Here were dozens of chimaera, and they were dead and naked—without, she noted, any visible wounds—and laid out cold on slabs in some kind of underground cathedral. Her own hamsas connected her to them in some way, but she couldn't imagine how.

She circled back around to the first table, the white-haired man, and leaned against it. She was conscious of the scented smoke from the thurible and had a moment of anxiety when she realized her hair would be infused with the smell and give her away to Yasri and Issa when she snuck back into the shop. The shop. The thought of climbing back up that interminable corkscrew made her want to sink down into fetal position. Her wounds throbbed. They were seeping through the bandages, and Yasri's balm was wearing off. She *hurt*.

But…this place. These dead. With her muddled head, Karou felt unequal to the mystery. The white-haired man's hand lay right before her, its hamsa taunting her. She laid her own beside it to compare the marks, but his lay in the shadow of his body, so she reached out to lift it into the light.

The marks were identical. She saw that as her mind worked at something else, a too-slow warning from her sluggish senses.

His hand, his dead hand…it was *warm*.

It was not dead.

He was not dead.

A whip-crack movement and he came upright, spinning on his knees. His hand, which had lain inert in hers, caught her throat and lifted her off her feet, slamming her down onto the stone table. Her head. Against stone. Her vision blurred. When it cleared again he was above her, eyes ice-pale, lips drawn back over fangs. She couldn't breathe. His hand still clutched her throat. She clawed at it, struggled to throw him off, managed to get her knees between them and kick out.

His grip loosened and she gasped a breath, tried to scream, but he was over her again, heavy and naked and bestial, and she fought him with everything in her, fought him with a wildness that plunged them over the edge of the table to the floor. It was chaos and thrashing, and bare limbs so strong Karou couldn't break free. He was on her, straddling her legs, staring, and some kind of crazed madness seemed to clear from his eyes. His lips eased from their snarl and he looked human again, almost, and beautiful, but still terrifying and... confused.

He gripped her by the wrists, forced open her hands to see her hamsas, then looked sharply at her face. His gaze roved over all of her so that she felt as if she were the naked one, and then he gave a thick growl that sent shudders through her. "Who are you?"

She couldn't answer. Her heart was pounding. Her wounds were on fire. And, as ever, she had no answer.

"Who are you?" He dragged her upright by her wrists and flung her back onto the stone table and was over her again. His movements were fluid and animal, his teeth sharp enough to rip out her throat, and all at once Karou saw how her trespass through the other door was going to end: in a pool of blood. She found her breath.

And screamed.

18

BATTLE NOT WITH MONSTERS

"Girl?" Izîl squinted up at Akiva. "You . . . you mean Karou?"

Karou? Akiva knew that word. It meant *hope* in the language of the enemy. So not only did she bear the hamsas, she had a chimaera name. "Who is she?" he demanded.

Clearly terrified, the old man pulled himself up a little straighter. "Why do you want to know, angel?"

"I'm asking the questions," said Akiva. "And I suggest you answer them." He was impatient to get on and meet the others, but loathe to leave with this mystery hanging over him. If he didn't find out who the girl was now, he would never know.

Eager to be helpful, Razgut supplied, "She tastes like nectar and salt. Nectar and salt and apples. Pollen and stars and hinges. She tastes like fairy tales. Swan maiden at midnight. Cream on the tip of a fox's tongue. She tastes like *hope*."

Akiva was stone-faced, unreasonably disturbed by the thought of this abomination *tasting* the girl. He waited until Razgut gibbered into silence before he said, his voice low in his throat, "I didn't ask what she tastes like. I asked who she *is*."

Izîl shrugged, fluttering his hands in an effort at nonchalance. "She's just a girl. She draws pictures. She's nice to me. What more can I tell you?"

His voice was glib, and Akiva saw that he thought he could protect her. It was noble, and laughable. Having no time to waste playing games, he decided on a more drastic approach. He seized Izîl by his shirtfront and Razgut by one of his jagged bone spurs and leapt airborne with the pair of them, hauling their combined weight as if it were nothing.

It was only a matter of wingbeats before all of Marrakesh glimmered below them. Izîl was screaming, his eyes squeezed shut, but Razgut was silent, his face displaying such unutterable longing it shot pity into Akiva's heart like a splinter — more painful, indeed, than the shard of wood Karou had stabbed him with. It surprised him. Over the years he had learned to deaden himself, and he had lived so long with the deadness that he believed pity and mercy were extinguished in him, but tonight he had experienced dull stabs of both.

Slowly spiraling downward like a bird of prey, he brought the two to rest on the domed peak of the city's tallest minaret. They scrabbled to hold on and failed, sliding down its slick surface, paddling frenziedly for handholds and footholds before coming to rest against a low, decorative parapet that was all that kept them from plummeting over the edge, several hundred feet to the rooftops of the mosque below.

Izîl's face was gray, his breathing thin. When Razgut shifted himself on the old man's back, they teetered perilously close to

118

the edge. Izîl let out a stream of panicked commands to stay low, not shift, hang on to something.

Akiva stood over them. Behind him, the serrated ridge of the Atlas Mountains shone in the moonlight. Breezes teased the flame-feathers that made up his wings, setting them dancing, and his eyes were the muted glow of embers. "Now. If you wish to live, tell me what I want to know. Who is the girl?"

Izîl, with a horror-struck glance over the edge of the roof, answered in a rush. "She's nothing to you, she's innocent—"

"Innocent? She bears the hamsas, traffics teeth for the devil sorcerer. She doesn't seem innocent to me."

"You don't know. She *is* innocent. She just runs errands for him. That's all."

Was that all she was, some kind of servant? It didn't explain the hamsas. "Why her?"

"She's the Wishmonger's foster daughter. He raised her from a baby."

Akiva processed this. "Where did she come from?" He knelt to bring his face closer to Izîl's. It felt very important that he know.

"I don't know. I don't! One day she was just there, cradled in his arm, and after that she was always there, no explanations. Do you think Brimstone told me things? If he had, maybe I would still be a man instead of a mule!" He gestured to Razgut and fell into lunatic laughter. "'Be careful what you wish for,' Brimstone said, but I didn't listen, and look at me now!" Tears sprang to the wrinkled corners of his eyes as he laughed and laughed.

Akiva was rigid. Trouble was, he believed what the hunchback said. Why would Brimstone tell his human minions anything, especially mad fools like this? But if Izîl didn't know, what hope did Akiva have of finding out? The old man was his only lead, and he had lingered too long already.

"Then tell me where to find her," he said. "She was friendly with you. Surely you know where she lives."

Woe flickered in the old man's eyes. "I can't tell you that. But...but...but I can tell you other things. Secret things! About your own kind. Thanks to Razgut, I know far more of seraphim than I do of chimaera."

He was bargaining, still hoping to protect Karou. Akiva said, "You think there's anything you can tell me about my kind?"

"Razgut has stories—"

"The word of the Fallen. Has he even told you why he was exiled?"

"Oh, *I* know why," said Izîl. "I wonder if *you* do."

"I know my history."

Izîl laughed. One cheek was pressed flat against the dome of the minaret, and his laugh came out as a wheeze. He said, "Like mold on books, grow myths on history. Maybe you should ask someone who was there, all those centuries ago. Maybe you should ask Razgut."

Akiva cast a cold eye over the quivering Razgut, who was whispering his unceasing chant of "Take me home, please, brother, take me home. I have repented, I have been punished enough, take me home...."

Akiva said, "I don't need to ask him anything."

"Ah, no? I see. A man once said, 'All you need in this life is ignorance and confidence; then success is sure.' Mark Twain, you know. He had a fine mustache. Men of wisdom so often do."

Something in the old man was shifting as Akiva watched. He saw him lift up his head to peer out over the stone lip that was keeping him from sliding to his death. His madness seemed to have abated, if indeed it hadn't all been an act to begin with. He was gathering up the tatters of his courage, which, under the circumstances, was not unimpressive. He was also stalling.

"Make this easy, old man," said Akiva. "I didn't come here to kill humans."

"Why *did* you come? Even the chimaera don't trespass here. This world is no place for monsters—"

"Monsters? Well, then. I am not a monster."

"No? Razgut doesn't think he is, either. Do you, monster of mine?"

He asked it almost fondly, and Razgut cooed, "Not a monster. A seraph, a being of smokeless fire, yes, forged in another age, in another world." He was looking hungrily at Akiva. "I'm like you, brother. I'm just like you."

Akiva did not enjoy the comparison. He said, "I'm nothing like you, cripple," in an acid tone that made Razgut flinch.

Izîl reached up to pat the arm that was like a vise around his own neck. "There, there," he said, his voice ringing hollow of compassion. "He can't see it. It is a condition of monsters that they do not perceive themselves as such. The dragon, you know, hunkered in the village devouring maidens, heard the townsfolk cry 'Monster!' and looked behind him."

"I know who the monsters are." Akiva's tiger eyes darkened. How well he knew. The chimaera had reduced the meaning of life to *war*. They came in a thousand bestial forms, and no matter how many of them you killed, more always came, and more.

Izîl replied, "A man once said, 'Battle not with monsters lest you become a monster, and if you gaze into the abyss, the abyss gazes also into you.' Nietzsche, you know. Exceptional mustache."

"Just tell me—" Akiva began, but Izîl cut him off.

"Have you ever asked yourself, do monsters make war, or does war make monsters? I've seen things, angel. There are guerrilla armies that make little boys kill their own families. Such acts rip out the soul and make space for beasts to grow inside. Armies *need* beasts, don't they? Pet beasts, to do their terrible work! And the worst is, it's almost impossible to retrieve a soul that has been ripped away. *Almost.*" He gave Akiva a keen look. "But it can be done, if ever . . . if ever you decide to go looking for *yours.*"

Fury flashed through Akiva. Sparks rained from his wings, to be borne by breezes over the rooftops of Marrakesh. "Why would I do that? Where I come from, old man, a soul's as useless as teeth to the dead."

"Spoken, I think, by one who still remembers what it was like to have one."

Akiva did remember. His memories were knives, and he was not pleased to have them turned against him. "You should worry about your own soul, not mine."

"My soul is clean. I've never killed anyone. But you, oh you. Look at your hands."

Akiva didn't take the bait, but he did curl his fingers reflexively into fists. The bars were etched along the tops of his fingers: Each represented an enemy slain, and his hands bore a terrible tally.

"How many?" Izîl asked. "Do you even know, or have you lost count?"

Gone entirely was the quivering madman Akiva had hauled up off the cobbles of the plaza. Izîl was sitting up now, or as near as he could come to it, encumbered as he was by Razgut, who looked back and forth in distress between his human mule and the angel he hoped had come to save him.

In fact, Akiva knew the precise number of kills recorded on his hands. "What about you?" he threw back at Izîl. "How many teeth, over the years? I don't suppose *you* kept count."

"Teeth? Ah, but I only took teeth from the dead!"

"And you sold them to Brimstone. You know what that makes you? A collaborator."

"Collaborator? They're just teeth. He makes necklaces, I saw him. Just teeth on strings!"

"You think he's making necklaces? Fool. You've had everything to do with our war, but you were too stupid to see it. You tell me that battling with monsters has made me a monster? Doing business with devils, what has that made you?"

Izîl stared at him, mouth hanging open, then stated in a rush of sudden understanding, "You know. You know what he does with the teeth."

Bitterly, Akiva breathed, "Yes, I know."

"Tell me—"

"Shut up!" Akiva commanded as the final tether of his patience snapped. "Tell me where to find her. Your life is nothing to me. Do you understand?" He heard the brutality in his own voice and saw himself as if from without, looming over these poor, broken creatures. What would Madrigal think if she could see him now? But she couldn't, could she? And that was the point.

Madrigal was dead.

The old man was right. He *was* a monster, but if he was, it was because of the enemy. Not just a lifetime at war—that hadn't managed to make Akiva what he was. It was one act that had done this, one unspeakable act that he could never forget or forgive, and for which, in vengeance, he had vowed to destroy a kingdom. He hissed. "Do you think I can't *make* you talk?"

To which Izîl replied with a smile, "No, angel. I don't think you can." And then he pitched himself off the minaret, carrying Razgut with him, to fall two hundred feet and shatter against the roof tiles below.

19

NOT WHO, BUT WHAT

The cathedral conducted Karou's scream and splintered it into a symphony of screams that echoed and collided so the vast vaulted space was alive with her voice. And then it wasn't. The chimaera silenced her with a backhand and she skidded off the stone slab, knocking down the metal crook and thurible, which sent up a clangor. He sprang down after her, and she thought he would tear out her throat with his teeth, his face was so close to hers, but then...he was dragged back as if plucked, and thrust away.

And Brimstone was there.

Karou had never been so happy to see him. "Brimstone..." she choked out, and then stopped. Her relief faltered. His crocodile pupils closed to black slashes, as they always did when he was angry, but if Karou thought she had seen him angry before, this was to be an education in rage.

The moment froze as he mastered his shock at seeing her

there, while for Karou, an eternity revolved in the space between heartbeats.

"Karou?" He snarled his incredulity, lips peeling back in a terrible grimace. His breath, fast, hissed through his teeth as he reached for her, claws flexed.

Behind him, the white-haired wolf chimaera demanded, "Who *is* that?"

Brimstone growled. "That is *no one*."

Karou thought maybe she should run.

Too late.

A lunge, and Brimstone caught her arm right over the blood-tinged bandage of her last angel slash, and crushed it in his grip. Light trembled behind Karou's eyelids and she gasped. He grabbed her other arm and picked her up, raising her so that her face was just inches from his own. Her bare feet paddled for purchase and found none. Her arms were pinned, his claws piercing her skin. She couldn't move. She could only stare back into his eyes, which had never in her life seemed so alien, so *animal*, as they did now.

"Give her to me," said the man.

Brimstone said, "You need rest, Thiago. You should still be sleeping. I'll take care of her."

"Take care of her? How?" Thiago demanded.

"She won't trouble us again."

Peripherally, Karou saw the familiar shape of Twiga with his long, hunched neck on sloping shoulders, and she turned to him, but the look on his face was worse than Brimstone's, because it was both appalled and afraid, as if he were about to witness something that he would rather not see. Karou started to panic.

"Wait," she gasped, writhing in Brimstone's grasp. "Wait, wait—"

But he was already moving, carrying her to the stairs, taking them fast, in leaps and lunges. He wasn't careful with her, and she felt what it must be like for a doll in a toddler's hands, whipped around corners and drubbed against walls, dropped and tossed like an inanimate thing. Sooner than she would have thought possible—or maybe she lost consciousness for a time—they were back at the shop door, and he hurled her through it. She didn't land on her feet but went sprawling, catching a chair with her cheek so that a firework detonated behind her eyes.

Brimstone slammed the door behind him and loomed over her. "What were you thinking?" he thundered. "You could not have done worse. Foolish child! And you!" He spun on Yasri and Issa, who had rushed out of the kitchen and were gaping, horrified. They flinched. "If we were going to keep her here, we said, there would be rules. Inviolable rules. Did we not all agree?"

Issa attempted an answer. "Yes, but—"

But Brimstone had rounded on Karou again and grabbed her up off the floor. "Did he see your hands?" he demanded. She had never heard his voice raised to this pitch. It was like stone grating against stone. She felt it in her skull. He was gripping her arms so hard. A whiteness washed across her vision, and she feared she was going to faint.

"Did he?" he repeated, louder.

She knew that no was the right answer, but she couldn't lie. She gasped, "Yes. Yes!"

He gave a kind of howl that chilled her worse than anything had during this whole terrible night. "Do you know what you've done?"

Karou did not know.

"Brimstone!" Yasri squawked. "Brimstone, she's injured!" The parrot-woman's arms were flapping like wings. She tried to pry the Wishmonger's hands from Karou's wound, but he shook her off.

He dragged Karou to the front door and wrenched it open, shoving her ahead of him into the vestibule.

"Wait!" cried Issa. "You can't put her out like that—"

But he wouldn't hear it. "Get out, now!" he snarled at Karou. "Get away!" He wrenched open the outer door of the vestibule— another measure of his rage; the doors were never opened together, *never*, it was a fail-safe against intrusion—and the last thing she saw was his face contorted with fury before he shoved her hard and slammed the door.

Released so suddenly, she took three or four reeling steps backward before tripping off the curb and collapsing, and there she sat, stunned, barefoot, and bleeding, light-headed and gasping, in a gutter stream of melting snow. She was torn between relief that he'd let her go—for a moment she'd feared far worse than this—and disbelief that he had thrown her out injured and barely dressed into the cold.

Dazed and dizzy, she hardly knew what to do. Shivering was setting in. It was frigid out, and she was soaked with gutter slush now in addition to blood. She picked herself up and stood there, uncertain. Her flat was a ten-minute walk. Already her feet burned with the cold. She stared at the door—unsurprised now to see a black handprint on its surface—and thought surely it must open. At the very least Issa would bring her coat and shoes.

Surely.

But the door didn't and didn't and still didn't open.

A car rumbled past at the end of the block, and here and there laughter and arguments drifted out windows, but no one was near. Karou's teeth chattered. She clutched her arms around herself, for all the good it did, and stayed fixed on the door, unable to believe that Brimstone would just *leave* her out here. Cold, awful moments ticked by and finally, outraged tears springing to her eyes, Karou turned away, hugging herself, and began to limp on numb feet in the direction of her flat. She got a few wide-eyed looks along the way, and some offers of help, which she ignored, and it wasn't until she reached her door, shivering convulsively, and reached for a coat pocket that wasn't there that she realized she didn't have her keys. No coat, no keys, and no shings, either, with which she would have been able to wish open the door.

"Damn damn damn," Karou cursed, tears icy on her cheeks. All she had were the scuppies around her wrist. She took one between her fingers and wished, but nothing happened. Unlocking doors exceeded a scuppy's small power.

She was about to buzz a neighbor awake when she sensed, behind her, a furtive movement.

She was beyond thinking. A hand came down on her shoulder, and she was all nerve and impulse. She seized the hand and threw her weight forward. The figure behind her was lifted— Karou registered a second too late the voice, concerned, saying,

"Jesus, Roo, are you okay?"—to catapult over her shoulder and through the plate glass of the door.

The glass shattered as Kaz sailed through it and hit the ground with an explosive grunt. Karou stood still, the awareness catching up to her that he hadn't even been trying to scare her this time, and now he was lying across the threshold in a litter of glass. She thought she should feel something— regret?—but she felt nothing at all.

The problem of the locked door, at least, was solved.

"Are you hurt?" she asked him, flat.

He just blinked, stunned, and she skimmed the scene with a cursory glance. No blood. The glass had broken into rectangular chunks. He was fine. She stepped over him and picked her way to the elevator. Throwing Kaz had cost her what little strength she had left, and she doubted she could walk up the six flights of stairs. The elevator doors opened and she got in, turning to face Kaz, who still hadn't moved. He was staring after her.

"What *are* you?" he asked.

Not *who*, but *what*.

She didn't answer. The elevator doors closed and she was alone with her reflection, in which she saw what Kaz had seen. She was wearing nothing but soaked jeans and a filmy white camisole gone see-through where it clung to her skin. Her hair clumped in blue coils around her neck, like Issa's serpents, and rust-streaked bandages hung loose from her shoulders. Against the blood, her skin looked translucent, almost blue, and she was curled over, clutching herself and shaking like some kind of junkie. All of that was bad enough, but it was her face that caught her. Her cheek was swelling from when Brimstone had flung her into the chair, and her head was set in a hard-jawed downward tilt so that her eyes were hooded in shadow. She looked like someone you'd go a long way to avoid walking past, she thought. She looked... not entirely human.

The elevator doors pinged open and she dragged herself down the hall. She had to climb out a window to get onto her balcony, and break a pane out of her balcony door to get into her apartment, and she managed it before her strength gave out or her shivering incapacitated her, and finally she was inside, stripping off her wet clothes. She dragged herself onto her bed, tugged a quilt around her, curled up in a ball, and sobbed.

Who are you? she asked herself, remembering the angel's question, and the wolf's. But it was Kaz's that reverberated through her, an echo that wouldn't die.

What are you?

What?

20

TRUE STORY

Karou spent the weekend alone in her apartment, feverish, bruised, sliced, slashed, and miserable. Rising from bed on Saturday was torture. Her muscles seemed to have been wound with winches, tight enough to snap. Everything hurt. Everything. It was hard to pick out one pain from the next, and she looked like a brochure on domestic violence, her cheek achieving coconut proportions and blooming blue to rival her hair.

She considered calling Zuzana for help but abandoned the idea when she realized she didn't have her phone. It was with her coat and shoes, bag, wallet, keys, and sketchbook, back at the shop. She could have e-mailed, but in the time it took to boot up her laptop she imagined how Zuzana would react to the sight of her, and she knew her friend wouldn't let things pass this time with evasions. Karou would have to tell her something. She was too tired to come up with a lie, so she ended up feeding herself Tylenol and tea and passing the weekend in a daze of chills and sweats, pain and nightmares.

She woke often to imagined sounds and looked to her windows, hoping as she had never hoped to see Kishmish with a note, but he didn't come, and the weekend went by with no one checking on her—not Kaz, whom she'd put through plate glass, and not Zuzana, whom she'd conditioned to accept her absences with wary silence. She had never felt so alone.

Monday came, and she still didn't leave the apartment. Erratically she kept up with the tea and Tylenol. Sleep was a carousel of nightmares, the same creatures coming around again and again—the angel, the thing on Izîl's back, the wolf chimaera, Brimstone in fury—and when she opened her eyes the light would have changed, but nothing else did except perhaps that her misery deepened.

It was dark when the buzzer rang. And rang. And rang. She pulled herself over to the console by the door and croaked, "Hello?"

"Karou?" It was Zuzana. "Karou, what the hell? Buzz me up, truant."

Karou was so glad to hear her friend's voice, so glad someone had come to check on her, that she burst into tears. When Zuzana came through the door she found Karou sitting on the edge of her bed, tears streaming down her battered face. She came to a halt, all five-almost-feet atop cartoonish platform boots, and said, "Oh. Oh. God. *Karou.*" She was across the tiny room in a streak. Her hands were cool from the wintry air, and her voice was soft, and Karou put her head on her friend's shoulder and cried for long minutes without stopping.

Things got better after that.

Zuzana got her settled without asking questions, then went out for supplies: soup; bandages; a box of butterfly closures for sealing the split flesh along Karou's collarbone, arm, and shoulder, where the angel's sword had cut her.

"These are going to be some serious scars," said Zuzana, bent over her doctoring with the same concentration she applied to building marionettes. "When did this happen? You should have gone to the hospital right away."

"I did," said Karou, thinking of Yasri's balm. "Sort of."

"And what—? Are these *claw marks?*" Both of Karou's upper arms were livid purple, darkest where Brimstone's fingers had sunk in, and pierced with scabbed puncture marks.

"Um," said Karou.

Zuzana regarded her in silence, then got up and heated the soup she'd brought. She sat on a chair beside the bed, and when Karou finished eating, she kicked her feet—bootless now—up on the mattress and folded her hands in her lap. "Okay," Zuzana said. "I'm ready."

"For what?"

"For a really good story that I hope will be the truth."

The truth. Karou attempted a subject change—"First tell me what happened Saturday with violin boy"—while she rolled the idea of truth around in her mind.

Zuzana snorted. "I don't think so. Well, his name is Mik, but that's all you're getting until you do some talking."

"His name! You got his name!" This morsel of normal life made Karou almost absurdly happy.

"Karou, I'm serious." She *was* serious. Her dark Slavic eyes took on a no-nonsense intensity that Karou had told her in the past would stand her in good stead as an interrogator with the secret police. "Tell me what the hell happened to you."

The thing was, Karou told the truth all the time, but she told it with that sardonic smile, as if she were being outrageous. Did she even have a facial expression that went with telling the truth in earnest? And what would she say? This wasn't a story she could ease into gently, like dipping a toe in cold water. She had to just jump.

"An angel tried to kill me," she said.

A beat, and then, "Uh-huh."

"No, really." Karou was conscious—too conscious—of her expression. She felt as if she were auditioning for the role of "truth teller" and trying way too hard.

"Did Jackass do this?"

Karou laughed, too quick and too hard, then winced and held her swollen cheek. The idea of Kaz hurting her was just silly. Well, hurting her *physically*, though now even the idea that he could have hurt her heart seemed silly, with everything else she had to worry about. "No. It wasn't Kaz. The cuts were made by a sword, when an angel tried to kill me Friday night. In Morocco. God, it was probably on the news. Then there was this wolf guy who I thought was dead but was most definitely *not*. The rest was Brimstone. And, oh. Um, everything in my sketchbooks is true." She held her wrists out, lined up so her tattoos spelled out *true story*. "See? It's a hint."

Zuzana was not amused. "Jesus, Karou—"

Karou plunged ahead. The truth, she found, felt *smooth*, like a skipping stone in the palm of your hand. "And my hair? I don't dye it. I wished it this color. And I speak twenty-six languages, and those were mostly wishes, too. Didn't you ever think it was weird that I speak Czech? I mean, who speaks Czech but Czechs? Brimstone gave it to me for my fifteenth birthday, right before I came here. Oh, and remember the malaria? I got it in Papua New Guinea, and it sucked. And I've been shot, too, and I think I killed the bastard, and I'm not sorry, and for some reason an angel tried to kill *me*, and he was the most beautiful thing I've ever seen and also the scariest, though that wolf guy was pretty freaking scary, too, and last night I pissed off Brimstone really bad and he threw me out, and when I got back here Kaz was waiting and I threw him through glass, which worked out great actually because I didn't have my key." Pause. "So I don't think he'll try scaring me again, which is about the only good thing to come of all this."

Zuzana said nothing. She scraped back her chair and pulled on her boots, setting each foot down with a *clomp*, and she surely would have left then—probably forever—if not for the *thunk* that rattled the glass panes of the balcony door.

Karou gave a strangled cry and jumped out of bed, mindless of her many hurts. She lunged for the door. It was Kishmish.

It was Kishmish, and he was on fire.

* * *

He died in her hands. She smothered the flames and cradled him, and he was raw and charred, the hummingbird fury of his heartbeat giving way to long pauses as she hunched over him saying, "No no no no no—" His forked tongue worked in and

136

out of his beak, and his frantic chirrups tapered away with his heartbeat. "No no no. Kishmish, no—" And then he died. Karou stayed hunched there, on her balcony, holding him. Her string of *nos* faded to whispers, but she didn't stop saying them until Zuzana spoke.

Her voice was weak. "Karou?"

Karou looked up.

"Is that...?" Zuzana gestured a jittery hand at Kishmish's lifeless form. She looked perplexed. "That's...um. That looks like—"

Karou didn't help her out. She looked back down at Kishmish and tried to make sense of this sudden intrusion of death. *He flew here on fire*, she thought. *He came to me.*

She saw that something was tied to his foot: a piece of Brimstone's thick notepaper, charred, which crumbled to ashes when she touched it, and...something else. Her fingers shook as she untied it, and then she held the object in her palm. Her heartbeat jumped with a child's ingrained fear: She wasn't supposed to touch it.

It was Brimstone's wishbone.

Kishmish had brought it to her. *On fire* he had brought it.

Out in the city a siren wailed, and it hurried a connection her mind had been slow to make. Burning. Black handprint. The portal. She struggled to her feet and rushed inside, pulled on a jacket and boots. Zuzana was there, asking, "What is it, Karou? What is that? What—?" but Karou barely heard her.

She went out the door and down the stairs, Kishmish still cradled in her arm, the wishbone tucked in her palm. Zuzana followed her into the street and all the way to Josefov, to the service door that had been Brimstone's Prague portal.

It was now a blue-white inferno impervious to the jets of the fire hoses.

At the same moment, though Karou didn't know it, across the world, at every door emblazoned with the black handprint, fires raged. They couldn't be doused, and yet they didn't spread. Flame ate away the doors and the magic that clung to them and then swallowed itself, leaving charred holes in dozens of buildings. Metal doors melted, so hot was the fire, and witnesses who stared at the flames saw, in the nimbus of their dazzled retinas, the silhouettes of wings.

Karou saw them and understood. The way to Elsewhere had been severed, and she was cast adrift.

Once upon a time,
a little girl was raised by monsters.

But angels burned the doorways to their world,
and she was all alone.

21

HOPE MAKES ITS OWN MAGIC

Once, when Karou was a little girl, she used a handful of scuppies to flatten the wrinkles out of a drawing that Yasri had sat on. Wrinkle by wrinkle, wish by wish — a painstaking procedure accomplished with total concentration, tongue peeking out at the corner of her lips.

"There!" She held it up, proud.

Brimstone made a sound that put her in mind of a disappointed bear.

"What?" she demanded, eight years old, dark-haired, dark-eyed, and skinny as the shadow of a sapling. "It's a good drawing. It deserved to be rescued."

It *was* a good drawing. It was a rendering of herself as a chimaera, with bat wings and a fox's tail.

Issa clapped with delight. "Oh, you'd look darling with a fox tail. Brimstone, can't she have a tail, just for today?"

Karou would rather have had the wings, but neither was to be. The Wishmonger, looking put-upon, breathed a weary *no*.

Issa didn't beg. She just shrugged, kissed Karou on the forehead, and tacked up the drawing in a place of honor. But Karou was taken with the idea, so she asked, "Why not? It would only take a lucknow."

"Only?" he echoed. "And what do you know of the value of wishes?"

She recited the scale in a single breath. "Scuppy shing lucknow gavriel bruxis!"

But that was not, apparently, what he meant. More disappointed bear sounds, like growls routed through the nose, and he said, "Wishes are not for foolery, child."

"Well, what do *you* use them for?"

"Nothing," he said. "I do not wish."

"What?" It had astonished her. "Never?" All that magic at his fingertips! "But you could have anything you wanted—"

"Not anything. There are things bigger than any wish."

"Like what?"

"Most things that matter."

"But a bruxis—"

"A bruxis has its limits, just like any wish."

A moth-winged hummingbird stuttered into the light and Kishmish launched off Brimstone's horn, plucked it from the air, and swallowed it whole—and just like that, the creature un-was. It was, and then it wasn't. Karou's stomach roiled as she contemplated the possibility of being so suddenly *not*.

Watching her, Brimstone added, "I *hope*, child, but I don't wish. There's a difference."

She turned this over in her mind, thinking that if she could come up with the difference, it might impress him. Something occurred to her, and she struggled to put it into words. "Because hope comes from *in* you, and wishes are just magic."

"Wishes are false. Hope is true. Hope makes its own magic."

She'd nodded as if she understood, but she hadn't then, and she didn't now, three months after the portals burned and amputated half her life. She'd been back to the doorway in Josefov at least a dozen times. It had been replaced, along with the wall around it, and they looked too clean, too new for their surroundings. She'd knocked and she'd hoped; she'd worn herself out hoping, and nothing. Again and again: nothing.

Whatever magic there was in hoping, she thought, it had nothing on a good, solid wish.

Now she stood at another door, this one belonging to a hunting cabin in nowhere, Idaho, and she didn't bother knocking. She just kicked it open. "Hello," she said. Her voice was bright and hard, and so was her smile. "It's been a while."

Inside, the hunter Bain looked up in surprise. He was cleaning a shotgun at his coffee table, and rose swiftly to his feet. "You. What do you want?"

Abominably, he was shirtless, showing an abundance of loose white gut, and his extraordinary beard bushed around his shoulders in clumps. Karou could smell it from across the room, sour as a mouse's nest.

She stepped uninvited into the cabin. She was dressed in black: slim-fitting wool trousers with boots, and a vintage leather trench belted at the waist. There was a satchel slung across her shoulder, her hair was smoothed back in a single braid, and she

143

wore no makeup. She looked tired. She *was* tired. "Killed anything fun lately?"

"Do you know something?" Bain asked. "Have the doors opened back up?"

"Oh. No. Nothing like that." Karou kept her voice light, as if she were paying a social call. It was a farce, of course. Even when she'd been running errands for Brimstone she had never visited here. Bain had always come into the shop himself.

"You weren't easy to find," she told him. He lived off the grid; as far as the Internet was concerned, he didn't exist. Karou had spent several wishes to track him down — low-grade wishes that she'd liberated from other traders.

She looked around the room. A plaid couch, some glazed-eyed elk heads mounted on the wall, and a Naugahyde recliner held together with duct tape. A generator hummed outside the window, and the room was lit by a bare bulb. She shook her head. "Gavriels to play with, and you live in a dump like this? Men."

"What do you want?" Bain asked, wary. "Do you want teeth?"

"Me? No." She perched on the edge of the recliner. Still with that hard, bright smile, she said, "*Teeth* are not what I want."

"What, then?"

Karou's smile disappeared, like flipping a switch. "I think you can guess what I want."

A beat. Then Bain said, "I don't have any. I used them all."

"Well. I don't think I'll take your word on that."

He gestured around the room. "Have a look, then. Knock yourself out."

"See, the thing is, I know where you keep them."

The hunter went still, and Karou considered the shotgun on

the table. It was disassembled, not a threat. The question was whether he had another gun within reach. Probably. He was not a one-gun kind of guy.

His fingers twitched almost imperceptibly.

Karou's pulse jumped in her hands.

Bain lunged for the couch. She was already moving. Smooth as dance, she leapt over the coffee table, caught his head with the flat of her palm and drove it against the wall. With a croak he collapsed onto the couch, and for an instant he was free to scrabble with both hands in the sofa cushions, frantic, and then he found what he was looking for.

He whipped around, pistol raised. Karou caught his wrist with one hand and grabbed a fistful of beard with the other. A crack; a bullet blazed over her head. She braced one foot against the sofa, heaved him by the beard, and swung him to the floor. The table tipped and shotgun parts scattered. Keeping her grip on his wrist, pistol pointed away, she came down hard on his forearm with her knee and heard bones grind. He yelped and released the gun. Karou took it up and pressed its muzzle into his eye socket.

"I'm going to forgive you for that," she said. "I do see, from your perspective, that this sucks. I just don't feel all that bad about it."

Bain was breathing hard and looking murder at her. Up close he smelled rancid. Still holding the gun to his eye, Karou steeled herself and reached into the greasy thatch of his beard to root around. Right away her hand encountered metal. So it was true. He kept his wishes in his beard.

She drew her knife from her boot.

"Do you want to know how I knew?" she asked him. He'd drilled holes in the wish coins and knotted his dirty hair right through them. She sliced them free one by one. "It was Avigeth. The snake? She had to circle your stinking neck, didn't she? I did *not* envy her that. Did you think she wouldn't tell Issa what you have hidden in this disgusting shrub of yours?"

It gave her a pang, remembering those casual nights in the shop, sitting cross-legged on the floor, sketching Issa and gossiping while Twiga's tools droned in the corner and Brimstone strung his endless necklaces of teeth. What was happening there now?

What?

Bain's wishes were mostly shings. There were a few lucknows, though, and best of all, heavy as hammers, there were two gavriels. That was good. That was very good. From the other traders she'd visited so far, she'd gotten only lucknows and shings. "I was hoping you wouldn't have spent these yet," Karou told him. "Thank you. Sincerely. *Thank you.* You don't know what this means to me."

"Bitch," he muttered.

"Well, that's brave," she said, conversational. "I mean, to say that to the girl with the gun against your eyeball." She went on sawing away hanks of beard as Bain lay rigid. He was probably twice her weight, but he didn't struggle. There was a wild light in her eyes and it cowed him. Plus, he'd heard rumors of St. Petersburg, and knew she wasn't shy with her knife.

She depleted his wish stash and, sitting back on her heels, used the barrel of the gun to peel back his lower lip. She grimaced when she saw his teeth. They were crooked and tobacco-brown. They were *real.* No hope of a bruxis, then.

146

"You know, you're the fifth one of Brimstone's traders I've tracked down, and you're the only one with your teeth."

"Yeah, well, I like meat."

"You like meat. Of course you do."

Of the other traders on whom she'd paid these "social calls," all had made the trade for a bruxis, and all had already spent them, mostly on long life. One, the hag matriarch of a clan of poachers in Pakistan, had botched the wish, forgetting to include youth and health, and she was a disaster of collapsing flesh, a testament to Brimstone's admonition that even a bruxis had limits.

Well, a bruxis would have been quite a score, but it was a pair of gavriels that Karou really needed, and now she had them. She gathered up all the wishes, along with the dirty beard hair that clung to them, and shoved the whole mess into her satchel. She kept one shing in her palm; she'd need it to make her exit.

"You think you can just do this?" Bain asked, low. "You piss off a hunter, you're gonna live like prey, little girl, always wondering who's tracking you."

Karou made a pondering gesture. "Hmm. Can't have that, can we?" She raised the pistol and sighted down the barrel at him, saw his eyes go wide and then squinch shut as she gave an enthusiastic little-boy "Kablam!" and then lowered the gun again. "Dummy. Lucky for you, I'm not that kind of girl."

She laid the gun on the sofa and, as he started to sit up, wished him to sleep. His head hit the floor with a thud and the shing vanished from her palm. Karou didn't look back. Her feet were heavy on the porch steps, and all the way down the dark gravel drive to where she'd left a cab idling at a clump of mailboxes.

She reached the mailboxes. There was no cab.

Karou sighed. The driver must have heard the gunshot and taken off. She could hardly blame him. It was like a scene out of a film noir: a girl pays him a ridiculous sum to drive her from Boise up into this no-man's-land, where she vanishes into a hunting cabin and a shot is fired. Who in his right mind would stick around to see how that played out?

With another sigh, she closed her eyes and almost rubbed them, then remembered she'd been handling Bain's filthy beard and wiped her hands on her pants instead. She was so tired. She reached into her bag. Judging it would take a lucknow to turn the cab around, she palmed one and was just about to make the wish when she stopped. "What am I thinking?" One cheek dimpled as her lips skewed into a smile.

She took out a gavriel instead. "Hello, you," she whispered to it. Weighing it on her palm, she tilted back her head and looked up at the sky.

22

A Piece of Empty Candy

Three months.

It had been three months since the portals burned, and Karou had had no word in all that time. How often had her thoughts, however otherwise occupied, suddenly skidded back to the scorched note in Kishmish's claws? Like a scratch in a record, the note had worn its groove in her mind. What had it said? What had Brimstone wanted to tell her as the portals burned?

What had the note said?

And then there was the wishbone, which she now wore around her neck, as Brimstone always had. It had occurred to her, of course, that *it* might be a wish, one more powerful even than a bruxis, and she had held it in her hand and wished on it—wished for a portal to peel open to Elsewhere—but nothing ever happened. There was something comforting in the feel of it in her hand, though. Its frail wings fit between her fingers as if it were meant to be held. But if it was anything more than a bone, she couldn't guess what, and as for why Brimstone had sent it to her, she feared she would never know. The fear festered alongside all her unanswered questions, and with it new fears, strange and undefinable.

Something was happening to her.

Sometimes when she looked in the mirror now, she experienced a moment of blank unfamiliarity, as if she were meeting the gaze of a stranger. Her name, called out to her, didn't always register, and even the lay of her shadow could strike her as foreign. Recently she'd caught herself testing it with quick gestures to see if it was hers. She was pretty sure this was not normal behavior.

Zuzana disagreed. "It's probably post-traumatic stress disorder," she'd said. "What would be weird is if you were fine. I mean, you lost your family."

Karou still marveled at the way in which Zuzana had accepted her whole bizarre story. Her friend was not, in practice, someone who believed in things, but after seeing Kishmish and getting a little scuppy demonstration she'd bought it all, and it was a good thing. Karou needed her. Zuzana was her anchor to her normal life. What remained of it, anyway.

She was still in school, if only technically. After the angel arsons it had taken about a week for her injuries to heal, at least enough that the yellow-green stage of her bruises could be concealed with makeup. She'd gone back to class for a couple of days, but it was a lost cause. She couldn't keep her focus, and her hand, clasping pencil or paintbrush, seemed incapable of delicacy. A furious energy built up in her, and more than ever before she was plagued by that phantom sense that she was meant to be doing something else.

Something else. Something else. Something *else*.

She made contact with Esther and other of Brimstone's less-vile associates around the world to confirm that the phenomenon was global: The portals were gone, every last one.

She also, in the process, discovered something quite unexpected: She was rich. Brimstone, it turned out, had established bank accounts for her over the course of her life. Juicy bank accounts overflowing with zeroes. She even owned real estate, such as the buildings in which, until recently, the portals had been. And *land*. A swamp, of all things. An abandoned medieval hill town in the lava path of Mount Etna. A mountain flank in the Andes where an amateur paleontologist claimed — to widespread scientific merriment — to have unearthed a cache of "monster skeletons."

Brimstone had seen to it that Karou would never worry about money, which was lucky, as she had to pay her "social calls" in the way of ordinary humans: airplanes, passport, overly friendly businessmen, and all.

She made it to school only sporadically after that, claiming family emergency. If not for all the extra work she did, the constant drawing in her new sketchbook — number ninety-three, which picked up where ninety-two, left behind in Brimstone's shop, had so abruptly cut off — she would surely have gotten the boot by now. As it was, she was hanging by a thread.

The last time she was there, Profesorka Fiala had been all frowns and judgment. Leafing through Karou's sketchbook, she paused on one drawing in particular, a rendering of the angel in Marrakesh, done from memory. It was of the moment Karou had first seen him up close in the alley. "This is *life* drawing class, Karou," said Fiala. "Not *fantasy* drawing."

Karou did a double take. She was pretty sure she'd left the wings out, and indeed, she saw, she had. "Fantasy?" she asked.

"No one is this perfect," said the teacher, skimming dismissively past the page.

Karou didn't argue, but later had said to Zuzana, "The funny thing is, I didn't even do him justice. Those *eyes*. Maybe a painting could capture those eyes, but a drawing never could."

"Yeah, well," said Zuzana, "he's one scary-looking beautiful bastard, is what he is."

"I know. You should have seen him."

"Well. I certainly hope I never do."

"I kind of hope I *do*, actually," said Karou, who no longer made the mistake of going out unarmed. She'd made a poor showing of herself in that fight, and cringed to think of the way she'd run away. If she were to see the angel again, she would stand her ground.

Where school was concerned, however, there was no ground to stand. She had no semester project to speak of and she couldn't squeak by on her sketchbook and feverish last-minute catch-ups anymore, and as hard as it was to just let it go, she had bigger things to worry about.

After the fires, her first trip had been to Marrakesh. She kept remembering what Izîl had yelled to her: "You must get to Brimstone. Tell him the seraphim are here. They've gotten back in. You must warn him!"

He knew something. It was the whole point of his bruxis:

knowledge. And while Karou had always wondered what he had learned, now she needed urgently to know. So she'd gone to find him, only to learn, to her great sadness, that he had thrown himself off the Koutoubia minaret later the same night she'd left him. Thrown *himself?* *Not likely,* she thought, vividly recalling the angel's soul-dead countenance, the bite of his blade, and the scars he'd left her to remember him by.

Zuzana had actually screen-printed her a T-shirt on the press at school that read: I MET AN ANGEL IN MOROCCO AND ALL I GOT WERE THESE LOUSY SCARS. She'd made another one, too: I SAW AN ANGEL AND YOU DIDN'T. SUCK IT, RAPTURE-MONKEYS!

The sentiment was a response to the worldwide fervor in the wake of the angel sightings. Though accounts of the encounters were initially brushed off as the ravings of drunks and children, the evidence had become too intriguing to ignore. Grainy video and a few photographs had gone viral on the Web and even crossed over to the mainstream media, with headlines like ANGELS OF DEATH: HARBINGERS OR HOAX? announced in drippy prime-time voices. The best footage came from a carpet merchant's phone and showed the attack on Karou, though she was, mercifully, just an unidentifiable silhouette in the background, blurred out by the heat shimmer of the angel's wings.

A far as she could tell, that was the only time that the angels—and there had been more than the one—had revealed their wings, but a number of witnesses claimed to have seen them fly, or at least to have seen their winged shadows. A nun in India had a burn in the shape of a feather on her palm, which was drawing throngs of pilgrims from around the world, hoping to be blessed by her. Rapture cults had packed their suitcases and were massing together in great vigils, waiting for the end. Online message boards were daily filled with new angel sightings, none of which rang true to Karou.

"All bogus," she'd told Zuzana. "Just crackpots waiting for the Apocalypse."

"Because how *fun*, right?" Zuzana had rubbed her hands together in mock glee. "Oh, boy, the Apocalypse!"

"Right? I know. How much does your life have to suck to want the Apocalypse?"

And with that, they had spent an entire evening at Poison—with Mik, incidentally, Zuzana's "violin boy" and now official boyfriend—drinking apple tea and playing the game *How much would your life have to suck to want the Apocalypse?*

"It would have to suck so much that your bunny slippers are your only friends."

"It would have to suck so much that your dog wags its tail when you *leave*."

"That you know all Celine Dion's lyrics."

"That you wish the *entire world* would end so you don't have to wake up one more day in your crappy house—which, by the way, has no art in it whatsoever—feed your surly kids, and go to a mind-numbing job where someone is sure to have brought doughnuts to make your ass even fatter. *That* is how much your life has to suck to want the Apocalypse."

That, for the win, was Zuzana.

Ah, Zuzana.

Out in the wilderness of Idaho now, as Karou spent her first-ever gavriel in the fulfillment of a lifelong wish—the gavriel vanished, and she rose smoothly off the ground—her first thought was, *Zuzana has got to see this.*

She was floating. She gave a delighted hoot and put her arms out for balance, sculling at the air as if she were floating in the sea, but...it wasn't the sea. It was *the air.* She was flying. Well, maybe not quite flying—*yet*—but floating at the threshold of *the whole freaking sky.* Which happened to wrap around *the whole freaking world.* Above her, night was huge and everywhere, full of stars and wild things—an infinitely deep, infinitely penetrable sphere, and she rose up higher and higher, claiming it.

She could see the roof of Bain's cabin from over the treetops now. Breezes whispered in her ears, cold but playful, seeming to welcome her to the high places. She couldn't help laughing. Once she started, she couldn't stop. It was a helpless, incredulous stream of giggles that sounded a little nuts, but who wouldn't sound a little nuts at a moment like this?

She was *flying.*

God, she wished there was someone here to share it with.

She would soon be sharing it with someone, but it was not, to say the least, the...er, *individual*...she would choose to share anything with, if all else were equal. But all else was not equal. There was only one individual in the entire world who could help her do what she needed to do, and that, unfortunately, was Razgut.

The thought of Izîl's creature made Karou shudder, but her fate was now tied up with his.

In Marrakesh, after learning of Izîl's death, she had wandered the lanes around the mosque in a desolation of disappointment. She'd been so sure Izîl would be able to tell her what was going on. She'd been counting on it with such intensity. She crumpled against a wall and gave in to tears that were a mixture of grief over the death of the poor, tortured man, and frustration for herself.

And then, echoing over the ground, came an unholy chuckle. Beneath a broken donkey cart something shifted, and Razgut dragged himself into the light. "Hello, lovely," he purred, and it was a testament to Karou's mental state that she was actually glad to see him.

"You survived the fall," she said.

But not unscathed. Bereft of his human, he was splayed out over the ground. One arm had been crushed; he cradled it to his chest and dragged himself with the other, legs limp behind him. And his head, his awful purple head, was flattened at the temple, crusted with dried blood, and still embedded with rocks and broken glass.

He gave an impatient flick of the hand. "I've fallen farther."

Karou was skeptical. The minaret towered overhead, the tallest structure in the city.

Seeing her glance up at it, Razgut chuckled again. It was a curdled sound: mingled misery and spite. "That's nothing, blue lovely. A thousand years ago, I fell *from heaven.*"

"Heaven. There is no heaven."

"Quibble, quibble. The sky, then, if you know so much. And I didn't exactly fall. That makes me sound clumsy, doesn't it? As though I tripped and fell into your world. No. I was thrown. Cast out. Exiled."

And that was how Karou had learned of Razgut's origin. It was hard to believe, looking at him and remembering the angel—that mythic, perfect being—that they were kin, but when she forced herself to really look at Razgut, she began to see it. And the splintered joints of his lost wings could not be denied. He was not a creature of this world.

She had also understood, finally, the twisted fulfillment of Izîl's bruxis. In wishing for knowledge of the other world, he had gotten himself saddled with Razgut, who could tell him everything that Brimstone would not.

"What happened to Izîl?" she asked. "He didn't really kill himself, did he? The angel—"

"Ah, well, you can blame him, he dragged us up the minaret, but the fool hunchback flung himself off, all to protect *you.*"

"*Me?*"

"My brother seraph was looking for *you*, lovely. Naughty boy, with all his questions. What does he want with you, I wonder."

"I don't know." It gave Karou a chill. "Izîl didn't tell him where I live?"

"Oh no, noble fool. He danced with the sky instead, and the sky dropped him like a rotten plum."

"Oh god." Karou slumped against the wall and hugged herself. "Poor Izîl."

"Poor him? Don't pity him, pity *me.* He's gone free, but look at me! Do you think mules are so easy to come by? I haven't even been able to trick a beggar." Razgut pushed himself upright and used his good arm to drag his legs around in front of him. His face contorted with pain, but as soon as Karou began to feel the smallest hint of pity for him, his pain turned to a leer.

"You'll help me, though, won't you, sweet?" he asked her, smiling. His teeth were incongruously perfect. "Give me a ride?"

He might have meant "a ride" such as Izîl had given him, but his tone caressed a lewder implication. "After all, this is your fault."

"My fault? Whatever."

Coaxing, he purred, "I'll tell you secrets, like I told Izîl."

"Ask for something else," Karou snapped. "I will not carry you. Ever."

"Oh, but I'll keep you warm. I'll braid your hair. You'll never be lonely again."

Lonely? Karou felt bare in that moment, to have this creature get at her substance like that. He went on, whispering: "All that beauty, it's wrapped around loneliness. You think I didn't taste it? You're practically hollow. A piece of empty candy to lick, but oh, you taste *so good*." His head fell back and he gave a groan, eyes half-lidded with remembered pleasure. Karou felt ill. "I could lick your neck forever, lovely," he moaned. *"Forever."*

Karou was a long, long way from desperate enough to strike that bargain. She pushed off the wall and began to walk away. "Nice chat. Good-bye."

"Wait!" Razgut called after her. "Wait!"

And she wouldn't have thought there was anything he could say that would make her stop. But then he called after her, "You want to see your Wishmonger again? I can take you there. I know a portal!"

She turned to look at him, suspicious.

His leer was gone, replaced by his singular sustaining emotion. It was one she recognized, and for the merest instant, she felt a link to the broken thing that he was. It was longing on his face. If her own substance was loneliness, Razgut's was longing.

"The portal they pushed me through, a thousand years ago. I know where it is. I'll show you, but you have to take me with you." A hitch in his breathing, and he whispered, "I just want to go home."

Karou's heart hummed with excitement. Another portal. "So let's go," she said. "Right now."

Razgut chuffed. "If it was that easy, do you think I'd still be here?"

"What do you mean?"

"It's in the sky, girl. We have to *fly* there."

And now, thanks to two greasy gavriels pillaged from a hunter's beard—one for her, and one for Razgut—they would.

❦ 23 ❦

INFINITE PATIENCE

Fairy-tale city. From the air, red rooftops hug a kink in a dark river, and by night the forested hills appear as spans of black nothing against the dazzle of the lit castle, the spiking Gothic towers, the domes great and small. The river captures all the lights and teases them out, long and wavering, and the side-slashing rain blurs it all to a dream.

This was Akiva's first sight of Prague; he hadn't been the one to mark this portal. That had been Hazael, who had remarked on it after, back in their own world. He'd said that it was beautiful, and it was. Akiva imagined that Astrae might have looked something like this in its golden age, before it was razed by the beasts. City of a Hundred Spires, the seraph capital had been called—a tower for each of the godstars—and the chimaera had torn down every one.

Many a human city had been demolished in war, too, but Prague had been lucky. It stood lovely and ghostly, its chapped stone worn smooth by centuries of storms, millions of rivulets of rain. It was wet and cold, inhospitable, but that didn't bother Akiva. He made his own heat. Moisture hissed on his invisible wings and vaporized, marking out the shape of them against the night in a diffuse halo. Nothing a glamour could do about that, any more than it could hide his wings from his shadow, but there was no one up here to see it.

He was perched on a rooftop in Old Town. The towers of Týn Church reared up like devil's horns behind the row of buildings across the street, in one of which was Karou's flat. Her window was dark. It had been dark, and her flat empty, for the two days since he'd found it.

Folded in his pocket, its creases worn smooth from much handling, was a page torn from a sketchbook — number ninety-two, as was printed on its spine. On the page, which had been the first in the book, a drawing showed Karou with her hands clasped in supplication, accompanied by the words: *If found, please return to Krâlodvorskâ 59, no. 12, Prague. You will be rewarded with cosmic goodwill and hard cash. Thank you.*

Akiva hadn't brought the whole book with him, just this one page with its ragged edge. He wasn't after cosmic goodwill or hard cash.

Just Karou.

With the infinite patience of one who has learned to live broken, he awaited her return.

24

FLYING IS EASY

Flying, Karou discovered to her delight, was easy. Exhilaration chased away her weariness, and with it the apathy that had settled over her after too many encounters with Brimstone's tooth-traders. She flew high, marveling at the stars and feeling as though she were among them. They were almost beyond belief. Give Bain that, at least. He might have no decorating sense, but he lived in the company of stars. The sky looked *sugared*.

She left the cabin behind and followed the road back in the direction of Boise. She dipped up and down, through tiers of wind. She toyed with speed—effortless, though it left her eyes streaming icy tears. It wasn't long before she overtook the taxi that had abandoned her to the wilds. Devious scenarios played in her mind. She might fly alongside and knock on the window, shake her fist before launching upward again.

Wicked girl, she thought, and she heard Brimstone's voice in her head, decrying such mischief as *reckless*. Well, maybe a little.

The wish itself, though—flying—and the plan that it was part of, what would he think of that? What would he think when Karou turned up on his doorstep, her hair mussed from the wind of two worlds? Would he be glad to see her, or would he still be furious, and roar at her that she was a fool, and cast her out once more? Was she supposed to find him, or did he want her to go on like a butterfly out a window, without a backward glance, as if she'd never even had monsters for a family?

If he expected her to do that, he didn't know her at all.

She was going to Morocco to find Razgut beneath whichever trash heap or donkey cart he was hiding, and together— *together!* It made her cringe to even *think* the word connecting herself to him—they would fly through a slash in the sky and emerge "Elsewhere."

It struck her that this was what Brimstone had meant by "hope makes its own magic." She hadn't been able to simply wish open a portal, but by the strength of her will, of her *hope*, when she might have given up her chimaera for lost, she had instead done this. She had found a way. Here she was, flying, and a guide waited to take her where she wanted to go. She was proud, and she believed that Brimstone would be, too, whether he showed it or not.

She shivered. It was cold in the sky, and her glee at flying was giving way to chattering teeth and the return of her exhaustion, so she set herself down in the middle of the road, making her first landing as easily as if she'd done it a thousand times, and waited for the taxi to catch up to her.

The driver, needless to say, was surprised to see her. He looked at her like she was a ghost, and spent more time peeking at her in the rearview mirror on the way back to the airport than he did watching the road. Karou was too tired to even think it was funny. She let her eyes close and reached into the collar of her coat for the wishbone, tucking its flanges neatly between her fingers.

She was almost asleep when her phone rang. Zuzana's name lit up its screen. Karou answered, "Hello, rabid fairy."

Snort. "Shut up. If anyone's a fairy, it's you."

"I'm not a fairy. I'm a monster. And guess what. Speaking of fairies, do I have a surprise for you." Karou tried to imagine Zuzana's face on seeing her rise into the air. Should she tell her, or surprise her? Maybe she could pretend to fall off a tower — or was that just mean?

"What?" asked Zuzana. "Did you get me a present?"

It was Karou's turn to snort. "You're like a kid when her parents come home from a party, checking their pockets for cake."

"Ooh, cake. I'll take cake. But not pocket cake, because yuck."

"I have no cake."

"Sigh. What kind of friend *are* you anyway? Besides the mostly absent kind."

"Right now, I'm the mostly *tired* kind. If you hear snoring, don't be offended."

"Where are you?"

"Idaho, on the way to the airport."

"Oh, yay, airport! You're coming home, aren't you? You didn't forget. I knew you wouldn't forget."

"Please. I've been looking forward to this for weeks. You don't even know. It's like, gross hunter, gross hunter, gross hunter, puppet show!"

"How go the gross hunters, anyway?"

"Grossly. But forget them. Are you all ready?"

"Yep. Freaked. Ready. The puppet's done and *magnificent*, if I do say so myself. Now I just need you to work your magic." She paused. "I mean, your nonmagical magic. Your ordinary Karou wizardry. When will you be back?"

"Friday, I think. I just have to stop in Paris really quick—"

"'Stop in Paris really quick,'" repeated Zuzana. "You know, a smaller soul than I might end our friendship on the grounds of you saying obnoxious things like 'I just have to stop in Paris really quick.'"

"There are smaller souls than you?" countered Karou.

"Hey! My body may be small, but my soul is large. It's why I wear platforms. So I can reach the top of my soul."

Karou laughed, a bright bell sound that drew the cab driver's eyes to her in the rearview mirror.

"And also for kissing," added Zuzana. "Because otherwise I could only date midgets."

"How's Mik, anyway? Besides not a midget?"

Zuzana's voice instantly went gooey. "He's goood," she said, stretching the word out like taffy.

"Hello? Who's there? Put Zuzana back on. Zuzana? There's this sappy chick on the line, pretending to be you—"

"Shut up," said Zuzana. "Just get here, okay? I need you."

"I'm coming."

"And bring me a present."

"*Tch.* Like you deserve a present."

Karou ended the call, smiling. Zuzana *did* deserve a present, and it was why she was stopping in Paris before going home to Prague.

Home. The word might still have air quotes around it, but half of Karou's life had been chopped off, and the other half—the normal half—was   ague. Her tiny flat with its rows and rows of sketchbooks;   a and marionettes; school, easels, naked old men with f   r boas; Poison Kitchen, statues in gas masks, bowls of go   steaming on coffin lids; even her jackass of an ex-boyfri   urking around corners dressed like a vampire.

So, okay. Normal-*is*

And though there   part of her that was anxious to go straight to Morocco,   t her gruesome traveling companion, and strike out for   ts Elsewhere, she couldn't bear the thought of just disapp   g, not with all that she'd already lost. She supposed she was   g back to say good-bye, and to refill her normal for the last time in the foreseeable future.

Plus, she wasn't about to miss Zuzana's puppet show.

25

Never Peace

Karou arrived back in Prague late Friday night. She gave the taxi driver her address, but as he neared her neighborhood, she changed her mind and asked him to let her off in Josefov, near the old Jewish Cemetery. It was the most haunted place she knew, the ground mounded high over centuries of dead, the tombstones as haphazard as bad teeth. Malign crows nested there, and the tree branches were like crone fingers. She loved drawing there, but it was closed, of course, and it wasn't her destination. She walked along its buckled outer wall, feeling the weight of its silence, and made her way to Brimstone's portal, nearby. Or, what had been his portal.

She stood across the street from it, daring herself to go up and knock. Suppose the door just opened, she thought. Suppose it creaked open and Issa was there with an exasperated smile on her face. "Brimstone is in a foul mood," she might say. "Are you sure you want to come in?"

As if it had all been some silly mistake. And wasn't it still possible?

She crossed the street. Her heartbeat a throb of hope, she lifted her hand and knocked, three sharp raps. No sooner had she done it than her hope crested painfully. She sucked a big breath and found herself holding it as her heart beat its *please please please* and her eyes pricked with gathering tears. If it opened or didn't, she would weep. The tears were ready for either disappointment or relief.

Silence.

Please please please.

And . . . nothing.

She breathed again, a slumping exhalation that unspooled a single track of tears from each eye, and still she waited, curling herself against the cold for minutes, minutes into minutes, before she finally gave up and headed home.

* * *

That night, Akiva watched her sleep. Her lips were softly parted, both hands curled childlike under one cheek, her breathing deep. *She's innocent,* Izîl had claimed. Asleep, she looked it. Was she?

Akiva had felt haunted by her these past months — her lovely face tilted up to look at him as she cowered in his shadow, believing she was going to die. The memory scalded him. Again and again it hit him, how close he had come to killing her. And what had stopped him?

Something about her had conjured another girl, long-ago

and long-lost, but what? It wasn't her eyes. They weren't loam-brown and warm as earth; they were black—black as a swan's, stark against the cream of her skin. And in her features he could pinpoint no resemblance to that other face, beloved, first seen through fog so long ago. Both were beautiful, that was all, but something had made a connection and stayed his hand.

Finally it came to him. It was a gesture: the birdlike way she had cocked her head to look at him. That was what had saved her. So small a thing as that.

Standing on her balcony, looking in the window, Akiva asked himself, *What now?*

Memories rose unbidden of the last time he had watched someone sleep. Then, there had been no glass between them frosted by his breath; he hadn't been on the outside looking in, but warm beside Madrigal, propped up on one elbow and testing himself to see how many minutes he could go without reaching for her.

Not even a whole minute. There had been an ache in his fingertips that could be assuaged only by touching her.

He had borne far fewer marks on his hands then, though he hadn't been free of his death ink. He was already a killer, but Madrigal had kissed his marked hands, knuckle by knuckle, and absolved him. "War is all we've been taught," she whispered, "but there are other ways to live. We can find them, Akiva. We can *invent* them. This is the beginning, here." She laid her palm against his bare chest—his heart jumped at her touch—and she brought his hand against her own heart, pressing it to the satin of her skin. "*We* are the beginning."

It had felt like a beginning, from that first stolen night with her — like the invention of a new way of living.

Akiva had never used his hands so softly as when he traced Madrigal's sleeping eyelids with his fingertip, imagining what dreams chased behind them and made them flutter.

She had trusted him enough to let him touch her while she slept. Even in recollection, it amazed him — that from the start she had trusted him to lie beside her and trace the lines of her sleeping face, her graceful neck, her lean, strong arms and the joints of her powerful wings. Sometimes he'd felt her pulse spike with jagged dreams; other times she'd murmured and reached for him, waking as she drew him against her and then, silkily, into her.

Akiva turned away from the window. What was it that made these memories of Madrigal rise so thick and fast?

The tendrils of an idea were unfurling in the deep reaches of his mind, beginning to probe for connections — a way to make the impossible possible — but he didn't admit it to himself. He wouldn't even have believed that somewhere in him lurked the capacity for hope.

What, he asked himself, had made him leave his regiment in the night, not even telling Hazael and Liraz, to come back into this world?

It would be nothing to break the window glass, or melt it. In seconds he could be beside Karou, waking her with a hand clamped over her mouth. He could demand to know...what, exactly? Did he think *she* would be able to tell him why he'd come? Besides, the idea of scaring her made him ill. Turning his back, he stalked to the balustrade and looked out over the city.

Hazael and Liraz would have realized by now that he was gone. "Again," they would be muttering to each other in low voices, even as they covered his absence with some quick story.

Hazael was his half brother, Liraz their half sister. They were children of the harem, offspring of the seraph emperor, whose hobby was breeding bastards to fight the war. Their "father"— and they spoke the word through clenched teeth—visited a different concubine each night, women given as tribute or hand-picked as they caught his eye. His secretaries kept a list of his progeny in two columns, girls and boys. Babies were always being added, and as they grew up and died on the battlefield, they were stricken unceremoniously off.

Akiva, Hazael, and Liraz had been added to the list in the same month. They had grown up together, babies in that place of women, and been given over at five to training. They'd managed to stay together since, always fighting in the same regiments, volunteering for the same missions, including the last: marking Brimstone's doorways with the incendiary handprints that had ignited all in an instant to destroy the sorcerer's portal.

This was the second time Akiva had vanished without explanation. The first time was years ago, and he'd been gone so long that time that his brother and sister thought he'd died.

A part of him had.

He had never told them or anyone where he'd been for those missing months, or what had happened to make him into who he was now.

Izîl had called him a monster, and wasn't he? He imag-ined what Madrigal would think if she could see him today, and see what he had made of the "new way of living" they had whispered about, long ago, in the quiet world of their own cupped wings.

For the first time since he'd lost her, his memory failed to conjure Madrigal's face. Another face intruded: Karou's. Her eyes were black and terrified, reflecting the blaze of his wings as he loomed above her.

He *was* a monster. The things he'd done, nothing could shrive.

He shook open his wings and lifted himself into the night. It was wrong, his being there at the window, a lurking threat while Karou slept so peacefully. He retreated again across the street to let himself sleep, too, and when he did at last, he dreamed he was on the other side of the glass. Karou—not Madrigal but *Karou*—smiled at him and pressed her lips against his knuckles one by one, each kiss erasing black lines until his hands were clean.

Innocent.

"There are other ways to live," she whispered, and he woke with bile in his throat, because he knew it wasn't true. There was no hope, only the executioner's ax, and vengeance. And there was no peace. Never peace. He ground the heels of his hands into his eyes as frustration built in him like a scream.

Why had he come here? And why couldn't he make himself leave?

26

A SOFT WRONGNESS

Saturday morning, Karou woke up in her own bed for the first time in weeks. She showered, brewed coffee, scavenged in the pantry for something edible, came up empty, and left her apartment with Zuzana's presents in a shopping bag. She texted her friend en route—*Peekaboo! Big day. I'm bringing breakfast*—and bought some croissants at her corner bakery.

A text came back—*If it's not chocolate, it's not breakfast*—and she smiled and doubled back to the bakery for some chocolate kolaches.

It was then, turning around in the street, that she began to feel that something was off. It was a soft sensation of wrongness, but it was enough that her steps stammered to a halt and she looked around. She remembered what Bain had said about living like prey, always wondering who was tracking her, and it raised her hackles. Her knife was in her boot, hard against the knob of her ankle, the discomfort giving her comfort.

She got Zuzana's kolaches and continued on, wary. She held her shoulders stiff and several times looked back, but saw nothing out of the ordinary. Soon enough she came to the Charles Bridge.

Icon of Prague, the medieval bridge crossed the Vltava between Old Town and the Little Quarter. Gothic bridge towers rose on both sides, and the whole span — pedestrian-only — was lined by monumental statues of saints. This early it was almost deserted, and by the slant of the young sun, the statues flung their shadows long and lean. Vendors and performers were arriving with handcarts to stake out the most coveted real estate in the city, and in the very middle, before the photo-perfect backdrop of Prague Castle on the hill, was the giant puppeteer.

"Oh my god, it's amazing," said Karou to no one, because the puppeteer sat alone, ten feet tall and sinister, with its cruel carved face and wooden hands the size of snow shovels. Karou peered behind it — it was clad in an immense trench coat — and no one was there, either. "Hello?" she called, surprised that Zuzana would have left her creation unattended.

But then, "Karou!" came from *inside* the thing, and the back seam of the trench coat parted like the opening of a teepee. Zuzana darted out.

And snatched the bag of pastries out of Karou's hand. "Thank god," she said, and fell to.

"Well. Good to see you, too."

"Mmph."

Mik emerged after her and gave Karou a hug. He said, "I'll be her translator. What she is saying, in the language of Zuzana, is thank you."

"Really?" asked Karou, skeptical. "It sounds kind of like *snarfle snarfle*."

"Exactly."

"Mmph," agreed Zuzana, nodding.

"Nerves," Mik told Karou.

"Bad?"

"Terrible." Stepping up behind Zuzana, he bent down to enfold her in a spoon-hug. "Ferociously, dreadfully awful. She's unbearable. You take her. I've had enough."

Zuzana batted at him, then squealed as he buried his face in the curve of her throat and made exaggerated kissing noises.

Mik was sandy-haired and fair-skinned, with sideburns and a goatee and the kind of knife-blade eyes that hinted at ancestors invading across the plains from Central Asia. He was handsome and gifted, he blushed easily and hummed when he concentrated, and he was soft-spoken but interesting—a good combination. He actually listened, rather than pretending to listen while waiting a suitable interval before it was his turn to talk again, the way Kaz had. Best of all, he was entirely dopey for Zuzana, who was dopey right back. They were cartoonish, the way they blushed and smiled—all they needed was hearts for eyes—and watching them made Karou both deeply happy and exquisitely miserable. She imagined she could practically see their butterflies—*Papilio stomachus*—dancing the sweet tango of new love.

For her own part, it was harder and harder to imagine anything fluttering to life inside herself. More than ever, she was the hollow girl, the emptiness seeming like an entity, malicious, taunting her with all the things she would never know.

No. She banished the thought. She *would* know. She was on her way to knowing.

Her smile was real when Mik began kissing Zuzana's neck, but after a moment it began to feel a little like a Mr. Potato Head smile, plastic and stuck on. "Did I mention," she said, clearing her throat, "that I have presents?"

That worked. "Presents!" squealed Zuzana, disengaging herself. She jumped up and down and clapped. "Presents, presents!"

Karou handed over the shopping bag. In it were three parcels wrapped in heavy brown paper and tied with twine. Atop the largest one, a letterpress card on vellum announced, MME. V. VEZERIZAC, ARTEFACTS. The parcels were elegant, and somehow consequential. As Zuzana took them out of the bag, her eyebrow did its thing. "What are these?" she asked, going serious. "*Artefacts?* Karou. By present, I meant, like, a stacking doll from the airport or something."

"Just open them," said Karou. "The big one first."

Zuzana opened it. And started to cry. "Oh my god, oh my god," she whispered, gathering it to her chest in a froth of tulle.

It was a ballet costume, but no ordinary ballet costume. "It was worn by Anna Pavlova in Paris in 1905," Karou told her, excited. Giving gifts was so much fun. She'd never had Christmases or birthday parties when she was little, but once she was old enough to leave the shop on her own, she'd loved to bring back little things for Issa and Yasri—flowers, weird fruit, blue lizards, Spanish fans.

"Okay, I totally don't know who that is—"

"*What?* She's only the most famous ballerina *ever.*"

Eyebrow.

"Never mind," sighed Karou. "She was famously tiny, so it should fit you."

Zuzana held it up. "It's...it's...it's...it's so Degas...." she stammered.

Karou grinned. "I know. Isn't it awesome? There's this woman at Les Puces flea market who sells vintage ballet stuff—"

"But how much did it cost? It must have cost a fortune—"

"Shush," said Karou. "Fortunes have been spent on stupider things. And besides, I'm rich, remember? Obnoxious rich. *Magic* rich."

One upshot of Brimstone's provisions on her behalf was that she could afford to give presents. She had given herself one in Paris, too, also an *artefact*, though not of the ballet. The knives had gleamed at her from a glass case and the instant she glimpsed them, she knew she had to have them. They were Chinese crescent-moon blades, one of her favorite weapons. Her own set, the ones she'd trained with, were still in Hong Kong with her sensei, where she hadn't been since the portals burned. In any case, these put that set to shame.

"Fourteenth-century—" Madame Vezerizac had begun her sales pitch, but Karou didn't need to hear it. It seemed disrespectful to the knives to haggle, so she paid the asking price without batting an eye.

Each knife was made up of two blades, like crescent moons interlocking, hence the name. The grips were in the middle, and when wielded the knives provided a number of piercing and slicing edges and, perhaps most important, blocking points. The crescent moons were an optimal weapon for taking on multiple opponents, especially opponents with long weapons like swords. If she'd had them in Morocco, the angel would not have overpowered her so easily.

She'd also bought Zuzana a pair of vintage toe shoes and a lovely headdress of forlorn silk rosebuds, also from the turn-of-the-century Paris stage. "Want to get ready?" Karou asked her, and Zuzana, *verklempt*, nodded yes. They squeezed inside the puppeteer and tossed her other, unremarkable costume aside.

An hour later tourists were trooping across the bridge, questing toward the castle with their guidebooks under their arms, and a not-insignificant number of them had formed an anticipatory half circle around the giant puppeteer. Karou and Zuzana huddled inside it.

"Stop squirming," said Karou, pausing with her makeup brush as Zuzana engaged in an unladylike tug-of-war beneath her tutu.

"My tights are crooked," Zuzana said.

"Do you want your cheeks to be crooked, too? Hold still."

"Fine." Zuzana held still while Karou painted perfect pink rouge circles onto her cheeks. Her face was powder-white, and her lips had been transformed to a doll's tiny Cupid's bow, with two fine black lines out from the corners of her mouth, simulating a marionette's hinged jaw. False eyelashes fringed her dark eyes, and she was dressed in the tutu, which did indeed fit, and the toe shoes, which had seen better days. Her white tights were laddered with runs and patched at the knees; one of the straps of her bodice hung broken; and her hair was a messy chignon crowned with faded rosebuds. She looked like a doll that had lain unloved in a toy chest for years.

A toy chest, in fact, stood open and ready to receive her as soon as her costume was squared away.

"All done," said Karou, surveying her work. She clapped her hands once in delight and felt like Issa when she fixed Karou with temporary horns fashioned of parsnips, or a tail out of a feather duster. "Perfect. You look adorably pathetic. Some tourist is sure to try to carry you home as a souvenir."

"Some tourist will rue the day," Zuzana said, upending her tutu and pursuing the tights tug-of-war with surly determination.

"Would you leave those poor tights alone? They're fine."

"I hate tights."

"Well, let me add them to the list. This morning you hate, let me see, men in hats, wiener dogs—"

"Wiener-dog *owners*," Zuzana corrected. "You'd have to have, like, a *lentil* for a soul to hate wiener dogs."

"Wiener-dog *owners*, hairspray, false eyelashes, and now tights. Are you finished?"

"Hating things?" She paused, reading some inner gauge. "Yes, I think I am. *For now.*"

Mik peered through the opening. "We've got a crowd," he said. It had been his idea to take Zuzana's semester project to the street. He sometimes played his violin for change, donning a patch over his perfectly good left eye to seem more "romantic," and he promised Zuzana she could make a few thousand crowns in a morning. He had his eye patch in place now, and looked somehow both roguish and darling.

"God, you're adorable," he said, his visible eye on Zuzana.

Usually *adorable* was not a word Zuzana relished. "Toddlers are adorable," she'd snap. But where Mik was concerned, all bets were off. She blushed.

"You give me wrong thoughts," he said, slipping into the crammed space, so Karou was trapped against the puppet's armature. "Is it weird that I'm turned on by a marionette?"

"Yes," said Zuzana. "Very weird. But it explains why you work at a marionette theater."

"Not all marionettes. Just you." He seized her around the waist. She squeaked.

"Careful!" Karou said. "Her makeup!"

Mik didn't listen. He kissed Zuzana lingeringly on her painted doll mouth, smearing the red of her lipstick and the white of her face makeup, and coming up at last with his own lips rosebud pink. Laughing, Zuzana wiped it away for him. Karou considered touching her up, but the smear actually suited the whole disheveled look perfectly, so she left it.

The kiss also worked wonders on Zuzana's nerves. "I think it's showtime," she announced brightly.

"Well, all right, then," said Karou. "Into the toy box with you."

And so it began.

The story Zuzana told with her body—of a discarded marionette brought out of its trunk for one last dance—was deeply moving. She started out clumsy and disjointed, like a rusty thing awakening, collapsing several times in a heap of tulle. Karou, watching the rapt faces of the audience, saw how they wanted to step forward and help the sad little dancer to her feet.

Over her the puppeteer loomed sinister, and as Zuzana twirled, its arms and fingers jittered and jumped as if *it* were controlling *her*, and not the other way around. The engineering was cunning and didn't draw attention to itself, so that the illusion was flawless. There came a point, as the doll began to rediscover her grace, that Zuzana rose slowly onto pointe as if drawn up by her strings, and she elongated, a glow of joy on her face. A Smetana sonata soared off Mik's violin strings, achingly sweet, and the moment went beyond street theater to touch something true.

Karou felt tears prick her eyes, watching. Within her, her emptiness *pounded*.

At the end, as Zuzana was forced back into the box, she cast toward the audience a look of desperate yearning and reached out one pleading arm before succumbing to her master's will. The lid of the trunk slammed shut, and the music bit off with a twang.

The crowd loved it. Mik's violin case filled fast with notes and coins, and Zuzana took a half dozen bows and posed for photos before vanishing inside the puppeteer's trench coat with Mik. Karou had no doubt they were doing grievous damage to her makeup job, and she just sat on the trunk to wait it out.

It was there, in the midst of the school-of-fish density of tourists on the Charles Bridge, that the wrongness crept back over her again, slow and seeping, like a shadow when a cloud coasts before the sun.

27

NOT PREY, BUT POWER

You're gonna live like prey, little girl.

Bain's words rang in Karou's ears as she looked around, searching faces in the throng surrounding her. Feeling exposed in the middle of the bridge, she squinted at the roofscapes on both riverbanks, her imagination running to the hunter sighting her through a rifle scope.

She shook it off. He wouldn't, would he? The feeling faded and she told herself it had only been paranoia, but over the rest of the day it came and went in scattered chills as Zuzana danced a dozen more times, gaining confidence with each performance, and Mik's violin case filled again and again, far exceeding his promised take.

He and Zuzana tried to coax Karou out to dinner with them, but she declined, pleading jet lag, which was not untrue but was also not foremost on her mind.

She was certain she was being watched.

Her fingertips fluttered against her palms. A prickle sparked there and traveled up her arms, and as she walked off the bridge and into the cobbled maze of Old Town, she knew she was being followed. She paused and knelt, pretending to adjust her boot as she pulled out her knife — her ordinary knife; her new crescent moons were in their case at her flat — and slipped it up her sleeve while scanning ahead and behind.

She saw no one, and kept going.

The first time she'd come to Prague, she'd gotten so lost exploring these streets. She'd passed an art gallery and a few blocks later doubled back to find it, and...couldn't. The city had swallowed it. In fact, she had *never* found it. There was a deceptive tangling of alleys that gave the impression of a map that shifted behind you, gargoyles tiptoeing away, stones like puzzle pieces rearranging themselves into new configurations while you weren't looking. Prague entranced you, lured you in, like the mythic fey who trick travelers deep into forests until they're lost beyond hope. But being lost here was a gentle adventure of marionette shops and absinthe, and the only creatures lurking around corners were Kaz and his cohorts in vampire makeup, ready with a silly thrill.

Usually.

Tonight Karou felt a real threat, and with each step she took, cool, precise, she willed it to manifest. She *wanted* to fight. Her body was a loaded spring. The way it so often taunted her with the phantom of what else it might be doing, at this moment, she was sure that in her phantom life she would *fight*.

"Come on," she whispered to her unseen pursuer, ducking her head and quickening her pace. "I have a surprise for you."

She was on Karlova, the major pedestrian route between the bridge and Old Town Square, and tourists continued thick as fish. She moved among them, darting and erratic, throwing looks back over her shoulder more to craft the illusion of fear than in the hope of catching a glimpse of her stalker. At the intersection of a quiet side alley, she ducked left, hugging close to the wall. She knew this territory well. It was riddled with lurking places for Kaz's tours. Just ahead, the curve of a medieval guildhall created a hidden niche where she had several times lain in wait in ghost garb. She moved into the shadows to tuck herself away.

And came face to face with a vampire.

"Hey!" said a sharp voice as Karou worked a quick reversal of momentum and tottered backward, out of the shadows. "Oh god," said the voice. "*You.*"

The vampire leaned back against the wall and crossed her arms in an attitude of bored superiority.

Svetla. Karou's jaw clenched at the sight of the other girl. She was model tall and thin, with a harsh kind of beauty that was sure to age scary. She was wearing white face paint and Goth eyeliner, with fake fangs and a dribble of blood at the corner of her ruby lips. Kaz's sexy vampire vixen to a T, black cape and all, and she was, most inconveniently, wedged into Karou's intended hiding place.

Stupid, Karou admonished herself. It was tour hour. Of course Kaz's hiding places would be stuffed with actors. It often amused her, as she walked through Old Town in the evening, to see bored ghosts leaning against walls, texting or tweeting while they waited for the next clutch of tourists to be led along.

"What are you doing here?" Svetla asked, her lip curling like she smelled something off. She was one of those beautiful girls with a knack for making herself ugly.

Karou glanced back to Karlova, then ahead to the next curve in the alley that could provide her with cover. It was too far down; she couldn't chance it. She could almost feel her stalker drawing nearer.

Svetla drawled, "If you're looking for Kaz, don't bother. He told me what you did."

Jesus, thought Karou. As if any of that mattered now. She said, "Svetla, shut up," and thrust herself into the niche right along with her, shoving the other girl back against the stones.

Svetla gasped and tried to shove her out. "What are you doing, freak?"

"I said shut up," Karou hissed, and when Svetla did not, she whipped her knife from her sleeve and held it up. It curved at the tip like the claw of a cat, and its edge caught a thread of light and glinted. Svetla gave a little gasp and fell silent, but not for long. "Oh, right. I'm so sure you're going to *stab* me—"

"Listen," said Karou, low. "Just be quiet for a minute and I'll fix your stupid eyebrows."

Shocked silence preceded a rasped *"What?"*

Svetla's hair was cut in a long, hard bang, so low it brushed her eyes, and it was shellacked with hairspray so it scarcely moved, all in order to hide her eyebrows, on which Karou had wasted a shing in a fit of spite around Christmastime. Black and bushy under her hair, they were likely not working any wonders for her modeling career.

Svetla's expression hovered somewhere between confusion

and outrage. There was simply no way that Karou could know about her eyebrows, always kept so carefully covered. She would think Karou had been spying on her. Karou didn't care what she thought. She just wanted silence. "I'm serious," she breathed. "But only if I'm still alive to do it, so *shut up*."

Voices drifted over from Karlova, along with strains of music from nearby cafes, and the purr of engines. She couldn't hear footsteps, but that didn't mean anything. Hunters understood stealth.

Svetla's expression remained aghast, but for the moment, at least, she was quiet. Karou stood rigid and fierce-eyed, listening intently.

Someone was coming. Footsteps like the ghosts of footsteps. Out in the alley, a shadow seeped into view. Karou watched it lengthen on the ground in front of her as its source drew nearer. Her palms throbbed; she clasped her knife tighter and peered at the shadow, trying to make sense of it.

She blinked, and words spilled across her thoughts. Not Bain's words, but Razgut's.

My brother seraph was looking for you, lovely.

The shadow. The shadow had *wings*.

Oh god, the angel. Karou's pulse went jagged. The distraction of Bain's warning lifted like smoke to reveal what had been there all along: in her palms, a coursing energy. Her hamsas were *on fire*. How could she not have realized sooner? She turned a ferocious warning glare on Svetla and mouthed, *Quiet*. Svetla dropped the snarl. She looked afraid.

The shadow advanced, and behind it, the angel. He was peering ahead, intense. His wings were glamoured, his eyes glowed in the gloom, and Karou had a clear view of his profile.

186

His beauty was as shocking as it had been the first time she'd seen him. *Fiala,* she invoked her drawing teacher, *if you could see this.* Though there was a pair of sheathed swords crossed on his back, his arms were passive at his sides, hands slightly raised and fingers splayed as if to demonstrate he was unarmed.

Good for you, thought Karou, tightening her grip on her knife. *I'm not.*

He drew even with the niche.

Karou gathered herself.

And leapt.

She had to launch herself upward to hook him around the neck—he was tall, six foot four at least—and she slammed into him hard and sent him staggering. She clung to him, feeling immediately what she couldn't see: the heat and mass of wings, invisible but real. She felt too the warmth and breadth of his shoulders and arms, and was keenly aware of their powerful vitality as she brought her blade against his throat.

"Looking for me?"

"Wait—" he said, making no move to fight her or throw her off.

"Wait," Karou scoffed, and, on impulse, she took the flat of her other hand and pressed its ink eye to the exposed skin of the angel's neck.

As in Morocco, when she had first directed the unknown magic of her hamsas at him, something happened. That time, it had hurled him through the air. Now, its awful force didn't hit and throw him—it went *into* him. Where Karou's tattoo touched him, she felt a shrieking in his skin that forced shudders down into his flesh and reverberated up her own arm, into the core of her, even the roots of her teeth. It was mind-splitting. Horrific. And that was her.

For him, it was much worse. Spasms wracked his powerful form, threatening to knock her loose. She hung on. He choked. The magic wracked him. It felt sick and wrong—what was it doing? He lurched, shaking violently, and tried to pry her hand away, but his fingers fumbled. Under Karou's hand, his skin was smooth and hot, so hot, so hot, and the heat was rising. The heat of his wings, too, like a bonfire whipped into a frenzy.

Fire, invisible fire.

Karou couldn't bear it. Her palm lost contact with his neck. As her hand came away, stinging with the heat, the angel rallied. He grabbed her wrist and pivoted hard, flinging her off.

She landed light and spun back to face him.

He stood slouched, breathing hard, one hand holding his neck as he stared at her with his tiger's eyes. She felt pinned in place, and for a long beat she could only stare back. He looked pained. Puzzlement drew a crease in his brow, like he was divining a mystery.

Like *she* was his mystery.

Then he moved, and the moment unfroze. He raised his hands, placating. His nearness pulsed at Karou. Her hamsas pulsed. Her heart, her fingertip, her memories: a slashing sword, Kishmish on fire, torched portals, Izîl the last time she'd seen him, wailing, *"Malak!"*

And when she raised her hands, it was not in peace. One gripped her knife; the other flashed its eye.

The seraph flinched and the hamsa buffeted him back several steps. "Wait," he said, straining against it. "I won't hurt you."

A laugh caught in Karou's throat. Just who was in danger of being hurt here? She felt powerful. Her phantom life had stopped taunting her, had slipped instead into her skin and possessed her. This was who she was: not prey, but *power*.

She launched herself at him, and he fell back. She pursued, he retreated. In all the sparring she'd done in years of training, she'd always held a little something back. Not now. Feeling strong, feeling *unleashed*, she delivered a whirling kata, landing blows to his chest, his legs, even his upheld, peacemaking hands, and with every contact she was reminded of his solidity—his firmly rooted physical presence. Angel or not—whatever that even meant—there was nothing ethereal about him. He was flesh.

"Why are you following me?" she growled in Chimaera.

"I don't know," he said.

Karou laughed. It really was kind of funny. She felt light as air and bright as danger. She attacked in a cool fury and still he barely defended himself, only parrying knife jabs and cringing under the force of her outfaced hamsa.

"Fight," she hissed at him when another kick hit home and he did nothing but absorb it.

He didn't. Instead, the next time she came at him, he gathered the air beneath him and took flight, lifting off the cobbles and out of her reach. "I just want to talk to you," he said from above her.

She threw her head back and looked up to where he hovered in the air. The draft of his wingbeats whipped her hair around her face in wild blue tendrils.

She smiled, savage, and sank into a crouch. "So talk," she said, and sprang into the air to meet him.

189

❧ 28 ❧

ATTITUDE OF PRAYER

In her hiding place, the vampire Svetla momentarily forgot how to breathe.

Down the alley at the junction with Karlova, a small tour group rounded the corner and came to a shocked halt. Gum fell from slack mouths. Kaz, sporting a top hat and carrying a wooden stake jauntily under one arm, perceived that his ex-girlfriend was *in midair*.

Honestly, he wasn't that surprised. There was something about Karou that activated an unusual credulity. Things you wouldn't dream of believing of others seemed, where Karou was concerned, not such a stretch. Karou, flying? Well, why not?

What Kaz felt wasn't surprise. It was jealousy. Karou was flying, sure, but she was not flying *alone*. She was with a man, a man who even Kaz — who claimed it was "gay" to recognize the attractiveness of other men — had to admit to himself was beautiful to the point of absurdity. Beautiful to the point of *completely overdoing it.*

Uncool, he thought, crossing his arms.

It couldn't exactly be described as flying, what the two were doing. They were up even with the roofline, but they were barely moving—circling like cats, staring at each other with extraordinary intensity. The air fairly throbbed between them, and Kaz felt it like a punch in the gut.

Then Karou attacked the guy, and he felt much better.

Later he would claim the airborne fight was part of his tour, and he'd rake in record tips. He'd refer to Karou as his girl-friend, infuriating Svetla, who would stalk home to glare at her eyebrows—still caterpillar-fat—in the mirror. But for now, they all just gawked at the two beautiful creatures fighting in the air with the rooftops of Prague behind them.

Well, Karou was fighting, anyway. Her opponent only dodged, with great grace and a strange kind of...gentleness?... and he seemed to shy away from her and flinch as if struck even when she hadn't touched him.

It went on like that for a few minutes as the crowd thickened on the ground, and then it happened that when she came at him, the guy seized her hands so she dropped her knife—it fell a long way and landed point down between cobblestones and stuck there—and he held her. It was strange: He held her palms pressed together in an attitude of prayer. She struggled, but he was clearly much stronger and held her with ease, his hands pressed over hers, like he was forcing her to pray.

He spoke to her and his words drifted down to the onlookers, foreign and richly tonal, rough and somehow a little . . . *animal.* Whatever he said to her, she gradually stopped struggling. Still, he kept her hands folded in his own for a long moment. Over in Old Town Square, the bells of Týn Church tolled nine, and it was only when the ninth hour echoed into silence that he released her and sculled backward in the air, tense and watchful, like one who has released a wild thing from a cage and doesn't know if it's going to turn on him.

Karou didn't turn on him. She drew away. The two spoke, gestured. Karou's movements in the air were languid, her long legs curled up beneath her, arms moving with a tidal rhythm, as if she were keeping herself afloat. It all looked so effortless — so possible — that several tourists cautiously tested the air with their own arms, wondering if they hadn't strayed into some pocket of the world where . . . well, where people could fly.

And then, just when they were becoming accustomed to the startling sight of the blue-haired girl and black-haired man floating overhead like a piece of magnificent performance art, the girl made a sudden move. The man sagged in the air and started to fall in fits and starts, struggling to stay aloft.

He lost the struggle and went limp. His head rolled back, loose on his neck, and, in a sizzle of sparks that gave the brief impression of the tail of a comet, he plunged to earth.

🌿 29 🌿

STARLIGHT TO THE SUN

When the angel thought he could get away simply by lifting ten feet off the ground, Karou took a devilish pleasure in surprising him. But if he was surprised, he didn't show it. She rose up into the air in front of him, and he looked at her. Just *looked*. His gaze was heat across her cheeks, her lips. It was *touch*. His eyes were hypnotic, his brows black and velvet. He was copper and shadow, honey and menace, the severity of knife-blade cheekbones and a widow's peak like the point of a dagger. All that and the muted snap of invisible fire, and facing him, Karou was jolted into the hum of blood and magic, and something else.

In her belly: a flutter of winged things shaking themselves fervently to life.

It brought a flush to her cheeks. The temerity of butterflies to trouble her now. What was she, some giddy girl to swoon at beauty?

"Beauty," Brimstone had scoffed once. "Humans are fools for it. As helpless as moths who hurl themselves at fire."

Karou would not be a moth. For the moments that they circled each other, she reminded herself that though the seraph wouldn't fight her now, he had spilled her blood before. He had left her scarred. Worse, he had burned the portals and left her *alone*.

She put on her anger like armor and attacked him again, surging at him in the air, and for a few minutes she was able to fool herself that she was a match for him, that she could... what? Kill him? She was barely even trying to use her knife. She didn't want to kill him.

What *did* she want? What did *he* want?

And then he grabbed her hands and in one smooth movement disarmed her and disabused her of any notion she might have had that she was winning. He pressed her palms together so she couldn't lash out with her hamsas again—up close she saw that his neck was welted white where she had touched him—and he was so strong, she couldn't break free. His hands were warm and enclosed hers completely. Her magic was trapped in her palms, one tattoo hot against the other, and her knife had fallen to the street below. She was caught. She experienced a frantic moment, remembering the way he had stood over her in Morocco, the deadness of his expression. But it wasn't dead now. Far from it.

He might have been someone else entirely, his look was so full of feeling. What feeling? Pain. He glistened with a fever sheen. His face bore the strain of endured agony, and his breathing was uneven. But that wasn't all. He blazed with intensity, leaning toward Karou in the air, looking, looking, alive with a searing, wide-eyed *searching*.

His touch, his heat, his gaze washed over her and, in an

instant, it was not butterflies she felt. That was small, the flut-terings of a giddy girl.

This new thing that sprang up between them, it was...*astral*. It reshaped the air, and it was *in* her, too—a warming and soft-ening, a *pull*—and for that moment, her hands in his, Karou felt as powerless as starlight tugged toward the sun in the huge, strange warp of space. She fought against it, trying to get away.

His voice low and hoarse, the angel said, "I'm not going to hurt you. What happened before, I'm sorry. Please believe me, Karou. I didn't come here to hurt you."

She startled at the sound of her name and stopped strug-gling. How did he know her name? "Why did you come?"

On his face, a helpless look. He said again, "I don't know," and this time it didn't strike her as funny. "Just...just to talk," he said. "To try to understand this...this..." He fumbled for words and trailed away, at a loss, but Karou thought she knew what he meant, because she was trying to understand it, too.

"I can't withstand more of your magic," he said, and she was aware again of his strain. She had really hurt him. As she *should*, she told herself. He was her enemy. The heat in her hands told her that. Her scars told it, and her severed life. But her body wasn't listening. It was focused on the contact of their skin, his hands on hers.

"But I won't hold you," he said. "If you want to hurt me, it's no more than I deserve."

He released her. His heat deserted her and the night rushed between them, colder than it had been before.

Clasping her hamsas in her fists, Karou backed away, barely aware that she was still floating.

Holy. What *was* that?

Remotely, she was conscious that she was flying in plain view of a gathered mass of people, and that more gawkers were coming in droves, as if the tourist route of Karlova had been diverted into this side channel. She sensed their pointing and amazement, saw the camera flashes, heard the shouts, but it was all muted muted muted, like it was playing on a screen, less real than the moment she was living.

She was on the cusp of something ineffable. When the seraph had held her hands, and when he had let her go, it was as if she had been *filled* and didn't realize it until he pulled away and the absence rushed back in. It pounded inside her now, cold and aching, void and wanting—*wanting*—and a desperate part of her had to be stilled from darting forward to grab his hands again. Wary of the extraordinary compulsion beating in her, she forced herself to resist. It was like fighting a tide, and in the fight was the same terror: of being swept into deep water, beyond all safety.

Karou panicked.

When the angel made as if to move toward her, she threw up her hands between them, both hands at once, and at close range. His eyes went wide and he faltered in the air, a breach in his perfect grace. Karou's breath caught. He tried to steady himself on the lintel of a fourth-story window, and failed.

His eyes rolled back and he dropped a few feet, sending up sparks. Was he losing consciousness? Karou spoke around a tight constriction in her throat. "Are you okay?"

But he wasn't, and he fell.

* * *

Akiva was dimly aware that he was no longer in the air. Beneath him, stone. In flashes he saw faces peering at him. Consciousness strobed. Voices in languages he couldn't understand, and at the edge of sight: blue. Karou was there. A roar rose up in his ears and he forced himself upright, and the roar was...applause.

Karou, her back to him, dropped a theatrical curtsy. With a flourish she plucked her knife from where it had embedded itself between cobbles, and sheathed it in her boot. She peered over her shoulder at him, seeming relieved to see him conscious, and then stepped back and...took his hand. Carefully, just her fingertips in his, so her marks wouldn't burn him. She helped him stand, and said, low in his ear, "Bow."

"What?"

"Just take a bow, okay? Let them think this was a performance. It'll be easier to get away. Leave them trying to figure out how we did it."

He gave an approximation of a bow and the applause thundered.

"Can you walk?" Karou asked.

He nodded.

It still wasn't easy getting away. People stood in their way, wanting to talk to them. Karou spoke; he didn't know what was said, didn't understand the language, but her answers were clipped. The onlookers were awed and delighted—except one of them, a young man in a tall hat who glared at Akiva and tried to take Karou's elbow. His proprietary air stirred old wrath in Akiva and made him want to throw the human into a wall, but Karou didn't need his intervention. She brushed the man aside and led Akiva out of the crowd. Her fingers were still in his; they were cool and small, and he was sorry when, turning a corner into a plaza of empty market stalls, she pulled away.

"Are you okay?" she asked, putting distance between them.

He steadied himself against a wall in the shadows beneath an awning. "Not that I didn't deserve it," he said. "But I feel as though an army has marched over me."

She paced, anxious energy fairly vibrating in her. "Razgut said you were looking for me. Why?"

"Razgut?" Akiva was startled. "But I thought he was—"

"Dead? He survived. Not Izîl, though."

Akiva looked at the ground. "I didn't know he would jump."

"Well, he did. But that doesn't answer my question. Why were you looking for me?"

Again, the helplessness. He groped for meaning. "I didn't understand who you were. *Are.* A human, marked with the devil's eyes."

Karou looked at her palms, then up at him, a confused vulnerability in her expression. "Why do they...do that? To you?"

He narrowed his eyes. Could she not know?

The eye tattoos were just one example of Brimstone's deviltry. The magic hit like a wall of wind, one that carried a fury of sickness and weakness, and Akiva had trained to resist it—all seraph soldiers did—but there was only so much he could take. If he'd been in battle, he'd have sliced off the enemy's hands before letting them focus so much of their evil energy at him.

198

But Karou...the last thing he wanted to do was hurt her again, so he had endured as much as he could.

Now more than ever she struck him like a fairy in a tale — a haunted one with shadowed eyes and a sting like a scorpion. The scorch of her touch on his neck felt like an acid splash, accompanying the dull, roiling nausea from her relentless assault. He felt enfeebled, and feared he might collapse again.

He said carefully, "They're the revenants' marks. You must know that."

"Revenant?"

He studied her face. "Do you really not know?"

"Know what? What's a revenant? Isn't it a ghost?"

"It's a chimaera soldier," he said, which was part of the truth. "The hamsas are for them." Pause. "Only."

She made tight, sudden fists. "Obviously not *only*."

He didn't answer.

Everything was between them, everything he'd felt suffuse the air while they faced each other over the rooftops. Being near her was like balancing on a tipping world, trying to keep your footing as the ground wanted to roll you forward, hurl you into a spiral from which there was no recovery, only impact, and it was a longed-for impact, a sweet and beckoning collision.

He'd felt this before and never wanted to feel it again. It could only diminish the memory of Madrigal; it already *was*. Again his memory failed to conjure her face. It was like trying to call up a melody while another song played. Karou's face was all he could see — shining eyes, smooth cheeks, the arc of soft lips pressed together in consternation.

He'd cut out feeling; it shouldn't even have been possible to feel this—this welter, this urgency and tumult, this *thrum*. And under it all, a crippled twist of thought he held prisoner in the shadows of his mind, so warped he didn't recognize it for what it was: a hope. A very small hope. And at its center: Karou.

She was a wingspan away, still pacing. They were prowling on the edges of their mutual compulsion, both afraid to draw nearer together. "Why did you burn the portals?" she asked.

He let out a deep breath. What could he say? For vengeance? For peace? Both were true in their way. Warily, he said, "To end the war."

"*War*? There's a war?"

"Yes, Karou. War is *all* there is."

She was taken aback, again, by his use of her name. "Are Brimstone and the others... are they okay?" There was a breathlessness in her voice Akiva realized was fear—fear of what his answer would be.

Under the roiling nausea from the hamsas, he felt another, deeper sickness—the beginnings of dread. "They're in the black fortress," he said.

"Fortress." Her voice lifted in hope. "With the bars. I was there, I saw it, the night you attacked me."

Akiva looked away. A wave of nausea went through him. The throbbing in his head was getting hard to focus past; only once before had he taken such sustained trauma from the devil's marks, a torture he had not expected to survive, and still didn't understand why he had. He was having a hard time holding his eyes open, and his body felt like an anchor trying to drag him down.

Voices.

Karou's head snapped around. Akiva looked. Some of their audience had traced them here and were pointing.

"Follow me," said Karou.

As if he could have done anything else.

30

YOU

She led him to her flat, all the while thinking, *Stupid, stupid, what are you doing?*

Answers, she told herself. *I'm getting answers.*

She hesitated at the elevator, unsure about being in so small a space with the seraph, but he wasn't in any state to climb stairs, so she pushed the button. He followed her in, seeming unfamiliar with the principle of elevators, and startled slightly when the mechanism chugged to life.

In her flat, she dropped her keys in a basket by the door and looked around. On the wall: her Angel of Extinction wings, uncannily like his wings. If he noticed the similarity, his face gave away nothing. The space was too small for the wings to be spread to their full span, so they were suspended like a canopy, half-sheltering the bed, which was a deep teak bench piled princess-and-the-pea with feather mattresses. It was unmade and lost in an avalanche of old sketchbooks that Karou had been leafing through the night before, keeping company in the only way she could with her family.

One lay open to a portrait of Brimstone. She saw the angel's jaw clench at the sight of it, and she grabbed it and clutched it to her chest. He went to the window and looked out.

"What's your name?" she asked.

"Akiva."

"And you know mine how?"

A long beat. "The old man."

Izîl. Of course. But...a thought struck her. Hadn't Razgut said Izîl leapt to his death to protect her? "How did you find me?" she asked.

It was dark outside, and Akiva's eyes reflected orange in the window glass. "It wasn't difficult," was all he said.

She was going to ask him to be specific, but he closed his eyes and leaned his brow against the glass. She said, "You can sit down," and gestured to her deep green velvet armchair. "If you're not going to burn anything."

His lips made a grim twist that was like the joyless cousin of a smile. "I won't burn anything."

He loosed the buckle on the leather straps that crossed his chest, and his swords, sheathed between his shoulder blades, fell to the floor with two thunks that Karou did not think her downstairs neighbor would appreciate. Then Akiva sat, or rather collapsed, in the chair. Karou shoved her sketchbooks aside to make a space for herself on the bed, and seated herself in lotus position facing him.

The flat was tiny — just room for the bed and the chair and a set of carved nesting tables, all atop Karou's splurge of a

Persian carpet, haggled for while it was still on the loom in Tabriz. One wall was all bookcases, facing one all of windows, and off the entry hall: a tiny kitchen, tinier closet, and a bathroom roughly the size of a shower stall. The ceilings were a fairly preposterous twelve feet, making even the main room taller than it was wide, so Karou had built a loft above the bookcases, which she had to climb to reach it, just deep enough to lounge on Turkish cushions and take in the view out the high windows: a direct line over the rooftops of Old Town to the castle.

She watched Akiva. He had let his head drop back; his eyes were closed. He looked so weary. He was rolling one shoulder gingerly, wincing as if it pained him. She considered offering him tea—she could have used some herself—but it felt too much like playing hostess, and she struggled to remember the dynamic between them: They were enemies.

Right?

She studied him, mentally correcting the drawings she'd done from memory. Her fingers itched to snatch up a pencil and draw him from life. Stupid fingers.

He opened his eyes and caught her looking. She blushed. "Don't get too comfortable," she said, discomposed.

He struggled upright. "I'm sorry. It's like this, after battle."

Battle. He watched guardedly as she processed the idea. She said, "Battle. With chimaera. Because you're enemies."

He nodded.

"Why?"

"Why?" he repeated, as if the notion of enemies needed no justification.

"Yes. Why are you enemies?"

"We have always been. The war had been going on for a thousand years—"

"That's weak. Two races can't have been born enemies, can they? It had to start somewhere."

A slow nod. "Yes. It started somewhere." He rubbed his face with his hands. "What do you know of chimaera?"

What *did* she know? "Not a lot," she admitted. "Until the night you attacked me, I didn't even know there were more than the four of them. I didn't know they were an entire race."

He shook his head. "They aren't one race. They're many, allied."

"Oh." Karou supposed that made sense, with how unalike they were. "Does that mean there are others like Issa, like Brimstone?"

Akiva nodded. The idea gave new shades of reality to the world Karou had glimpsed. She imagined scattered tribes in vast landscapes, a whole village of Issas, families of Brimstones. She wanted to see them. Why had she been kept from them?

Akiva said, "I don't understand what your life has been. Brimstone raised you, but just in the shop? Not in the fortress itself?"

"I didn't even know what was on the other side of the inner door until that night."

"He took you inside, then?"

Karou pursed her lips, remembering the Wishmonger's fury. "Sure. Let's say that's what happened."

"And what did you see there?"

"Why would I tell you that? You're enemies, in which case, you're my enemy, too."

"I'm not your enemy, Karou."

"They're my family. Their enemies are mine."

"Family," Akiva repeated, shaking his head. "But where did you come from? Who are you, really?"

"Why does everybody ask me that?" Karou asked, animated by a flash of anger, though it was something she had wondered herself almost every day since she was old enough to understand the extreme oddness of her circumstances. "I'm *me*. Who are *you*?"

It was a rhetorical question, but he took it seriously. He said, "I'm a soldier."

"So what are you doing here? Your war is there. Why did you come here?"

He took a deep, shuddering breath, sank back once more into the chair. "I needed...something," he said. "Something apart. I have lived war for half a century—"

Karou interrupted him. "You're *fifty*?"

"Lives are long, in my world."

"Well, you're lucky," said Karou. "Here, if you want long life, you have to yank out all your teeth with pliers."

The mention of teeth brought a dangerous flicker to his eyes, but he said only, "Long life is a burden, when it's spent in misery."

Misery. Did he mean himself? She asked him.

His eyes fluttered shut as if he'd been struggling to keep them open and abruptly abandoned the fight. He was silent for so long that Karou wondered if he'd fallen asleep, and gave up on her question. It felt intrusive, anyway. And she sensed he *had* meant himself. She thought of the way he'd looked in

206

Marrakesh. What made the life go out of somebody's eyes like that?

Again the caretaker impulse came to her, to offer him something, but she resisted it. She let herself stare at him — the cut of his features, the deep black of his brows and lashes, the bars inked on his hands, which were splayed open on the chair arms. With his head tilted back, she could see the welt on his neck and, a little higher up, the steady pulse of his jugular vein.

Once more his physicality struck her, that he was a flesh-and-blood being, though unlike any she had ever seen or touched. He was a melding of elements: fire and earth. She would have thought an angel would have something of air, but he didn't. He was all substance: powerful and rugged and real.

His eyes opened and she jumped, caught staring once again. How many times was she going to blush, anyway?

"I'm sorry," he said, his voice faint. "I think I fell asleep."

"Um." She couldn't help it. "Do you need some water?"

"Please." He sounded so grateful she felt a pang of guilt for not offering sooner.

She untangled her legs from their lotus, rose, and brought him a glass of water, which he drained in a draft. "Thank you," he said in a weirdly heartfelt way, as if he were thanking her for something much more profound than a glass of water.

"Uh. Uh-huh," she said, awkward. She felt like she was hovering, standing there. There was really nowhere in the room to go except the bed, so she scooted back onto it. She kind of wanted to take off her boots, but that was something you didn't do if there was any chance you might have to quickly flee or kick someone. Judging from Akiva's plain exhaustion, she didn't think she was in danger of either. The only danger was of foot smell.

She kept her boots on.

She said, "I still don't get why you burned the portals. How does that end your war?"

Akiva's hands tightened on the empty water glass. He said, "There was magic coming through the doorways. Dark magic."

"From *here*? There's no magic here."

"Says the flying girl."

"Okay, but that's because of a wish, from your world."

"From Brimstone."

She acknowledged this with a nod.

"So you know that he's a sorcerer."

"I...Uh. Yeah." She'd never really thought of Brimstone as a sorcerer. Did he do more than manufacture wishes? What did she know, really, and how much did she *not* know? Her ignorance was like standing in pure dark that could be either a closet or a vast, starless night.

A kaleidoscope of images whirled in her mind. The fizz of magic when she stepped into the shop. The array of teeth and gems, the stone tables in that underground cathedral, laid out with the dead...the dead who were not, as Karou had learned the hard way, actually dead. And she remembered Issa admonishing her not to make Brimstone's life any harder—his "joyless" life, as she had said. His "relentless" work. What work?

She picked up a sketchbook at random, fanning past drawings of her chimaera so that they made a jerky kind of animation. "What was the magic?" she asked Akiva. "The dark magic."

He didn't answer, and she expected when she looked up to

208

see that he had fallen asleep again, but he was watching the images flash past in her sketchbook. She snapped it closed, and his eyes fixed on her instead. Again, that vivid *searching*.

"What?" she asked, discomfited.

"Karou," he said. "*Hope*."

She raised her eyebrows, as if to say *So?*

"Why did he give you that name?"

She shrugged. It was getting tiring, not knowing anything. "Why did your parents name you Akiva?"

At the mention of his parents, Akiva's face hardened, and the vivid watchfulness of his gaze glazed back to fatigue. "They didn't," he said. "A steward named me from a list. Another Akiva had been killed. The name opened up."

"Oh." Karou didn't know what to make of that. It made her own strange upbringing seem cozy and familial by comparison.

"I was bred to be a soldier," Akiva said in a hollow voice, and he closed his eyes again, tightly this time, as if gripped by a wave of pain. He was silent for a long time, and when he spoke again, he said far more than she expected.

"I was taken from my mother at five years old. I don't remember her face, only that she did nothing when they came for me. It's my earliest memory. I was so small that they were just legs, these looming soldiers surrounding me. They were the palace guard, so their shin plates were silver, and I could see myself mirrored in them, in all of them, my own terrified face over and over. They took me to the training camp, where I was one of a legion of terrified children." He swallowed. "Where they punished our terror and taught us to conceal it. And that became my life, the concealment of terror, until I didn't feel it anymore, or anything else."

Karou couldn't help imagining him as a child, afraid and forsaken. Tenderness welled up in her like tears.

In a fading voice, he said, "I exist only because of war—a war that began a thousand years ago with a massacre of my people. Babies, elders, no one spared. In Astrae, the capital of the Empire, the chimaera rose up to massacre the seraphim. We are enemies because the chimaera are monsters. My life is blood because my world is beasts.

"And then I came here, and humans..." A dreamlike wonder shaded into his tone. "Humans were walking freely, weaponless, gathering in the open, sitting in plazas, laughing, growing old. And I saw a girl...a girl with black eyes and gemstone hair, and...sadness. She had a sadness that was so deep, but it still could turn to light in a second, and when I saw her smile I wondered what it would be like to *make* her smile. I thought...I thought it would be like the discovery of smiling. She was connected to the enemy, and though the only thing I wanted to do was look at her, I did what I was trained to do and I...I hurt her. And when I went home, I couldn't stop thinking about you, and I was so grateful that you had defended yourself. That you didn't let me kill you."

You. Karou did not miss the pronoun shift. She sat unblinking, barely breathing.

"I came back to find you," Akiva said. "I don't know why. Karou. Karou. I don't know why." His voice was so faint she could barely hear him. "Just to find you and be in the world that you're in..."

Karou waited, but he didn't say any more, and then...something happened in the air around him.

A shimmer, like an aura at first, brightening to light and becoming *wings*—open and upthrust from his shoulder blades to sprawl over the armchair and sweep the carpet in great arabesques of fire. His glamour had given way, and Karou almost gasped to see his wings revealed, but the flame didn't catch. It was smokeless, somehow self-contained. The subtle shifts of the fire-feathers were hypnotic, and Karou breathed again, deeply, and sat watching them for minutes as Akiva's features relaxed into something like peacefulness. This time he was truly asleep.

She got up and took the water glass from his hands. She turned off the light. His wings were sufficient illumination, even for drawing. She got out her sketchbook and a pencil, and she drew Akiva asleep at the locus of his vast wings, and then from memory, with his eyes open. She tried to capture the precise shape of them; she used charcoal for the heavy black kohl that rimmed them and made him look so exotic, and she couldn't take leaving his fiery irises colorless. She grabbed a watercolor box and painted. She drew and painted for a long time, and he didn't move except for the soft rise and fall of his chest and the glimmer of his wings, which cast the room in a firelight glow.

Karou didn't plan to sleep, but some time after midnight she subsided, still half on the landslide of her sketchbooks, to "rest her eyes" for a moment. She fell into dreams, and when she woke just before dawn—something woke her, a quick, bright sound—the room around her was, for a blink, entirely unfamiliar. Only the wings on the wall over her were not, and gave her a surge of pleasure, and then it all slid away as dreams do.

She was in her flat, of course, on her bed, and the sound that had awakened her was Akiva.

He was standing over her, and his eyes were molten. They were wide, his orange irises ringed around in white, and he was holding, one in each hand, her crescent-moon knives.

❧ 31 ❧

RIGHT

Karou sat up with a suddenness that sent sketchbooks skidding off the bed. Her pencil was still in her hand, and the thought struck her: always with the ridiculous weapon, where this angel was concerned. But even as she adjusted her grip on it, ready to stab, Akiva was backing away, lowering the knives.

He set them where he had found them, where she had left them, in their case, atop the nesting tables. They would have been practically under his nose when he woke.

"I'm sorry," he said. "I didn't mean to frighten you."

Just then, lit only by the flicker of his wings, the sight of him was so . . . *right*, somehow. He was *right*. It made no sense at all, but the feeling flooded through Karou, and whatever it was, it was as sweet as a patch of sun on a glossy floor and, like a cat, she just wanted to curl up in it.

She tried to pretend she hadn't been about to stab him with a pencil. "Well," she said, stretching and letting it drop casually out of her hand. "I don't know your customs, but here, if you don't want to frighten someone, you don't go looming over their sleeping body with *knives.*"

Was that a smile? No. A twitch at the corners of his stern mouth; it didn't qualify.

She caught sight of the sketchbook open before her, the evidence of her late-night portrait session right there for him to see. She flipped it quickly shut, though he'd of course have seen it while she was still sleeping.

How could she have fallen asleep with this stranger in her flat? How could she have *brought* this stranger to her flat?

He didn't feel like a stranger.

"They're unusual," Akiva said, gesturing to the knife case.

"I just got them. Beautiful, aren't they?"

"Beautiful," he agreed, and he might have been talking about the knives, but he was looking straight at her.

She flushed, suddenly conscious of her appearance — mussed hair, sleep drool? — then got angry. What did it matter what she looked like? What exactly was going on here? She shook herself and climbed off the bed, trying to find a space in the tiny room outside his radiant aura. It was impossible.

"I'll be right back," she said, and stepped into the hall and then the tiny bathroom. Separated from him, she experienced a sharp fear that she would return to find him gone. She relieved herself, wondering if seraphim were above such mundane needs — though judging from the duskiness of his jaw, Akiva was not above the need for a razor — then splashed water on her face and brushed her teeth. She ran a brush through her hair, and every moment she lingered, her anxiety grew that when she returned she would find just an empty room, balcony door standing open and the whole universe of sky above, giving no hint which way he'd gone.

But he was still there. His wings were glamoured gone again, his swords strapped in place at his back, innocuous in their decorative leather sheaths.

"Um," she said, "bathroom's in there, if, uh..."

He nodded and went past her, awkward as he tried to wedge his invisible wings into the tiny space and get the door closed.

Karou hurriedly changed into clean clothes, then went to the window. It was still dark out. The clock said five. She was starving, and knew from her previous morning's foraging that there was nothing even remotely edible in the kitchen. When Akiva emerged, she asked, "Are you hungry?"

"As if I might die of it."

"Come on, then." She picked up her coat and keys and started toward the door, then paused and changed direction. She went out onto the balcony instead, climbed up onto the balustrade, glanced back over her shoulder at Akiva, and stepped right off.

Six stories to the street, she landed light as hopscotch, unable to suppress a smile. Akiva was right beside her, unsmiling as ever. She couldn't quite imagine him smiling; he was so somber, but wasn't there something in the way he looked at her? There, in that sidelong glance: a hint of wonder? She recalled the things he'd said in the night, and now, seeing flickers of feeling interrupt the sad gravity of his face, it shot a pang through her heart. What had his life been like, given over so young to war? *War.* It was an abstraction to her. She couldn't conceptualize its reality, not even the edges of its reality, but the way Akiva had been—dead-eyed—and the way he looked at her now, it made her feel as if he was coming back from the dead *for her*, and that seemed a tremendous thing, and an intimate one. The next time their eyes met, she had to look away.

She took him to her corner bakery. It wasn't open yet, but the baker sold them hot loaves through the window—honey-lavender, fresh from the oven and still steaming in their crinkly brown bags—and then Karou did what anyone would do if they could fly and found themselves out on the streets of Prague at dawn with loaves of hot bread to eat.

She flew, gesturing to Akiva to follow, up into the sky and over the river, to perch on the high, cold cupola of the cathedral bell tower, and watch the sun rise.

* * *

Akiva kept close behind her, watching the snap of her hair, its long tendrils taking on the damp of dawn. Karou had been wrong to suppose her flying didn't surprise him. It was only that he had learned over many years to crush down all feeling, all reaction. Or he thought he had. In the presence of this girl, it seemed, nothing was certain.

There was a neatness in the way she sliced through the air. It was magic—not glamoured wings, but simply the will to fly made manifest. A wish, he supposed, from Brimstone's own supply. Brimstone. The thought of the sorcerer came on like an ink splash, a black thought against the brightness of Karou.

How could something as light as Karou's graceful flight come from the evil of Brimstone's magic?

They flew above casual observation, over the river and veering in the direction of the castle, where they circled down toward the cathedral at its heart. It was a Gothic beast, carved and weathered like some tortured cliff battered by ages of storms. Karou alighted upon the cupola of the bell tower. It was not a kind perch. The wind scoured past, full of ice and ill will, and Karou had to gather her hair in her hands and hold it off her face. She produced a pencil—the same one she had brandished at him?—knotted her hair, and shoved the pencil through it; an all-purpose implement. Blue wisps escaped the arrangement and danced across her brow, blowing over her eyes and catching on her lips, which were smiling with uncomplicated, childlike delight. "We're on the cathedral," she said to him.

He nodded.

"No. *We're on the cathedral*," she said again, and he thought he was missing something, some nuance lost in language, but then he realized: She was just amazed. Amazed to be perching atop the cathedral, high on the hill above Prague with everything below her. She hugged her arms around the warm bread and stood looking out, and on her face was a naked awe more potent than Akiva could ever recall feeling, even when flying was new. It was likely he had never felt any such thing. His own early flights weren't occasion for awe or joy—only discipline. But he wanted to be part of the moment that was making her face shine like that, so he moved to her side and looked out.

It *was* a remarkable sight, the sky beginning to flush pale at the roots, all the towers bathed in a soft glow, the streets of the city still shadowed and aglitter with fireflies of lamplight and the weaving, winking beams of headlights.

"You haven't come up here before?" he asked.

She turned to him. "Oh, yes, I bring all the boys up here."

"And if they don't meet with approval," he said, "you can always push them off."

It was the wrong thing to say. Karou's expression darkened. No doubt she was thinking of Izîl. Akiva admonished himself for making an effort at humor. Of course it would come off all wrong. It had been a long time since he'd had the will to banter.

"The truth is," Karou said, letting it pass, "I only made the wish for flying a few days ago. I haven't had a chance to enjoy it yet."

Again he was surprised; it must have shown this time, because Karou caught his look and said, "What?"

He shook his head. "You were so smooth in the air, and the way you stepped off your balcony without a second's pause, as if flying is just a part of you."

She said, "You know, it didn't occur to me that the wish could wear off. That would have been some punishment for showing off, wouldn't it? Splat." She laughed, untroubled by the thought, and said, "I should be more careful."

"Do the wishes wear off?" he asked.

She shrugged. "I don't know. I don't think so. My hair has never changed back."

"That's a wish? Brimstone let you use magic on . . . that?"

"Well. He didn't exactly approve." She skewed him a glance that was both sheepish and defiant. "It's not like he ever let me have any real wishes. Just enough to make minor mischief— Oh." A thought struck her. "Oops."

"What?"

"I made a promise last night and forgot all about it." She rummaged in her coat pocket and pulled out a small coin, on which Akiva glimpsed Brimstone's likeness. It was there on her palm when she closed her hand; when she opened it, it was gone. "Magic," she said. "Poof."

"What did you wish?" he asked.

"Just something stupid. A mean girl somewhere down there is going to wake up happy. Not that she deserves it. Hussy." She stuck out her tongue at the city, a flash of childish whimsy. "Oh. Here." She turned to Akiva and thrust one of the bakery bags at him. "You know, so you don't die."

While they ate, he saw that she was shivering, and he opened his wings — invisible — so the wind would catch their heat and fan it around her. It seemed to help. She sat down, dangling her legs over the edge, and kicked them casually while she pulled little pieces of bread off her loaf and ate them. He went into a crouch at her side.

"How are you feeling, by the way?" she asked.

"That depends," he said, feeling sly, as if Karou's whimsy were catching.

"On?"

"On whether you're asking because you're concerned for my well-being, or because you mean to keep me weak and helpless."

"Oh. Weak and helpless. Definitely."

"In that case, I feel awful."

"Good." She said it seriously enough, but with a glint in her eye. Akiva realized that she had been taking care with her hamsas, to not accidentally turn them in his direction. He was

219

moved, as he had been when he'd awakened to find her sleeping just feet from him, so lovely and vulnerable, and her trust, like Madrigal's, so unearned.

"I'm feeling better," he said softly. "Thank you."

"Don't thank me. I'm the one who hurt you."

Shame engulfed him. "Not...not like I hurt you."

"No," Karou agreed. "Not like that."

The wind was spiteful; with an insurgent gust it freed her hair, then danced in to seize it; in an instant it was everywhere, as if a pod of air elementals were trying to make off with it, to line their nests with its blue silk. She scrambled to contend with it; the pencil was lost over the roof's edge, plunging between flying buttresses, so she held her hair with both hands.

Akiva waited for her to say she was ready to get down out of the wind, but she didn't. The sun climbed above the hills and she watched as its glow herded night into the shadows where it gathered, all the darker for its density—all of night crowded into the slanting places beyond the reach of the dawn.

After a while she said, "You know last night, you said your earliest memory was of the soldiers coming for you—"

"I told you that?" He was startled.

"What, don't you remember?" She turned to him, eyebrows twin quirks, cocoa-dark, raised in surprise.

He shook his head, searching his mind. He'd been so ill from the devil's marks, it was all a fugue, but he couldn't believe he'd spoken of his childhood, and that day of all days. It made him feel as if he'd dragged that bereft little boy out of the past—as if, in a moment of weakness, he had *become* him again. He asked, "What else did I say?"

Karou cocked her head. It was the gesture that had saved her in Marrakesh, the quick birdlike tilt, to regard him almost sideways, and Akiva's heart sped up. "Not much," she said, after a moment. "You fell asleep after that." She was clearly lying.

What had he said to her in the night?

"Anyway," she went on, not meeting his eyes, "you got me thinking, and I was trying to remember my own earliest memory." She levered herself back to her feet from the roof's edge, a move that required releasing her hair, which sprang wild back into the wind.

"And?"

"Brimstone." A hitch in her breathing, a fond and infinitely sad smile. "It's Brimstone. I'm sitting on the floor behind his desk, playing with the tuft of his tail."

Playing with the tuft of his tail? That didn't fit with Akiva's own idea of the sorcerer, which had been forged by his deepest anguish, seared into his soul like a brand.

"Brimstone," he said, bitter. "He was good to you?"

Karou was fierce in her reply. Her hair a blue torrent, her eyes hungry, she said, "Always. Whatever you think you know of chimaera, you don't know him."

"Isn't it possible, Karou," he said slowly, "that it's *you* who don't really know him?"

"What?" she asked. "What exactly don't I know?"

"His magic, for one thing," said Akiva. "Your wishes. Do you know what they come from?"

"Come from?"

"It's not free, Karou. Magic has a price. The price is *pain.*"

❧ 32 ❧

Both Place and Person

Pain.

As Akiva explained, Karou felt sick. She thought of every nonsensical wish she'd ever made—why had Brimstone never told her? The truth would have achieved what all his grumpy looks never did. She would never have made another wish if she'd known.

"To take from the universe, you must give," said Akiva.

"But... why *pain*? Couldn't you give something else? Like... joy?"

"It's a balance. If it were something easy to give, it would be meaningless."

Karou said, "You really think joy is easier to come by than pain? Which have *you* had more of?"

He gave her a long look. "That's a good point. But I didn't create the system."

"Who did?"

"My people believe it was the godstars. The chimaera have as many stories as races."

Troubled, Karou asked, "Well . . . where does the pain come from? Is it his own pain?"

Akiva said, "No, Karou. It is not his own pain." He enunciated each word carefully, and the implication hung there: If it wasn't his own pain, whose was it?

She felt queasy. An image came to her of bodies laid out on tables. No. That could be something else completely. She knew Brimstone, didn't she? She might not know . . . well, anything about him . . . but she knew *him*, trusted *him*, not this angel.

Swallowing a lump in her throat, she said, "I don't believe you."

Not ungently, he said, "Karou, what were the errands you did for him?"

She opened her mouth to answer and closed it again. A slow wave of understanding began to creep over her, and she wanted to push it away. Teeth: one of the great mysteries of her life. Carcasses, pliers, death. Those Russian girls with their bloody mouths. For as long as she had been aware of Brimstone's trafficking, she had held on to the idea that he needed the teeth for something vital, and that pain was a sad and desperate corollary of it. But . . . what if pain was *the whole point*? If it was how Brimstone paid for his power, for wishes, for everything?

"No," she said, and shook her head, but the conviction had gone out of her.

A little while later, when she stepped back off the cathedral and into the air, her pleasure in flying was gone. Whose pain, she wondered, had paid for it?

They went to a teahouse on Nerudova, the long, winding

223

road down from the castle, and Akiva proceeded to tell her about his world. Empire and civilization, uprising and massacre, cities lost and taken, lands burned, walls battered, sieges where the children starved first, no matter that their parents gave them all they had and perished soon after.

He talked of bloodshed and terror in a land of failing beauty. "The ancient forests have gone to build ships, siege engines; or they've been torched so they couldn't be turned to ships and siege engines."

Of hulking, ruined cities, mass graves, treachery.

Beast armies that kept coming and kept coming, never dwindling, never breaking.

There were other things—epic, terrible things—that he didn't tell her but skirted around, like caressing the edges of a wound, hesitant, testing for pain.

Karou, listening wide-eyed, horror-struck at the brutality, wished that some time in the last seventeen years Brimstone had seen fit to give her a lesson in Elsewhere. It occurred to her to ask, "What's it called, your world?"

"Eretz," Akiva said, which caused Karou's eyebrows to shoot up.

"That's *Earth*," she said. "In Hebrew. Why do our worlds have the same name?"

"Once, the magi believed the worlds were layered, like rock sediment, or the rings of trees," said Akiva.

"Uh, okay," said Karou, brow furrowed. And then, "Magi?"

"The seraph sorcerers."

"You said 'once.' What do they believe now?"

"They believe nothing. The chimaera slaughtered them all."

224

"Oh." Karou pursed her lips. What could you say to something like that? "Well." She pondered the idea of the worlds. "Maybe we just stole the name *Eretz* from you way back when, the way we built our religions on the look of you." It was what Brimstone had called a quilt of fairy tales, which humans had patched together out of glimpses. "Beauty equals good; horns and scales, evil. Simple."

"And, in this case, true."

Behind the counter, the waitress was staring back and forth between them. Karou wanted to ask her what she was looking at, but didn't. "So basically," she said to Akiva, trying to gather all the things he'd told her into a simple strand, "the seraphim want to rule the world, the chimaera don't want to be ruled, and that makes them evil."

His jaw worked; he was displeased with the simplification. "They were nothing but barbarians in mud villages. We gave them light, engineering, the written word—"

"And took nothing for it, I'm sure."

"Nothing unreasonable."

"Uh-huh." Karou wished she'd paid closer attention in her own human history classes so she could better imagine a context for the vast scope of what he was telling her. "So, a thousand years ago, for no good reason, the chimaera rose up and slaughtered their masters, and took back control of their lands."

He objected. "The land had never been theirs. They had small farm holdings, stone hovels. At the most, villages. The cities were built by the Empire, and not just cities. Viaducts, harbors, roads—"

"But it was where they'd been born and died since, like, the beginning of everything? Where they fell in love, raised their babies, buried their elders. So what if they hadn't built cities on it? Wasn't it still theirs? I mean, unless you're going on the rule that what's yours is what you can defend, in which case anyone is within their rights at any time to try to take anything from anyone else. That's hardly civilization."

"You don't understand."

"No, I don't."

Akiva took a deep breath. "We built the world, in good faith. We lived alongside them—"

"As equals?" Karou asked. "You keep calling them 'beasts,' so I have to wonder."

He didn't answer right away. "What have you seen of them, Karou? Did you say *four* chimaera, and none of them warriors? When you have seen your brothers and sisters gored by mino-taurs, mauled by lion-dogs, ripped to pieces by dragons, when you have seen your—" Whatever he was about to say, he bit it off hard, with a look of agony. "When you have been tortured and forced to witness the execution of…loved ones…then you can speak to me of what makes a beast."

Loved ones? He didn't mean brothers and sisters, the way he said that. Karou felt a pang of…surely it wasn't jealousy. What did it matter who he loved, or had loved? She swallowed. What could she say? She couldn't contradict a thing he'd told her. Her ignorance was entire, but that didn't mean she had to just believe him, either. "I'd like to hear Brimstone's side," she said quietly. Something occurred to her then, something big. "You could take me there. *You* could take me back."

He blinked, startled, then shook his head. "No. It's no place for humans."

"And this is a place for angels?"

"It's not the same. It's safe here."

"Oh, really? Tell my scars how safe it is here." She pulled the collar of her shirt out of shape to reveal the puckered slash of scar tissue across her collarbone. Akiva winced at the sight of it, ugly and of his own making, and Karou set her collar back in place. "Besides," she argued, "there are more important things than safety. Like ... *loved ones.*" She felt cruel, using his words, like she was twisting a knife.

"Loved ones," he repeated.

"I told Brimstone I would never just leave him, and I won't. I'm going, even without your help."

"How do you plan to do that?"

"There are ways," she said, cagey. "But it would be easier if you would take me." Easier indeed. What a preferable traveling companion Akiva would be to Razgut.

But he said, "I can't take you. The portal is guarded. You'd be killed on sight."

"You seraphim do a lot of that, killing on sight."

"The monsters have made us who we are."

"Monsters." Karou thought of Issa's laughing eyes, Yasri's excitable flutter and soothing touch. She called them monsters herself sometimes, but fondly, the same way she called Zuzana rabid. From Akiva's mouth, the word was just ugly. "Beasts, devils, monsters. If you'd ever known any chimaera, you couldn't dismiss them like that."

He dropped his eyes and didn't answer, and the thread of their conversation was lost in a tense silence. She thought he looked pale, still unwell. The tea mugs were big earthen affairs without handles, and Karou cupped hers with both hands. She kept her palms flat against it, both to warm them up after the frigid hours atop the cathedral and to prevent herself from inadvertently flashing any painful magic at Akiva. Across the table, his pose mirrored her own, his hands also wrapped around his mug, so that she couldn't help seeing *his* tattoos: the repeating black bars across the tops of his fingers.

Each one was slightly raised, like scar tissue, and Karou thought that, unlike hers, they were just cuts rubbed in lampblack—a primitive procedure. The longer she looked at them, the more she was seized with a strange sense of knowing something, or almost knowing it. It was as if she was at the cusp of an awareness, vibrating between knowing and not knowing, so fast that she couldn't quite register what it was—like trying to see the wings of a bee in flight. She couldn't fix on it.

Akiva saw her staring, and it made him self-conscious. He shifted, covering one hand with the other, as if he could blot out the tattoos.

"Do yours have magic in them, too?" Karou asked.

"No," he said, she thought, a little gruffly.

"What, then? Do they mean something?"

He didn't answer and she reached out, unthinking, to trace them with her fingertip. They were in a classic five-count pattern: For every four lines, the fifth was a diagonal strikethrough. "It's a count," she said, as her fingertip moved lightly from one five-count to the next on his right index finger—five, ten, fifteen, twenty—and each time she touched him it was like a leaping spark and a call, a call to entwine her fingers in his, and even—god, what was *wrong* with her?—to lift his hands to her lips and *kiss* the [mar]ks there....

And then, out of nowher[e sh]e knew. She knew what they tallied, and snatched back [her h]and. She stared at him and he sat there, unguarded, read[y to] accept whatever judgment she would lash at him.

"They're kills," she said, fa[intly.] "They're *chimaera*."

He didn't deny it. As when [she] had attacked him, he wouldn't defend himself. His hands sta[yed] where they were, still as bones, and Karou knew he was figh[ting] the urge to hide them.

She was shaking, staring [at] those marks, thinking of the ones she'd touched—twen[ty on] one index finger alone. "So many," she said. "You've kill[ed so] many."

"I'm a soldier."

Karou imagined her own four chimaera dead and put a hand over her mouth, afraid she might be sick. When he'd been telling her of the war, it was a world away. But Akiva was real and right in front of her, and the fact that he was a killer was real now, too. Like teeth spilled across Brimstone's desk, all those marks stood for blood, death—not of wolves and tigers, but the blood and death of chimaera.

She was looking at him, fixed on him, and... she saw something. As if the moment split like an eggshell to reveal another moment inside it, almost indistinguishable from it—almost— and then it was gone, and time stood intact. Akiva was just as he had been and nothing at all had happened, but that glimpse...

Karou heard herself say, in a vague voice that might have emanated from within that eggshell moment, "You have more now."

"What?" Akiva regarded her, blank—then, like lightning strike, *not* blank. He sat sharply forward, his eyes wide and flashing, the sudden movement upsetting his tea. *"What?"* he said again, louder.

Karou drew back. Akiva seized her hand. "What do you mean, I have more now?"

She shook her head. More marks, she'd meant. She had seen something in that spliced moment. There was the real Akiva, sitting before her, and there was a flash of the impossible, too: Akiva *smiling*. No grim twist of the lips but, warm with wonderment, a smile so beautiful it ached. There were crinkles at the corners of his eyes, which were merry and asquint with unselfconscious happiness. The change was profound. If he was beautiful when grave—and he was—smiling, he was nothing short of glorious.

But Karou would swear that he had *not* smiled.

And that impossible Akiva, who had existed for that instant— there had been something else: his hands had carried fewer marks, some of his fingers entirely bare of them.

Her hand was still in his, resting in the puddle of his spilled tea. The waitress came out from behind the counter and stood poised with a towel, uncertain. Karou extricated her hand and sat back to let her wipe up the mess, which she did, still glancing back and forth between them. When she was finished she asked, hesitantly, "I was just wondering...I was wondering how you did it."

230

Karou looked at her, uncomprehending. The waitress was a girl about her own age, full-cheeked and flushed. "Last night," she clarified. "The flying."

Ah. The flying. "You were there?" Karou asked. It seemed a strange coincidence.

"I wish," said the girl. "I saw it on TV. It's been on the news all morning."

Oh, thought Karou. *Oh*. Her hand went to her phone, which had been giving off snippy snorts and buzzes for the past hour or so, and she checked its screen. Missed calls and texts spooled across it, most from Zuzana and Kaz. Damn.

"Were there wires?" the waitress asked. "They couldn't find any wires or anything."

Karou said, "No wires. We were really flying," then gave her trademark wry smile.

The girl beamed back, thinking she was part of a joke. "Don't tell me, then," she said, mock-angry, and she left them alone except to bring Akiva more tea.

He was still sitting back, regarding Karou with those lightning-strike wide eyes and that vivid, searching wariness.

"What?" she asked, self-conscious. "Why are you looking at me like that?"

He lifted his hands and raked his nails through his dense, cropped hair, holding on to his head for a beat. "I can't help it," he said, abashed.

Karou experienced a fizz of pleasure. She realized that over the course of the morning all the hardness had gone from his face, or nearly. His lips were softly parted, his gaze unguarded, and now that she'd seen — imagined? — that impossible flash of

231

a smile, it wasn't so difficult to imagine it could happen again, and for real this time.

For her, maybe.

Oh god. *Be that cat!* she reminded herself. The one that stayed out of reach, and never—*ever*—purred. Sitting back, she composed her features in what she hoped was the human version of feline disdain. She gave him the gist of what she'd learned from the waitress, though she wasn't sure he really understood about television, let alone the Internet. Or phones, for that matter. "Can you give me a minute?" she asked him, and she dialed Zuzana, who picked up on the first ring.

Her voice exploded in Karou's ear. *"Karou?"*

"It's me—"

"Oh my god! Are you all right? I saw you on the news. I saw *him.* I saw...Holy Jesus, Karou, do you realize that you were *flying?"*

"I know. Isn't it awesome?"

"It is *not awesome!* Un-awesome! I thought you were dead somewhere." She was on the edge of hysteria, and it took Karou a few minutes to calm her, all the while mindful of Akiva's eyes on her, and trying to keep her feline cool.

"You're really okay?" Zuzana asked. "He doesn't have, like, a knife to your throat, forcing you to say you are?"

"He doesn't even speak Czech," Karou assured her, then gave her a quick rundown of the previous night, letting her know he hadn't tried to hurt her—had gone to extremes of passiveness to *not* hurt her—and finishing with, "We, um, watched the sun rise from the top of the cathedral."

"The hell? Was it a date?"

"No, it wasn't a date. Honestly, I don't know what it was. *Is.* I don't know what he's doing here...." Her voice faltered as she looked at him. It wasn't just the smile, or the marks on his hands. She knew, somehow, that his right shoulder was a mass of scar tissue. He favored it; she'd seen that. That must be how she knew. Why, then, did she know what the scars looked like?

Felt like?

"Karou? Hello? *Karou?*"

Karou blinked and cleared her throat. It had happened again: her own name, floating right past, unconnected to herself. She sensed from Zuzana's agitation that she had been missing in action for a few beats past any acceptable span of zoning out. "I'm here," she said.

"*Where?* I keep asking you. Where are you?"

Karou had momentarily forgotten. "Um. Oh. The teahouse on Nerudova."

"Sit. Stay. I'm coming there."

"No, you're not—"

"Yes, I am."

"Zuze—"

"*Karou.* Don't make me hurt you with my tiny fists."

"Fine," Karou relented. "Come on, then."

Zuzana boarded with a widow aunt in Hradčany, not far away. "I'll be there in ten," she said.

Karou couldn't resist telling her, "It's faster if you fly."

"Freak. Don't you dare leave. And don't let him leave, either. I have threats to deliver. Judgments to pass."

"I don't think he's going anywhere," said Karou, and she

233

looked straight at Akiva as she said it, and he looked back, molten, and she knew it was true, but she didn't know why.

He wasn't human. He wasn't even from her world. He was a soldier with scores of kills on his hands, and he was the enemy of her family. And yet, something tied them together, stronger than any of that, something with the power to conduct her blood and breath like a symphony, so that anything she did to fight against it felt like discord, like disharmony with her *self*.

As far back as she could remember, a phantom life had mocked her with its impenetrable "something else," but now it was the opposite. Here, in the circle of Akiva's presence, even as they spoke of war and siege and enduring enmity, she felt herself being drawn into the warm absoluteness and rightness of him, like he was both place and person and, contrary to all reason, exactly where she was supposed to be.

33

PREPOSTEROUS

"My tiny scary friend is coming here," Karou told Akiva, drumming her fingers on the table.

"The one from the bridge."

Karou recalled that he had been following her yesterday, and would have seen Zuzana perform. She nodded. "She knows about your world, a little. And she knows you tried to kill me, so..."

"Should I be afraid?" Akiva asked, and for a second Karou thought he was serious. He always looked so serious, but it was another hint of dry humor, like atop the cathedral when he had surprised her with his joke about pushing off bad dates.

"Terribly afraid," she replied. "All cower before her. You'll see."

Her mug was empty, but she kept her palms on it, less now for fear of flashing magic at Akiva than to keep her hands from making any more unsanctioned sallies across the table to touch his. She should have been repelled by his hands with their death count, and she was, but not only. Side by side with the horror was . . . the *pull.*

She knew he felt it, too, that his hands were fighting their own battle not to reach for hers. He kept looking at her, and she kept blushing, and their conversation stuttered along until the door opened and Zuzana stomped in.

She came straight to the table and stood facing Akiva. She was fierce, ready to scold, but when she saw him, really saw him, she faltered. Her expression warred with itself—ferocity with awe— and awe won out. She cast a sidelong glance at Karou and said, in helpless amazement, "Oh, hell. Must. Mate. Immediately."

It was so unexpected, and Karou was already so on edge, that laughter burst from her. She sank back in her chair and let it pour out: soft, glittering laughter that worked another change in Akiva's countenance as he watched her with a hopeful, piercing scrutiny that made her tingle, she felt so . . . *seen.*

"No, really," said Zuzana. "Right now. It's, like, a biological imperative, right, to get the best genetic material? And *this*"— she made spokesmodel hands at Akiva—"is the best genetic material I have ever seen." She pulled up a chair beside Karou, so the two of them were like a gallery observing the seraph. "Fiala would so eat her words. You should bring him in to model on Monday."

"Right," said Karou. "I'm sure he wouldn't mind stripping for a bunch of humans—"

"*Disrobing,*" said Zuzana, prim. "For *art.*"

"Are you going to introduce us?" Akiva asked. The chimaera tongue, which they had been using all along, now sounded out of place, like a rough echo from another world.

Karou nodded, fanning away laughter. "I'm sorry," she said, and made a cursory introduction. "Of course, I'll have to translate if you want to say anything to each other."

"Ask him if he's in love with you," said Zuzana at once.

Karou almost choked. She turned her whole body in her chair to face Zuzana, who held up a hand before she could protest. "I know, I know. You're not going to ask him that. And you don't even need to. He so *is*. Look at him! I'm afraid he's going to set you on fire with his crazy orange eyes."

It did feel like that, Karou had to admit. But *love?* That was preposterous. She said so.

"You want to know what's preposterous?" said Zuzana, still studying Akiva, who looked bemused by her appraisal. "That widow's peak is preposterous. *God.* It really makes you feel the sad dearth of widow's peaks in daily life. We could, like, use him as breeding stock to seed widow's peaks into the populace."

"My god. What's with all the mating and seed talk?"

"I'm just saying," Zuzana said reasonably. "I'm crazy about Mik, okay, but that doesn't mean I can't do my part for the proliferation of widow's peaks. As a favor to the gene pool. You would, too, right? Or maybe..." She shot Karou a sidelong glance. "You already *have?*"

"What?" Karou was aghast. "No! What do you think I am?"

She was certain Akiva couldn't understand, but there was an amused quirk to his mouth. He asked what Zuzana had said, and Karou felt her face flame crimson.

"Nothing," she told him in Chimaera. In Czech she added, sternly, "She. Did not say. Anything."

"Yes, I did," piped Zuzana, and like a child who has gotten a reaction for naughty antics, she merrily repeated, "Mating! Seed!"

"Zuze, stop, please," begged Karou, helpless and so very glad the two had no common language.

"Fine," said her friend. "I can be polite. Observe." She addressed Akiva directly. "Welcome to our world," she said with exaggerated gestures. "I hope that you are enjoying your visit."

Chewing on a smile, Karou translated.

Akiva nodded. "Thank you." To Karou, "Would you tell her, please, that her performance was beautiful?"

Karou did. "I know," agreed Zuzana. It was her standard acceptance of a compliment, but Karou could tell she was pleased. "It was Karou's idea."

Karou didn't convey that. She said instead, "She's an amazing artist."

"So are you," Akiva replied, and it was Karou's turn to be pleased.

She told him they went to a school for the arts, and he said they had nothing like that in his world; only apprenticeships. She told him that Zuzana was kind of like an apprentice, that she came from a family of artisans, and she wondered if he was from a family of soldiers. "In a manner of speaking," he replied. His siblings were soldiers, and so had his father been in his day. He said the word *father* with an edge, and Karou sensed animosity and didn't press, and talk shifted back to art. The conversation, filtered through Karou—and Zuzana, even on her best behavior, required a high degree of filtering—was surprisingly easy. Too easy, she thought.

Why was it so easy for her to laugh with this seraph, and

keep forgetting the image of the fiery portal, and Kishmish's little raw body as his heartbeat went wild and then failed? She had to keep reminding herself, chastening herself, and even so, when she looked at Akiva, it all wanted to slip away—all her caution and self-control.

After a moment, he remarked, nodding toward Zuzana, "She's not actually very scary. You had me worried."

"Well, you disarm her. You have that effect."

"I do? It didn't seem to work on you, yesterday."

"I had more reason to fight it," she said. "I have to keep reminding myself we're enemies."

It was as if a shadow fell over them. Akiva's expression turned remote again, and he put his hands under the table, removing his tattoos from her sight.

"What did you just say to him?" Zuzana asked.

"I reminded him that we're enemies."

"*Tch.* Whatever you are, Karou, you are *not* enemies."

"But we are," she said, and they *were*, no matter how powerfully her body was trying to convince her otherwise.

"Then what are you doing, watching sunrises and drinking tea with him?"

"You're right. What *am* I doing? I don't know what I'm doing." She thought of what she *should* be doing: getting herself to Morocco to find Razgut; flying through that slash in the sky to...Eretz. A chill snaked through her. She'd been so focused on getting gavriels that she'd avoided thinking too much about what it would be like to actually *go*, and now with Akiva's depiction of his world fresh in her mind—war-torn, bleak—dread crept over her; suddenly, she didn't want to go anywhere.

What was she supposed to do when she got there, anyway? Fly up to the bars of that forbidding fortress and politely ask if Brimstone was at home?

"Speaking of enemies," Zuzana said, "Jackass was on TV this morning."

"Good for him," said Karou, still in her own thoughts.

"No. Not good. *Bad. Bad* Jackass."

"Oh no. What did he do?"

"Well, while you've been watching sunrises with your *enemy*, the news has been all over you, and a certain actor has been most helpful, preening for the camera and telling the world all about you. Like, um, *bullet scars*? He's made you out to be some kind of gangster's moll—"

"*Moll?* Please. If anything, I'm the gangster—"

"*Anyway*," Zuzana cut her off. "I'm sorry to say that whatever anonymity you might have had, blue-haired girl, your flying stunt put an end to it. The police are probably at your flat—"

"*What?*"

"Yeah. They're calling your fight a 'disturbance' and saying they just want to talk to the, er, *people* involved, if anyone knows their whereabouts."

Akiva, seeing her distress, wanted to know what was being said; she quickly translated. His look darkened. He stood and moved to the door, glancing out. "Will they come for you here?" he asked. Karou saw the protectiveness in his stance, shoulders hunched and tense, and she realized that in his world, such a threat might be much more dire.

"It's okay," she assured him. "It's not like that. They would just ask questions. Really." He didn't move away from the door.

240

"We didn't break any laws." She turned to Zuzana and switched to Czech. "It's not like there's a law against flying."

"Yes there is. The law of *gravity*. The point is that you are looked for." She shot a glance at the waitress, who was skulking nearby and most certainly eavesdropping. "Isn't that right?"

The waitress blushed. "I haven't called anyone," she was quick to say. "You're okay to stay here. Do...do you want more tea?"

Zuzana waved her off and told Karou, "You can't stay here forever, obviously."

"No."

"So what's the plan?"

Plan. Plan. She *had* a plan, and it was near its fruition. All she had to do now was *go*. Leave her life here, leave school, her flat, Zuzana, Akiva...No. Akiva was *not* part of her life. Karou looked at him, watchful in the doorway, ready to protect her, and she tried to imagine walking away from the...*placeness*... of him, the rightness, the patch of sunlight, the *pull*. All she had to do was get up and leave. Right?

A moment passed in silence, and Karou's body did not so much as twitch in response to the idea of leaving.

"The plan," she said, exerting a massive effort of will and facing up to it. "The plan is to go away."

Akiva had been looking out the door, and only when he pivoted to face her did she realize she'd spoken in Chimaera, addressing this to him.

"Away? Where?"

"Eretz," she said, standing up. "I told you. I'm going to find my family."

Dismay spread over his face as understanding dawned. "You really have a way to get there."

"I really do."

"How?"

"There are more portals than just yours."

"There were. All knowledge of them was lost with the magi. It took me years to find this one—"

"You're not the only one who knows things, I guess. Though I would rather *you* showed me the way."

"Than who?" He was thinking, trying to figure it out, and Karou saw by the flicker of disgust when he did. "The Fallen. That *thing*. You're going to that thing."

"Not if you take me instead."

"I truly can't. Karou. The portal is under guard—"

"Well then. Maybe I'll see you on the other side sometime. Who knows?"

A rustle from his unseen wings sent sparks shivering across the floor. "You can't go there. There's no kind of life there, trust me."

Karou turned away from him and picked up her coat, slipping it on and fanning out her hair, which had a damp mermaid quality to it and lay in coils over her shoulders. She told Zuzana that she was leaving town, and she was fending off her friend's inevitable queries when Akiva took her elbow.

Gently. "You can't go with that creature." His expression was guarded, hard to read. "Not alone. If he knows another portal, I can come with you and make sure you're safe."

Karou's first impulse was to refuse. *Be that cat. Be that cat.* But who was she fooling? That wasn't the cat she wanted to be.

She didn't want to go alone—or alone with Razgut, which was worse. Her heart hammering, she said, "Okay," and once the decision was made, a tremendous burden of dread lifted.

She wouldn't have to part with Akiva.

Yet, anyway.

❧ 34 ❧

WHAT'S A DAY?

What's a morning? Karou asked herself. A part of her was already flying into the future, imagining what her reunion with Brimstone would be like, but another part of her was settled firmly in her skin, mindful of the heat of Akiva's arm against her shoulder. They were walking down Nerudova with Zuzana, against the flow of tourists heading up to the castle, and they had to press close to navigate a horde of Germans in sensible shoes.

She had her hair tucked away in a hat, borrowed from the waitress, so her most obvious feature was disguised. Akiva was still drawing an inordinate amount of attention, but Karou thought it was mostly because of his otherworldly beauty, and not recognition from the news.

"I have to stop by school," Zuzana said. "Come with me."

Karou wanted to go there anyway — it was part of her good-bye program — so she agreed. She'd have to wait until nightfall anyway to get back in her flat, if the police were watching it.

After dark she could return by way of sky and balcony, instead of street and elevator, and get the things she'd need for her journey.

What's a day? she asked herself, and there was a buzzing happiness in her that she had to admit had a lot to do with the way Akiva had stood in the teahouse doorway, and the solidity of him beside her now in all its rightness.

There was wrongness, too, faint and flickering, but she attributed that to nerves, and as the morning went by in its buzz of unlooked-for happiness, she kept brushing it aside, unconsciously, as one might fan at a fly.

* * *

Karou said her good-byes to the Lyceum—in her head only, not wanting to alarm Zuzana—and, afterward, to Poison Kitchen. She laid a fond hand on the marble flank of Pestilence, and ran her fingers over the slightly ratty velvet of the settee. Akiva took the place in with a puzzled expression, coffins and all, and called it "morbid." He ate a bowl of goulash, too, but Karou didn't think he would be asking for the recipe anytime soon.

She saw her two haunts with new eyes, being there with him, and was humbled to think how little she had really internalized the fact of the wars that had shaped them. At school, some joker had scrawled a red graffiti *volnost*—liberty—where freedom fighters had once written it in Nazi blood, and in Poison she had to explain gas masks to Akiva, and that they came from a different war than the *volnost* did.

"These are from World War One," she said, putting one on. "A hundred years ago. The Nazis came later." She gave him a tart sideward glance. "And just so you know, the invaders are always the bad guys. Always."

Mik joined them, and it was a little strained at first, because he didn't know anything of other worlds and other races, and believed Karou was just eccentric. She told him the truth — that they had really been flying, and that Akiva was an angel from another world — but in her accustomed manner, so that he thought she was teasing him. But his eyes kept going to Akiva with the same kind of astonished appraisal as everyone else's did, and Karou, watching, saw that it made Akiva uncomfortable. It struck her that there was nothing in his manner at all to suggest he knew the power of his beauty.

Later the four of them walked onto the Charles Bridge. Mik and Zuzana were a few steps ahead, entwined as if nothing could ever shoehorn them apart, Karou and Akiva trailing.

"We can leave for Morocco tonight," Karou said. "I was going to take an airplane, but I don't think that's an option for you."

"No?"

"No. You'd need a passport, a document saying your nationality, which tends to assume you are from this actual world."

"You can still fly, yes?"

Karou tested her ability, rising a discreet few inches off the ground and coming right back down. "It's a long way, though."

"I'll help you. Even if you couldn't fly, I could carry you."

She imagined crossing the Alps and the Mediterranean in Akiva's arms. It wasn't the worst thing she could think of, but still. She was no damsel in distress. "I'll manage," she said.

Up ahead, Mik dipped Zuzana into a back-bending kiss, and Karou came to a halt, flustered by their display. She turned to the bridge railing and looked out over the river. "It must be weird for you just doing nothing all day."

Akiva nodded. He was looking out, too, leaning on the railing, one of his elbows against hers. It didn't escape Karou's notice that he found subtle ways of touching her. "I keep trying to imagine my own people living like this, and I can't."

"How do they live?" she asked.

"War is all. If they're not fighting it, they're providing for it, and living in fear, always. There is no one without loss."

"And the chimaera? What are their lives like?"

He hesitated. "There's no good life there for anyone. It's not a safe place." He laid a hand on her arm. "Karou, your life is here, in this world. If Brimstone cares about you, he can't want you to go to that broken place. You should stay." His next words were a whisper. She barely heard them, and afterward wasn't entirely sure she had. He said, "I could stay here with you."

His grip was firm and it was soft; his hand on her arm was warm and it was right. Karou let herself pretend, just for a moment, that she could have what he had whispered: a life with him. Everything she had always craved was right here: solidity, a mooring, love.

Love.

The word, when it came to her, wasn't jarring or preposterous, as when Zuzana had uttered it that morning at the teahouse. It was tantalizing. Karou didn't think. She reached for Akiva's hand.

And shocked a pulse into it.

She jerked back. Her hamsa. She'd laid it full against his skin. Her palm burned, and Akiva had been knocked back a step. He stood there holding his magic-scorched hand to his body as a shudder passed through him. His jaw was clenched with the endurance of pain.

Pain, again.

"I can't even touch you," Karou said. "Whatever Brimstone wants for me, it's not you, or he wouldn't have given me these." Her own hands, clasped tight to her chest, felt evil to her in that moment. She reached into her collar and fished up her wishbone, took it into her hand and held it tight, for comfort.

Akiva said, "You don't have to want what he wants."

"I know that. But I have to know what's happening there. I have to know." Her voice was ragged; she wanted him to understand, and he did. She saw it in his eyes, and with it the helplessness and anguish she'd seen in glints and glimmers since he had come into her life the night before. Only the night before. It was unbelievable it had been so short a time.

"You don't have to come with me."

"Of course I'm coming with you. Karou..." His voice was still whisper-soft. "*Karou.*" He reached out and eased the hat from her head so that her hair spilled out in a splash of blue, and he tucked an errant strand behind her ear. He took her face in his hands and a sunburst went off in Karou's chest. She held herself quiet, her motionlessness belying the rushing within her. No one had ever looked at her like Akiva was right now, his eyes held wide as if he wanted take more of her into himself, like light through a window.

One of his hands slipped softly around to the nape of her

neck, twining through her hair and sending frissons of longing through her body. She felt herself giving way, melting toward him. One booted foot slid forward so her knee brushed his and settled against it, and the remaining space between them—negative space, it was called in drawing—called out to be closed.

Was he going to kiss her?

Oh god, did she have goulash breath?

Never mind. He had it, too.

Did she *want* him to kiss her?

His face was so close she could see the sun dusky on his lashes, and her own face centered in the deep black of his pupils. He was gazing into her eyes as if there were worlds within her, wonders and discoveries.

Yes. She did want him to kiss her. Yes.

His hand slipped down her throat to find her hand, which was still cupping the wishbone on its cord.

Its flanges protruded through the webbing of her fingers, and when Akiva felt them there, he stopped. Something in his gaze froze. He looked down. His breath caught; with a hitch he inhaled and opened Karou's hand with no caution for her hamsas.

The wishbone was there, a small bleached relic of another life. He gave a cry that was amazement and...what? Something deep and painful wrenched out of him like nails splintering wood as they pulled free.

Karou jumped, startled. "What?"

"Why do you have this?" He had gone pale.

"It's...it's Brimstone's. He sent it to me as the portals burned."

"Brimstone," he repeated. His face was alive with furious thought, and then understanding. *"Brimstone,"* he said again.

"What? Akiva—"

What he did then made Karou falter into silence. He sank to his knees. The cord around her neck gave way and the wishbone came away in his hand, and for an instant she felt bereft without it. But then he leaned into her. He pressed his face against her legs, and she felt the heat of it through her jeans. She stood astonished, looking down at his powerful shoulders as he curled into her, letting go of his glamour so his wings sprang visible.

From around them on the bridge came gasps and cries. People stopped in their tracks, gaping. Zuzana and Mik broke from their embrace and spun to stare. Karou was only distantly aware of them. Gazing down at Akiva, she saw that his shoulders were shaking. Was he crying? Her hands fluttered, wanting to touch him, afraid of hurting him. Hating her hamsas, she bent over him and stroked his hair with the backs of her fingers, his hot, hot brow with the backs of her hands.

"What is it?" she asked. "What's wrong?"

He straightened, still on his knees, and looked up at her. She was curved over him like a question mark. He held her legs, and she could feel tremors shaking his hands, the wishbone in his grip where he clasped the back of her knee. His wings unfolded; they came around like a pair of great fans so the two of them were in a room of fire, more than ever in a world all their own.

He searched her face, looking stunned and, Karou thought, terribly sad.

And he told her, "Karou, I know who you are."

35

THE TONGUE OF ANGELS

I know who you are.

Akiva, gazing up into Karou's face, saw what his words did to her. The hope at odds with the fear of hoping, her black eyes tear-glossed and shining with fire. Only then, seeing the reflection in her eyes, did he realize he'd dropped his glamour. There was a time when such carelessness could have gotten him killed. Now, he just didn't care.

What? Karou's lips moved but no sound came out. She cleared her throat. "What did you say?"

How could he just tell her? He was reeling. Here was the impossible, and it was beautiful, and it was terrible, and it flayed open his chest to show that his heart, numb for so long, was still vital and beating...just so it could be ripped out again, after all these years?

Was there any fate more bitter than to get what you long for most, when it's too late?

"Akiva," implored Karou. Wide-eyed, distraught, she sank to her knees in front of him. "Tell me."

"Karou," he whispered, and her name taunted him — *hope* — so full of promise and recrimination that he almost wished he was dead. He couldn't look at her. He gathered her to him and she let herself be gathered, supple as love. Her wind-mussed hair was like tousled silk, and he buried his face in it and tried to think what to tell her.

All around, a weave of murmurs and the weight of being watched, and Akiva registered almost none of it until one sound fought its way forward. A throat was cleared, caustic and theatrically loud. A prickling of unease, and before any words were spoken, he'd already begun to turn.

"Akiva, really. Pull yourself together."

So out of place here — that voice, that language. *His* language.

There, with swords sheathed at their sides and wearing twin expressions of dismay, stood Hazael and Liraz.

Akiva couldn't even register surprise. The appearance of the seraphim was small next to the shocks that had been coming one after another all morning: the crescent-moon knives, Karou's strange reaction to his tattoos, the dreamlike music of her laughter, and now the undeniable: the wishbone.

"What are you doing here?" he asked them. His arms were still around Karou, who had lifted her head from his shoulder to stare at the intruders.

"What are *we* doing here?" repeated Liraz. "I think, all things considered, that question belongs to us. What in the name of the godstars are *you* doing here?" She looked dumbfounded, and Akiva saw himself as she was seeing him: on his knees, weeping, entwined with a human girl.

And it struck him how important it was that they think Karou was just that: a human girl. However strange it might seem, it was only that: strange. The truth would be much worse.

He straightened, still on his knees, and turned, ushering Karou behind him. Quietly, so his brother and sister wouldn't hear him speak the language of the enemy, he murmured, "Don't let them see your hands. They won't understand."

"Understand what?" she murmured back, not taking her eyes from them, as they didn't take theirs from her.

"Us," he said. "They won't understand *us*."

"I don't understand us, either."

But thanks to the wishbone, fragile in his fist, Akiva finally did.

Karou lapsed into tense silence, keeping her eyes on the two seraphim. They had their wing glamours in place, but even so, their presence on the bridge seemed unnatural, and not a little unnerving—Liraz especially. Though Hazael was more powerful, Liraz was more frightening, she always had been; perhaps she'd had to be, being female. Her pale hair was scraped back in severe plaits, and there was something coolly sharklike about her beauty: a flat, killer apathy. Hazael had more life in his eyes, but just now it was mostly a frank bafflement as he regarded Akiva before him, still on his knees.

"Get up," he said, not unkindly. "I can't stand the sight of you like that."

Akiva rose, drawing Karou up with him and keeping her behind the shield of his wings.

"What's going on?" Liraz demanded. "Akiva, why did you come back here? And...who *is* that?" She made a wild gesture of disgust toward Karou.

"Just a girl." Akiva heard himself echo Izîl, sounding just as unconvincing as the old man had.

"Just a girl who flies," amended Liraz.

A heartbeat's pause, and then Akiva said, "You've been following me."

"What did you think," Liraz spat, "that we'd let you vanish again? The way you were acting after Loramendi, we knew something was coming. But...this?"

"What exactly *is* this?" Hazael asked, clearly still hoping for some explanation that would make it all okay. Akiva felt split down the middle. Here before him were his closest allies, and they felt like enemies, and it was his fault.

If Akiva had a family, it was not his mother, who had turned away when the soldiers came to take him; and it was certainly not the emperor. His family was these two, and there was no answer he could give them to make this make sense. There was nothing he could say to Karou, either, who stood behind him desperate to know what had been kept from her all her life—a secret so big and so strange he couldn't begin to find words to frame it. So he stood there mute, the languages of two races useless to help him explain anything.

"I don't blame you wanting to get away," said Hazael, always the peacemaker. He and Liraz bore a sibling resemblance they didn't share with Akiva. They were fair-haired and blue-eyed, with a blush to their honey skin. Hazael had an ease to him, almost a slouch, and for a resting expression a lazy smile that could almost fool you into misjudging him. He was, always, a soldier—reflexes and steel—but at heart he had managed somehow to retain something childlike that training and years of war worked hard to stamp out. He was a dreamer. He said, "I had thoughts myself, of coming back to this world after everything—"

"But you didn't," snapped Liraz, who had within her no dreamer at all. "*You* didn't vanish in the night, leaving others to make up stories to cover for you, not knowing when or even *if* you'd come back this time."

"I didn't ask you to cover for me," said Akiva.

"No. Because then you'd have had to tell us you were going. Instead you snuck off, just like before. And were we to wait for you to come back broken again, and never tell us what had broken you?"

"Not this time," he said.

Liraz gave him a brittle smile, and Akiva knew that under her iciness she was hurt. He might never have returned; they might never have known what had happened to him. What did that say for the decades they had protected one another? Hadn't it been Liraz, years ago, who had risked her life to return to the battlefield at Bullfinch? Against any expectation that he might still be alive, and with chimaera crawling over their victory and spitting the wounded on pikes, she had returned and found him, and borne him away. She had risked her life for him, and would again without hesitation, and so would Hazael, and Akiva would for them. But he couldn't tell them why he'd come here, or what he'd found.

"Not this time *what?*" Liraz demanded. "You're not coming back broken? Or you're not coming back at all?"

"I didn't plan anything. I just couldn't stay there." He groped to explain; he owed them the effort, at least. "After Loramendi, an end was reached, and it was like the edge of a cliff. There was nothing else I wanted, nothing except..." He left the rest unsaid. He didn't need to say it; they'd seen him on his knees. They fixed their eyes on Karou.

"Except *her*," said Liraz. "A human. If that's what she is."

"What else would she be?" he said, covering a spark of fear.

"I have a theory," she said, and Akiva's heart lurched. "Last night, when she attacked you, there was something strange about that fight, wasn't there, Hazael?"

"Strange," agreed Hazael.

"We weren't close enough to feel any...magic...but it certainly seemed as though *you* were feeling it."

Akiva's thoughts spun furiously. How could he get Karou away from here?

"You seem to have forgiven her for it, though." Liraz came a step closer. "Is there anything you want to tell us?"

Akiva retreated, keeping Karou behind him. "Leave her alone," he said.

Liraz advanced. "If you have nothing to hide, let us see her."

In a sorrowful voice that was worse than Liraz's sharp tone, Hazael said, "Akiva, just tell us it isn't what it looks like. Just tell us she isn't..."

Akiva felt a kind of rushing around him, years of secrets catching him up like a wind—a wind, he wished with a wild kind of surrender, that could just bear him away, with Karou, to a place without seraphim and chimaera and their talent for hate, without humans to stand around and gape, without anyone to come between them, ever again. "Of course she isn't," he said. It came out as a snarl, and Liraz took it as a challenge to prove it—what Karou was and what she wasn't—and her eyes flashed with a look Akiva knew too well, a hard fury she harnessed on the battlefield. She came closer.

Adrenaline surged hot as his hands seized into fists, the wishbone bowing under the pressure, and he braced himself for what must come next. Sick incredulity washed over him, that it had come to this.

But whatever he expected to happen, it was not for Karou to speak up in a clear, cool voice and ask, "What? What am I not?"

Liraz halted, her fury blinking to shock. Hazael looked startled, too, and it took Akiva a beat to realize why, but, with a start, he did.

Karou's words. They were as smooth as falling water. They were in his language. She had spoken the tongue of angels, which she had no way, earthly or elsewise, of knowing. In the hesitation wrought by her question, she stepped out from the shelter of his wings and stood exposed before Liraz and Hazael.

Then, with the same bright savagery she had smiled at Akiva when she attacked him the night before, she said to Liraz, "If you want to see my hands, all you have to do is ask."

❦ 36 ❦

TO DO ELSE THAN KILL

All it took was a lucknow from her pocket and a whispered wish, and the words of the seraphim swam from melodious flow into meaning—another language for Karou's collection, and it was a prize. She already knew, from the hard, darting eyes of the female seraph and the protective stance of Akiva, that they were talking about her.

"Just tell us she isn't..." said the male, letting his words trail into some unspoken horror, as if he were pleading with Akiva to disprove their suspicions about her.

Who did they think she was? Was she to stand here mute while they talked her over?

"What?" she asked. "What am I not?" She saw their faces freeze in shock as she stepped out from behind Akiva. The female angel was just paces away, staring. She had the dead eyes of a jihadist, and Karou felt a tremor of vulnerability with Akiva no longer between them. She thought of her crescent-moon knives sitting useless in her flat, and then she realized she didn't need them. She had a weapon tailored just to seraphim.

She *was* a weapon tailored just to seraphim.

The smile rose unbidden from her phantom self, and she said, with a leaping, dark excitement, "If you want to see my hands, all you have to do is ask."

And then, there on the Charles Bridge in full view of gawkers, their upheld phones and cameras capturing it for the world, and with the police approaching, wary and grim-faced, all hell broke loose.

* * *

"No!" cried Akiva, but it was too late.

Liraz moved first, like the slash of a knife, and she was fast, but Karou matched her with a knifelike speed of her own. She threw up her hands and the air rippled with the expulsion of magic. It made a slow-motion tracery, hanging there for a second like a warp, and then it hit. Its fringes shivered wide to catch Hazael and Akiva, and they both staggered. Liraz, though, was hurled back like a flicked bug. She twisted, acrobatic, and landed on her feet with a concussive force that shook the bridge. In the aftermath of the blast, only Karou stood straight. Her hair had been caught as in a backdraft, sucked forward and then turned loose, and it floated on the churning air.

She was still smiling, cold. With her drifting hair, and her palms outfaced with their staring ink eyes, she looked malevolent, even to Zuzana, like some species of fell goddess

259

in the unconvincing guise of a girl. Zuzana, Mik, and the other onlookers faltered back. Liraz dropped her glamour, and it was as though the veil that had cloaked them was drawn away to reveal a raging fire. Hazael dropped his glamour, too, and moved to his sister's side, and a battle line was drawn, the two angels facing Karou, their heads lowered against the misery her hamsas were pulsing at them.

Akiva stood between them, stricken. He had to move to one side or the other. A step or two in either direction, just that, and it was a choice that would define him forever. He looked rapidly back and forth between his comrades and Karou.

"Akiva," hissed Liraz. She expected him to come to them. It had always been the three of them, advancing against the enemy, killing, and afterward drawing the rough tally marks on one another's hands with knife tips and campfire soot. To them, Karou was just another tattoo waiting to happen, a line to be carved.

And then there was Karou, so ready to raise her hands and unleash Brimstone's noxious magic.

"It doesn't have to be like this," Akiva said, but his voice was thin, as if he didn't believe it himself.

"It *is* like this," said Liraz. "Don't be a child, Akiva."

He was still between them, straddling two possible futures.

Liraz said, "If you can't kill her yourself, then go. You don't have to see it. We'll never speak of it again. It's over. Do you hear me? *Go home.*"

She spoke with urgency and resolution. She really believed she was taking care of him, and that this—this thing with Karou, so beyond her ken—was some madness to be forcibly forgotten.

He said, "I'm not going home."

Hazael. "What do you mean, you're not going home? After all you've done? All you've fought for? It's a new age, brother. *Peace*—"

"It's not peace. Peace is more than the absence of war. Peace is accord. Harmony."

"Harmony with beasts, you mean?" Mistrust shaded into Hazael's expression, and disgust, and still, still, the hope that it was all a misunderstanding.

When Akiva answered, he knew he was crossing a final border, beyond all possibility of misinterpretation or return. It was a border he should have crossed a long time ago. Everything had gotten so twisted; *he* had gotten so twisted. "Yes. That's what I mean."

Karou broke her gaze away from the two intruders to glance at him. The hard smile had left her face already, and now, as she sensed his turmoil, even her upheld hands faltered. Thoughts of herself, her answers, her emptiness were forgotten, all overshadowed by Akiva's anguish, which she felt like it was her own.

The police arrived. They hesitated in the face of this other-worldly tableau. Karou saw their baffled faces, their nervous guns, and she saw the way they looked at *her*. There were angels on the Charles Bridge, and she was their foe. She: enemy of angels, in her black coat and evil tattoos, with her lashing blue hair and black eyes. They: so golden, the very image of church frescoes come to life. She was the demon in this scene, and she half expected, glancing at her shadow sharp before her, to see that it had *horns*. It did not. Her shadow was a girl's shadow, and seemed in that moment to have nothing at all to do with her.

Akiva, who a moment ago had pressed his face against her legs and wept, stood stock-still, and Karou felt fear for the first time since the two angels had come upon them. If he should take their side...

"Akiva," she whispered.

"I'm here," he said, and when he moved, it was to her. There had never been any doubt, only a hope that somehow the choice wouldn't be forced, that the moment could be backed away from, but it was too late for that. So he stepped into his future, coming between Karou and his brother and sister, and he said to them in a low but steady voice, "I won't let you harm her. There are other ways to live. We have it in us to do else than kill."

Hazael and Liraz stared at him. Unthinkably, he had chosen the girl. Liraz's shock quickly turned to bitterness. "Do we?" she flung back at him. "That's a convenient position to take now, isn't it?"

Karou had lowered her hands when Akiva came before her. She reached out, just her fingertips to his back, because she couldn't help it.

He told her, "Karou, you have to go."

"Go? But—"

"Get away from here. I'll keep them from following you." His voice was grim with what that would mean, but his decision was made. He gave her a quick look over his shoulder; his face was strained but set. "I'll meet you in the place we first saw each other. Promise me you'll wait for me there."

The place they first saw each other. The Jemaa el-Fna, heart of Marrakesh, where she had caught his burning gaze through the chaos of a crowd and been pierced through the soul by it. Akiva said, in a voice hoarse with urgency, "Promise me. Karou, promise you won't go with Razgut until I find you. Until I explain."

Karou wanted to promise. She saw that he had thrown his allegiance to her, even against his own kind. He had surely saved her life—could she have survived an attack by two armed seraphim?—in addition to which, he had *chosen* her. Wasn't that what she had always wanted, to be chosen? Cherished? He had given up his place in his own world for her, and he was asking that she wait for him in Marrakesh.

But something unyielding in her shrank from the promise. He might have chosen her, but that didn't mean that she would do the same if she were faced with the same choice—against Brimstone, Issa, Yasri, Twiga. She had told Brimstone, "I want you to know I would never just leave you," and she wouldn't. She would choose her family. Anything else was unthinkable, though even now the idea of turning and leaving Akiva behind brought on physical pain.

She said, "I'll wait for you as long as I can. That's the best I can do."

And she thought the brilliance of his burning wings dimmed just a little. He said in a hollow voice, still faced away from her, "Then that will have to be good enough."

Liraz drew her sword, and Hazael followed suit. The police responded by falling back, raising their guns, shouting in Czech for the angels to drop their weapons. The onlookers cried out

263

in a kind of ecstatic terror. Zuzana, jostled among them, kept her eyes on Karou.

Akiva, whose swords were less obvious in their crossed sheaths between his wings, reached double-handed over his shoulders and drew them with a harmonic ringing. Without looking back, he urged, "Karou. Go."

She gathered herself into a crouch, and just before she sprang skyward to vanish into the ether in a streak of blue and black she said, both choked and pleading, "Come and find me, Akiva."

And then she was gone, and he was left alone to face the fallout of his shattering choice.

Once upon a time,
an angel lay dying in the mist.

And a devil knelt over him and smiled.

❧ 37 ❧

DREAM-LOST

Akiva was helpless to keep his blood in his body. It pulsed up under his fingers and escaped, riding the tide of his heartbeat out in hot spurts. He couldn't stop the bleeding. The wound was a mauling, and clutching at it was a little like gathering a fistful of meat scraps to fling to a dog.

He was going to die.

Around him, the world had lost its horizons. Sea mist choked Bullfinch beach, and Akiva heard waves breaking but could see only as far as the nearest corpses: gray hummocks obscured by the fog. They might have been chimaera or seraphim — except for the nearest one, he couldn't tell. That one lay only a few yards away, with his own sword embedded in it. The beast had been part hyena, part lizard, a monstrosity, and it had raked him open from collarbone to biceps, rending his mail as easily as cloth. It had clung to him, its teeth meeting through the flesh of his shoulder, even after he'd skewered it through its barrel chest. He'd twisted his blade, thrust deeper, twisted again. The beast had screamed deep in its throat, but didn't let him go until it died.

Now, as Akiva lay waiting to die, the post-battle silence was split by a roar. He stiffened and clasped his wound tighter. Later, he would wonder why he'd done that. He should have let go, tried to die before they could reach him.

The enemy was stalking the field, killing the wounded. They had taken the day, driven the seraphim back to the fortifications at Morwen Bay, and they had no interest in prisoners. Akiva should have hurried his dying, slipped away in the calm of blood loss, like falling asleep. The enemy would be far less kind.

What made him wait? The hope of killing one more chimaera? But if that was it, why didn't he try to drag himself over to retrieve his sword? He just lay there, holding his wound, living those extra few minutes for no reason that he could fathom.

And then he saw her.

She was just a silhouette at first. Vast bat wings, long ridged gazelle horns as sharp as pikes—the bestial parts of the enemy. Black loathing filled Akiva and he watched her pause beside first one corpse and then the next. She came to the body of the hyena-lizard and stood there a long moment—what was she doing? Death rites?

She turned and prowled toward Akiva.

She came clearer with every step. She was slender, her legs long—lean human thighs that gave way, below the knee, to the sleek taper of gazelle's legs, the fine cloven hooves making her seem to balance on pins. Her wings were folded, her gait both graceful and tense with suppressed power. In one hand she held a crescent-moon blade; another just like it was sheathed at her thigh. With the other hand she raised a long staff that was not a weapon. It was curved like a shepherd's crook, with some-thing silver—a lantern?—suspended from the end.

No, not a lantern. It gave off not light, but smoke.

A few steps, hooves sinking into the sand, then the mist revealed her face to him, and his to her. She stopped abruptly when she saw he was alive. He braced for a snarl, a sudden lunge, and new pain as he was gutted by her blade, but the chi-maera girl didn't move. For a long moment they just looked at each other. She cocked her head to one side, a quizzical, bird-like gesture that spoke not of savagery, but curiosity. There was no snarl on her lips. Her face was solemn.

Unaccountably, she was beautiful.

She took a step closer. He watched her face as she drew nearer. His gaze slipped down her long neck to the ridges of her collarbones. She was finely made, elegant and spare. Her hair was short as swan's down, soft and dark and close as a cap, so the architecture of her face was unobscured; perfect. Black greasepaint made a mask around her eyes, which Akiva could see were large—brown and bright, vivid and sorrowful.

He knew the sorrow was for her fallen comrades and not for him, but he still found himself transfixed by the compassion in her gaze. It made him think that perhaps he had never really looked at a chimaera before. He saw slaves often enough, but they kept their eyes on the ground, and warriors like this he only ever met while dodging a killing blow or dealing one,

269

half-blind with the blood rage of battle. If he ignored the fact of her bloodied blade and her closely fitted black armor, her devilish wings and horns, if he focused just on her face—so unexpectedly lovely—she looked like a girl, a girl who had found a young man dying on the beach.

For a moment, that's what he was. Not a soldier, not anyone's enemy, and the death that was upon him seemed meaningless. That they lived as they did, angels and monsters locked in a volley of killing and dying, dying and killing, seemed an arbitrary choice.

As if they might just as well choose *not* to kill and die.

But no. That was all there was between them. And this girl was here for the same reason he was: to slay the enemy. And that meant *him*.

Why, then, didn't she do it?

She knelt at his side, doing nothing to protect herself from any sudden move he might make. He remembered the knife at his hip. It was small, nothing like her own fantastical double-crescent, but it could kill her. In one motion he could embed it in the soft curve of her throat. Her perfect throat.

He made no move.

He was dream-lost by then. Blood-lost. Gazing up at the face above him, he was beyond wondering whether this was real. It could be a dying dream, or she could be a reaper sent from the next life to cull his soul. The silver censer hung on its crook, exhaling a fume of smoke that was both herbal and sulfurous, and as its scent wafted down to him, Akiva felt a tug, a *lure*. Dizzy, he thought he wouldn't mind following this messenger into the next realm.

He imagined her guiding him by the hand, and with that serene image cradled in his mind, he let go of his wound to reach for her fingers, caught them in his, which were slippery with blood.

Her eyes went wide and she snatched her hand away.

He'd startled her; he hadn't meant to. "I'll go with you," he said, speaking in Chimaera, which he knew enough of to give orders to slaves. It was a rough tongue, a cobbling together of many tribal dialects that the Empire had brought under one roof, and which had been melded over time into a common language. He could scarcely hear his own voice, but she made out his words well enough.

She glanced at her censer, then back at him. "That's not for you," she said, taking it away and planting it in the mud where the breeze would tease the smoke downwind. "I don't think you want to go where I'm going." Even under the animal inflections of the language, her voice was as pretty as a song.

"Death," said Akiva. His life was leaving him fast now that he no longer held his wound. His eyes just wanted to drift closed. "I'm ready."

"Well, I'm not. I hear it's dull, being dead."

She said it lightly, amused, and he peered up at her. Had she just made a joke? She smiled.

Smiled.

He did, too. Amazed, he felt it happening, as if her smile had triggered a reflex in him. "Dull sounds nice," he said, letting his eyes flutter closed. "Maybe I can catch up on my reading."

She muffled a laugh, and Akiva, drifting, began to believe that he *was* dead. It would be less strange than if this were really happening. He could no longer feel his torn shoulder, so he didn't realize that she was touching him until he felt a tight pain. He gasped as his eyes flew open. Had she stabbed him after all?

No. She had winched a tourniquet above his wound. That was the pain. He looked wonderingly up at her.

She said, "I recommend living."

"I'll try."

Then, voices nearby, guttural. Chimaera. The girl froze, held a finger to her lips and breathed, "Shhh."

One last look passed between them. The fog diffused the sun behind her, limning her horns and wings in radiance. Her shorn hair was velvet nap — it looked as soft as a foal's throat — and her horns were oiled, gleaming like polished jet. In spite of her wicked greasepaint mask, her face was *sweet*, her smile *sweet*. Akiva was unfamiliar with sweetness; it pierced him in the center of his chest, in some deep place that had never given any hint before that it was a locus of feeling. It was as new and strange as if an eye had suddenly peeled itself open in the back of his head, seeing in a new dimension.

He wanted to touch her face but held back because his hand was covered with blood, and besides, even his uninjured arm felt so heavy he didn't think he could lift it.

But she had the same impulse. She reached out, hesitated, then trailed the tips of cool, cool fingers down his fever-hot brow, over the ridge of his cheek to rest against the soft pulse point of his throat. She left them there a moment, as if reassuring herself that life still beat in his blood.

Did she feel how his pulse quickened at her touch?

And then, in a bound, she was up and gone. Those long legs with their gazelle hooves and lean long muscles propelled her away through the mist in fluid leaps that were nearly flight, her wings half-folded and held aloft like kites so her descent from each leap was a balletic drift. At a distance, Akiva saw her shadow-shape meet others in the fog—hulking beasts with none of her lithe grace. Voices carried toward him, full of snarls, and hers in their midst, calming. He trusted that she would lead them away from him, and she did.

Akiva lived, and was changed.

"Who tied this tourniquet?" Liraz asked him later, when she found him and got him to safety. He said he didn't know.

He felt as if his life to that point had been spent wandering in a labyrinth, and on the battlefield at Bullfinch he'd finally found its center. His own center—that place where feeling had pulsed up from numbness. He'd never even suspected the place existed until the enemy knelt beside him and saved his life. He remembered her with the softness of a dream, but she was not a dream.

She was real, and she existed in the world. Like animal eyes shining from a nighttime wood, she was out there, a brief shimmer of radiance in the all-encompassing dark.

She was out there.

38

UNGODLY

After Bullfinch, Madrigal's existence — it would be two years before he learned her name — had called to Akiva like a voice adrift in a great silence. As he lay near death in the battle encampment at Morwen Bay, he dreamed again and again that the enemy girl was kneeling over him, smiling. Each time he woke to her absence, to see instead the faces of his kith and kin, they seemed less real than this eidolon who haunted him. Even as Liraz fended off the doctor who wanted to amputate his arm, his mind was called back to the mist-shrouded beach at Bullfinch, to brown eyes and oiled horns and that shock of sweetness.

He had trained to withstand the devil marks, but not this. Against this, he found he had no defense.

Of course, he told no one.

Hazael came to his bedside with his kit of tattoo tools to mark Akiva's hands with his Bullfinch kills. "How many?" he asked, heating up his knife blade to sterilize it.

Akiva had slain six chimaera at Bullfinch, including the hyena monstrosity that had taken him down. Six new ticks would fill out his right hand, which, thanks to Liraz, was still attached to his body. The arm lay useless at his side. Severed nerves and muscles had been reattached; he wouldn't know for some time if it would ever function again.

When Hazael picked up the lifeless hand, knife at the ready, all Akiva could think of was the enemy girl, and how she might end up a black mark on some seraph's knuckle. The thought was unendurable. With his good hand, he wrested his arm from Hazael and was immediately swamped with pain. "None," he gasped. "I didn't kill any."

Hazael squinted. "You did. I was with you against that phalanx of bull centaurs."

But Akiva wouldn't take the marks, and Hazael went away.

Thus, had begun the secret that, over the years, grew into a rift between them, and that, in the skies of the human world, threatened to tear them apart forever.

* * *

When Karou exploded off the bridge, Liraz followed, and Akiva surged up to block her. Their blades clashed. He crossed his two swords close to the hilt and put his strength behind them with a steady pressure that forced his sister back. He kept Hazael in sight, afraid he would pursue Karou, but his brother was still standing on the bridge, staring up at the unimaginable sight of Akiva and Liraz with swords crossed.

Liraz's arms trembled with the effort at holding her

ground—her air—and her wings worked at furious backbeats. Her face was livid, clench-jawed and lurid with striving, and her eyes were so wide that her irises were spots in staring white orbs.

With a banshee wail she threw Akiva off, swung her freed sword in a cyclone around her head, and brought it hacking down.

He blocked it. Its force jarred his bones. She wasn't holding back. The ferocity of her attack shocked him—would she really try to kill him? She hacked again, and he blocked, and Hazael finally came unfrozen and leapt toward them.

"Stop," he cried, aghast. He started to dart in but had to dodge when Liraz swung wild. Akiva parried the blow, knocking her off balance, and she whirled around before fumbling to a hover. She gave him a look that glittered with malice, and instead of coming at him again, she surged upward. Her wings gave off a fireball burst that brought a collective gasp from the onlookers, and then she was speeding in the direction Karou had gone.

The sky gave no hint of Karou, but Akiva didn't doubt that Liraz could track her. He sped after her. Precipitously, the rooftops receded, and humanity with them. There was just the rushing air, the flare of wings, and—he caught up to his sister and grabbed her arm—strife.

She spun on him again, slashing, and their swords rang out, again and again. As in Prague, when Karou had attacked him, Akiva only parried, dodged, and did not return attack.

"Stop!" barked Hazael again, coming up on Akiva and giving him a hard shove that put distance between him and Liraz. They were high above the city now, in airy silence echoing with the ring of steel. "What are you doing?" Hazael demanded in a tone of disbelief. "You two, fighting—"

"I'm not," said Akiva, backing away. "I won't."

"Why not?" hissed Liraz. "You might as well slit my throat as stab me in the back."

"Liraz, I don't want to hurt you—"

She laughed. "You don't want to, but you will if you have to? Is that what you're saying?"

Was it? What would he do to protect Karou? He couldn't harm his sister or brother; he could never live with that. But he couldn't let them hurt Karou, either. How could these be his only two choices?

"Just...forget her," he said. "Please. Just let her go."

The thick emotion in his voice made Liraz's eyes narrow with scorn. Looking at her, Akiva thought that he might as well appeal to a sword as to her. And wasn't that what they were all three bred to be, and all the emperor's other bastards, too? Weapons forged in flesh. Unthinking instruments of age-old enmity.

He couldn't accept that. They were more than that, all of them. He hoped. He took a risk. He sheathed his swords. Her eyes like slashes, Liraz watched in silence.

"At Bullfinch," he said, "you asked who tied my tourniquet."

She waited. Hazael, too.

Akiva thought of Madrigal, remembered the feel of her skin, the surprising smoothness of her leathern wings, and the light of her laughter—so like Karou's laughter—and he recalled what Karou had said to him that morning: If he'd ever known any chimaera, he couldn't dismiss them as monsters.

But he had, both. He had known and loved Madrigal, and still he had become what he had become — the dead-eyed husk that had almost slain Karou on impulse. Grief had grown its ugly blooms in him: hate, vengeance, blindness. The person he was now, Madrigal would have regretted ever saving his life. But in Karou, he had another chance — for peace, that is. Not for happiness, not for him. It was too late for him.

For others, maybe there could still be salvation.

"It was a chimaera," he told his sister and brother. He gulped a breath of air, knowing that this would sound ungodly to them. They had been taught from the cradle that chimaera were vile, crawling things, devils, *animals*. But Madrigal...she had managed to unchain him in an instant from his bigotry, and it was time he tried to do the same. "A chimaera saved my life," he said. "And I fell in love with her."

❧ 39 ❧

Blood Will Out

After Bullfinch, everything changed for Akiva. When he sent Hazael and his tattoo kit away, an idea took hold: When he saw the chimaera girl again, he would be able to tell her that he had not used the life she had given him to kill any more of her kindred.

That he would ever see her again was extravagantly unlikely, but the notion took up residence in his mind — a darting, fugitive thing he couldn't seem to chase away — and he became accustomed to its lurking presence. He grew comfortable with it, and the thing morphed from a wild notion into a *hope* — a sustaining hope, and the one that would change the course of his life: to see the girl again, and thank her. That was all, just thank her. When he imagined the moment, his mind went no further.

It was enough to keep him going.

He wasn't long in Morwen Bay after the battle. The battle

surgeons sent him back to Astrae to see what the healers there could do for him.

Astrae.

Until the Massacre a millennium past, the seraphim had ruled the Empire from Astrae. For three hundred years it had been, by all accounts, the light of the world, the most beautiful city ever built. Palaces, arcades, fountains, all pearl marble quarried in Evorrain, broad boulevards paved in quartz, over-reached by the honey-scented boughs of gilead. It perched above its harbor on striated cliffs, with the emerald Mirea coast as far as the eye could see. Like in Prague, spires pointed to the heavens, one for each of the godstars—the godstars that had ordained seraphim as guardians of the land and all its creatures.

The godstars that had looked on as it all fell into chaos.

At three hundred years, Akiva thought, the citizens of Astrae must have felt that it had always been and would always be. Now, ten centuries later, its golden age seemed like the long-ago blink of some dead god's eye, and little remained of the original city. The enemy had razed it: toppled the towers, burned everything that would catch fire. They would have torn the very stars from the heavens if they could. Such savagery had no precedent in history. At the end of the first day, the magi lay dead, even their youngest apprentices, and their library was swallowed by fire, with every magical text in all of Eretz.

Strategically, it made sense. Seraphim had come to rely so heavily on magic that in the aftermath of the Massacre, with not a single magus left alive, they were very nearly helpless. Any angels who hadn't escaped Astrae were sacrificed on an altar by the light of the full moon, and the seraph emperor, ancestor of Akiva's father, was among them. So many angels had bled out their lives on that altar stone that their blood rolled down the temple steps like monsoon rains and drowned small creatures in the streets.

The beasts held Astrae for centuries, until Joram—Akiva's father—waged an all-out campaign early in his reign and won back all the territory up to the Adelphas Mountains. He had consolidated power and begun to rebuild the Empire, with its heart where, as he said, it belonged: in Astrae.

Where Joram had not made much headway was with magic. With the library burned and the magi dead, the seraphim had been knocked back to the most basic of manipulations, and in all the intervening centuries, they hadn't progressed much beyond them.

Akiva had never given much thought to magic. He was a soldier; his education was limited. He presumed it a mystery for other, brighter minds. But his sojourn in Astrae changed that. He had the time to discover that his mind, soldier's though it was, burned brighter than most, and that he possessed something the would-be magi of Astrae did not. In truth, he had two things they didn't. He had the blood for it, though it took a malicious comment from his father for him to know it. And he had the most critical thing, the crux.

He had pain.

The pain in his shoulder was a constant, and so was his eidolon, the enemy girl, and the two were linked. When his shoulder burned, coming slowly back to life, he couldn't help but think of her fine hands on it, winching the tourniquet that had saved him.

281

The healers of Astrae spurned the drugs of the battle surgeons, which didn't help matters, and they made him use his arm. A slave—chimaera—was employed for the purpose of stretching it to keep the muscles supple, and Akiva was ordered onto the practice field to work his left arm in swordsmanship, in case the right never fully recovered. Against expectation, it did, though the pain did not diminish, and within a few months he was a more formidable swordsman than he had been before. He visited the palace armorer about a set of matched blades, and soon he reigned on the practice field. Fighting two-handed, he drew crowds to the morning bouts, including the emperor himself.

"One of mine?" asked Joram, appraising him.

Akiva had never been in his father's immediate presence. Joram's bastards were legion; he couldn't be expected to know them all. "Yes, my Lord," said Akiva with bowed head. His shoulders still heaved from the exertion of sparring, his right sending out the flares of agony that were just a part of living now.

"Look at me," ordered the emperor.

Akiva did, and saw nothing of himself in the seraph before him. Hazael and Liraz, yes. Their blue eyes came straight from Joram, as did the set of their features. The emperor was fair, his golden hair going to gray, and though broad, he was of modest height and had to look up at Akiva.

His look was sharp. He said, "I remember your mother."

Akiva blinked. He hadn't been expecting that.

"It's the eyes," said the emperor. "They're unforgettable, aren't they?"

It was one of the few things Akiva did remember about his

mother. The rest of her face was a blur, and he'd never even known her name, but he knew that he had her eyes. Joram seemed to be waiting for him to answer, so he acknowledged, "I remember," and felt a tug of loss, as if, by admitting it, he was handing over the one thing he had of her.

"Terrible what happened to her," said Joram.

Akiva went still. He'd had no knowledge of his mother after he was taken from her, as surely the emperor knew. Joram was baiting him, wanting him to ask, *What? What happened to her?* But Akiva didn't ask, only clenched his teeth, and Joram, smiling knives, said, "But what can you expect, really, of Stelians? Savage tribe. Almost as bad as the beasts. Watch that the blood doesn't out, soldier."

And he walked away, leaving Akiva with the burn of his shoulder and a new urgency to know what he had never cared about before: *What blood?*

Could his mother have been Stelian? It made no sense that Joram would have had a Stelian concubine; he had no diplomatic relations with the "savage tribe" of the Far Isles, renegade seraphim who would never have given their women as tribute. How, then, had she come to be there?

The Stelians were known for two things. The first was their fierce independence — they were not part of the Empire, having steadfastly refused, over the centuries, to come into the fold with their seraph kindred.

The second was their sympathy with magic. It was believed, in the deep murk of history, that the first magi had been Stelian, and they were rumored still to practice a rarified level of magic unknown in the rest of Eretz. Joram hated them because he could neither conquer nor infiltrate them, at least not while needing to focus his forces on the Chimaera War. There was no doubt, though, in the gossip that swirled through the capital, of where he would set his sights once the beasts were broken.

As for what had happened to his mother, Akiva never found out. The harem was a closed world, and he couldn't even confirm that there had ever been a Stelian concubine, let alone what had become of her. But for himself, something grew out of his encounter with his father: a sympathy with those strangers of his blood, and a curiosity about magic.

He was in Astrae for more than a year, and besides physical therapy, sparring, and some hours each day in the training camp drilling young soldiers in arms, his time was his own. After that day, he made use of it. He knew about the pain tithe, and thanks to his wound, he now had a constant reservoir of pain to draw on. Observing the magi—to whom he, a brute soldier, was as good as invisible—he learned the fundamental manipulations, starting with summoning. He practiced on bat-crows and hummingbird-moths in the dark of night, directing their flight, lining them up in Vs like winter geese, calling them down to perch on his shoulders, or in his cupped hands.

It was easy; he kept going. He quickly came up against the boundary of the known, which wasn't saying much—what passed for magic in this age was little more than parlor tricks, illusions. And he never fooled himself that he was a magus, or anywhere close, but he was inventive, and unlike the courtly fops who called themselves magi, he didn't have to flog or burn or cut himself to dredge up power—he had it, low and constant. But the real reason he surpassed them was neither his pain nor his inventiveness. It was his motivation.

The idea that had grown from a wild thing into a hope—to see the chimaera girl again—had become a plan.

It had two parts. Only the first was magical: to perfect a glamour that could conceal his wings. There was a manipulation for camouflage, but it was rudimentary, only a kind of "skip" in space that could trick the eye—at a distance—into overlooking the object in question. Invisibility it was not. If he hoped to pass in disguise among the enemy—which was exactly what he hoped—he would have to do better than that.

So he worked at it. It took months. He learned to go into his pain, like it was a place. From within it, things *looked* different—sharp-edged—and felt and sounded different, too, tinny and cool. Pain was like a lens that honed everything, his senses and instincts, and it was there, through relentless trial and repetition, that he did it. He achieved invisibility. It was a triumph that would have garnered him fame and the emperor's highest honors, and it gave him a cold satisfaction to keep it to himself.

Blood will out, he thought. *Father*.

The other part of his plan was language. To master Chimaera, he perched on the roof of the slave barracks and listened to the stories they told by the light of their stinking dungfire. Their tales were unexpectedly rich and beautiful, and, listening, he couldn't help imagining his chimaera girl sitting at a battle campfire somewhere telling the same stories.

His. He caught himself thinking of her as *his,* and it didn't even seem strange.

By the time he was sent back to his regiment at Morwen Bay, he could have used a little more time to perfect his Chimaera accent, but he thought he was basically ready for what came next, in all its bright and shining madness.

🌿 40 🌿

Almost Like Magic

Back then, it had been Madrigal's existence that had called to him across space. Now it was Karou's. Then, Loramendi had been his destination, the caged city of the beasts. Now it was Marrakesh. Once again he left Hazael and Liraz behind, but this time he didn't leave them in ignorance. They knew the truth about him.

What they would do about it, he couldn't guess.

Liraz had called him a traitor, said he made her sick. Hazael had just stared, pale and repulsed.

But they had let him go without bloodshed — his or theirs — and that was the best he had hoped for. Whether they would tell their commander — or even the emperor — come back hunting for him, or cover for him, he couldn't know. He couldn't think about it. Flying over the Mediterranean with the wishbone in his hand, his thoughts belonged to Karou. He imagined her waiting for him at the mad Moroccan square where he'd first locked eyes with her. He could picture her so clearly, down to the way she would keep lifting her hand to her throat, reaching for the wishbone before she remembered, with a fresh pang every time, that she didn't have it.

He had it. Everything it meant, to the past, to the future, was right here in his hand—almost like magic, as Madrigal had told him once.

Until the night that he had finally seen Madrigal again, he hadn't even known what a wishbone was. She wore one on a cord around her neck, so incongruous a thing against her silk gown, her silken skin.

"It's a wishbone," she'd told him, holding it out. "You hook your finger around the spur, like this, and we each make a wish and pull. Whoever gets the bigger piece gets their wish."

"Magic?" Akiva had asked. "What bird does this come from, that its bones make magic?"

"Oh, it's not magic. The wishes don't really come true."

"Then why do it?"

She shrugged. "Hope? Hope can be a powerful force. Maybe there's no actual magic in it, but when you know what you hope for most and hold it like a light within you, you can make things happen, almost like magic."

He was lost in her. The radiance of her eyes kindled something in him that made him aware he had passed his life in a haze of half-living, at best half-feeling. "And what do you hope for most?" he asked, wanting—whatever it was—to give it to her.

She was coy. "You're not supposed to tell. Come, wish with me."

Akiva reached out and hooked one finger around the bone's slender spur. The thing he wished for most was a thing he had never wished for at all, not until he had discovered her. And it came true that night, and many nights after. A brief and shining span of happiness, it was the pivot point around which his whole life spun. Everything he had done since, it had been because he had loved Madrigal, and lost her, and lost himself.

And now? He was flying toward Karou with the truth in his hand, this thing so fragile, "almost like magic."

Almost? Not this time.

This wishbone *seethed* magic. Brimstone's signature was as powerful on it as on the portals that set Akiva's teeth on edge. In the bone was the truth, and with it, the power to make Karou hate him.

And if it were to vanish—such a tiny thing to drop in an ocean—what then? Karou never needed to know anything. He could have her then; he could love her. More to the point, if there were no wishbone, *she* could love *him*.

It was a poisonous thought, and it filled Akiva with self-loathing. He tried to quell it, but the bone taunted him. *She never has to know*, it seemed to say, lying there on his open hand. And the Mediterranean far below, dappled and sun-dazzled and fathoms deep, affirmed it.

She never has to know.

🌿 41 🌿

ALEPH

Karou was exactly where Akiva had imagined her to be, at a cafe table at the edge of the Jemaa el-Fna, and also as he had imagined, she was unquiet in the absence of the wishbone. Once, her fingers would have needed no occupation but the holding of her pencil. Now her sketchbook lay open before her, white pages blinding in the North African sun, and she fidgeted, unfocused, unable to keep her eyes from searching the plaza for Akiva.

He would come, she told herself, and he would bring back the wishbone. He would.

If he was alive.

Would they have harmed him, those other seraphim? It had been two days already. What if . . . ? No. He was alive. To imagine him otherwise . . . Karou's mind couldn't approach it. Absurdly, she kept remembering Kishmish, years ago, gulping down that hummingbird-moth—the stark suddenness of it: alive, not alive. Just like that.

No.

Her thoughts veered away, finding focus on the wishbone. What did it mean, that it had had that effect on Akiva? And... what could he have to tell her that had made him fall to his knees? The mystery of her self took on a dark tint and she felt a shiver of apprehension. She couldn't help remembering Zuzana and Mik, the looks on their faces—stunned and afraid. Of *her.* She had called Zuzana from her airport layover in Casablanca. They had argued.

"What are you doing?" Zuzana had demanded to know. "Let's not regress to the time of mysterious errands, Karou."

There wasn't much point being cagey now, so she'd told her. Zuzana, unsurprisingly, had taken Akiva's line that it was too dangerous, and Brimstone wouldn't want it.

"I want you to take my flat," said Karou. "I already called the landlord. He has a key for you, and it's paid for the rest of—"

"I don't want your stupid flat," Zuzana said. Zuzana, who boarded with a cabbage-cooking elder aunt and joked not infrequently about killing Karou just *for* her flat. "Because *you* live in it. You are not just going to vanish like this, Karou. This isn't some goddamn Narnia book."

There was no reasoning with her. The conversation ended badly, and Karou was left sitting with her phone warm in her hands and no one else to call. It struck her with terrible clarity how few people were in her life. She thought of Esther, her fake grandmother, and that just made her sad, that her mind would default to a stand-in. She almost tossed the phone in the trash right there—she didn't have the charger, anyway—but was very glad the next morning that she hadn't. It vibrated in her pocket at the cafe, on the regs of its juice, and disclosed the message:

*No. Food. Anywhere. Thanks a lot for starving me. *croak expire**

She laughed, and held her face, and even cried a little, and when an old man asked her if she was okay, she wasn't quite sure.

Two days she had been sitting here now; two nights she had tried to sleep in her rented room nearby. She had tracked down Razgut, just to know where he was when she was ready to go, and had left him again, wailing for his gavriel, which she did not give him. She would make his wish for him when the time came to go.

To go. With or without Akiva, with or without her wishbone. How long would she wait?

Two days and two unending nights, and her eyes were darting, hungry. Her heart was gasping, empty. Whatever resistance had been in her, she gave it up. Her hands knew what they wanted: They wanted Akiva, the spark and heat of him. Even in the warmth of the Moroccan spring she was cold, as if the only thing with a chance of warming her was him. On the third morning, walking through the souks to the Jemaa el-Fna, she made a curious purchase.

Fingerless gloves. She saw them in a vendor's stall, densely knit things of striped Berber wool, reinforced with leather at the palms. She bought them and pulled them on. They covered her hamsas entirely, and she couldn't deceive herself that she'd bought them for warmth. She knew what she wanted. She wanted what her hands wanted: to touch Akiva, and not just with her fingertips, and not with caution, and not with fear of causing him pain. She wanted to hold him and be held, in soft perfect unity, like slow-dancing. She wanted to fit herself to him, breathe him, come alive against him, discover him, hold his face as he had held hers, with tenderness.

With *love.*

"It will come, and you will know it," Brimstone had promised her once, and though he had surely never dreamed it would come to her as the enemy, she knew now he hadn't been wrong. She did know it. It was simple and total, like hunger or happiness, and when she looked up from her tea on the third morning and saw Akiva in the square, standing some twenty yards off and looking at her, it thrilled through her like her nerves were channeling starlight. He was safe.

He was here. She rose from her chair.

It struck her, the way he was just standing there at a distance.

And when he came to her, it was with a heavy tread and a closed expression, slowly, reluctantly. Her certainty vanished. She did not reach for him, or even step out from behind the table. All the starlight shrank back up her nerve endings, leaving her cold, and she stared at him — the heavy slowness, the flatness of his look — and wondered if she had imagined everything between them.

"Hi," she said in a small voice, hesitant and with an uplift of hope that she might be misreading him, that he might still mirror back at her the starburst that the sight of him had ignited in her. It was what she had always wanted and thought that she'd found: someone who was *for her*, as she was for him, whose blood and butterflies sang to hers and answered them, note for note.

But Akiva answered nothing. He gave a tight nod and made no move to come closer.

"You're okay," she said, and her voice didn't begin to convey her gladness.

"You waited," he said.

"I...I said I would."

"As long as you could."

Was he bitter that she hadn't promised? Karou wanted to tell him that she hadn't known then what she knew now—that "as long as she could" was a long time indeed, and that she felt as if she'd been waiting for him all her life. But she was silenced by his closed expression.

He thrust out his hand and said, "Here," and there was her wishbone, dangling by its cord.

She took it, managing a whispered *thank you* as she slipped it over her head. It settled back into its place at the base of her throat.

"I brought these, too," Akiva said, and placed on the table the case that held her crescent-moon knives. "You'll need them."

It sounded hard, almost like a threat. Karou just stood there, blinking back tears.

"Do you still want to know who you are?" Akiva asked. He wasn't even looking at her. He was looking past her, at nothing.

"Of course I do," she said, though it wasn't what she had been thinking. What she wanted right now was to go back in time, to Prague. She had believed then, with a certainty that was both thrill and refuge, that Akiva was coming back from some dark night of the soul *for her*. Now it was like he was dead again, and though she had her wishbone back, and though she was going to learn, finally, the answer to the question at the core of her being, she felt dead, too.

"What happened?" she asked. "With the others?"

He ignored the question. "Is there somewhere we can go?"

"Go?"

Akiva gestured to the crowds in the square, the vendors building their pyramids of oranges, the tourists toting cameras and parcels of shopping. "You'll want to be alone for this," he said.

"What...what do you have to tell me that I'll want to be alone to hear it?"

"I'm not going to tell you anything." Akiva had been gazing past her, unfocused, this whole time, so that she'd begun to feel like some kind of blur, but he fixed his eyes on her now. Their brilliance was like the sun in topaz, and she saw, before he looked away again, the bare glint of a yearning so deep it hurt to behold. Her heart leapt.

"We're going to break the wishbone," he said.

* * *

And then she would know everything, and she would hate him. Akiva was trying to prepare himself for the way she would look at him once she understood. He had watched her from the square for a handful of seconds before she looked up, and he witnessed the way her face was transformed by the sight of

295

him—from anxious, lost expectancy, to...light. It was as if she had emitted a pulse of radiation that reached him even where he stood, and it bathed him and it burned him.

All that he didn't deserve and could never have was in that instant. All he wanted now was to fold her against him, lose his hands in her hair—which was clean and combed straight as rivers over her shoulders—lose himself in the fragrance and softness of her.

He remembered a story Madrigal had told him once: the human tale of the golem. It was a thing shaped of clay in the form of a man, brought to life by carving the symbol *aleph* into its brow. Aleph was the first letter of an ancestral human alphabet, and the first letter of the Hebrew word *truth*; it was the beginning. Watching Karou rise to her feet, radiant in a fall of lapis hair, in a woven dress the color of tangerines, with a loop of silver beads at her throat and a look of joy and relief and... *love*...on her beautiful face, Akiva knew that she was his aleph, his truth and beginning. His soul.

His wing joints ached with the desire to beat, once, and propel him to her, but instead he walked, heavy and heartsick. His arms felt banded by iron, keeping them from reaching for her. The way the light went out of her at the cold manner of his approach, the hesitation and hope in her voice—it was killing him by degrees. It was better this way. If he gave in and let himself have what he wanted, she would only hate him more once she knew what he really was. So he held himself remote, aching, preparing for the moment he knew must come.

"Break it?" Karou asked now, looking at the wishbone in surprise. "Brimstone never did—"

"It wasn't his," said Akiva. "It was never his. He was just keeping it. For you."

He hadn't been able to drop it in the sea. That he had even considered it made him sick with himself—more evidence of his unworthiness of her. She deserved to know everything, in all its heartbreak and brutality, and if he was right about the wishbone, she very soon would.

She seemed to sense something of the magnitude of the moment. "Akiva," she whispered. "What is it?"

And when she looked at him with her bird-black eyes, frightened and imploring, he had to turn away again, so powerful was the longing that twisted through him. Not touching her in that moment was one of the hardest things he had ever done.

* * *

And it might have gone on between them in that terrible, false way, but Karou had seen what she had seen, and felt it, too—Akiva's yearning, meeting her own in a deep place—and when he turned away she experienced a sudden unspooling, like the snap of a cable and all her restraints giving way, and she couldn't bear it anymore. She reached for him. Her half-gloved hand, hamsa covered, took his arm, gently and full against his skin, and turned him back to her. She stepped close, tipping back her head to gaze up at him, and took his other arm.

"Akiva," she murmured, her tone no longer fearful, but low and ardent and sweet. "What is it?" Her hands climbed him, over the steel of his arms and shoulders, up ramps of trapezius to his throat, his rough-smooth jaw, and then her fingertips were on his lips, so soft by comparison. She felt them tremble. "Akiva," she repeated. "Akiva. *Akiva.*" She seemed to be saying, *Enough of this; stop pretending.*

And so, with a shudder, he did. He dropped the pretense, and dropped his head, so his brow came to rest against the sun-warmed top of hers. His arms went around her and drew her in, and Karou and Akiva were like two matches struck against each other to flare starlight. With a sigh, she softened, and it was pure homecoming to melt against him and rest. She felt the coarseness of his unshaven throat at her cheek as he tested, against his own, the perfect water-smoothness of her hair. They stood like that for a long time, and they were quiet but their blood and nerves and butterflies were not—they were rampantly alive, rushing and thrumming in a wild and perfect melody, matched note for note.

The wishbone, small but sharp, was trapped between them.

🌿 42 🌿

ACHE AND SALT AND ALLNESS

"In here," Karou said, leading Akiva to a sky-blue door set in a dusty wall. Their fingers were laced together. They couldn't not touch, and guiding him through the medina, Karou had felt like she was floating. They might have hurried, but instead they drifted, pausing to watch a carpet-maker, to peer into a basket of puppies, to test the points of ornamental daggers with their fingertips — anything but haste.

But as slowly as they went, they still arrived at their destination. Akiva followed Karou down a dark passage, where they were spilled into the light of a courtyard, a hidden world open only to the sky. It was fringed with date palms and brilliant with *zelij* tiles, a fountain plashing in its center. A balcony ran around the second story, and Karou's room was up a twist of stairs. It was bigger than her flat, with a high, timbered ceiling. The walls were vermillion *tadelakt* with a deep, earthen glow, and a Berber blanket on the bed spelled out some mysterious blessing in a language of symbols.

Akiva closed the door and let go of Karou's hand, and the moment that she had been pushing ahead of them, forestalling— the breaking of the wishbone . . . It was here.

This was it.

This was it.

Akiva paced away from her, looked out a window, raised his hands and raked his fingers through his hair in a gesture that was becoming familiar, then turned back to her. "Are you ready, Karou?"

No.

Suddenly, *no*. She was not ready. Panic, like a chaos of wings in her rib cage. "We can wait," she said with artificial brightness. "We don't want to fly until nightfall anyway." The plan was to fetch Razgut once the sun went down, and to fly with him under cover of darkness to the portal, wherever it might be.

Akiva came back toward her, a few halting steps, and stopped just out of reach. "We could wait," he agreed, seeming lured by the idea. Then he added, very softly, "But it won't get any easier."

"You'd tell me, wouldn't you, if it was something awful?"

He came closer, reached up and stroked her hair, once, slowly. Feline, she leaned into his touch. He said, "You don't have to be afraid, Karou. How could it be awful? It's *you*. You can only be beautiful."

A shy smile tugged at her lips. She took a breath and said with resolve, "Okay then. Should I, um, sit down?"

"If you like."

She went to the bed and climbed to its center, curling her legs under her and tucking down the hem of her orange dress, which she'd bought in the souk with the thought of Akiva seeing her in it. She had bought more practical apparel, too, for the journey and whatever might come after. It was packed in a new bag and ready to go, along with such mundane necessaries as she'd had to leave Prague without, having fled town so abruptly. She was glad Akiva had brought her knives — glad to have them, that is, and afraid of needing them.

He sat facing her, his legs long and easy, shoulders rolled forward in a way that accentuated their breadth.

It was then that Karou had another flash, a split in the surface of time, and a glimpse, within, of Akiva. He was sitting just like this, his shoulders heavy and relaxed in just that way, but ... they were *bare*, as was his chest, and he was all tawny muscle, the right shoulder a snarl of scar tissue. Again, on his face, the smile that hurt with its beauty. Again, an instant and it was gone.

She blinked, cocked her head, and murmured, "*Oh.*"

"What?" Akiva asked.

"Sometimes I think I see you, in another time or something. ... I don't know." She shook her head and waved it off. "Your shoulder. What happened to it?"

He touched it, watching her intently. "What did you see?"

She blushed. There had been something so sensual about that moment, him sitting there shirtless and happy. She said only, "You ... smiling. I haven't seen you smile like that, not really."

"It's been a long time."

"I wish you would," she said. "For me."

He didn't. Pain flashed over his face and he looked down at his knuckles and then back up at her. "Come here," he said, and reached out, easing the wishbone's cord up and over her head. He hooked a finger around it. "Like this."

She didn't take it. She said in a rush, "Whatever happens, we don't have to be enemies. Not if we don't want to be. It's up to us, isn't it?"

"It will be up to *you*," he said.

"But I already know—"

He shook his head, sorrowful. "You can't know. You can't know until you know."

She let out an exasperated breath. "You sound like Brimstone," she muttered, and set about composing herself. And then, finally, she lifted her hand to slip her pinkie around the wishbone's free spur. Her knuckle came to rest against Akiva's, and even that small contact kicked off an effervescence all through her.

Now, all they had to do was pull. Karou waited a beat, thinking Akiva would lead, but then she thought he was waiting for her. She checked his eyes—they were on hers, searing—and tensed her hand. The only way to do it was to do it. She started to pull.

This time, it was Akiva who jerked his hand away. "Wait," he said. "Wait."

He reached for her face, and Karou covered his hand with hers, pressing it to her cheek.

He said, "I want you to know…" He swallowed. "I need you to know that I was drawn to you—to *you*, Karou—before the

302

wishbone. Before I knew, and I think...I think I would always find you, no matter how you were hidden." He was focused on her with extraordinary intensity. "Your soul sings to mine. My soul is yours, and it always will be, in any world. No matter what happens—" His voice cracked, and he took a breath. "I need you to remember that I love you."

Love. Karou felt bathed in light. The cherished word leapt to her own lips to answer him, but he beseeched her, "Tell me you'll remember. Promise me."

Here was a promise she *could* make, and did. Akiva fell silent, and Karou, sitting forward, breathless, thought that that was all—that he would just say something like that and then not kiss her. Which was absurd, and she would have protested had it come to that, but it did not.

One of his hands was already at her cheek; he lifted the other. He cradled her face in his hands, and then it was as smooth as inevitability: a gliding together. His mouth brushed hers. A dip, a touch like a whisper—a gentle, gentle grazing of Akiva's full lower lip across both of Karou's in an upward lilt, and then there was space between them again, so small a space, their faces so close. They breathed each other's breath as the pull gathered between and around and in them, astral, and then the space was gone again, and all there was was the kiss.

Sweet and warm and trembling.

Soft and hard and deepening.

Mint on Karou's breath, salt on Akiva's skin.

His hands in her hair, plunged to the wrists like it was water; her palms at his chest, the wishbone forgotten in the discovery of his heartbeat.

Sweetness gave way to something else. Pulse. Pleasure. What overwhelmed Karou was the *realness*, the deep physical *trueness* of Akiva—salt and musk and muscle, flame and flesh and heartbeat—the feeling of *allness*. The taste of him and the feel of him against her lips—his mouth and then his jaw, his neck and the soft place beneath his ear, and how he shivered when she kissed him there, and somehow her hands slipped under his shirt and up, so that only her half gloves were between her hands and his chest. Her fingertips danced over him and he shook and crushed her to him and the kiss was so much more than a kiss now.

It was Karou who leaned back, drawing him down with her, over her, and the feel of all of him against all of her was total and burning and…*familiar*, too, and she was herself but not herself, arching into him with a soft animal mewl.

And Akiva broke away.

It was quick as shattering—a lurch and he was up, leaving behind the jagged edges of the moment. Karou sat up fast. She didn't know where her breath had gone. Her dress was bunched at her thighs; the wishbone lay abandoned on the blanket, and Akiva stood at the foot of the bed, faced away from her with his hands on his hips and his head lowered. His breathing matched hers in rhythm, even now. Karou sat silent, overcome by the power of what had possessed her. She had never felt anything like it. With space between them now, she was chastened— what had made her take things so far?—but she also wanted it back, the ache and salt and allness of it.

"I'm sorry," said Akiva, strained.

"No, it was me, and it's all right. Akiva, I love you, too—"

"It's not all right," he said, turning back, his tiger eyes violently ablaze. "It's not all right, Karou. I didn't mean for that to happen. I don't want you to hate me more than you already—"

"*Hate* you? How could I ever—"

"Karou," he said, cutting her short. "You have to know the truth, and you have to know it *now*. We have to break the wishbone."

* * *

And so, at last, they did.

❧ 43 ❧

Snap

Such a little thing, and brittle, and the sound it made: a sharp, clean *snap*.

44

Whole

Snap.

Rushing, like wind through a door, and Karou was the door, and the wind was coming home, and she was also the wind. She was all: wind and home and door.

She rushed into herself and was filled.

She let herself in and was full.

She closed again. The wind settled. It was as simple as that.

* * *

She was whole.

🌿 45 🌿

MADRIGAL

She is a child.

She is flying. The air is thin and miserly to breathe, and the world lies so far below that even the moons, playing chase across the sky, are seen from above, like the shining crowns of children's heads.

* * *

She is no longer a child.

She slips down from the sky, through the boughs of requiem trees. It is dark, and the grove is alive with the *hish-hish* of evangelines, night-loving serpent-birds that drink the requiem blooms. They're drawn to her—*hish-hish*—and dart around her horns, stirring the blossoms so pollen sifts down, golden, and settles on her shoulders.

* * *

Later, it will numb her lover's lips as he drinks her in.

* * *

She is in battle. Seraphim plummet from the sky, trailing fire.

* * *

She is in love. It is bright within her, like a swallowed star.

* * *

She mounts a scaffold. A thousand-thousand faces stare at her, but she sees only one.

* * *

She kneels on the battlefield beside a dying angel.

* * *

Wings enfold her. Skin like fever, love like burning.

* * *

She mounts the scaffold. Her hands are tied behind her, her wings pinioned. A thousand-thousand faces stare; feet stamp, hooves; voices shriek and jeer, but one rises above them all. It is Akiva's. It is a scream to scour ghosts from their nests.

* * *

She is Madrigal Kirin, who dared imagine a new way of living.

* * *

The blade is a great and shining thing, like a falling moon. It is sudden —

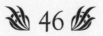 46

SUDDEN

Karou gasped. Her hands flew to her neck and wrapped around it, and it was intact.

She looked at Akiva and blinked, and when she breathed his name, there was a new richness in her voice, an infusion of wonder and love and entreaty that made it seem to rise out of time. As it did. "Akiva," she breathed with the fullness of her self.

With longing, with anguish, he watched her, and waited.

She dropped her hands from her neck and they trembled as she stripped off her gloves to reveal her palms. She stared at them.

They stared back.

They stared back — two flat indigo eyes — and she understood what Brimstone had done.

* * *

She finally understood everything.

Once upon a time,
there were two moons, who were sisters.

Nitid was the goddess of tears and life,
and the sky was hers.
No one worshipped Ellai but secret lovers.

🌿 47 🌿

EVANESCENCE

Madrigal ascended the scaffold. Her hands were tied behind her, her wings pinioned so she couldn't fly away. It was an unnecessary precaution: Overhead arched the iron bars of the Cage. The bars were there to keep seraphim *out*, not chimaera *in*, but today they would have served that purpose. Madrigal was not going anywhere but to her death.

"That is unnecessary," Brimstone had objected when Thiago ordered the pinion. His voice had come out as a scraping almost too low to hear, like something being dragged across the ground.

Thiago, the White Wolf, the general, the Warlord's son and right hand, had ignored him. He knew it was unnecessary. He wanted to humiliate her. Madrigal's death wasn't enough for him. He wanted her abject, penitent. He wanted her on her knees.

He would be disappointed. He could bind her hands and wings, he could force her to her knees, and he could watch her die, but it was not in his power to make her repent.

She was not sorry for what she had done.

On the palace balcony, the Warlord sat in state. He had the head of a stag, his antlers tipped in gold. Thiago was in his place at his father's side. The seat at the Warlord's left hand belonged to Brimstone, and was empty.

A thousand-thousand eyes were on Madrigal, and the cacophony of the crowd was sharpening to something dark, the voices cresting to jeers. Feet stamped, thunderous. There had not been an execution in the plaza in living memory, but those gathered knew what to do, as if hate were an atavism just waiting to resurface.

A shrieked accusation: "Angel-lover!"

Some in the crowd were stricken, uncertain. Madrigal was a beauty, a joy—could she really have done this unthinkable thing?

And then Akiva was brought out. It was Thiago's order that he be forced to watch. The guards knocked him to his knees on a platform opposite hers, from which his view would be unobscured. Even bloodied and shackled and weak from torture, he was glorious. His wings flared radiant; his eyes were fire, and they were fierce, and fixed on her, and Madrigal was filled with a warmth of memories and tenderness, and with sharp regret that her body would never again know his, her mouth never again meet his, that their dreams would never come to their fruition.

Her eyes filled with tears. She smiled across space to him, and it was a look of such unmistakable love that no one watching could continue to doubt her guilt.

Madrigal Kirin was guilty of treason—of loving the enemy—sentenced to death and worse, a sentence that had not been handed down for hundreds of years: evanescence.

Unmaking.

She was alone on the scaffold with the hooded executioner. Head held high, she stepped toward the block and sank to her knees, and it was then that Akiva started to scream. His voice soared over the pandemonium—a scream to scour the souls of all gathered, a sound to drive ghosts from their nests.

It drilled through Madrigal's heart, and she yearned to gather him in her arms. She knew Thiago wanted her to break and scream and beg, but she wouldn't. There was no point. There was not the slightest hope of life. Not for her.

One last look to her love, and she laid her head down on the block. It was black rock, like everything in Loramendi, and it was hot as an anvil against her cheek. Akiva screamed, and Madrigal's heart answered it. Her pulse raced—she was about to *die*—but she kept calm. She had a plan, and it was what she held on to as the executioner raised his blade—a great and shining thing, like a falling moon—because she had work ahead of her, and she couldn't afford to lose her focus. She wasn't finished yet.

After she died, she was going to save Akiva's life.

❧ 48 ❧

PURE

Madrigal Kirin was Madrigal *of the* Kirin, one of the last winged tribes of the Adelphas Mountains. The Adelphas were the natural bastion between the Seraph Empire and the free holdings—the defended chimaera territory—and it had been centuries since anyone had dwelt safely in their peaks. The Kirin, flash-fast and superb archers, lasted longer than most. They were annihilated only a decade ago, when Madrigal was a child. She grew up in Loramendi, a child of towers and rooftops, not mountains.

Loramendi—the Cage, the Black Fortress, the Warlord's Nest—was home to some million chimaera, creatures of all aspects who would never, but for the seraphim, have lived together or fought side by side, or even spoken the same language. Once, the races had been scattered, isolated, sometimes trading with one another, sometimes skirmishing—a Kirin like Madrigal having no more in common with an Anolis from

Iximi, for example, than a wolf did with a tiger—but the Empire had changed all that. In naming themselves the world's keepers, the angels had given the creatures of the land a common enemy, and now, centuries into their struggle, they shared heritage and language, history, heroes, a cause. They were a nation—of which the Warlord was leader, and Loramendi capital.

It was a port city, its broad harbor filled with warships, fishing vessels, and a stout trade fleet. Ripples in the surface of the water gave evidence of amphibious creatures who, part of the alliance, escorted the ships and fought on their side. The city itself, within the massive black walls and bars of the fortress, was shared by a multifarious population, and though they had been stirred together over the centuries, still they tended to settle in neighborhoods like with like, or near enough, and a caste system prevailed, based on aspect.

Madrigal was of high-human aspect, as was said of races with the head and torso of man or woman. Her horns were a gazelle's, black and ridged, flowing up off her brow and back in a scimitar sweep. Her legs shifted at the knees from flesh to fur, the gazelle portion giving them an elegant, exaggerated length, so that when she stood to her full height she was nearly six feet, not including horns, and an undue portion of that was leg. She was slender as a stem. Her brown eyes, spaced wide, were as large and glistening as a deer's but with none of a deer's vacantness. They were keen and immediate and intelligent, leaping like sparks. Her face was oval, smooth and fair, her mouth generous and mobile, made for smiling.

By anyone's measure, she was beautiful, though she made as

little as possible of her beauty, keeping her dark hair short as fur and wearing no paint or ornament. It didn't matter. She was beautiful, and beauty would be noticed.

Thiago had noticed.

❖ ❖ ❖

Madrigal was hiding, though she would deny it if accused. She was on the roof of the north barracks, stretched out on her back like she'd fallen from the sky. Or, not the sky. If she had fallen from the sky, she would have landed on iron bars. She was within the Cage, on a rooftop, her wings splayed wide on either side of her.

All around, she felt the manic rhythms of the city, and heard and smelled them, too—excitement, preparations. Meat roasting, instruments being tuned. A firework test fizzled past like a misbegotten angel. She should have been preparing, too. Instead she lay on her back, hiding. She wasn't dressed for festivity, but in her usual soldier's leathers—breeches that fit like a skin to the knee, and a vest that laced in the back, accommodating wings. Her blades, shaped in homage to the sister moons, were at her sides. She looked relaxed, even limp, but her stomach was churning, her hands clasped in fists.

The moon wasn't helping. Though the sun was out—it was full, effulgent afternoon—Nitid had already appeared in the sky, as if Madrigal actually needed a sign. Nitid was the bright moon, the elder sister, and there had been a belief among the Kirin that when Nitid rose early it meant she was eager, and that something was going to happen. Well, this evening some-

320

thing was certainly going to happen, but Madrigal did not yet know what.

It was up to her. Taut within her, her unmade decision felt like a bow strung too tight.

A shadow, a wing-stirred wind, and her sister Chiro was sweeping down to land beside her. "Here you are," she said. "Hiding."

"I'm not—" Madrigal started to protest, but Chiro wasn't hearing it.

"Get up." She kicked Madrigal's hooves. "Up up up. I've come to take you to the baths."

"Baths? Are you trying to tell me something?" Madrigal sniffed herself. "I'm almost sure I don't smell."

"Maybe not, but between *shining cleanliness* and *not smelling*, there is a vast gray area."

Like Madrigal, Chiro had bat wings; unlike her, she was of creature aspect, with the head of a jackal. They were not blood sisters. When Madrigal was orphaned by the slave raid that claimed her tribe, the survivors had come to Loramendi—a handful of elders with the few babes they'd managed to hide in the caves, and Madrigal. She was seven, and had not been taken only because she wasn't there. She'd been up the peak gathering the shed skins of air elementals from their abandoned nests, and had returned to ruin, corpses, loss. Her parents were among the taken, not the dead, and for a long time she had dreamed she would find them and set them free, but the Empire was vast, and swallowed its slaves whole, and it got harder to hold on to that dream as she grew up.

In Loramendi, Chiro's family, of the desert Sab race, had been chosen to foster her chiefly because, being winged, they could keep up with her. She and Chiro had grown up side by side, as good as sisters in all but blood.

Chiro's haunches were cat, caracal to be precise, and when she melted to a crouch beside Madrigal, her pose was sphinx-like. "For the ball," she said, "I would hope that you would aspire to *shining cleanliness*."

Madrigal sighed. "The ball."

"You did not forget," said Chiro. "Don't pretend you did."

She was right, of course. Madrigal had not forgotten. How could she?

"Up." Chiro kicked her feet again. "Up up up."

"Stop it," muttered Madrigal, staying where she was and halfheartedly kicking back.

Chiro said, "Tell me you've at least got a dress and a mask."

"When would I have gotten a dress and a mask? I've only been back from Ezeret for—"

"For *a week*, which is plenty of time. Honestly, Mad, it's not like this is just another ball."

Exactly, Madrigal thought. If it were, she wouldn't be hiding on the roof, trying to block out the thing that loomed over her, that sent her heartbeat skittering like scorpion-mice whenever she thought of it. She would be getting ready, excited for the biggest festival of the year: the Warlord's birthday.

"Thiago will be looking at you," Chiro said, as if it could possibly have slipped her mind.

"*Leering*, you mean." Leering, peering, licking his teeth, and waiting for a gesture.

"As you deserve to be leered at. Come on, it's *Thiago*. Don't tell me it doesn't excite you."

322

Did it? The general Thiago — "the White Wolf" — was a force of nature, brilliant and deadly, bane of angels and architect of impossible victories. He was also beautiful, and Madrigal's flesh was ever unquiet around him, though she couldn't exactly tell if it was arousal or fear. He had let it be known he was ready to marry again, and who it was he favored: *her*. His attention made her feel warm and skittish, pliant and inconsequential and at the same time rebellious, as if his overwhelming presence was something that needed to be worked against, lest she lose herself in the grand, consuming shadow of him.

It was left to her to encourage his suit or not. It wasn't romantic, but she couldn't say that it wasn't exhilarating.

Thiago was powerful and as perfectly muscled as a statue, of high-human aspect, with legs that changed at the knees not to antelope legs as her own did, but to the huge padded paws of a wolf, covered in silken white fur. His hair was silken white too, though his face was young, and Madrigal had once glimpsed his chest, through a gap in the curtain of his campaign tent, and knew it, also, was furred white.

She'd been striding past as a steward rushed out, and she'd seen the general being suited in his armor. Flanked by attendants, his arms outstretched in the moment before his leather chestplate was fitted into place, his torso was a stunning V of masculine power, narrowing to slim hips, breeches clinging low beneath the ridges of perfect abdominal muscles. It was only a glimpse, but the image of him half-clad had stayed in Madrigal's mind ever since. A whisper of a thrill came over her at the thought of him.

"Well, maybe a *little* excited," she admitted, and Chiro

323

giggled. The girlish sound struck a false note, and Madrigal thought with a pang that her sister was jealous. It made her more sensible of the honor of being Thiago's choice. He could have anyone he wanted, and he wanted her.

But did *she* want *him*? If she did, truly, wouldn't it be easy? Wouldn't she be at the baths already, getting perfumed and oiled and daydreaming of his touch? A small shudder went through her. She told herself it was nerves.

"What do you think he would do if... if I rejected him?" she ventured.

Chiro was scandalized. "Reject him? You must be feverish." She touched Madrigal's brow. "Have you eaten today? Are you *drunk*?"

"Oh, stop," said Madrigal, pushing Chiro's hand away. "It's just... I mean, can you picture, you know... *being* with him?" When Madrigal pictured it, she imagined Thiago heavy and breathing and... *biting*; it made her want to back into a corner. But then, she didn't have much to go on by way of experience; maybe she was simply nervous, and altogether wrong about him.

"Why would *I* imagine it?" asked Chiro. "It's not like he'd have *me*." There was no detectable bitterness in her voice. If anything, it was a touch too bright.

She meant, of course, her aspect—chimaera races did intermarry, though such unions were restricted by aspect—but there was more to it than that. Even if she were high-human, Chiro would not satisfy Thiago's other criterion. That one was not a matter of caste. It was his own fetish, and it was Madrigal's luck—good luck or bad, she hadn't yet decided—to qualify. Unlike Chiro's, her own hands were not marked by the hamsas, with all that they signified. She had never awakened on a stone table to the lingering scent of revenant smoke. Her palms were blank.

She was still "pure."

"It's such hypocrisy," she said. "His fetish for purity. He isn't pure himself! He isn't even—"

Chiro cut her off. "Yes, well, he's Thiago, isn't he? He can be whoever he wants. Unlike some of us." There was a barb in that, directed at Madrigal, which accomplished what all her kicking had not. Madrigal sat up abruptly.

"*Some of us*," she replied, "should learn to appreciate what they have. Brimstone said—"

"Oh, Brimstone said, Brimstone said. Has the almighty Brimstone deigned to give you any advice about Thiago?"

"No," said Madrigal. "He has not."

She supposed Brimstone must know that Thiago was courting her, if you could call it that, but he hadn't brought it up, and she was glad. There was a sanctity in Brimstone's presence, a purity of purpose possessed by no one else. His every breath was devoted to his work, his brilliant, beautiful, and terrible work. The underground cathedral, the shop with its dust-laden air pervaded by the whispering vibrations of thousands of teeth; not least its tantalizing doorway, and the world to which it led. It was, all of it, a fascination to Madrigal.

She spent as much of her free time with Brimstone as she could get away with. It had taken her years of badgering, but she had actually succeeded in getting him to teach her—a first for him—and she felt far more pride in his trust than she did in Thiago's lust.

325

Chiro said, "Well, maybe you should ask him, if you really can't decide what to do."

"I'm not going to ask him," said Madrigal, irritated. "I'll deal with this myself."

"*Deal* with it? Poor you with your problems. Not everyone gets such a chance, Madrigal. To be Thiago's wife? To trade in leathers for silks, and barracks for a palace, to be safe, to be loved, to have status, to bear children and grow old..." Chiro's voice was shaking, and Madrigal knew what she was going to say next. She wished she wouldn't; she was already ashamed. Her problem was no problem at all, not to Chiro, who wore the hamsas.

Chiro, who knew what if felt like to die.

Chiro's hand went with a flutter to her heart, where a seraph arrow had pierced her in the siege of Kalamet last year, and killed her. She said, "Mad, you have a chance to grow old in the skin you were born in. Some of us have only more death to look forward to. Death, death, and death."

Madrigal looked at her own bare palms and said, "I know."

🌿 49 🌿

Teeth

It was the secret at the core of the chimaera resistance, the thing that plagued angels, kept them awake at night, strummed at their minds and clawed at their souls. It was the answer to the mystery of beast armies that, like nightmares, kept coming and coming, never diminishing, no matter how many of them the seraphim slaughtered.

When Chiro took the arrow at Kalamet a year ago, Madrigal was at her side. She held her while she died, blood frothing at her sharp dog teeth as she kicked and jerked and finally fell still. Madrigal did what she had trained to do, and what she had done many times before, though never for so close a friend.

With steady hands, she lit the incense in the thurible that hung, lantern-like, from the end of her gleaning staff—the long, curved crook that chimaera soldiers carried strapped to their backs—and she waited as the smoke wreathed around Chiro. Arrows rained down, profuse and dangerously near, but she didn't leave until it was done. Two minutes to be certain; that was the standard. Two minutes felt like two hours in the thickness of arrows, but Madrigal didn't retreat. There might not be another chance. A furious seraph sally was driving them back from the Kalamet wall. She could drag Chiro's body with her, or she could complete the gleaning and leave it behind.

What was not an option was to leave it with Chiro's soul trapped in it.

When Madrigal did finally fall back, she took her foster sister's soul with her, safe within her thurible, just one of many souls she would glean that day. The bodies were left to rot. Bodies were just bodies, just things.

Back in Loramendi, Brimstone would already be making new ones.

* * *

Brimstone was a resurrectionist.

He didn't breathe life back into the torn bodies of the battle-slain; he *made* bodies. This was the magic wrought in the cathedral under the earth. Out of the merest relics—teeth— Brimstone conjured new bodies in which to sleeve the souls of slain warriors. In this way, the chimaera army held up, year after year, against the superior might of the angels.

Without him, and without teeth, the chimaera would fold. It wasn't even a question. They would fall.

"This is for Chiro," Madrigal had said, handing Brimstone a necklace of teeth. Human, bat, caracal, and jackal. She had labored over it for hours, neither sleeping nor eating since her return from Kalamet. Her eyelids were lead weights. She had handled every jackal tooth in the jar and listened to each until she was certain she had the most favorable—the cleanest, smoothest, sharpest, strongest. The same with the other teeth, and the gems strung with them: jade for grace, diamonds for strength and beauty. Diamonds were a luxury not usually accorded a common soldier, but Madrigal had used them defiantly, and Brimstone let her.

He needed only hold the necklace for a moment to see that it was correct. As he had taught her, she had strung teeth and gems in careful configuration for the conjuring of a body. If they were strung in a different order, the body would manifest accordingly: bat head, perhaps, instead of jackal, human legs instead of caracal. It was part recipe and part intuition, and Madrigal was certain this necklace was perfect.

Resurrected, Chiro would look almost exactly as she had in her original flesh.

"Well done," Brimstone said, and then he did something rare: He touched her. One big hand came to rest briefly on the back of her neck before he turned away.

She blushed, proud; Issa saw and smiled. A "well done" from Brimstone was uncommon enough; the touch was something special. Everything between the two of them was uncommon, really, and hard-won on Madrigal's part.

Brimstone was a hermit, rarely seen outside his domain in Loramendi's west tower. When he did make an appearance, it was at the left hand of the Warlord, and he inspired equal reverence, though of a different sort. The two of them were living myths, almost gods. It was they, after all, who had orchestrated the uprising in Astrae that left their angel masters dead in lakes of blood, and the survivors foundering for years to come as the chimaera found their footing as a people and gouged huge swaths of land back from the Empire to establish the free holdings.

The Warlord's role was clear—he had been the general, the face and voice of the rebellion, and he was beloved as the father of the allied races. But Brimstone's part in things was shadowier, and his fearsome persona rendered him a figure of mystery and speculation, rather than adulation. He was the subject of many imaginative rumors—some of which hit on the truth, others nowhere near.

He did not, for example, eat humans.

He *did* have a doorway to their world, as Madrigal had occasion to learn firsthand when, at the age of ten, she was assigned to be his page.

The youth mistress selected her because of her wings; pure chance. She might as easily have chosen Chiro, but she didn't. She chose Madrigal, three years an orphan, skinny and inquisitive and lonely, and sent her off with an abstracted command to do as she was told, and keep quiet about what she learned.

What was she going to learn? The secrecy of it at once set young Madrigal's mind on fire, and it was with wide eyes and jitters that she presented herself in the west tower, to be ushered

330

into the shop by a sweet-faced Naja woman—Issa—and offered tea. She accepted it but didn't drink, so preoccupied was she with staring at everything: Brimstone, for one thing, bigger up close than she had imagined from her few distant glimpses of him. He hulked behind his desk, ignoring her. In the shadows, his tufted tail switched like a cat's, making her nervous. She looked around at the shelves and dusty books; she looked at the broad door on its scrollwork bronze hinges that maybe, just maybe, opened to another world; and, of course, she looked at the teeth.

That was unexpected. Everywhere, the *clitter-clack* of teeth strings, the dusty jars of them, sharp teeth and blunt, huge and strange and tiny as hailstones. Her young fingers itched to touch, but no sooner did the thought enter her mind than, as if he heard it flittering there, Brimstone cut her a look with those slit-pupil eyes of his, and the impulse froze dead. Madrigal froze. He looked away, and she sat rigid for at least an entire minute before venturing one finger out to tap a curled boar tusk—

"Don't."

Oh, his voice! What a thing it was, deep as a catacomb. She should have been afraid, and maybe she was, a little, but the fire in her mind was primary. "What are they all for?" she asked, awed. The first question of many. Very, very many. Brimstone didn't answer. He only finished the message he was writing out on thick cream paper and sent her off with it to the Warlord's steward. That was all he wanted her for, to carry messages and run errands, to save Twiga and Yasri scurrying up and down the long spiral stairs. He certainly wasn't looking for an apprentice.

But once Madrigal learned the fullness of his magic—resurrection! It was nothing less than immortality, the preservation of chimaera and all hope for their freedom and autonomy, forever — she was not content to be a page.

"I could dust the jars for you."

"I could help. I could make some necklaces, too."

"Are these alligator or crocodile? How can you tell?"

By way of proving her value, she presented him with sheaves of drawings of possible chimaera configurations. "Here's a tiger with bull's horns, see? And this one is a mandrill-cheetah. Could you make that? I bet I could make that."

She was eager, piping. "I could help."

Wistful, entranced. "I could learn."

Determined, incorrigible. "I could *learn*."

She didn't understand why he wouldn't teach her. Later, she would realize it was that he didn't want to share the burden with anyone — that it was beautiful, what he did, but terrible, too, and the terrible bountifully outweighed the beautiful. But by the time she understood that, she didn't care. She was in it.

"Here. Sort these," Brimstone said to her one day, shoving a tray of teeth across his desk to her. She had been with him a few years, as page, and he had been steadfast in keeping her in that role. Until now.

Issa, Yasri, and Twiga all stopped what they were doing and swung their heads around to stare. Was it . . . a test? Brimstone ignored them, busy with something in his strongbox, and Madrigal, almost afraid to breathe, slid the tray in front of her and quietly got to work.

They were bear teeth. Brimstone probably expected her to sort them by size, but Madrigal had been watching him for years by then. She held each tooth and . . . listened to it. She listened with her fingertips, and picked out the few that didn't feel right—decay, Brimstone told her later—discarded them, and shifted the others into piles by feeling, not size. When she slid the tray back to him, she had the tremendous satisfaction of seeing his eyes go wide and lift up to regard her in an entirely new way.

"Well done," he told her then, for the first time. Her heart gave a strange surging pang while, in the corner, Issa dabbed at her eyes.

After that, and all the while pretending he was doing no such thing, he began to teach her.

She learned that magic was ugly—a hard bargain with the universe, a calculus of pain. A long time ago, medicine men had flagellated themselves, flaying open their own flesh to access the power of their agony, or even maiming themselves, crushing bones and setting them wrong on purpose to create lifelong reservoirs of pain. There had been a balance then, a natural check when it was one's own harm that was harvested. Along the way, though, some sorcerers had worked ways to cheat the calculus and draw on the pain of others.

"That's what teeth are for? A way to cheat?" It seemed a little unsporting. "Poor animals," Madrigal murmured.

Issa gave her an unusually hard look. "Perhaps you would prefer to torture slaves."

It was so awful, and so uncharacteristic, that Madrigal could only stare at her. It would be years before she learned what Issa meant—it would be the eve of her own death when Brimstone finally talked freely to her—and she would be ashamed that she had never figured it out for herself. His scars. That should have made it obvious—the network of scars, so ancient-seeming on his hide, fine crisscrossed whip splits all over his shoulders and back. But how could she have guessed? Even with all that she had seen—the sack of her mountain village, the dead and the lost, and the sieges she had fought in—she had no foundation for the horror that had been Brimstone's early life, and he did not enlighten her then.

He taught her teeth and how to draw power from them, how to manipulate the residue of life and pain in them to bring forth bodies as real as natural flesh. It was a magic of his own devising, not something he'd learned, but invented, and the same with the hamsas. They weren't tattoos at all, but a part of the very conjuring, so that bodies came into existence already marked, infused with magic in a way no natural body could be.

Revenants—as the resurrected were called—didn't have to tithe pain for power; it was already done. The hamsas were a magical weapon paid for with the pain of their last death.

It was the lot of soldiers to die again and again. "Death, death, and death," as Chiro put it. There were just never enough of them. New soldiers were always coming up—the children of Loramendi and all of the free holdings, trained from the time they could grip a weapon—but the battle tolls were high. Even with resurrection, chimaera existed at the edge of annihilation.

"The beasts must be destroyed," thundered Joram after his every address to his war council; the angels were like the long shadow of death, and all chimaera lived in its chill.

When the chimaera won a battle, the gleaning was easy. The survivors went over land and city for all the corpses of the slain and drew out every soul to bring back to Brimstone. When they were defeated, though they risked death to save the souls of their fallen comrades, many were left behind and lost forever.

The incense in the thuribles lured the souls from their bodies. In a thurible, properly sealed, souls could be preserved indefinitely. In the open, prey to the elements, it was only a matter of days before they evanesced, teased apart like breath on wind, and ceased to exist.

Evanescence was not, in itself, a grim fate. It was the way of things, to be unmade; it happened in natural death, every day. And to a revenant who had lived in body after body, died death after death, evanescence could seem like a dream of peace. But the chimaera could ill afford to let soldiers go.

"Would you want to live forever," Brimstone had asked Madrigal once, "only to die again and again, in agony?"

And over the years, she saw what it did to him, to thrust that fate on so many good creatures who were never let to go to their rest, how it bowed his head and wearied him and left him staring and morose.

Becoming a revenant was what Chiro spoke of, hard-eyed, while Madrigal tried to decide whether to marry Thiago. It was a fate she could choose now to escape. Thiago wanted her "pure"; he would see that she stayed that way—already, he was manipulating his commanders to keep her battalion away from danger. If she chose him, she would never bear the hamsas. She would never go into battle again.

And maybe that would be for the best—for herself, and for her comrades, too. She alone knew how unfit she was for it. She hated to kill—even angels. She had never told anyone what she'd done at Bullfinch two years earlier, sparing that seraph's life. And not just sparing it, but *saving* it! What madness had come over her? She had bound his wound. She had caressed his face. A wave of shame always rose in her at the memory—at least she chose to call it shame that quickened her pulse and flushed her face with delicate color.

How hot the angel's skin had been, like fever, and his eyes, like fire.

She was haunted with wondering if he had lived. She hoped he had not, and that any evidence of her treason had died right there, in the Bullfinch mist. Or so she told herself.

It was only in moments of waking, with the lace edge of a dream still light in her grasp, that the truth came clear. She dreamed the angel alive. She *hoped* him alive. She denied it, but it persisted, rising in flashes to startle her, always accompanied by a quickening of the blood, a flush, and strange, rushing frissons of sensation all the way to her fingertips.

She sometimes thought that Brimstone knew. Once or twice when the memory had caught her unaware, that rush and shiver, he had looked up from his work as if something had captured his attention. Kishmish, perched on his horn, would look, too, and both of them would stare at her unblinking. But whatever Brimstone knew or didn't know, he never said a word about it, just as he didn't say a word about Thiago, though he had to know that Madrigal's choice was heavy in her mind.

And that evening, at the ball, it would be decided, one way or the other.

Something is going to happen.

But what?

She told herself that when she stood before Thiago, she would know what to do. Blush and curtsy, dance with him, play the shy maiden while smiling an unmistakable invitation? Or stand aloof, ignore his advances, and remain a soldier?

"Come on," said Chiro, shaking her head as if Madrigal were a lost cause. "Nwella will have something you can wear, but you'll have to take what she gives you, and no complaining."

"All right," sighed Madrigal. "To the baths, then. To make ourselves *shiningly clean.*"

Like vegetables, she thought, *before they go in the stew.*

❦ 50 ❦

SUGARED

"No," said Madrigal, looking in the mirror. "Oh no. No no. *No.*"

Nwella did indeed have a gown for her. It was midnight-blue shot silk, a form-skimming sheath so fine it felt like a touch could dissolve it. It was arrayed with tiny crystals that caught the light and beamed it back like stars, and the whole back was open, revealing the long white channel of Madrigal's spine all the way to her tailbone. It was alarming. Back and shoulders and arms and chest. Far too much chest. "No." She started to shrug out of it, but Chiro stopped her.

"Remember what I said: no complaining."

"I take it back. I reserve my right to complain."

"Too late. It's your fault, anyway. You had a week to get a gown. You see what happens when you dither? Others make your choices for you."

Madrigal thought that she wasn't talking about the gown. "What? Is this a punishment, then?"

At her other side, Nwella chuffed. She was a frail thing of lizard aspect who had been with Madrigal and Chiro at school, but parted from them when they went to battle training and she into royal service. "Punishment? Making you stunning, you mean? Look at yourself."

Madrigal did look, and what she saw was skin. The most delicate interweaving of individual silk strands climbed around her neck, invisibly holding the gown to her body. "I look naked."

"You look *astonishing*," said Nwella, who was seamstress to the Warlord's younger wives, the very youngest of whom were, to put it kindly, unyoung. The Warlord had seen fit to stop imposing himself on new brides some centuries earlier. Like Brimstone, he was of natural flesh, and looked it. Thiago, his firstborn, was some hundreds of years old, though he wore the skin of a young man, and the hamsas to go with it.

As Madrigal had said, the general's fetish for purity was hypocrisy: He himself had been through many resurrections, and his hypocrisy was twofold — not only was he not "pure," he had not been born high-human.

The Warlord was Hartkind, with a stag's head: creature aspect, as were his wives, and so had been Thiago, originally. It wasn't that it was unusual for a revenant to resurrect in a body unlike his or her natural one; Brimstone couldn't always match them. It was a matter of time and tooth supply. But Thiago's bodies were another matter. They were crafted to his precise specifications, and even before they were needed, so that he could examine them for flaws and give his approval. She had seen it once: Thiago checking over a naked replica of himself — the husk that would receive him the next time he died. It had been macabre.

She tested her gown with little tugs, feeling certain that too heavy a hand in dancing could pull it clean off. "Nwella," she implored, "don't you have something more...substantial?"

"Not for you," Nwella said. "A figure like that, why would you want to cover it?" She whispered something to Chiro.

"Stop conspiring," Madrigal said. "Can't I have a shawl at least?"

"No," they said together.

"I feel almost as naked as at the baths."

She had never in her life felt so exposed as when she'd walked through the steam and thigh-deep water with Chiro that afternoon. Everyone knew now that she was Thiago's choice, and every pair of eyes in the women's bath had inspected her, so that she wanted to sink down out of sight, leaving just her horns spiking through the surface of the water.

"Let Thiago see what he's getting," Nwella said, devilish.

Madrigal stiffened. "Who said he's getting it?" *It*, she heard herself say. The word felt appropriate, as if she were some inanimate thing, a gown on a hanger. "*Me*," she corrected. "Who said he's getting *me*?"

Nwella laughed off the idea that Madrigal might refuse him. "Here." She came forward with a mask. "We *will* permit you to cover your face." It was a bird with its wings spread, carved of lightweight kaza wood, black and embellished with dark feathers that fanned out from the sides of her face. In shifts of light, rainbows of iridescence rippled over the feathers.

"Ah. Good. No one will know who I am *now*," Madrigal remarked, wry. Her wings and horns eluded disguise.

The Warlord's ball was a masquerade, a "come-as-you-aren't."

Chimaera of human aspect wore the faces of creatures, while those of beast aspect wore carven human likenesses, exaggerated to ridiculous proportion. It was the one night of the year for folly and pretend, the one night that fell outside normal life, but for Madrigal, this year, it was anything but. It was, rather, a night to *decide* her life.

With a sigh, she gave in to her friends' ministrations. She sat on a stool and let them define her eyes with kohl, rouge her lips with rose-petal paste, and string lengths of ultrafine gold chain between her horns in tiers, suspended with tiny crystal drops that winked in the light. Chiro and Nwella giggled as if they were preparing a bride for her wedding night, and it struck Madrigal that it well could be, if not in ceremony, at least in one way.

If she accepted Thiago, it was unlikely she would be returning to the barracks tonight.

She shivered, imagining his clawed hands on her flesh. What would it be like? She had never made love — in that way, too, she was "pure," as she imagined Thiago must know. She thought about it, of course she thought about it. She was of age; her body coursed with urges, just like anyone's, and chimaera weren't puritanical about sex. Madrigal had just never come to a moment when it had felt right.

"There. You're finished," said Chiro. She and Nwella pulled Madrigal to her feet and stood back from her to survey their work. "Oh," breathed Nwella. There was a pause, and when Chiro spoke again, her voice was flat. She said, "You're beautiful."

It didn't sound like a compliment.

After Kalamet, when Chiro had awakened in the cathedral, Madrigal was there beside her. "You're all right," she assured her, as Chiro's eyes fluttered open. It was Chiro's first resurrection, and revenants said it could be disorienting. Madrigal hoped that in matching the new body so closely to her sister's original flesh, she could ease her transition. "You're all right," she said again, clasping Chiro's hand with its hamsa, symbol of her new status. She told her, "Brimstone let me make your body. I used diamonds." Conspiratorial. "Don't tell anyone."

She helped Chiro sit up. The fur of her cat haunches was soft, and the flesh of her human arms was, too. Jerkily, Chiro touched her new skin—hips, ribs, human breasts. Her hand climbed eagerly up her neck to her head, felt the fur there, and the jackal muzzle, and froze.

The sound she made was like choking, and at first Madrigal thought it was only the problem of a newly made throat and a mouth that had never yet formed speech. But it wasn't.

Chiro threw off Madrigal's hand. "*You* did this?"

Madrigal backed up a step. "It's... it's perfect," she said, faltering. "It's almost exactly like your real—"

"And that's all I merit? Beast aspect? Thank you, my sister. *Thank you.*"

"Chiro—"

"You couldn't have made me high-human? What are a few teeth to you? To Brimstone?"

The idea had never even entered Madrigal's mind. "But... Chiro. This is *you.*"

"*Me.*" Her voice was changed; it had a deeper tone than her original voice, and Madrigal couldn't tell how much of this was its newness, but whatever else it was, it was acid, and ugly. "Would *you* want to be me?"

Hurt and confused, Madrigal said, "I don't understand."

"No, you wouldn't," said Chiro. "You're beautiful."

* * *

Later, she had apologized. It was the shock, she said. The new body had felt tight, unyielding; she could barely breathe. Once she grew accustomed to it, she praised its strength, its lithe movement. She could fly faster than before; her movements were whip-quick, her teeth and eyesight sharper. She said she was like a violin that had been tuned—the same, but better.

"Thank you, my sister," she said, and seemed to mean it.

But Madrigal remembered the spiteful way she had said, "You're beautiful." She sounded like that now.

Nwella was more exuberant. "So beautiful!" she sang. A frown creased her scaled brow, and she plucked at the charm that hung around Madrigal's neck. "This, of course, will have to go," she said, but Madrigal pulled away.

"No," she said, closing her hand around it.

"Just for tonight, Mad," coaxed Nwella. "It just isn't fit for the occasion."

"Leave it," said Madrigal, and that was that. The tone of her voice dissuaded Nwella from pressing the issue.

"Okay," she said with a sigh, and Madrigal spilled her

wishbone from her cupped palm so that it settled back in its place, where her clavicles met. It wasn't beautiful or fine, just a bone, and she saw plainly that it did not do justice to her decolletage, but she didn't care. It was what she wore.

Nwella regarded it, pained, and then turned to rummage in her drawer of cosmetic tubes and ointments. "Here, then. At the very least." She came up with a silver bowl and a big soft brush, and before Madrigal knew what was happening Nwella had dusted her chest, neck, and shoulders with something that glittered.

"What—?"

"Sugar," she said, giggling.

"Nwella!" Madrigal tried to brush it off, but it was dust-fine and it clung: sugar powder, which girls wore when they planned to be tasted. If her rose-petal lips and naked back were not enough invitation to Thiago, Madrigal thought, this certainly was. Its telltale shimmer might as well have been a sign that said LICK ME.

"You don't look like a soldier now," said Nwella.

It was true. She looked like a girl who had made her choice. Had she? Everyone thought she had, which almost felt like the same thing. But it wasn't too late. She could decide not to go to the ball at all—that would send quite the opposite message of showing up *sugared*. She had only to decide what she wanted.

She held herself framed in the mirror for a long beat. She felt dizzy, as if the future were rushing at her.

It was, though at that moment, she could have no notion that it was coming for her with invisible wings and eyes that no mask could disguise, and that her choices, such as they were,

344

would soon be swept away like dust on a wingbeat, leaving in their place the unthinkable.

Love.

"Let's go," she said, and she linked arms with Chiro and Nwella, and went out to meet it.

❦ 51 ❦

THE SERPENTINE

Loramendi's main thoroughfare, the Serpentine, became a processional route on the Warlord's birthday. The custom was to dance its length, moving from partner to masked partner all the way to the agora, the city's gathering place. The ball was there, under thousands of lanterns strung like stars from the bars of the Cage, making it, for a night, a miniature world with its own firmament.

Madrigal plunged into the crowd with her friends, as she had in years past, but this year, she realized at once, things were different.

She might have been masked, but she was not disguised — her appearance was far too distinctive — and she might have been sugared, but no one took the sparkle of her shoulders as an invitation. They knew she was not for them. In the wild merriment of the street, she was as apart as if she were drifting along in a crystal sphere.

Again and again, Chiro and Nwella were swept into strangers' embraces and kissed, mask to mask. That was tradition: a spinning, stamping dance punctuated liberally with kisses, to celebrate unity among the races. Musicians were grouped at intervals so that merrymakers were passed from melody to melody as from hand to hand, with never a lull. Wild music spun them along, but no one swept Madrigal up. Several times some soldier started toward her—one even grabbed her hand—but always there was a friend there to pull him back and whisper a warning. Madrigal couldn't hear what was said, but she could imagine it.

She is Thiago's.

No one touched her. She drifted through the revelry alone.

Where was Thiago, she wondered, her eyes darting from mask to mask. She would get a glimpse of long white hair or wolf aspect and her heart would jump at the thought that it was him, but each time it was someone else. The long white hair belonged to an old woman, and Madrigal had to laugh at her own skittishness.

Every citizen of Loramendi was in the streets, but somehow space opened around her and she moved alone, following in her friends' wake toward the agora. Thiago would be there, she guessed, probably standing with his father on the palace balcony, watching the crowd surge as the procession spilled wave after wave of chimaera into the square.

He would be watching for her.

Unconsciously, she slowed her steps. Nwella and Chiro went whirling on ahead in their masks, kissing. For the most part they just touched the lips of their masks to the lips—beaks,

347

muzzles, maws—of other masks, but there were real kisses, too, with no regard to aspect. Madrigal knew what it was like from previous festivals, the grasswine breath of strangers, the nuzzle of a tiger's whiskered jaw, or a dragon's, or a man's. But not tonight.

Tonight, she was in isolation—eyes were on her but not hands, and certainly not lips. The Serpentine seemed a very long stretch to go alone.

Then someone took her elbow. The touch jarred her, coming as it did to end her apartness. Thinking it must be Thiago, she stiffened.

But no. The one at her side wore a horse mask of molded leather that covered his true head completely. Thiago would never wear a horse head, or any other mask to conceal his face. He wore the same thing to the ball every year: a real wolf's head atop his own, its lower jaw removed so that it made a sort of headdress, its eyes replaced with blue glass, dead and staring.

So who was this? Someone foolish enough to touch her? Well then. He was tall, a head above even her own height, so that Madrigal had to tilt her face up, laying her hand on his shoulder, to nudge his horse muzzle with the beak of her bird mask. A "kiss," to prove that she still belonged to herself.

And as if some spell had been broken, she was part of the crowd again, spinning in the graceless stamping of the revel, with the stranger for a partner. He moved her along, guarding her from the shoving of larger creatures. She could feel his strength; he might easily have buoyed her without her feet even touching the ground. He ought to have turned her loose after a twirl or two, but he didn't. His hands—gloved—kept hold of her. And since she didn't think anyone else would dance with her if he let her go, she didn't move away. It felt good to be dancing, and she gave herself over to it, and even forgot her anxieties about her dress. Fragile as it seemed, it was holding up fine, and when she whirled it rose in waves around her gazelle hooves, weightless and lovely.

Part of a seething, living tide, they streamed along. Madrigal lost track of her friends, but the horse-masked stranger didn't abandon her, and when the procession neared the end of the Serpentine, it began to bottleneck. The dancing slowed to a sway and she found herself standing with him, their breathing quick. She looked up, flushed and smiling behind her bird mask, and said, "Thank you."

"My lady, thank *you*. The honor is mine." His voice was rich, his accent strange. Madrigal couldn't place it. The eastern territories, perhaps.

She said, "You're braver than the rest, to dance with me."

"Brave?" His mask was expressionless, of course, but his head quirked to one side, and from his tone, Madrigal realized he didn't know what she meant. Was it possible he didn't know who she was—*whose* she was? He asked, "Are you so ferocious?" and she laughed.

"Terrifying. Apparently."

Again, that tilt of the head.

"You don't know who I am." She was strangely disappointed. She had thought he might be a bold soul, flouting the general fear of Thiago, but it seemed he was only ignorant of the risk.

His head bent toward her, his mask muzzle brushing her ear. In his nearness, there was an aura of warmth. He said, "I know who you are. I came here for you."

"Did you?" She felt slightly giddy, as if she had been drinking grasswine, though she hadn't had so much as a sip. "Tell me then, Sir Horse. Who am I?"

"Ah, well, that's not entirely fair, Lady Bird. You never told me your name."

"You see? You don't know. But I have a secret." She tapped her beak and whispered, smiling, "This is a mask. I am not really a bird."

He reared back in feigned surprise, though his hand didn't leave her arm. "Not a bird? I am deceived."

"So you see, whatever lady you're looking for, she is all alone somewhere, waiting for you." She was almost sorry to send him away, but the agora wasn't far off now. She didn't want him to catch Thiago's disfavor, not after he'd rescued her from dancing the whole length of the Serpentine alone. "Go on," she urged. "Go and find her."

"I've found who I'm looking for," he said. "I may not know your name, but I know you. And I have a secret, too."

"Don't tell me. You're not really a horse?" She was looking up at him; his voice had struck her as familiar, but the familiarity was distant and vague, like something she'd dreamt. She tried to see through his mask but he was too tall; at the angle of her sight, all she could make out through the eye apertures was shadow.

"It's true," he confessed. "I am not really a horse."

"And what are you?" She was really wondering now—who was he? Someone she knew? Masks made for mischief, and many a sly game was played on the Warlord's birthday, but she didn't think anyone would be playing games with her tonight.

His answer was swallowed by an upsurge of piping as they drew near the last musicians along the route. Trills like bird calls, a twanging lute, the throat-deep ululation of singers, and beneath it all, like a heartbeat under skin, the cadence of drums carrying the urgency to dance. Bodies were close on all sides, the stranger's closest of all. A swell in the crowd pressed him against Madrigal and she felt the mass and breadth of his shoulders through his cloak.

And heat.

She was conscious of her bareness and sugar glitter, and, plainly, her own rushing heartbeat, her own rising heat.

She flushed and stepped away, or tried to, but was shoved back into him. His scent was warm and full: spice and salt, the pungent leather of his mask, and something rich and deep that she couldn't identify but that made her want to lean into him, close her eyes, and breathe. He kept an arm around her, pushed back against the crush and kept her from being jostled, and there was nowhere to go but onward with the crowd as it funneled into the agora. They were in the funnel, and there was no turning back.

The stranger was behind her, his voice low. "I came here to find you," he said. "I came to thank you."

"Thank me? For what?" She couldn't turn. A centaur flank hemmed her in on one side, a Naja coil on the other. She thought she caught a glimpse of Chiro in the whirl. She could see the agora now—straight ahead, framed by the armory and the war college. The lanterns overhead were like constellations, their flicker blotting out the real stars, and the moons, too. It crossed Madrigal's mind to wonder if Nitid—curious, peering Nitid—could see *in*.

Something is going to happen.

"I came to thank you," said the stranger, close to her ear, "for saving my life."

Madrigal had saved lives. She had crept in darkness over fields of the fallen, slipped through seraphim patrols to glean souls that would otherwise be lost to evanescence. She had led a strike on an angel position that had her comrades trapped in a gully, and bought them time to retreat. She had shot an angel's arrow out of the sky as it made its deadly glide toward a comrade. She had saved lives. But all those memories passed through her consciousness in the space of a finger snap, leaving only one.

Bullfinch. Mist. *Enemy.*

"I took your recommendation," he said. "I lived."

Instantly, it was as if her veins were conducting fire. She whipped around. His face was only inches from her own, his head tilted down so that now she could see into his mask.

His eyes blazed like flames.

She whispered, *"You."*

52

MADNESS

The living tide sucked them into the agora, a backwash of elbows and wings, horns and hide, fur and flesh, and she was carried along, stricken dumb with disbelief, her hooves scarcely skimming the cobbles.

A seraph, inside Loramendi.

Not *a* seraph. *This* seraph. Whom she had touched. *Saved.* Here, in the Cage, his hands on her arms, hot even through the leather of his gloves, this angel who was alive because of her.

He was *here.*

It was such madness, it made a churning of her thoughts, more chaotic than the churning all around her. She couldn't think. What could she say? What should she *do*?

Later it would strike her that not for an instant had she considered doing what anyone else in the entire city would have done without a thought: unmasking him and screaming, "Seraph!"

She drew a long, uneven breath and said, "You're mad to be here. Why did you come?"

"I told you, I came to thank you."

She had a terrible thought. "Assassination? You'll never get close to the Warlord."

Earnestly, he said, "*No.* I wouldn't tarnish the gift you gave me with the blood of your folk."

The agora was a massive oval; it was big enough for an army to mass, many phalanxes abreast, but tonight there were no troops at its center, only dancers moving in the intricate patterns of a lowland reel. Those spilling from the Serpentine eddied out around the edges of the square where the density of bodies was greatest. Casks of grasswine stood amid tables laden with food, and folk gathered in clusters, children on their shoulders, everyone laughing and singing.

Madrigal and the angel were still caught in the churning delta of the Serpentine. He was anchoring her, as steady as a breakwall. In the blank, gasping aftermath of shock, Madrigal didn't try to move away.

"Gift?" she said, incredulous. "You hold that gift lightly, coming *here*, into certain death."

"I'm not going to die," he said. "Not tonight. A thousand things might have stopped me from being here right now, but instead, a thousand things *brought* me here. Everything lined up. It has been easy, as if it were meant—"

"Meant!" she said, amazed. She spun to face him, which, in the crush, brought her against his chest as if they were still dancing. She fought backward for space. "As if *what* were meant?"

"You," he said. "And me."

His words sucked the breath from her lungs. Him and her? Seraph and chimaera? It was preposterous. All she could think to say was, again, "You're mad."

"It's your madness, too. You saved my life. Why did you do it?"

Madrigal had no answer. For two years she had been haunted by it, by the feeling, when she had found him dying, that somehow he was hers to protect. Her. And now here he was, alive and, impossibly, *here*. She was still grappling with disbelief, that it was him, his face—of which he remembered every plane and angle—hidden behind that mask.

"And tonight," he said, "a million souls in the city, I might not have found you at all. I might have searched all night and never so much as glimpsed you, but instead, there you were, like you were set down in front of me and you were alone, moving through the crowd and apart in it, like you were waiting for me...."

He went on speaking, but Madrigal stopped hearing. At his mention of her apartness, the reason for it came thundering back to her, having been momentarily forgotten in her shock. Thiago. She looked to the palace, up at the Warlord's balcony. At this distance, the figures on it were only silhouettes, but they were silhouettes she knew: the Warlord, the hulking shape of Brimstone, and a gaggle of the ruler's antlered wives. Thiago was not there.

Which could only mean he was down *here*. A thrill of fear shot through her from hooves to horns. "You don't understand," she said, pirouetting to scan the crowd. "There was a reason no one was dancing with me. I thought you were brave. I didn't know you were mad—"

"What reason?" the angel asked, still near. Still too near.

"Trust me," she said, urgent. "It isn't safe for you. If you want to live, leave me."

"I've come a long way to *find* you—"

"I'm spoken for," she blurted, hating the words even before they were out.

This brought him up short. "Spoken for? Betrothed?"

Claimed, she thought, but she said, "As good as. Now go. If Thiago sees you—"

"*Thiago?*" The angel recoiled at the name. "You're betrothed to *the Wolf?*"

And at the moment he pronounced those words—*the Wolf*—arms came around Madrigal's waist from behind and she gasped.

In an instant, she saw what would happen. Thiago would discover the angel, and he wouldn't just kill him, he would make a spectacle of it. A seraph spy at the Warlord's ball— such a thing had never happened! He would be tortured. He would be made to wish that he had never lived. It all flashed through her, and horror rose like bile in her throat. When she heard, close to her ear, a *giggle*, the relief almost left her limp.

It wasn't Thiago, but Chiro. "There you are," said her sister. "We lost you in the crush!"

Madrigal's blood made a roaring in her ears, and Chiro glanced from her to the stranger, whose heat suddenly felt to Madrigal like a beacon. "Hello," Chiro said, peering with curiosity at the horse mask, through which Madrigal could still make out the orange burn of his tiger's eyes.

It hit her anew that he had come in such thin disguise into

the den of the enemy *for her*, and she felt a queer constriction in her chest. For two years she had reflected on Bullfinch as a momentary madness, though it hadn't felt like madness then, and it didn't now, to wish this seraph to live — and she did wish it. She pulled herself together and turned to Chiro. Nwella was right behind her.

"Some friends you are," she chided them. "To dress me like this and then abandon me to the Serpentine. I might have been mauled."

"We thought you were behind us," said Nwella, breathless from dancing.

"I was," said Madrigal. "*Far* behind you." She had turned her back on the angel without a second glance. She began to casually herd her friends away from him, using the motion of the crowd to put space between them.

"Who was that?" Chiro asked.

"Who?" asked Madrigal.

"In the horse mask, dancing with you."

"I wasn't dancing with anyone. Or perhaps you didn't notice: No one *would* dance with me. I am a pariah."

Scoffing, "A pariah! Hardly. More like a princess." Chiro threw a skeptical look back, and Madrigal was wild to know what she saw. Was the angel looking after them, or had some sense of self-preservation kicked in and made him disappear?

"Have you seen Thiago yet?" Nwella asked. "Or rather, has *he* seen *you*?"

"No —" Madrigal started to say, but then Chiro burst out with, "There he is!" and she went cold.

There he was.

He was unmistakable, with the hewn-off wolf head atop his own, his grotesque version of a mask. Its fangs curved over his brow, its muzzle drawn back in a snarl. His snow-white hair was brushed and arranged over his shoulders, his vest ivory satin — so much white, white upon white, framing his strong, handsome face, which was bronzed by the sun, making his pale eyes seem ghostly.

He hadn't seen her yet. The crowd parted around him, not even the drunkest of the revelers failing to recognize him and make way. The mob seemed to shrivel as he passed with his retinue, who were of true wolf aspect, and moved like a pack.

The meaning of this night caught up to Madrigal: her choice, her future.

"He's magnificent," breathed Nwella, clinging to Madrigal on one side. Madrigal had to agree, but she placed the credit for it with Brimstone, who had crafted that beautiful body, not with Thiago, who wore it with the arrogance of entitlement.

"He's looking for you," said Chiro, and Madrigal knew she was right. The general was unhurried, his pale eyes sweeping the crowd with the confidence of one who gets what he wants. Then his gaze came to rest on her. She felt impaled by it. Spooked, she took a step back.

"Let's go dance," she blurted, to the surprise of her friends.

"But —" Chiro said.

"Listen." A new reel was starting up. "It's the Furiant. My favorite."

It was not her favorite, but it would do. Two lines of dancers were forming, men on one side, women on the other, and before Chiro and Nwella could say another word, Madrigal had spun to flee toward the women's file, feeling Thiago's gaze on the back of her neck like the touch of claws.

She wondered: *What of other eyes?*

The Furiant began with a light-footed promenade, Chiro and Nwella rushing to join in, and Madrigal went through the steps with grace and a smile, not missing a beat, but she was barely there. Her thoughts had flown outward, darting and dipping with the hummingbird-moths that flocked by the thousands to the lanterns hanging overhead, as she wondered, with a wild, timpani heart, where her angel had gone.

🌿 53 🌿

Love Is an Element

In the patterns of the Furiant, no one bypassed Madrigal's hand as they had in the Serpentine—it would have been too obvious a slight—but there was a formal stiffness in her partners as she passed from one to the next, some barely skimming her fingertips with their own when they were meant to be clasping hands.

Thiago had come up and stood watching. Everyone felt it, and the gaiety of the dance was tamped down. It was his effect, but it was her fault, Madrigal knew, for running from him and trying to hide here, as if it were possible to hide.

She was just buying time, and the Furiant was good for that at least, as it went on a full quarter of an hour, with constant shifts in partner. Madrigal went from a courteous elder soldier with a rhinoceros horn to a centaur to a high-human in a dragon mask who scarcely touched her, and with each revolution she was brought past Thiago, whose eyes never left her.

Her next partner's mask was tiger, and when he took her hand...he actually took her hand. He clasped it firmly in his own gloved hand. A thrill went up Madrigal's arm from the warming touch, and she didn't have to look at his eyes to know who it was.

He was still here—and with Thiago so near. *Reckless*, she thought, electrified by his nearness. After a moment, steadying her breathing and her heart, she said, "Tiger suits you better than horse, I think."

"I don't know what you mean, lady," he replied. "This is my true face."

"Of course."

"Because it would be foolish to still be here, if I were who you thought."

"It would. One might suppose you had a death wish."

"No." He was solemn. "Never that. A *life* wish, if anything. For a different sort of life."

A different sort of life. If only, Madrigal thought, her own life and choices—or lack of them—hemming her in. She kept her voice light. "You wish to be one of us? I'm sorry, we don't accept converts."

He laughed. "Even if you did, it wouldn't help. We are all locked in the same life, aren't we? The same war."

In a lifetime of hating seraphim, Madrigal had never thought of them as living the same life as she, but what the angel said was true. They were all locked in the same war. They had locked the entire world in it. "There is no other life," she said, and then she tensed, because they had come around to the place where Thiago stood.

The pressure of the angel's grip on her hand increased ever so slightly, gently, and it helped her bear up under the general's gaze until she turned away from it again, and could breathe.

"You need to go," she said quietly. "If you're discovered..."

The angel let a beat pass in silence before asking, just as quietly, "You're not really going to marry him, are you?"

"I... I don't know."

He lifted her hand so that she could circle beneath the bridge of their arms; it was a part of the pattern, but her height and horns interfered, and they had to release fingers and join them again after the spin.

"What is there to know?" he asked. "Do you love him?"

"*Love?*" The question was a surprise, and a laugh escaped Madrigal's lips. She quickly composed herself, not wanting to draw Thiago's scrutiny.

"It's a funny question?"

"No," she said. "Yes." Love Thiago? Could she? Maybe. How could you know a thing like that? "What's funny is that you're the first one to ask me that."

"Forgive me," said the seraph. "I didn't realize that chimaera don't marry for love."

Madrigal thought of her parents. Her memory of them was hazed with a patina of years, their faces blurred to generalities— would she even know them, if she found them?—but she did remember their simple fondness for each other, and how they had seemed always to be touching. "We do." She wasn't laughing now. "My parents did."

"So you are a child of love. It seems right, that you were made by love."

She had never thought of herself in that way, but after he said it, it struck her as a fine thing, to have been made by love, and she ached for what she had lost, in losing her family. "And you? Did your parents love each other?"

She heard herself ask it, and was overcome by the dizzying surreality of the circumstance. She had just asked a seraph if his parents loved each other.

"No," he said, and offered no explanation. "But I hope that my children's parents will."

Again he lifted her hand so that she could circle under the bridge made by their arms, and again her horns got in the way, so they were briefly parted. Turning, Madrigal felt a sting in his words, and when they were facing each other once more, she said, in her defense, "Love is a luxury."

"No. Love is an element."

An *element*. Like air to breathe, earth to stand on. The steady certainty of his voice sent a shiver through her, but she didn't get a chance to respond. They had concluded their pattern, and she still had gooseflesh from the effect of his extraordinary statement as he handed her on to her next partner, who was drunk and uttered not a syllable for the entirety of their contact.

She tried to keep track of the seraph. He should have partnered Nwella after herself, but by then he was gone, and she saw no tiger mask in the whole of the array. He had melted away, and she felt his absence like a space cut from the air.

The Furiant wound down to its final promenade, and when it ended in a brazen gypsy tinkling of tambourines, Madrigal was delivered, as if it had been orchestrated that way, virtually into the White Wolf's arms.

363

🌿 54 🌿

MEANT

"My lord," Madrigal's throat went dry so her words were a rasp, near enough a throaty whisper to be mistaken for one.

Nwella and Chiro crowded behind her, and Thiago smiled, lupine, the tips of fangs appearing between his full red lips. His eyes were bold. They didn't meet hers, but roved lower, with no effort at subtlety. Madrigal's skin went hot as her heart grew cold, and she dropped into a curtsy from which she wished that she never had to rise and meet his eyes, but rise she must, and did.

"You're beautiful tonight," said Thiago. Madrigal needn't have worried about meeting his eyes. If she had been headless, he would not yet have noticed. The way he was looking at her body in the midnight sheath made her want to cross her arms over her chest.

"Thank you," she said, fighting the impulse. A return of compliment was called for, so she said simply, "As are you."

He looked up then, amused. "I am beautiful?"

She inclined her head. "As a winter wolf, my lord," she said, which pleased him. He seemed relaxed, almost lazy, his eyes heavy-lidded. He was entirely sure of her, Madrigal saw. He wasn't looking for a gesture; there was not the smallest kernel of uncertainty in him. Thiago got what he wanted. Always.

And would he tonight?

A new tune struck up, and he tilted his head to acknowledge it. "The Emberlin," he said. "My lady?" He held out his arm to her, and Madrigal went still as prey.

If she took his arm, did that mean it was done, that she accepted him?

But to refuse it would be the grossest of slights; it would shame him, and one simply did not shame the White Wolf.

It was an invitation to dance, and it felt like a trap, and Madrigal stood paralyzed a beat too long. In that beat she saw Thiago's gaze sharpen. His easy lethargy fell away to be replaced by . . . she wasn't sure. It didn't have time to take form. Disbelief, perhaps, which would have given way in its turn to ice-cold fury had not Nwella, with a panicked squeak, placed her palm in the small of Madrigal's back and shoved.

Thus propelled, Madrigal took a step, and there was nothing for it. She didn't take Thiago's arm so much as she collided with it. He tucked hers beneath his own, proprietary, and escorted her into the dance.

And certainly, as everyone thought, into the future.

He grasped her by the waist, which was the proper form of the Emberlin, in which the men lifted the ladies like offerings to the sky. Thiago's hands almost completely encircled her slim midriff, his claws on her bare back. She felt the point of each one on her skin.

There was some talk between them—Madrigal must have asked after the Warlord's health, and Thiago must have answered, but she could scarcely have related what was said. She might have been a sugared shell, for all that she was present in her skin.

What had she done? What had she just done?

She couldn't even fool herself that it was the product of an instant and Nwella's tiny shove. She had let herself be dressed like this; she had come here; she had *known*. She might not have admitted to herself that she knew what she was doing, but of course she had. She had let herself be carried along on the certainty of others. There had been a piquant satisfaction in being chosen...envied. She was ashamed of it now, and of the way she had come here tonight, ready to play the trembling bride, and accept a man she did not love.

But...she had *not* accepted him, and she thought now that she wouldn't have. Something had changed.

Nothing had changed, she argued with herself. *Love is an element,* indeed. The angel coming here, the risk of it! It stunned her, but it changed nothing.

And where was he now? Each time Thiago lifted her she glanced around, but she saw no horse or tiger mask. She hoped he had gone, and was safe.

Thiago, who up until now had seemed satisfied with what his hands could hold, must have sensed that he was not commanding her attention. Bringing her down from a lift, he intentionally let her slip so he had to catch her against him. At the surprise, her wings spontaneously sprang open, like twin spinnakers filling with wind.

"My apologies, my lady," Thiago said, and he eased her down so her hooves found the ground again, but he didn't loosen his hold on her. She felt the rigid surface of his muscled chest against her own chest. The wrongness of it stirred a panic that she had to fight down to keep from wrenching herself from his arms. It was hard to fold her wings again, when what she really wanted to do was take flight.

"This gown, is it cut from shadow?" the general asked. "I can barely feel it between my fingers."

Not for want of trying, thought Madrigal.

"Perhaps it is a reflection of the night sky," he suggested, "skimmed from a pond?"

She supposed that he was being poetic. Erotic, even. In return, as unerotically as possible — more like complaining of a stain that wouldn't come out — she said, "Yes, my lord. I went for a dip, and the reflection clung."

"Well. Then it might slip away like water at any moment. One wonders what, if anything, is beneath it."

And this is courtship, thought Madrigal. She blushed, and was glad of her mask, which covered all but her lips and chin. Choosing not to address the matter of her undergarments, she said, "It is sturdier than it looks, I assure you."

She did not intend a challenge, but he took it as one. He reached up to the delicate threads that, like gossamers of a spider's web, secured the gown around her neck, and gave a short,

367

sharp tug. They gave way easily to his claws, and Madrigal gasped. The dress stayed in place, but a cluster of its fragile fastenings were severed.

"Or perhaps not so sturdy," said Thiago. "Don't worry, my lady, I'll help you hold it up."

His hand was over her heart, just above her breast, and Madrigal trembled. She was furious at herself for trembling. She was Madrigal of the Kirin, not some blossom caught in a breeze. "That's kind of you, my lord," she replied, shrugging off his hand as she stepped away. "But it is time to change partners. I'll have to manage my gown on my own."

She had never been so glad to be handed on to a new partner. In this case it was a bull-moose of a man, graceless, who came near to treading on her hooves any number of times. She barely noticed.

A different sort of life, she thought, and the words became a mantra to the melody of the Emberlin. *A different sort of life, a different sort of life.*

Where was the angel now, she wondered. Yearning suffused her, full as flavor, like chocolate melting on her tongue.

Before she knew it, the bull-moose was returning her to Thiago, who claimed her with his clutching hands and pulled her into him.

"I missed you," he said. "Every other lady is coarse next to you."

He talked to her in that bedroom purr of his, but all she could think was how clumsy, how effortful his words seemed after the angel's.

Twice more Thiago passed her to new partners, and twice she was returned to him in due course. Each time was more unbearable than the last, so that she felt like a runaway returned home against her will.

When, turned over to her next partner, she felt the firm pressure of leather gloves enfold her fingers, it was with a lightness like floating that she let herself be swept away. Misery lifted; wrongness lifted. The seraph's hands came around her waist and her feet left the ground and she closed her eyes, giving herself over to feeling.

He set her back down, but didn't let her go. "Hello," she whispered, happy.

Happy.

"Hello," he returned, like a shared secret.

She smiled to see his new mask. It was human and comical, with jug ears and a red drunkard's nose. "Yet another face," she said. "Are you a magus, conjuring masks?"

"No conjuring needed. There are as many masks to choose from as there are revelers passed out drunk."

"Well, this one suits you least of all."

"That's what you think. A lot can happen in two years."

She laughed, remembering his beauty, and was seized by a desire to see his face again.

"Will you tell me your name, my lady?" he asked.

She did, and he repeated it—"Madrigal, Madrigal, Madrigal"—like an incantation.

How odd, Madrigal thought, that she should be overcome by such a feeling of...fulfillment...from the simple presence of a man whose name she didn't know and whose face she couldn't see. "And yours?" she asked.

"Akiva."

"Akiva." It pleased her to say it. She may have been the one whose name meant music, but his sounded like it. Saying it made her want to sing it, to lean out a window and call him home. To whisper it in the dark.

"You've done it, then," he said. "Accepted him."

Defiantly, she replied, "No. I have not."

"No? He's watching you like he owns you."

"Then you should certainly be elsewhere—"

"Your dress," he said, noticing it. "It's torn. Did *he*—?" Madrigal felt heat, a ripple of anger flashing off him like a draft off a bonfire.

She saw that Thiago was dancing with Chiro, and was staring right between Chiro's sharp jackal ears at her. She waited until the revolutions of the dance brought Akiva's broad back between them, shielding her face, before answering. "It's nothing. I'm not used to wearing such fragile fabric. This was chosen for me. I crave a shawl."

He was tense with anger but his hands remained gentle at her waist. He said, "I can make you a shawl."

She cocked her head. "You knit? Well. That's an unusual accomplishment in a soldier."

"I don't knit," he said, and that's when Madrigal felt the first feather-soft touch on her shoulder. She didn't mistake it for Akiva's touch, because his hands were at her waist. She looked down and saw that a gray-green hummingbird-moth had settled on her, one of the many fluttering overhead, drawn to the expansiveness of lantern light that must seem like a universe to them. The feathers of its tiny bird body gleamed, jewel-like, as its furred moth wings fanned against her skin. It was followed

370

shortly by another, this one pale pink, and another, also pink, with orange eyespots on its lacework wings. More floated out of the air, and in a moment, a fine company of them covered Madrigal's chest and shoulders.

"There you are, my lady," said Akiva. "A living shawl."

She was amazed. "How—? You *are* a magus."

"No. It's a trick, only."

"It's *magic.*"

"Not the most useful magic, herding moths."

"Not useful? You made me a *shawl.*" She was awed by it. The magic she knew through Brimstone had little whimsy in it. This was beautiful, both in form—the wings were a dozen twilight colors, and as soft as lamb's ears—and in purpose. He had covered her. Thiago had torn her dress, and Akiva had covered her.

"They tickle." She laughed. "Oh no. *Oh.*"

"What is it?"

"Oh, make them go." She laughed harder, feeling tiny tongues dart from tiny beaks. "They're eating my sugar."

"*Sugar?*"

The tickling made her wriggle her shoulders. "Make them go. Please."

He tried to. A few lifted away and made a circle around her horns, but most stayed where they were. "I'm afraid they're in love," he said, concerned. "They don't want to leave you." He lifted one hand from her waist to gently brush a pair from her neck, where their wings fanned against her jaw. Melancholy, he said, "I know just how they feel."

Her heart, like a fist clenching. The time had come for Akiva to lift her again, and he did, though her shoulders were

371

still cloaked in moths. From above the heads of the crowd, she was grateful to see that Thiago was turned away. Chiro, though, whom he was lifting, saw her and did a double take.

Akiva brought Madrigal back down, and just before her feet touched ground they looked at each other, mask to mask, brown eyes to orange, and a surge went between them. Madrigal didn't know if it was magic, but most of the hummingbird-moths took flight and swirled away as if carried by a wind. She was down again, her feet moving, her heart racing. She had lost track of the pattern, but she sensed that it was drawing to its conclusion and that, any second, she would come around again to Thiago.

Akiva would have to hand her back into the general's keeping.

Her heart and body were in revolt. She couldn't do it. Her limbs were light, ready to flee. Her heartbeat sped to a fast staccato, and the remnants of her living shawl burst from her as if spooked. Madrigal recognized the signs in herself, the readying, the outward calm and inner turmoil, the rushing that filled her mind before a charge in battle.

Something is going to happen.

Nitid, she thought, *did you know all along?*

"Madrigal?" asked Akiva. Like the hummingbird-moths, he sensed the change in her, her quickened breath, the muscles gone taut where his warm hands encircled her waist. "What is it?"

"I want..." she said, knowing what she wanted, feeling pulled toward it, arching toward it, but hardly knowing how to say it.

"What? What do you want?" Akiva asked, gentle but urgent.

He wanted it, too. He inclined his head so that his mask came briefly against her horn, sparking a flare of sensation through her.

The White Wolf was only wingspans away. He would see. If she tried to flee, he would follow. Akiva would be caught.

Madrigal wanted to scream.

And then, the fireworks.

Later, she would recall what Akiva had said about everything lining up, as if it were meant. In all that was to happen, there would be that feeling of inevitability and rightness, and the sense that the universe was conspiring in it. It would be easy. Starting with the fireworks.

Light blossomed overhead, a great and brilliant dahlia, a pinwheel, a star in nova. The sound was a cannonade. Drummers on the battlements. Black powder bursting in the air. The Emberlin broke apart as dancers shucked masks and threw back their heads to look up.

Madrigal moved. She took Akiva's hand and ducked into the moil of the crowd. She kept low and moved fast. A channel seemed to open for them in the surge of bodies, and they followed it, and it carried them away.

❧ 55 ❧

CHILDREN OF REGRET

Once upon a time, before chimaera and seraphim, there was the sun and the moons. The sun was betrothed to Nitid, the bright sister, but it was demure Ellai, always hiding behind her bold sister, who stirred his lust. He contrived to come upon her bathing in the sea, and he took her. She struggled, but he was the sun, and he thought he should have what he wanted. Ellai stabbed him and escaped, and the blood of the sun flew like sparks to earth, where it became seraphim — misbegotten children of fire. And like their father, they believed it their due to want, and take, and have.

As for Ellai, she told her sister what had passed, and Nitid wept, and her tears fell to earth and became chimaera, children of regret.

When the sun came again to the sisters, neither would have him. Nitid put Ellai behind her and protected her, though the sun, still bleeding sparks, knew Ellai was not as defenseless as she seemed. He pled with Nitid to forgive him but she refused, and to this day he follows the sisters across the sky, wanting and wanting and never having, and that will be his punishment, forever.

Nitid is the goddess of tears and life, hunts and war, and her temples are too many to count. It is she who fills wombs, slows the hearts of the dying, and leads her children against the seraphim. Her light is like a small sun; she chases away shadows.

Ellai is more subtle. She is a trace, a phantom moon, and there are only a handful of nights each year when she alone takes the sky. These are called Ellai nights, and they are dark and star-scattered and good for furtive things. Ellai is the goddess of assassins and secret lovers. Temples to her are few, and hidden, like the one in the requiem grove in the hills above Loramendi.

That was where Madrigal took Akiva when they fled the Warlord's ball.

* * *

They flew. He kept his wings veiled, but it didn't prevent his flying. By land, the requiem grove was unreachable. There were chasms in the hills, and sometimes rope bridges were strung across them — on Ellai nights, when devotees went cloaked to worship at the temple — but tonight there were none, and Madrigal knew they would have the temple to themselves.

They had the night. Nitid was still high. They had hours.

"*That* is your legend?" Akiva asked, incredulous. Madrigal had told him the story of the sun and Ellai while they flew. "That seraphim are the blood of a rapist sun?"

375

Madrigal said blithely, "If you don't like it, take it up with the sun."

"It's a terrible story. What a brutal imagination chimaera have."

"Well. We have had brutal inspiration."

They reached the grove, and the dome of the temple was just visible through the treetops, silver mosaics glinting patterns through the boughs.

"Here," said Madrigal, slowing with a backbeat to descend through a gap in the canopy. Her whole body thrilled with night wind and freedom, and with anticipation. In the back of her mind was fear of what would come later — the repercussions of her rash departure. But as she moved through the trees, it was drowned out by leaf rustle and wind music, and by the *hish-hish* all around. *Hish-hish* went the evangelines, serpent-birds who drank the night nectar of the requiem trees. In the dark of the grove, their eyes shone silver like the mosaics of the temple roof.

Madrigal reached the ground, and Akiva landed beside her in a gust of warmth. She faced him. They were still wearing their masks. They could have stripped them off while flying, but they hadn't. Madrigal had been thinking of this moment, when they would stand face-to-face, and she had left her mask on because in her imagining, it was Akiva who took hers off, as she did his.

He must have imagined the same thing. He stepped toward her.

The real world, already a distant thing — just a crackle of fireworks at horizon's edge — faded away entirely. A high, sweet thrill sang through Madrigal as if she were a lute string. Akiva took off his gloves and dropped them, and when he touched her, fingertips trailing up her arms and neck, it was with his bare hands. He reached behind her head, untied her mask, and lifted it away. Her vision, which had been narrowed all night to what she could see through its small apertures, opened, and Akiva filled her sight, still wearing his comical mask. She heard his soft exhalation and murmur of "so beautiful," and she reached up and took off his disguise.

"Hello," she whispered, as she had when they had come together in the Emberlin and happiness had bloomed in her. That happiness was like a spark to a firework, compared with what filled her now.

He was more perfect even than she remembered. At Bullfinch he had lain dying, ashen, slack, and still beautiful for all that. Now, in the full flush of health and the blood-thrum of love, he was golden. He was ardent, gazing at her, hopeful and expectant, inspired, beguiled, *glad*. He was so *alive*.

Because of her, he was alive.

He whispered back, "Hello."

They stared, amazed to be facing each other after two years, as if they were figments conjured out of wishing.

Only touching could make the moment real.

Madrigal's hands shook as she raised them, and steadied when she laid them against the solidity of Akiva's chest. Heat pulsed through the fabric of his shirt. The air in the grove was rich enough to sip, full enough to dance with. It was like a presence between them — and then not, as she stepped close.

His arms encircled her and she tilted up her face to whisper, once more, "Hello."

This time when he said it back, he breathed it against her lips. Their eyes were still open, still wide with wonder, and they only let them flutter shut when their lips finally met and another sense — touch — could take over in convincing them that this was real.

❧ 56 ❧

THE INVENTION OF LIVING

Once upon a time, there was only darkness, and there were monsters vast as worlds who swam in it. They were the Gibborim, and they loved the darkness because it concealed their hideousness. Whenever some other creature contrived to make light, they would extinguish it. When stars were born, they swallowed them, and it seemed that darkness would be eternal.

But a race of bright warriors heard of the Gibborim and traveled from their far world to do battle with them. The war was long, light against dark, and many of the warriors were slain. In the end, when they vanquished the monsters, there were a hundred left alive, and these hundred were the godstars, who brought light to the universe.

They made the rest of the stars, including our sun, and there was no more darkness, only endless light. They made children in their image—seraphim—and sent them down to bear light to the worlds that spun in space, and all was good. But one day, the last of the Gibborim, who was called Zamzumin, persuaded them that shadows were needed, that they would make the light seem brighter by contrast, and so the godstars brought shadows into being.

But Zamzumin was a trickster. He needed only a shred of darkness to work with. He breathed life into the shadows, and as the godstars had made the seraphim in their own image, so did Zamzumin make the chimaera in his, and so they were hideous, and forever after the seraphim would fight on the side of light, and chimaera for dark, and they would be enemies until the end of the world.

*　*　*

Madrigal laughed sleepily. "Zamzumin? That's a name?"

"Don't ask me. He's your forefather."

"Ah, yes. Ugly Uncle Zamzumin, who made me out of a shadow."

"A hideous shadow," said Akiva. "Which explains your hideousness."

She laughed again, heavy and lazy with pleasure. "I always wondered where I got it. Now I know. My horns are from my father's side, and my hideousness is from my huge, evil monster uncle." After a pause, Akiva nuzzling her neck, she added, "I like my story better. I'd rather be made from tears than darkness."

"Neither is very cheerful," said Akiva.

"I know. We need a happier myth. Let's make one up."

They lay entwined atop their clothes, which they had draped over a bank of shrive moss behind Ellai's temple, where a delicate rill burbled past. Both moons had slipped beyond the canopy of the trees, and the evangelines were falling silent as the requiem blooms closed their white buds for the night. Soon Madrigal would have to leave, but they were both pushing the thought away, as if they could deny the dawn.

"Once upon a time..." said Akiva, but his voice trailed off as his lips found Madrigal's throat. "Mmm, sugar. I thought I got it all. Now I'll have to double-check *everywhere*."

Madrigal squirmed, laughing helplessly. "No, no, it tickles!"

But Akiva would retaste her neck, and it didn't really tickle so much as it *tingled*, and she stopped protesting soon enough.

It was some time before they got back around to their new myth.

"Once upon a time," Madrigal murmured later, her face now resting on Akiva's chest so that the curve of her left horn followed the line of his face, and he could tilt his brow against it. "There was a world that was perfectly made and full of birds and striped creatures and lovely things like honey lilies and star tenzing and weasels—"

"*Weasels?*"

"Hush. And this world already had light and shadow, so it didn't need any rogue stars to come and save it, and it had no use for bleeding suns or weeping moons, either, and most important, it had never known war, which is a terrible, wasteful thing that no world ever needs. It had earth and water, air and fire, all four elements, but it was missing the last element. Love."

Akiva's eyes were closed. He smiled as he listened, and stroked the soft down of Madrigal's fur-short hair, and traced the ridges of her horns.

"And so this paradise was like a jewel box without a jewel. There it lay, day after day of rose-colored dawns and creature sounds and strange perfumes, and waited for lovers to find it and fill it with their happiness." Pause. "The end."

"The end?" Akiva opened his eyes. "What do you mean, the end?"

She said, smoothing her cheek against the golden skin of his chest, "The story is unfinished. The world is still waiting."

He said wistfully, "Do you know how to find it? Let's leave before the sun rises."

The sun. The reminder stilled Madrigal's lips from their new course up the curve of Akiva's shoulder, the one scarred with the reminder of their first meeting, at Bullfinch. She thought how she might have left him bleeding, or worse, finished him, but some ineluctable thing had stopped her so that they might be here, now. And the idea of disentangling, dressing, *leaving*, gave rise to a reluctance so powerful it hurt.

There was dread, too, of what her disappearance might have stirred up back at Loramendi. An image of Thiago, angry, intruded into her happiness, and she pushed it away, but there was no pushing away the sunrise. In a mournful voice, she said, "I have to go."

Akiva said, "I know," and she lifted her face from his shoulder and saw that his wretchedness matched her own. He didn't ask, "What will we do?" and she didn't, either. Later they would talk of such things; on that first night, they were shy of the future and, for all that they had loved and discovered in the night, still shy of each other.

Instead, Madrigal reached up for the charm she wore around

her neck. "Do you know what this is?" she asked him, untying the cord.

"A bone?"

"Well, yes. It's a wishbone. You hook your finger around the spur, like this, and we each make a wish and pull. Whoever gets the bigger piece gets their wish."

"Magic?" Akiva asked, sitting up. "What bird does this come from, that its bones make magic?"

"Oh, it's not magic. The wishes don't really come true."

"Then why do it?"

She shrugged. "Hope? Hope can be a powerful force. Maybe there's no actual magic in it, but when you know what you hope for most and hold it like a light within you, you can make things happen, almost like magic."

"And what do you hope for most?"

"You're not supposed to tell. Come, wish with me."

She held up the wishbone.

It was part whimsy and part impudence that had made her put the thing on a cord. She had been fourteen, four years in Brimstone's service, but also now in battle training and feeling full of her own power. She'd come into the shop one afternoon while Twiga was plucking newly minted lucknows from their molds, and she had wheedled for one.

Brimstone had not yet educated her about the harsh reality of magic and the pain tithe, and she still regarded wishing as fun. When he refused her—as he always did, not counting scuppies, which cost a mere pinch of pain to create—she'd had a small, dramatic meltdown in the corner. She couldn't even remember now what wish had been of such dire importance to her fourteen-year-old self, but she well remembered Issa extracting a bone from the remains of the evening meal — a grimgrouse in sauce — and comforting her with the human lore of the wishbone.

Issa had a wealth of human stories, and it was from her that Madrigal came by her fascination with that race and their world. In defiance of Brimstone, she took the bone and made an elaborate show of wishing on it.

"That's it?" Brimstone asked, when he heard what petty desire had inspired her tantrum. "You would have wasted a wish on that?"

She and Issa were on the verge of breaking the bone between them, but they stopped.

"You're not a fool, Madrigal," Brimstone said. "If there's something you want, pursue it. Hope has power. Don't waste it on foolish things."

"Fine," she said, cupping the wishbone in her hand. "I'll save it until my hope meets your high expectations." She put it on a cord. For a few weeks she made a point of voicing ridiculous wishes aloud and pretending to ponder them.

"I wish I could taste with my feet like a butterfly."

"I wish scorpion-mice could talk. I bet they know the best gossip."

"I wish my hair was blue."

But she never broke the bone. What started as childish defiance turned into something else. Weeks became months, and the longer she went without breaking the wishbone, the more important it seemed that when she did, the wish — the *hope*, rather — should be worthy of her.

In the requiem grove with Akiva, it finally was.

She formed her wish in her mind, looking him in the eyes, and pulled. The bone broke clean down the middle, and the pieces, when measured against each other, were of exactly the same length.

"Oh. I don't know what that means. Maybe it means we both get our wishes."

"Maybe it means that we wished for the same thing."

Madrigal liked to think that it did. Her wish that first time was simple, focused, and passionate: that she would see him again. Believing she would was the only way she could bring herself to leave.

They rose from their crushed clothes. Madrigal had to wriggle back into the midnight gown like a serpent back into a shed skin. They went into the temple and drank water from the sacred spring that rose in a fount from the earth. She splashed her face with it, too, paid silent homage to Ellai to protect their secret, and vowed to bring candles when she came again.

Because of course she would come again.

Parting was almost like a stage drama, an exaggerated physical impossibility—to fly away and leave Akiva there—the difficulty of which she would not, before this moment, have believed. She kept turning and returning for one last kiss. Her lips, unaccustomed to such wear, felt mussed and obvious, carnal, and she imagined herself red with the evidence of how she had spent her night.

Finally she flew, trailing her mask by one of its long ribbon ties like a companion bird winging at her side, and the dawn-touched land rolled beneath her all the way back to Loramendi.

The city lay quiet in the aftermath of celebration, pungent and hazy with the residue of fireworks. She went in by a secret passage to the underground cathedral. Its interlocking gates were keyed by Brimstone's magic to open to her voice, and there was no guard to see her come in.

It was easy.

That first day she was hesitant, cautious, not knowing what had passed in her absence, or what wrath might await her. But the fates were weaving their unguessable threads, and a spy came that morning from the Mirea coast with news of seraph galleons on the move, so that Thiago was gone from Loramendi almost as soon as Madrigal returned to it.

Chiro asked her where she'd been and she gave a vague lie, and from then on her sister's manner toward her changed. Madrigal would catch her watching her with a strange, flat affect, only to turn away and busy herself with something as if she hadn't been watching her at all. She saw her less, too, in part because Madrigal was adrift in her new and secret world, and in part because Brimstone had need of her help in that time, and so she was excused from her other duties, such as they were. Her battalion was not mobilized in response to the seraph troop movements, and she thought, ironically, that she had Thiago to thank for it. She knew that he'd been keeping her from any potential danger that might relieve her of her "purity" before he had a chance to marry her. He must not have had time to countermand the orders before his departure.

So Madrigal spent her days in the shop and cathedral with Brimstone, stringing teeth and conjuring bodies, and she spent her nights — as many as she could — with Akiva.

She brought candles for Ellai, and cones of frangible, the moon's favorite spice, and she smuggled out food fit for lovers, which they ate with their fingers after love. Honey sweets and sin berries, and roasted birds for their ravenous appetites, and always they remembered to take the wishbone from its place in the bird's breast. She brought wine in slender bottles, and tiny cups carved from quartz to sip it from, which they rinsed in the sacred spring and stored in the temple altar for the next time.

Over each wishbone, at each parting, they hoped for a next time.

Madrigal often thought, as she sat quietly working in Brimstone's presence, that he knew what she was doing. His goldgreen gaze would rest on her, and she would feel pierced, exposed, and tell herself that she couldn't go on as she was, that it was madness and she had to end it. Once she even rehearsed what she was going to say to Akiva as she flew to the requiem grove, but as soon as she saw him it went out of her mind, and she slipped without struggle into the luxury of joy, in the place they had come to think of as the world from her story—the paradise waiting for lovers to fill it with happiness.

And they did fill it. For a month of stolen nights and the occasional sun-drenched afternoon when Madrigal could get away from Loramendi by day, they cupped their wings around their happiness and called it a world, though they both knew it was not a world, only a hiding place, which is a very different thing.

After they had come together a handful of times and begun to learn each other in earnest, with the hunger of lovers to know everything—in talk and in touch, every memory and thought, every musk and murmur—when all shyness had left them, they admitted the future: that it existed, that they couldn't pretend it didn't. They both knew this wasn't a life, especially for Akiva, who saw no one but Madrigal and spent his days sleeping like the evangelines and longing for night.

Akiva confessed that he was the emperor's bastard, one of a legion bred to kill, and he told her of the day the guards had come into the harem to take him from his mother. How she had turned away and let them, as if he wasn't her child at all, but only a tithe she had to pay. How he hated his father for breeding children to the task of death, and in flashes she could see that he blamed himself, too, for being one of them.

Madrigal smoothed the raised scars on his knuckles and imagined the chimaera represented by each line. She wondered how many of their souls had been gleaned, and how many lost.

She did not tell Akiva the secret of resurrection. When he asked why she bore no eye tattoos on her palms, she invented a lie. She couldn't tell him about revenants. It was too great a thing, too dire, the very fate of her race balanced upon it, and she couldn't share it, not even to assuage his guilt for all the chimaera he had killed. Instead, she kissed his marks and told him, "War is all we've been taught, but there are other ways to live. We can find them, Akiva. We can *invent* them. This is the beginning, here." She touched his chest and felt a rush of love for the heart that moved his blood, for his smooth skin and his scars and his unsoldierly tenderness. She took his hand and pressed it to her breast and said, "*We* are the beginning."

They began to believe that they could be.

Akiva told her that, in the two years since Bullfinch, he had not slain another chimaera.

"Is it true?" she asked, hardly believing it.

"You showed me that one might choose not to kill."

Madrigal looked down at her hands and confessed, "But *I* have killed seraphim since that day," and Akiva took her chin and tilted her face up to his.

"But in saving *me*, you changed me, and here we are because of that moment. Before, could you have thought it possible?"

She shook her head.

"Don't you think others could be changed, too?"

"Some," she said, thinking of her comrades, friends. The White Wolf. "Not all."

"Some, and then more."

Some, and then more. Madrigal nodded, and together they imagined a different life, not just for themselves, but for all the races of Eretz. And in that month that they hid and loved, dreamed and planned, they believed that this, too, was meant: that they were the blossoms set forth by some great and mysterious intention. Whether it was Nitid or the godstars or something else altogether, they didn't know, only that a powerful will was alive in them, to bring peace to their world.

When they broke their wishbones now, that was what they hoped for. They knew they couldn't hide in the requiem grove and daydream forever. There was work to be done; they were just beginning to make it real, with such passion in their hope that they might have wrought miracles—*begun* something— had they not been betrayed.

❦ 57 ❦

REVENANT

"Akiva," breathed Karou with the fullness of her self.

Mere seconds had passed since they had broken the wishbone, but in that space of time, years had come home to her. Seventeen years ago, Madrigal had ended. All that had happened since was another life, but it was hers, too. She was Karou, and she was Madrigal. She was human and chimaera.

She was revenant.

Within her, something was at work: a swift concrescence of memories, two consciousnesses that were really one, coming together like interlacing fingers.

She saw her hamsas and knew what Brimstone had done. In defiance of Thiago's sentence of evanescence, he had somehow gleaned her soul. And because she could not have a life in her own world, he had given her one here, in secret. How had he extracted her memory from her soul? The life she had lived as

Madrigal—he had taken it all and put it in the wishbone, and saved it for her.

It came to her what Izîl had said the last time she saw him, when he offered her baby teeth and she rejected them. *"Once,"* he'd said, and she hadn't believed him. "Once he wanted some."

She believed it now.

Revenants were made for battle; their bodies were always conjured fully grown, from mature teeth. But Brimstone had made her a baby, a human, named her *hope* and given her a whole life, far away from war and death. Sweet, deep, fond love filled her. He had given her a childhood, a world. Wishes. *Art.* And Issa and Yasri and Twiga, they had known and helped; hidden her. Loved her. She would see them soon, and she wouldn't stand back from Brimstone as she always did, cowed by his gruffness and his monstrous physical presence. She would throw her arms around him and say, finally, *thank you.*

She looked up from her palms—from one wonder to another—and Akiva was before her. He still stood at the foot of the bed on which, just a moment earlier, they had fallen back together, all of him against all of her, and Karou understood that the aching allness rose from what she had shared with him in another body, another life. She had fallen in love with him twice. She loved him now with both loves, so overpowering it was almost unbearable. She beheld him through a prism of tears.

"You escaped," she said. "You lived."

She uncoiled from the bed, flashed toward him, threw herself against the remembered solidity of him, the heat.

A hesitation, then his arms came around her, tight. He

didn't speak, but held her against him and rocked back and forth. She felt him shake, weeping, his lips pressed to the crown of her head.

"You escaped," she repeated, sobbing, but laughing now, too. "You're alive."

"I'm alive," he whispered, choked. "*You're* alive. I never knew. All these years, I never thought—"

"We're alive," Karou said, dazed. The wonder of it swelled within her, and she felt like their myth had come to life. They had a world; they were in it. This place that Brimstone had given her, it was half her home, and the other half lay waiting through a portal in the sky. They could have both, couldn't they?

"I saw you die," Akiva said, helpless. "Karou... Madrigal... My love." His eyes, his expression. He looked as he had seventeen years ago, on his knees, forced to watch. He said again, "I saw you die."

"I know." She kissed him tenderly, remembering the scouring horror of his scream. "I remember it all."

* * *

As did he.

The hooded executioner: a monster. The Wolf and the Warlord, looking on from their balcony, and the crowd, their stamping riot, their roars and bloodlust: monsters all, making a mockery of the dream of peace Akiva had nurtured since Bullfinch. Because one among them had touched his soul, he had believed them all worthy of that dream.

And there she stood in shackles—the one; *his* one—her

392

wings in their pinion crimped cruelly out of shape, and the sham dream was gone. This was what they did to their own. His beautiful Madrigal, graceful even now.

He watched in helpless horror as she sank to her knees. Laid her head on the block. *Impossible*, screamed Akiva's heart. This couldn't happen. The will, the mystery that had been on their side... where was it now? Madrigal's neck, stretched vulnerable, her smooth cheek to the hot black rock, and the blade, raised high and poised to fall.

His scream was a thing. It clawed its way out of him, gutting him from the inside. It ripped and tore; there was pain, pain to summon, and he tried to work it into magic, but he was too weak. The Wolf had seen to that: Even now Akiva was flanked by revenant guards, their hamsas aimed at him and flooding him with their debilitating sickness. Still he tried, and ripples went through the crowd as the very ground beneath their feet shifted. The scaffold rocked, the executioner had to take a step to steady himself, but it wasn't enough.

The effort burst the blood vessels in his eyes. Still he screamed. Tried.

The blade glinted its descent, and Akiva fell forward on his hands. He was shredded, empty. Love, peace, wonder: gone. Hope, humanity: gone.

All that remained was vengeance.

❖ ❖ ❖

The blade was a great and shining thing, like a falling moon. It bit, and Madrigal was unsheathed.

She was aware of the falling away of flesh.

She still was. She *was*, but she was not corporeal. She didn't want to see her head's disgraceful tumble, but couldn't help it. Her horns hit the platform first with a clatter, and then there was the ungodly thud of meat before it came to rest, the horns preventing it from rolling.

From this strange new vantage point above her body, she saw it all. She couldn't not. The eyes had been the body's apparatus, with their selective focus and lids for closing. She had no such ability now. She saw everything, with no fleshly boundary to divide herself from the air all around her. It was a muted kind of seeing, all directions at once as if her entire being were an eye, but a hazy one. The agora, the hateful crowd. And on the platform facing her own, his scream still warping the air around her: Akiva on his knees, pitched forward and wracked with sobs.

Below her she saw her own body, headless. It swayed to one side and collapsed. It was finished. Madrigal felt tethered to it. She had expected that; she knew souls stayed with their bodies for several days before beginning to ebb. Revenants who had been snatched back from the verge of evanescence had said it felt like a tide carrying them out.

Thiago had ordered her body left on the platform to rot, under guard, so that no one might attempt to glean her soul. She was sorry for the treatment of her body. For all that Brimstone might call bodies "envelopes," she loved the skin that had carried her through her life, and she wished it could have a more respectful end, but it couldn't be helped, and anyway, she didn't intend to be here to see it break down. She had other plans.

She wasn't certain that it could be done, this idea she clung to. She had nothing but a hint to go on, but she wrapped all her will around it, and all her longing and passion. Everything that she and Akiva had dreamed about, now thwarted, she directed into this one last act: She was going to set him free.

To which end, she would need a body. She had one picked out. It was a good one; she'd made it herself.

She had even used diamonds.

❧ 58 ❧

VICTORY AND VENGEANCE

"What's going on with you, Mad?"

A week earlier, Madrigal had been with Chiro in the barracks. It was dawn, and she had crept into her bunk a mere half hour earlier from a night with Akiva. "What do you mean?"

"Do you ever sleep anymore? Where were you last night?"

"Working," she said.

"All night?"

"Yes, all night. Though I may have fallen asleep in the shop for a couple of hours." She yawned. She felt safe in her lies because no one outside Brimstone's inner circle knew what went on in the west tower, or even knew about the secret passageway through which she came and went. And it was true that she had slept for a little while—just not in the shop. She'd dozed curled against Akiva's chest and woken to him watching her.

"What?" she'd asked, bashful.

"Good dreams? You were smiling in your sleep."

"Of course I was. I'm happy."

Happy.

She thought that was what Chiro really meant when she asked, "What's going on with you?" Madrigal felt *remade*. She had never guessed how deep happiness could go. In spite of the tragedy in her childhood and the ever-present press of war, she had mostly considered herself happy. There was almost always something to take delight in, if you were trying. But this was different. It couldn't be contained. She sometimes imagined it streaming out of her like light.

Happiness. It was the place where passion, with all its dazzle and drumbeat, met something softer: homecoming and safety and pure sunbeam comfort. It was all those things, intertwined with the heat and the thrill, and it was as bright within her as a swallowed star.

Her foster sister was scrutinizing her in silence when a trumpet blast in the city caused her to turn to the window. Madrigal went to her side and looked out. Their barracks were behind the armory, and they could just see the facade of the palace on the far side of the agora, where the Warlord's gonfalon hung, a vast silk banner that indicated he was in residence. It bore his heraldry—antlers sprouting leaves to signify new growth— and beside it, as Madrigal and Chiro watched, another gonfalon unfurled. This one was blazoned with a white wolf, and though it was too distant to read, they both knew its motto well.

Victory and vengeance.

Thiago had returned to Loramendi.

Chiro's hands fluttered so that she had to steady them against the window ledge. Madrigal saw her sister's excitement, even as she fought her own rising bile. She had chosen to take Thiago's departure and absence as a sign—of fate conspiring in her happiness. But if his absence had been a sign, what did his return signify? The sight of his banner was like a splash of icy water. It couldn't douse her happiness, but it made her want to curl around it and protect it.

She shivered.

Chiro noticed. "What's the matter? Are you afraid of him?"

"Not afraid," Madrigal said. "Only anxious that I gave offense, disappearing like I did." Her story had been that she'd drunk too much grasswine and, overcome by nerves, had hidden in the cathedral, where she'd fallen asleep. She studied her sister's expression and asked, "Was he . . . very angry?"

"No one likes to be rejected, Mad."

She took that as a yes. "Do you think it's over now, though? That he's through with me?"

"One way you could make sure," said Chiro. She was glib, jesting—surely—but her eyes were bright. "You could die," she said. "Resurrect ugly. He'd leave you alone then."

Madrigal should have known then—to take care, at least. But she hadn't the soul for suspicion. Her trust was her undoing.

❦ 59 ❦

The World Remade

"I can't save you."

Brimstone. Madrigal looked up. She was on the floor in the corner of her barren prison cell, and didn't expect saving. "I know."

He approached the bars, and she held herself still, chin raised, face blank. Would he spit at her, as others had? He didn't have to. The simple fact of Brimstone's disappointment was worse than anything others could hurl at her.

"Have they hurt you?" he asked.

"Only by hurting him."

Which was worse a torture than she could have believed. Wherever they were keeping Akiva, it was just near enough that she could hear his screams when they crested into full agony. They rose, wavering audible at irregular intervals, so she never knew when the next one was coming, and had lived the past days in a state of sick expectancy.

Brimstone studied her. "You love him."

She could only nod. She'd held up so well until now, high dignity and a hard veneer, not letting them see how inside she was dissolving, as if her evanescence had already begun. But under Brimstone's scrutiny, her lower lip began to tremble. She crushed her knuckles against it to still it. He was silent, and once she thought she could trust her voice, she said, "I'm sorry."

"For what, child?"

Was he mocking her? His ovine face had always been impossible to read. Kishmish was on his horn, and the creature's posture mimicked his master's, the tilt of his head, the hunch of his shoulders. Brimstone asked, "Are you sorry for falling in love?"

"No. Not for that."

"Then what?"

She didn't know what he wanted her to say. In the past, he had told her that all he ever wanted was the truth, as plain as she could make it. So what was the truth? What was she sorry for?

"For getting caught," she said. "And... for making you ashamed."

"Should I be ashamed?"

She blinked at him. She would never have believed that Brimstone would taunt her. She had thought he just wouldn't come, that her last sight of him would be on the palace balcony as he awaited her execution along with everyone else.

He said, "Tell me what it is you have done."

"You know what I've done."

"Tell me."

It was to be taunting, then. Madrigal bowed to it. She gave him a recitation. "High treason. Consorting with the enemy.

400

Endangering the perpetuity of the chimaera race and everything we've fought for for a thousand years—"

He cut her off. "I know your sentence. Tell me in your own words."

She swallowed, trying to divine what he wanted. Haltingly, she said, "I...I fell in love. I—" She shot him an abashed glance before revealing what she had so far told no one. "It started at the Battle of Bullfinch. The fighting was over. It was after, during the gleaning. I found him dying and I saved him. I didn't know why; it felt like the only thing. Later...later I thought it was because we were meant for something." Her voice dropped and her cheeks flamed as she whispered, "To bring peace."

"Peace," Brimstone echoed.

How childish it seemed, considering where she was now, to have believed there was some divine intention in their love. And yet, how beautiful it had been. What she had shared with Akiva could not be touched by shame. Madrigal lifted her voice to say, "We dreamed together of the world remade."

There followed a long silence, Brimstone just looking at her, and if she hadn't made a game of trying to outstare him as a child she would have been ill-equipped to endure it. Even so, she was burning to blink by the time he finally spoke. "And for that," he said, "I should be ashamed of you?"

All the cogs of misery within Madrigal froze. It felt as if her blood stopped moving. She didn't hope...she didn't dare. What did he mean? Would he say more?

No. He breathed a heavy sigh, and said again, "I can't save you."

"I...I know."

"Yasri sent you these." He thrust a cloth bundle through the bars, and Madrigal took it. It was warm, fragrant. She unwrapped it and saw the horn-shaped pastries Yasri had been stuffing her with for years in a vain effort to fatten her up. Tears sprang to her eyes.

She laid them gently aside. "I can't eat," she said. "But... tell her I did?"

"I will."

"And... Issa and Twiga." An ache swelled in her throat. "Tell them..." She had to press her knuckles to her lips again. She was barely holding it together. Why was it so much more difficult in Brimstone's presence? Before he came in, anger had kept her hard.

Though she had yet to give him a message to relay, he said, "They know, child. They already know. And they aren't ashamed of you, either."

Either.

It was as close as he would come, and it was good enough. Madrigal burst into tears. She leaned into the bars, head down, and wept, and she felt his hand settle on her neck, and wept harder.

He stayed with her, and she knew that no one but Brimstone—save the Warlord himself—could have overridden Thiago's direct order that she have no visitors. He had power, but even he couldn't overrule her sentence. Her crime was just too grave, her guilt too plain.

After she had cried, she felt at once hollow and... better, as if the salt of all her unshed tears had been poisoning her, and now she was cleansed. She leaned against the bars; Brimstone was hunkered down on the other side. Kishmish started chirping regular little snips that Madrigal knew were a combination boss/beg, so she broke off bits of Yasri's pastry and fed them to him.

"Prison picnic," she said, with a weak effort at a smile, which then bit off abruptly.

They both heard it at the same time—a scream of such pure wretchedness that Madrigal had to fold over herself, press her face to her knees and her hands to her ears, pitching herself in darkness, silence, denial. It didn't work. This fresh scream was already in her skull, and even after it stopped, its echo stayed inside her.

"Who will be first?" she asked Brimstone.

He knew what she meant. "You. With the seraph watching."

In a moment of strange detachment, she said, "I thought he would decide the opposite, and make me watch."

"I believe," said Brimstone with some hesitation, "that he isn't...finished with him yet."

A small sound escaped Madrigal's throat. How long? How long would Thiago make him suffer?

She asked Brimstone, "Do you remember the wishbone, when I was younger?"

"I remember."

"I finally made a wish on it. Or...a *hope*, I suppose, as there was no real magic in it."

"Hope *is* the real magic, child."

Images flashed through her mind. Akiva smiling his smile of light. Akiva beaten to the ground, his blood running into the sacred spring. The temple in flames as the soldiers dragged them away, the requiem trees starting to catch fire, too, and all the evangelines that lived in them. She reached into her pocket and produced the wishbone she had brought to the grove that last time. It was intact. They had never gotten the chance to break it.

She thrust it at Brimstone. "Here. Take it, trample it, throw it away. There is no hope."

"If I believed that," Brimstone said, "I wouldn't be here now."

What did that mean?

"What do I do, child, day after day, but fight against a tide? Wave after wave upon the shore, each wave licking farther up the sand. We won't win, Madrigal. We can't beat the seraphim."

"What? But—"

"We can't win this war. I've always known it. They are too strong. The only reason we've held them off this long is because we burned the library."

"The library?"

"Of Astrae. It was the archive of the seraph magi. The fools kept all their texts in one place. They were so jealous of their power, they didn't allow copies. They didn't want any upstarts to challenge them, so they hoarded their knowledge, and they took only apprentices they could control, and kept them close. That was their first mistake, keeping all their power in one place."

Madrigal listened, rapt. Brimstone, telling her things. History. *Secrets.* Almost afraid to break the spell, she asked, "What was their next mistake?"

"Forgetting to fear us." He was silent a moment. Kishmish hopped back and forth from one of his horns to the other. "They needed to believe we were animals, to justify the way they used us."

"Slaves," she whispered, hearing Issa's voice in her head.

"We were pain thralls. *We* were the source of their power."

"Torture."

"They told themselves we were dumb beasts, as if that made it all right. They had five thousand beasts in their pits who weren't dumb at all, but they believed their own fiction. They didn't fear us, and that made it easy."

"Made what easy?"

"Destroying them. Half the guards didn't even understand our language, were happy to believe it was just grunts and roars we screamed in our agony. They were fools, and we killed them, and we burned everything. Without magic the seraphim lost their supremacy, and all these years, they have not recovered it. But they will, even without the library. Your seraph is proof that they are rediscovering what they lost."

"But...No. Akiva's magic, it isn't like that—" She thought of the living shawl he'd made her. "He would never use it as a weapon. He only wanted peace."

"Magic isn't a tool of peace. The price is too high. The only way I can keep using it, cycling souls through death after death, is by believing that we are keeping alive until...until the world can be remade."

Her words.

He cleared his throat. It sounded like gravel churning. Was it possible, was he telling her that he...?

He said, "I dream it, too, child."

Madrigal stared.

"Magic won't save us. The power it would take to conjure on such a scale, the tithe would destroy us. The only hope...is

405

hope." He still held the wishbone. "You don't need tokens for it — it's in your heart or nowhere. And in your heart, child, it has been stronger than I have ever seen." He slipped the bone into his breast pocket, then rose from his lion-haunched crouch and turned. Madrigal's heart cried out at the thought that he was leaving her alone.

But he only paced to the small window on the far wall and looked out. "It was Chiro, you know," he said, an abrupt change of subject.

Madrigal knew.

Chiro, who had the wings to follow her, and who hid in the grove, and saw.

Chiro, who, like Thiago's lapdog, betrayed her for a pat on the head.

"Thiago promised her human aspect," Brimstone said. "As if it were a promise he could keep."

Stupid Chiro, thought Madrigal. If that was her hope, she had chosen her alliance poorly. "You won't honor his promise?"

With a dark look, Brimstone replied, "She should make best efforts to never need another body. I have a string of moray eel teeth I never thought I would be tempted to use."

Moray eel? Madrigal couldn't tell if he was serious. Probably. She felt almost sorry for her sister. Almost. "To think I wasted diamonds on her."

"You were true to her, even if she was not to you. Never repent of your own goodness, child. To stay true in the face of evil is a feat of strength."

"Strength," she said with a little laugh. "I gave *her* strength, and look what she did with it."

He scoffed. "Chiro is not strong. Her body may have been wrought with diamonds, but her soul within will be a soft mollusk thing, wet and shrinking."

It was an unlovely image, but it felt just about right.

Brimstone added, "And easily pushed aside."

Madrigal cocked her head. "What?"

Out in the corridor: sounds. Was someone coming? Was it time? Brimstone spun toward her. "The revenant smoke," he said, quick and clipped. "You know what is in it."

She blinked. Why was he talking about the smoke? There would be none of it for her. But he was looking at her so intently. She nodded. Of course she knew. The incense was arum and feverfew, rosemary, and asafetida resin for the sulfur smell.

"You know why it works," he said.

"It makes a path for the soul to follow, to the vessel. The thurible, or the body."

"Is it magic?"

Madrigal hesitated. She'd helped Twiga make it often enough. "No," she said, distracted, as the sounds in the corridor grew louder. "It's just smoke. Just a path for the soul."

Brimstone nodded. "Not unlike your wishbone. It isn't magic, just a focus for the will." He paused. "A powerful will might not even need it."

His look burned at her, steady. He was trying to tell her something. What?

Madrigal's hands started to shake. She didn't understand, quite, but something was starting to take shape, out of magic and will. Smoke and bone.

At the door, the bolts drew back. Madrigal's heart pounded.

Her wings made the ineffectual fluttering of a caged bird. The door opened and Thiago framed himself in it like a picture. As ever, he was clad all in white, and Madrigal realized for the first time *why* he wore white: It was a canvas for the blood of his victims, and now his surcoat was livid with it.

With Akiva's blood.

Thiago's face flashed anger when he saw Brimstone in the room. But he didn't risk a battle of wills he couldn't win. He inclined his head to the sorcerer and faced Madrigal. "It's time," he said. His voice, perversely, was soft, as if he were coaxing a child to sleep.

She said nothing, fought for calm. Thiago wasn't fooled. His wolf senses could smell the tang of her fear. He smiled, turning to the guards who awaited his command. "Bind her hands. Pinion her wings."

"That is unnecessary." Brimstone.

The guards hesitated.

Thiago faced the resurrectionist and the two stared at each other, their enmity confined to the flaring of nostrils, clenching of jaws. The Wolf repeated his order in precise syllables, and the guards scurried to carry it out: into the cell, wrestling Madrigal's wings together and piercing them through with iron clips to secure them. Her hands were easier; she didn't struggle. Once she was fully trussed, they shoved her toward the door.

Brimstone had one last surprise. He told Thiago, "I have designated someone to bless Madrigal's evanescence."

The blessing was a sacred ritual that she had assumed she would be denied. Thiago, apparently, had assumed the same.

408

He narrowed his eyes and said, "You think you're getting any-one close enough to glean her—"

Brimstone cut him short. "Chiro," he said. Madrigal flinched. To Thiago, he said, "I can't imagine you would object to her."

Thiago did not. "Fine." To the guards, he said, "Go."

Chiro. It was so deeply wrong, so profane, that Madrigal's betrayer should be the one to grant her soul peace, that for an instant she thought she had misconstrued everything that Brimstone had just said to her, that this was one final punish-ment heaped upon the others. Then he smiled. A wily uplift of the line of his stern ram's mouth, and it struck her. It exploded behind her eyes.

Soft mollusk thing. Easily pushed aside.

The guard gave Madrigal another shove and she was out the door, her mind racing to encompass this wild new notion in the short time that was left to her.

❧ 60 ❧

IF FOUND, PLEASE RETURN

It had never been done, not that she had heard of. Never even speculated on, and it surely would not have been possible with a natural body. A body accretes to its soul like nacre to a grain of sand, forming a perfect, unified entity that only death can unwork. There is no *gap* within a natural body for guests, or for hijackers. But Chiro's body was a vessel, as Madrigal well knew, having made it herself.

She might not need smoke to guide her, but she did need proximity. She couldn't move through space; she had no control or propulsion. Chiro would have to come to her, and, because Brimstone had selected her to perform the blessing, she did. With heavy steps up the scaffold to kneel beside the pieces that had been her sister. Shaking, she raised her eyes to the air above the body.

She whispered, "I'm sorry, Mad. I didn't know it would be evanescence. I'm so sorry."

Madrigal, who could not block out the sight of her own severed head or the memory of Akiva's screams, was unmoved. What had Chiro hoped for? A lesser sentence? Resurrection of low aspect, perhaps? Maybe she hadn't been thinking of Madrigal at all, except as a means of drawing Thiago's attention. Love made a person do strange things, as Madrigal well knew. There was nothing stranger than what she was about to do.

There was no smoke to guide her. As Brimstone had said, she wouldn't need it. With a powerful thrust of will, she funneled herself into the body that she had made with such loving care.

There was even less resistance than she had expected—a sensation of surprise, a feeble struggle. Chiro's soul was a sullen thing made weak by envy. It was no match for Madrigal's, and subsided almost at once. It wasn't expelled, only shoved writhing into its own depths. The vessel remained, to all eyes, Chiro.

She trembled violently, performing the blessing, but no one watching thought it strange—her sister lay dead at her feet. And if she was rigid descending the scaffold, her movements jerky, no one questioned that, either.

There was no suspicion because there was no precedent. After Chiro left, there was nothing tethered to the broken body on the platform. The soldiers who stood watch the next three days guarded only meat and air—no soul.

The only one who could have sensed its lack was Brimstone, and he wasn't inclined to tell.

* * *

It was through Chiro's eyes that Madrigal had her last sight of Akiva. He was on a rack of sorts, his wings and arms wrenched back and secured by rings to the wall. His head had fallen forward, and when she entered his cell, he lifted it to look at her with dead eyes.

The whites were full bloodred from the effort at magic that had burst capillaries, but it wasn't only that. The gold in them—the exquisite fire—had burned low, and Madrigal had the impression of a soul in cinders. It was the worst thing yet— worse even than her own death.

Now, in Marrakesh, as Karou patched together memories of both her lives, she remembered that same deadness from the first time she had seen him. She had wondered what had happened to make him look like that, and now she knew. It was a splinter in her heart to think that all these years that she had been growing up in a new body, a world apart, childish and blithe and spending wishes on foolish things, he had been soul-dead, grieving for her.

If only he could have known.

In the prison cell, she had rushed to free his arms. She was glad then of Chiro's diamond strength. Akiva's chains were pulled so taut that his arms must have been straining at their sockets. She feared that he would be too weak to fly, or to craft the glamour that would enable him to make it out of the city unseen, but she shouldn't have feared. She knew Akiva's power. When the chains fell slack, he didn't slump off the rack. He sprang like a predator that had been lying in wait. He turned on her, seeing only Chiro and in no state to wonder why this stranger had set him free. He hurled her against the wall before she had a chance to speak, and she was engulfed in the darkness of unconsciousness.

The memories ended there. Karou wouldn't know how Brimstone had found and gleaned her soul until she could ask him. She only knew that he had, because she was here.

"I didn't know," Akiva said. He was stroking her hair, smoothing it over the contours of her head and neck down to her shoulders, lovingly and lingeringly. "If I had known he saved you..." He clutched her tight against him.

"I couldn't tell you it was me," Karou said. "How would you have believed me? You didn't know about resurrection."

He swallowed. Said quietly, "I did know."

"What? How?"

They were still standing together at the foot of the bed. Karou was lost in sensation. The sifting together of memories. The simple, profound joy of being with Akiva. The curious dueling familiarity and...lack. Her body: her seventeen-years skin, utterly *hers*, and also new. The absence of wings, the flexion of human feet with all their complicated muscles, her hornless head light as wind.

And there was something else, a kind of buzzing, an alarm, an awareness she couldn't yet quite finger.

"Thiago," Akiva said. "He...he liked to talk while he... Well. He gloated. He told me everything."

Karou could believe that. Another set of memories slotted into sense: the Wolf awakening on the stone table as she—Karou— held his hamsa-marked hand in her own. He might have killed her then, she thought, if not for Brimstone. She understood Brimstone's fury now. All these years he'd hidden her from Thiago, and she had waltzed right down to the cathedral and held his hand. Which had been every bit as beastly as she remembered.

She nestled against Akiva. "I could have said good-bye, then," she said. "I wasn't even thinking. I only wanted to see you free."

"Karou..."

"It's okay. We're here now." She breathed the remembered smell of him, warm and smoky, and set her lips against his throat. It was heady. Akiva was alive. *She* was alive. So much lay ahead of them. Her lips made a trail up his throat to the line of his jaw, remembering, rediscovering. She was soft in his arms the way she had once known—that marvelous way bodies can melt together and erase all negative space. She found his lips. She had to take his head in her hands to angle it down to hers.

Why did she have to do that?

Why... why wasn't Akiva kissing her back?

Karou opened her eyes. He was looking at her, not with desire but... *anguish.*

"What?" she asked. "What is it?" A terrible thought came to her and she stepped back, letting him go and hugging her arms around herself. "Is it... is it because I'm not pure? Because I'm a... a made thing?"

Whatever was plaguing him, her question made it worse. "No," he said, wretched. "How could you think that? I'm not Thiago. You promised to remember, Karou. You promised to remember that I love you."

"Then what is it? Akiva, why are you acting so weird?"

He said, "If I'd known...Oh, Karou. If I had known that Brimstone saved you..." He raked his fingers through his hair and began to pace the room. "I thought he was with them, against you, and it was *worse*, his betrayal, because you loved him like a father—"

"No. He's like us, Akiva. He wants peace, too. He can help us—"

His look stopped her. So desolate. He said, "I didn't know. If I'd known, Karou, I would have believed in redemption. I never... I *never* would have..."

Karou's heartbeat went arrhythmic. Something was very, very wrong. She knew it, and was afraid of it, didn't want to hear it, needed to hear it. "Never would have what? Akiva, *what?*"

He halted his pacing, stood with his hands on his head, gripping it. "In Prague," he said, forcing out each word. "You asked how I found you."

Karou remembered. "You said it wasn't difficult."

He reached into his pocket and produced a folded paper. With palpable reluctance, he handed it to her.

"What—?" she began, but stopped. Her hands started to shake uncontrollably, so that as she unfolded it, the page tore along a well-worn crease, right down the center of her self-portrait, and she was holding two halves of herself, and the plea, in her own script, *If found, please return.*

It was from her sketchbook, which she had left in Brimstone's shop. Comprehension was instant and blinding. There was only one way Akiva could have this.

She gasped. Everything clicked into place. The black handprints, the blue infernos that had devoured the portals and all their magic, putting an end to Brimstone's trade. And the echo of Akiva's voice, telling her why.

To end the war.

When she had dreamed with him, long ago, of ending the war, they had meant by bringing *peace*. But oh, peace wasn't the only way to end a war.

She saw it all. Thiago had told Akiva the chimaera's deepest secret, believing it would die with him, but she — *she* — had turned him loose with it.

"What have you done?" she asked, unbelieving, her voice breaking.

"I'm sorry," he whispered.

Black handprints, blue infernos.

An end to resurrection.

Akiva's hands, his hands that had held her in dance, in sleep, and in love, his knuckles that she had kissed and forgiven — they were newly etched. They were full. She cried out, *"No!"* the word pulled long and pleading, and then she was grabbing his shoulders, nails digging in, grabbing and holding him and forcing him to look at her.

"Tell me!" she screamed.

In a husk of a voice — such pure sorrow, such deep shame — Akiva said, "They're dead, Karou. It's too late. They're all dead."

 Epilogue

A slash in the sky, that's all it was, nothing like Brimstone's cunning portal with its aviary doors. There was no door at all, and no guardian. Its only protection was its nowhereness, high above the Atlas Mountains, and its narrowness, less than a seraph's wingspan.

It was remarkable that Razgut had managed to find it after so long.

Or, Karou thought, looking at the creature, perhaps not so remarkable, that the worst moment of one's life could be seared into the memory, brighter than any joy. She understood now why pain was the tithe for magic: It *was* more powerful than joy. Than anything.

Than hope?

She saw the pyre in Loramendi as if she'd been there herself: chimaera corpses fed to the flames like scraps of flung cloth, and Akiva watching it all from a tower, breathing the ashes of her people. She tasted ash, and imagined it had still lingered on his flesh when she'd kissed him.

Because of her, he had lived to do this.

And still, she hadn't been able to kill him, though he had brought her knives from Prague himself, and would have fallen to his knees to make it easier for her.

She left him, and even after everything, the distance between them felt like a sphere pulled out of proportion. *Wrong,* that growing distance. Aching, the void that had been her new fullness. A miserable part of her wanted to unknow Akiva's treachery, go back to before, to the incandescent happiness before it all came crashing down.

"Are you coming?" Razgut asked, shouldering his way through the gash in the world, so that half his body disappeared into the ether of Eretz.

Karou nodded. The rest of him vanished, and she breathed deep of the raw air, gathering herself to follow. There was no more happiness. But under the misery, there was hope.

That the name Brimstone had given her was more than a whim.

That this was not the end.

…to be continued

✿ ACKNOWLEDGMENTS ✿

My first thanks are for Kathi Appelt, Coe Booth, Carolyn Coman, Nancy Werlin, and Gene Luen Yang, for changing my life as a writer. Deepest, deepest thanks, forever.

To Alexandra Saperstein and Stephanie Perkins, for reading every inch of this book many times over, and managing to stay excited about it. Every writer should have readers like you. But they can't have *you*. You're mine. Mwa-ha-ha-ha-ha!

To Jane Putch, who is so much more than an agent: Thank you. *Thank you.* This one is for you.

To my darling Clementine, for being an easy baby—I dare say, a *perfect* baby. If it weren't so, finishing this book would have been a very different experience.

And of course, for Jim Di Bartolo, my wonderful husband. For everything from reading and encouragement, to making playlists and coffee, to sharing the baby duties and holding down the fort while I was "Elsewhere." My cherished partner in things both creative and mundane—books, laughing, travel, diaper-changing—I couldn't do it without you, and wouldn't want to.

Mountains and fountains of gratitude for Alvina Ling and the whole amazing crew at Little, Brown, my new home. This has been so amazingly *fun* so far. Your creativity and enthusiasm brighten my horizon. Thank you. In every language real and imaginary: Thank you.

Lastly—and this is kind of goofy, but so what—thank you to the world for being a wild and inspiring place, full of odd creatures, strange people, and mysterious cities. I hope by and by to know you better.